Bones and Blades

L.L. Gray

Heroic Rose Publishing

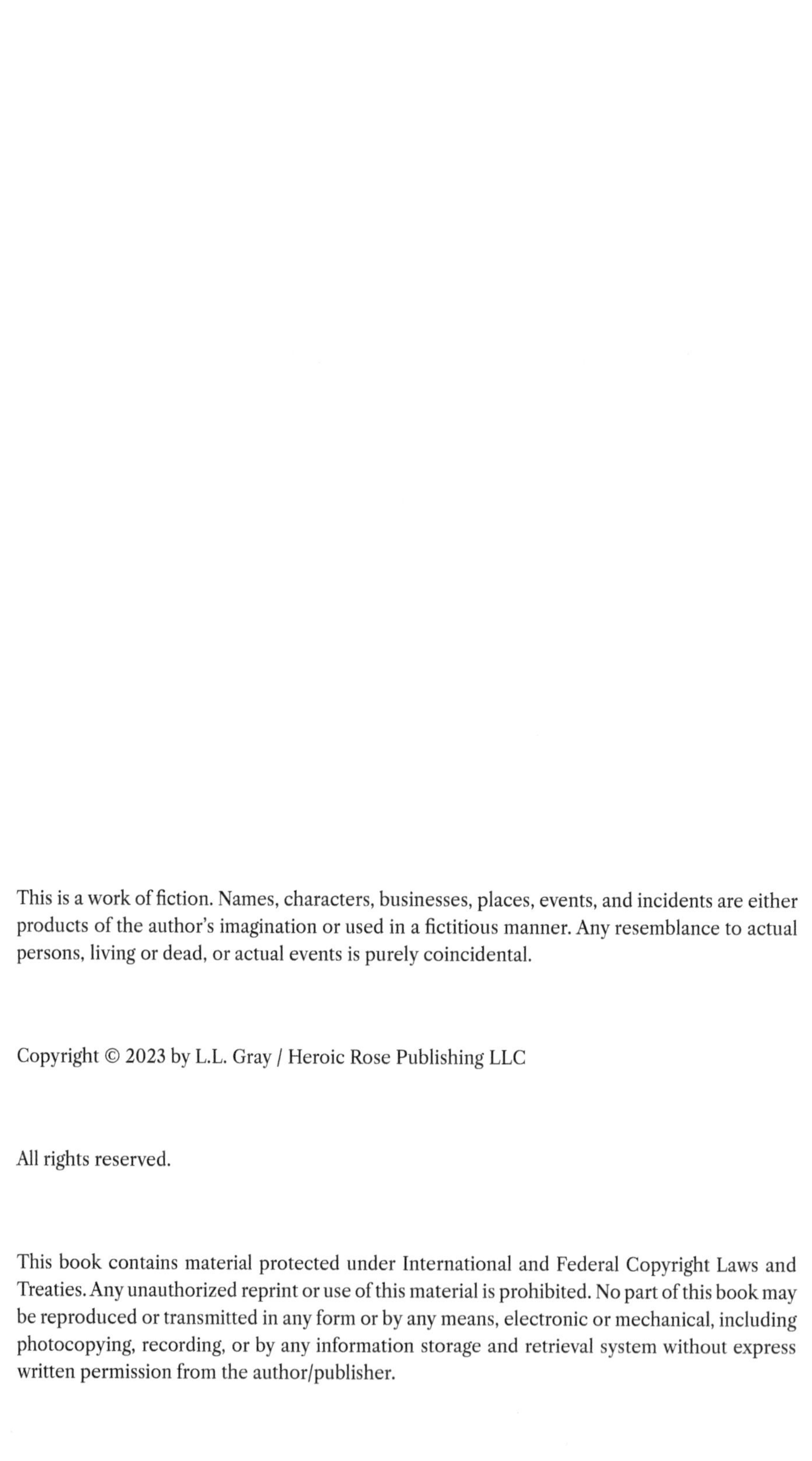

Your FREE book is waiting

**A killer pair of shoes, a party of a lifetime, and a demon.
What could possibly go wrong?**

Cameron Blaze owes a demon a favor and what better way to pay off a debt than to have a girl's night out? The plan was simple. Find a killer pair of heels, go to a great bar, and party into the early hours of the morning. Cameron thinks that she has everything planned. The shoes on are, the drinks are poured, and the party is in full swing. She just forgot to account for one small thing. Magic going haywire.

Suddenly, gods are out of control, myths are throwing punches, and Cameron is running for her life. Will she be able to stop the magical mayhem in time or has the clock run out for Cameron and her friends?

Sign up here to get your free book!

https://www.subscribepage.com/llgray

Contents

Chapter 1

I was a born hunter, with a sharp tongue and an even sharper blade. I had always been able to take care of myself, but now I needed to learn something new. I needed to learn magic. And the only being that could teach me was a disembodied voice at the other end of a mysterious charm who claimed to be a djinn. An ancient creature of fire and smoke who was not only familiar with my unusual brand of shadow magic, but also willing to tutor me.

Barqan.

How did I know all this? Because I wasn't any better than Pandora when it came to not opening ancient magical secrets. Hey! I did my due diligence and researched the hell out of the djinn online. I'd even discretely asked around about them. Nothing I'd uncovered had disproved his claims. If anything, the information I'd dug up reinforced them.

But does that mean I trusted him? Far from it. I wasn't an idiot. However, he had two things I desperately wanted—information about my mom and knowledge about my unique brand of shadow magic. Despite years of looking for answers to both, the mysterious possible djinn, but definitely dangerous sorcerer, was the best source of information I'd found. I was determined to find out the truth about my mother's death, and if that meant learning magic from a dangerous djinn, then so be it.

"Have you practiced your shadow cloaking?" his deep voice rumbled out of the tiny charm in the palm of my hand.

I tried to imagine what he might look like, but the only image that sprang to mind was something akin to the feeling you get when you are walking alone down a road at night and you hear ominous footsteps behind you. Add in some menacing, glowing eyes peering intently out of the darkness, and that about summed up my impression of Barqan from our chats.

I cleared my throat, speaking directly into the charm. "My shadow cloaks are getting stronger. It helps that I've had a chance to heal after that thing with the vampires. Now, when I cloak, I'm only a hazy smudge in full light and nearly invisible at night. It's getting much easier to pull the shadow magic to me when I need it."

"It sounds like you are close to mastery of that skill," Barqan observed, his resonant voice reverberating out of the charm and making it vibrate slightly in my hand.

I closed my eyes, imagining that I was on that lonely road. Barqan's voice echoing out of the darkness made me shiver and my heart rate ratcheted up. It felt like I was being stalked by a dangerous predator and I didn't have my knives.

"And what about the smoke form we've been working on?" he asked.

In my mind, the glowing eyes flared to life in the fog behind me, turning their full, unwavering attention towards me.

"I have been able to, I don't know how to describe it. Fade out? Dissolve? But not completely," I said.

Barqan grunted. "You have to fully commit to the smoke form, or it won't work. Either you do it or you fail."

"Do or do not, there is no try?" I said, quoting my favorite green movie character of all time. Kermit was cool and could play the guitar, but he had nothing on Yoda in my mind.

"Precisely," Barqan said crisply, either ignoring or not recognizing the reference.

I inhaled deeply as the glowing eyes seemed to creep closer. "What if I dissolve into smoke and can't return?" I asked, finally giving voice to my fear about this spell.

His voice was cool. "We would know that you are not very good with shadow magic, wouldn't we?"

"That doesn't sound very comforting!" I protested indignantly.

"There would be one immediate positive that would come from such a situation," Barqan mused, as if I hadn't spoken.

"Which is?" I asked. The glowing eyes blinked at me in my mind.

"I wouldn't waste any more of my time," Barqan replied matter-of-factly.

"Great! Good for you!" The sarcasm dripped thickly off my tongue.

"I agree," Barqan said, ignoring my tone. "Which is why I said it."

I rolled my eyes, but in my mind, the glowing eyes grew larger with every passing moment. The predator was creeping closer.

"Well, if you do not want to proceed with the smoke form, I suppose I could always teach you another spell," Barqan offered. His voice was overly casual.

My heightened senses started blaring an internal warning at air-raid siren level. Supernatural survival tip: Never, *ever* interact with a sentient, inanimate object. You found a talking book? Great! Burn it. Throw the ashes in the deepest lake you can find and run the other way. A sword whispers about making you the King of England? It's *lying*! Leave it in the stone to rust! You find a charm engraved in an ancient language that supposedly connects you to a mysterious, powerful being? Run away. Which is what I knew I should do now. But...

"What kind of spell are we talking about here?" I asked, curiosity getting the better of me.

"How to make a shadow blade."

"What was that now?" I asked, excitement burbling to life within me.

"I can teach you how to pull on your magic to form any kind of weapon you can imagine with a mere thought." Barqan said it simply, like it was the easiest thing in the world.

As soon as he said it, a burning desire to know the spell lit within my gut. To never be without a weapon? To magic any blade out of thin air? Cool didn't even begin to cover it!

"Now that is my type of spell! Why hasn't that been on the syllabus before?" I asked hungrily.

Barqan's chuckle was that of a spider drawing a willing victim into his web. "Because it is very advanced magic. Nothing as simple as a shadow cloak or a smoke form. To teach you, this would require... remuneration."

I knew a negotiation when I heard one. "What kind of payment are we talking about here?" I asked cautiously.

The glowing eyes in my mind blinked and I imagined a Cheshire Cat smile appearing out of the fog. One filled with jagged, razor-sharp teeth. "A trade. A favor for a favor," Barqan said.

I wasn't an idiot. I saw the trap. He'd lured me in with knowledge and lesser spells before offering something he knew would be almost irresistible to me in exchange for... for what, exactly?

"What do you want?" I asked.

The Cheshire smile grew. "An even trade, that's all. You desire information so ancient it has nearly been lost to the tides of time. As do I."

When he didn't elaborate further, I scoffed, "Really? That's all you're giving me?"

I heard the smile in Barqan's voice. "For now."

A lump formed in my throat. He'd played his game well. I really wanted to know that shadow blade spell, but I wasn't ready to agree to an unspecified favor for it. Regretfully, I shook my head. "No deal."

If Barqan was disappointed, he didn't show it. "Very well. Back to your training, then. To master the smoke form, you must be able to dissolve completely and reform in an instant should you so choose. This will not be easy," the supposed djinn said.

"I'm ready for it," I said confidently.

"No, you are not," Barqan said with equal confidence. "It is going to hurt."

And then my training began in earnest.

Chapter 2

I dragged myself out of bed the next morning and limped toward the shower. Barqan hadn't lied, which I guess was something. I hurt. Even though I hadn't moved from my bed during my entire training session, my muscles screamed at me with every moment. I ached all over. It felt like I'd been a lifelong couch potato, content to let my only exercise be surfing channels and then, one day, just decide, *you know what? Instead of heading to the fridge to get myself a beer, I'm going to run a marathon. Right now. No prep. No stretching. Just shoes on and go.*

Yeah. It wasn't a good choice. Neither, apparently, was jumping into the distance learning of advanced shadow magic with a testy teacher. I hoped, for everyone's sake, that Barqan's day job had nothing to do with educating children. Unless the goal was to break their spirits and make them cry. Then, he'd do great.

Despite, or perhaps because of, his harsh teaching methods, I'd partially dematerialized into a slightly hazy version of myself. Barqan told me he knew children who could manage better smoke forms than I could. Repeatedly and creatively. On time twenty-seven, I told him to shove it where the sun didn't shine. He didn't like that at all and ended our training abruptly. I had the feeling the repercussions would have been worse had we been face to face.

Towel drying my long hair, I headed towards the kitchen and the promise of breakfast and caffeine. I flicked the kettle on and pulled my favorite mug off the shelf for my morning tea. I tossed the towel on the table and pulled open the fridge to figure out what I could put in the gnawing pit that used to be my stomach. Bare wire racks met my eyes. I groaned. I'd forgotten to go shopping. Again. Aside from half a stick of butter, some mustard, and a nearly empty carton of milk, there was only bright light and empty cold air in my fridge. I sighed and banged my head lightly against the door. Before I could decide what to do, my phone rang in the other room. I hurried to answer the call, ignoring the angry grumbling of my stomach.

When I looked at the caller id, I smiled. This might solve my breakfast problems in the best imaginable way. I flicked the accept button and answered the call.

"Hello Mama," I said.

"Cam, child. So good to hear your voice. How are things?" Mama Atli's warm, Southern drawl eased me into a better mood. She wasn't really my mother, but everyone I knew called Atli, Mama. Maybe it was because she had a natural, motherly way about her or because she baked for half the city of New Orleans, but she was and forever would be simply 'Mama' in these parts.

I tugged on some clothes as I talked. "I'm doing just fine, Mama. Beautiful morning, the sun is shining, what more could you ask for? How are you today?"

"I've been better," Mama said distractedly.

"Oh, no! What's going on?" I asked, concern rising. Mama was usually the very definition of cheerfulness. You could probably open a dictionary and see her picture right next to the word.

"It's just that silly old fool of a necromancer! He's exasperating, that's what he is," Mama said. I smiled, the image of Ben's wild white hair and perpetual grin dancing in front of my eyes.

"What's he done now?" I asked.

"Well, I asked him to run to the grocery store for me because I had a hankering for some blueberry and cream cheese Danishes. You know the ones I made for the Fourth of July last year? Well, instead of two punnet boxes of berries, Ben showed up with two pounds. Pounds! What am I supposed to do with two pounds of blueberries?"

"Make a lot of Danishes?" I asked with a smile.

"Ben said the same thing! You two are peas in a pod, you are!" Mama exclaimed. "But who's going to eat them before they get all soggy and lose their flake?"

"Me!" Ben's voice sounded faint over the phone. He must be shouting from a safe distance away from Mama. "They're delicious, by the way, Cam!"

"Shush you!" Mama hissed.

I suppressed a chuckle that this was the big emergency of Mama's morning. I was already convinced that Ben's 'mistake' had been nothing of the kind. "What about this, Mama? I'm low on provisions myself and need some breakfast, anyway. I'll swing by and take a couple off of your hands. Any others that you have going spare, I'll take down to the local shelter for you. How about that?"

"Oh, Cam, what a wonderful idea! Would you? That would be amazing! I know those folks down there do such good work and I'm going to have Danishes coming out of my ears before long. That Ben!"

I imagined her shaking a wrinkled fist coated in flour at the necromancer and barely held back another giggle. "I'll be there in about a half hour. Make sure you set at least one out of Ben's reach for me," I said.

"Impossible! She's too short for that!" Ben shouted at the phone.

"Aren't you already in enough trouble without opening your mouth, mister?" Mama's voice was faint. She'd obviously tried to muffle the phone and failed. Her voice came back louder over the line. "That'd be splendid of you, child. A real savior in my time of need. Thank you kindly!"

"I'll see you soon Mama," I said, barely keeping my chuckles in check as I hung up the phone. The promise of blueberry Danishes on an empty stomach spurred me to get out the door as quickly as possible. So fast, in fact, that I was halfway to Mama's before I realized I'd forgotten to grab my trusty karambits. Oh well. It was a sunny morning and Mama's wasn't that far away. Besides, the lure of pastries was strong.

I was still chuckling at Ben's ploy when I knocked on their front door, but knew enough to school my features before Mama opened the door.

There was no way I was going to risk upsetting her. Not with blueberry Danishes on the line.

Mama swung the door wide for me. A flour-dusted apron covered in bright pineapples wrapped around her plump midsection. A smear of the white powder streaked from her cheek to the corner of her eye. "Oh, good! There you are! I was running out of places for these pastries to cool, and I really want to get the next batch in the oven."

"Hello to you too, Mama," I said as I bent to give her a hug.

"Yes, yes. Hello to you too, child." She patted my back distractedly. "Come inside. You know I can't leave Ben alone in a kitchen. Not with sweets on the line. They will either be devoured, or he will have found a way to upend them all over the place, the clumsy man!"

I chuckled. "Still in the doghouse, is he?"

"Of course!" Mama led the way through their cozy house into the kitchen, from which was drifting the most delicious smells of hot pastries. "And he knows it. Although I have my suspicions that this was an honest-to-goodness mistake," she grumbled.

"Call it dishonest-to-goodness then," Ben called out as Mama swept into the kitchen. "Because from my dishonesty sprang all this goodness." He swept an arm around the room. "You're welcome."

My mouth gaped open. Cooling pastries covered every available surface, looking flaky, sweet, and delicious. If I could imagine a perfect paradise, this would be it. "He's not wrong, Mama. These look amazing," I said almost reverently as I took in the decadent display of Mama's talents.

"Oh, go on with you!" Mama exclaimed, but I could see a faint blush of pride sweep up her wrinkled cheeks.

"Good to see you, Cam," Ben said, standing up from the table. Or, at least, he tried. His foot got caught on the rungs of the chair. He toppled forward in slow motion, arms flailing like an off-kilter windmill towards an enormous plate of Danishes.

"Look out!" Mama cried, snatching the pastries out of the way.

I sprang forward and caught his arm, hauling him to his feet before he could cause any damage. My shoulder twinged slightly, but it was healing nicely after that fight with the vampires. It barely even bothered me now. Except for when I needed to save breakfast from a necromancer, apparently.

Ben patted himself down. I think it somewhat surprised him to not have blueberries smashed all over his shirt. "Thanks for that," he said, looking bemused.

Mama set the plate back on the table. "I'll grab you a tea, Cam. Just a moment." She bustled off.

Ben lowered his voice. "And thanks for distracting her," he whispered, jerking his thumb over his shoulder. "You really saved my bacon!"

"That's what family's for, isn't it?" I said with a smile.

"And this is why you'll always be my favorite almost-daughter. 'Cause you help me get a buttload of Danishes and get away scot-free." He winked at me.

I swatted at his arm gently. "You're a terror, Ben."

"Only if you are a pastry slathered in blueberries and cream!"

"Oh, hush you, and drink your tea," Mama said, settling steaming mugs in front of both of us. She went back for her own and returned with a generous slice of bacon and mushroom quiche, which she set in front of me.

"When you said you hadn't eaten, I whipped this up. I know you're young and think you can live on sugar and carbs alone, but trust me, look after yourself now or it catches up with you when you get to be my age," Mama said as she set a fork down next to my plate.

"Today, I feel about ten years older, and it's not because of sugar," I said. I snagged a pastry and bit into it. My eyes rolled back in my head. It tasted even better than it smelled. "In fact, sugar might be the cure after all," I said past the sweet ooze of blueberries and smooth creaminess of the cheese.

"That's what I keep tellin' her, but she just won't listen!" Ben said, slamming a fist down on the table in his excitement. The thump caused hot tea to splash out of his mug. A sharp look from Mama sent Ben hurrying for a cloth to mop up the mess.

"Is something troubling you, child? Anything you want to talk about?" Mama asked.

I shook my head. "Nothing new. Just training with Barqan. He taught me a new spell last night. Which is probably why I feel like I've been run through a washing machine full of tennis balls this morning." I forked up a generous helping of the quiche and started chewing. The crust melted on my tongue, allowing for the savory saltiness of the quiche to overwhelm my senses. I let out a little moan of pleasure.

Mama smiled with pride as I shoveled another large bite in. "Slow down there! Give your stomach a chance. There's plenty more if you want it."

"What's this about Barqan?" Ben said from the other side of the kitchen. "You know I don't think he's any good. Lower than a snake's belly in a wagon rut, if you ask me."

"You know nothing about him," I protested.

"Don't need to," Ben sniffed. "Any feller worth his salt wouldn't hide in no necklace. No siree-Bob! He'd be out there, face to face, shakin' hands and sayin' hello."

"Maybe he can't. Maybe he really is locked away in some sort of magical prison. I don't know! Besides, who else do you know who can teach me how to use my shadow magic?" I threw my hands up in the air, exasperation getting the better of me. We'd had this conversation before. No matter what I said, Ben was set in his ways. He didn't trust Barqan in the slightest.

Mama patted my hand. "Maybe so, but you've got to understand, we're just concerned for you. We don't want to see anything bad happen to you, child."

A blush of embarrassment crept up my cheeks as I hung my head. "I know you mean well. I'm sorry. It's just, well, I want some answers about my past. And Barqan is the first person I've met that might have some. He knew my mom, you know."

Mama leaned forward. "Did he tell you that?"

"Not in so many words, but it was a pretty easy inference to make," I said.

"Tell us everything," Ben said, settling down with a fresh pastry in hand. Mama shot him a dirty look, which he studiously ignored.

I spent the next twenty minutes bringing them up to speed on my training from last night. It should've only taken me about five, but there were pastries and quiche. I have my priorities and they are absolutely in the right place. Pastries first. Everything else could wait.

Unfortunately, Mama and Ben had nothing new to add. After making rehashing Ben's distrust of Barqan and making small talk, I needed to get on my way to deliver Mama's latest creations to the local shelter. I waved an awkward farewell around a giant white box filled with fresh blueberry pastries. Although our chat was pleasant, they hadn't been able to offer any more insight on my training sessions with Barqan, other than to tell me to proceed with caution. Again. Actually, Ben told me I shouldn't proceed at all, but we both knew that wasn't going to happen.

I lived close enough to Mama and Ben that I could walk home, which was a good thing. I couldn't imagine trying to balance the box for the shelter on my motorcycle and I didn't have a car. Maybe I could convince Sloane to play taxi for me and the pastries. Knowing my best friend, she definitely wouldn't mind exchanging a car ride for some of Mama's baked goods. Plus, that meant we could hang out this afternoon. I hadn't seen her very much recently, so a catch up would be nice.

An empty house caught my eye. I knew the family who used to live there had recently moved, and it hadn't yet sold. Not that I was house hunting. But if I cut through the backyard, the alley behind the house would shave about ten minutes off my walk. With the awkwardly large box in my arms, I was all in favor of the shortcut.

I carefully balanced the box on one palm and fiddled with the latch on the iron gate surrounding the yard, hoping it was unlocked. It was. I smiled and leaned my shoulder into the gate, swinging it wide so it didn't accidentally knock into the box of pastries.

Which was when something heavy and smelling faintly of sulfur smashed into my back. I watched in horror as the lid of the box flew open and the Danishes intended for the homeless shelter splattered to the ground. Anger bubbled inside me. I whirled around to see who had just ruined all of Mama's hard work. What I saw behind me turned my rage to icy fear in a split second.

I turned and ran.

Chapter 3

*S*tupid, stupid, stupid!

I chastised myself as I sprinted away from the demon behind me. Unfortunately, it was a demon I recognized. If you ever get to a point where you can recognize demons, you took a wrong turn somewhere in life. Probably more than one. Although, come to think of it, I don't know if there would be a fortunate time to recognize a demon.

Not the point right now. Right now, the point was to survive a demon attack. Without my weapons.

Stupid! Why hadn't I brought my knives? Idiot!

I felt something brush at the hair on the back of my head. This was no time for self-recrimination. Survival first. Then I could beat myself up over my poor life choices. I threw myself into a diving forward roll around the corner of the deserted house to avoid the demon's claws digging into my scalp. When I scrambled to my feet, I saw a child's play set in front of me.

Thank all the gods the family already moved!

I didn't even want to imagine a scenario where a child walked out to find a demon in his or her backyard. Now wasn't the time to be thinking of that, though. Now was the time to get the hell away from the demon. Quick as I could, I scrambled up the cheap plastic slide to the raised wooden platform shaped like a miniature castle tower and turned to look at my opponent. The red-skinned demon below me had the muscled torso of a gym rat and the hairy hindquarters of a goat, complete with cloven hooves. Come to think of it, maybe that wasn't so different from some of the gym rats I'd known.

The demon curled his clawed hands at me and charged. His hooves tore up the grass as he ran at the play structure. I don't know if he'd intended on running up the slide like I had or what, but children's play equipment wasn't built for demons. Instead of tearing up the slide like I had, he tore straight *through* it. Green plastic shards flew in all directions. I shielded my eyes to protect them.

A reverberating crunch sounded off to the right and behind me. I spun to see the demon clutching his horned head and staggering next to the tower. The high wooden security fence that ringed the yard had an impressive dent in the middle that looked to be perfectly demon sized. I glanced around, sizing up my surroundings in a desperate search for impromptu weaponry.

Unfortunately, whoever had lived here had been a responsible adult and not left weapons lying about for the kiddies to play with. I swore softly under my breath. Sometimes, responsibility's not all it's cracked up to be.

Something caught my eye, and an idea sparked. Without a moment's hesitation, I slid down the firefighter's pole, which brought me level with the demon. He shook his head like a maddened bull. However, when the demon tried to focus on me, he swayed drunkenly back and forth. That collision with the fence must've really rung his bell.

I backed up slowly until I felt my secret weapon bump against my back. With that slight advantage bolstering me with more confidence than I had any right to, I taunted a demon in the tried-and-true method that started more than one playground fight. I stuck my thumbs in my ears, waggled my fingers at the demon and said, "Neener, neener, come and get me, you big baby!"

Shock was swiftly replaced by incandescent fury as the demon registered my words. He crouched and let out a terrifying howl of rage. This close, I could see straight down his throat. Distantly, I noticed that his tongue was still missing from where I'd cut it off in our last meeting. But that realization was almost immediately swept away on a blast of stanky-ass breath that smelled like he brushed his teeth with a mixture of sulfur, farts, and rotten eggs.

I waved a hand in front of my nose and tried not to gag. "Dude! It's halitosis, not hell-a-tosis! Seriously! Haven't you ever heard of mouthwash?"

The demon let out a garbled response, made entirely unintelligible because of his missing tongue.

I cupped a hand around my ear. "Sorry, couldn't understand that. Try enunciating. Slow and clear now," I encouraged mockingly. I wanted him good and angry, so he wouldn't expect what I had planned. Now, if only I could get the bastard to charge me.

I got my wish. The demon lowered his head, wickedly sharp horns pointed right at my chest. He actually pawed the ground twice with his hooves before racing to close the distance between us.

The moment he took his eyes off me, I scrabbled for the swing at my back. This wasn't one of those flimsy plastic swings. This swing was a sturdy piece of oak. As the demon charged, I dodged to the side, bringing the plank of a swing up over my shoulder. Using the full momentum of my body, I swung the swing at the back of the demon's head as he charged into the space I'd been standing a moment before. The plank cracked in half and the demon went sprawling into the grass.

If I had my knives with me, I would've ended the fight right then. However, I didn't like my chances in a bare-handed wrestling match with this creature. Deciding to live to fight another day, I scrambled back up the firefighter's pole to put some distance between me and the demon. I tugged my phone out of my pocket and shouted into the microphone.

"Call Damon Lykaios!"

Damon was the Alpha of the New Orleans Pack. He was also a member of the Collective, the supernatural council that kept the peace among the local Supes and kept the Norms from finding out that supernatural creatures lived among them. A demon in the middle of residential New Orleans in the middle of the day was definitely the Collective's problem. Or at least it would be if Damon would just pick up his godsdamned phone!!

The demon groggily shoved to his knees, swaying from side to side with every breath he took. I watched him tensely as the phone clicked over to voicemail.

Damn it!

"Call Magnus Donovan!" I shouted into the phone. Magnus was a werewolf too, but he and I... well, there was something between us. I just didn't know what it was yet and with the events of the past few weeks, I hadn't had the time to sort out my thoughts and now there was this demon and...

"Hello?"

I sucked in a breath. "Magnus! Oh, thank all the gods!"

"Cam! What's wrong?"

"It's a demon. No, *the* demon. The same one as before!"

Magnus' voice was tight, but calm. "Deep breath, Cam. Tell me where you are."

I rattled off the street. "It's the white house. The one that's up for sale. Get the Pack here as soon as you can!"

The demon's head swiveled towards the sound of my voice. With no other weapons at my disposal, I hurled words at him. "That's right! The entire Pack of werewolves is on their way here!"

The creature's horned head swiveled wildly back and forth. He staggered to his feet and stumbled towards the alleyway behind the house.

"Yeah! You'd better run! They're gonna be here any minute and when they get here, they'll rip you to shreds!" I shouted after the demon as it disappeared around the corner. The clippity-clop of his cloven hooves on the pavement faded as Magnus' voice rang over the phone.

"Cam! Stay where you are! I'm on my way!"

I pulled myself up onto the wooden wall that formed the tower of the play set, craning my neck to get a better look at where the demon had disappeared. "I think it's gone," I said into the phone.

"What are you saying? Is there a demon or isn't there?" Magnus demanded.

"No, there was definitely a demon. There's a demon-sized dent in the fence to prove that, but it's gone."

"Gone, like *poof!* It disappeared?" Magnus asked.

"Nope. Gone like he ran away," I said, still craning my neck to see if this was some kind of trick and the demon was coming back for another ambush.

"Ran away?"

"Yep. Trust me, I'm just as confused as you are," I said.

"What did you do to him?"

"Hit him with a kid's swing," I said, distractedly.

"What?! Never mind. Stay there. I'm coming to get you."

I shook my head. "I don't think he's coming back. The bigger problem is that there is a demon loose in New Orleans right now, and Damon isn't answering his phone. You've got to find your Alpha. Tell him to get the Collective's collective asses in gear to track this thing down."

"What about you?" Magnus asked, sounding obviously torn.

Aw, that was sweet of him to worry about me. "I'm close to home. I'll get there, grab some weapons and then meet you at the Forge. Get Damon and we can make a plan, ok?"

"Wait. Did I just understand you right? You tackled a demon *without weapons?*"

"Well, technically, he tried to tackle me. And I had a swing."

"You're not making any sense!"

I ran my hand through my hair in frustration. "Look, we can talk about this later. Get Damon. I'll see you at the Forge in an hour. Sooner if I can make it."

"Fine. Keep your head down and stay safe," Magnus said, but didn't sound like he liked it.

"You too." I ended the call. I took another quick look around to ensure the neighborhood was demon-free before sliding down the pole again and sprinting towards the front gate. Mama's pastries squished underfoot as I rounded the corner of the house and sprinted down the street towards my apartment.

I doubted she would hold the demolition of her pastries against me, but when I told her this story, I was one hundred percent blaming the demon for everything.

I ran all the way back to my apartment, keeping an eye out for any flashes of red, horns, or goat butt as I ran. Luckily, there was nothing.

The entire way back to my home, one thought hammered through my skull again and again.

How had he found me?

I pounded up the stairs, taking them two at a time. Whatever the answer to that question, I'd feel much better once I had my weapons in my hands. I unlocked the door with a shaking hand. It swung wide. I moved to enter the apartment but froze mid-step with my hand on the door.

A demon sat at my kitchen table, but I knew this one. Meridiana.

"We need to talk," the demoness said, seriously.

Chapter 4

What do you do when a demoness invites herself into your apartment right after you beat up one of her brethren with a child's plaything? Scream? Fight? Throw a scalding hot mug of tea and hope the demon thinks you carry holy water around at all times?

Come to think of it, with demons running around town, maybe I should start doing that. Where could one buy blessed water in bulk? Was there a way I could get Mannanan Mac Lir, the Irish god of the sea, to bless more water for me so I could have an unending supply? I wondered what he might charge for something like that.

Focus, Cam! Important things first. Unexpected demon at your kitchen table. Wholesale holy water could wait.

Before you ask, I'm not sure if an unexpected demon is worse than an expected demon. I just know that my heart rate jumped from couch potato to Olympic-gold-medal-sprinter level to see a demon in what I thought was an empty apartment. Well, a demoness. Meridiana. And she looked like shit.

The adrenaline spike over the demon attack hadn't fully left my system. That, combined with her sudden appearance, froze me in place. My subconscious was having problems deciding if it wanted me to fight or flee. It took a second for me to remember to breathe and another few for my heart rate to come down to something resembling normal.

During that time, I took in the Meridiana's gaunt appearance. She wasn't exactly a friend, but she wasn't an enemy, either. She was more of an excellent drinking buddy with definite friend potential. Despite being a demoness, she was good people. Meridiana was a demon who specialized in lust, a succubus. I didn't know if it was part of her job description or personal choice, but she always appeared as a beautiful redheaded seductress. She had melt-your-soul chocolate brown eyes, a petite but curvy figure, and a wicked smile that often showed off teeth that were just a bit too sharp for my liking.

Now, she looked like she'd been chewed up and spat out by something ugly and mean. Her luxurious red hair was limp and oily. Her chocolate brown eyes looked sunken and haunted. Bruises mottled her pale skin as it stretched and pulled tightly across her bones, showing off a disturbing number of cuts and scrapes. Her typical sexy-chic outfit was torn and bore dark stains that might have been blood. I shuddered to think what could have done that to the demoness.

"Where have you been? And what did that to you?" I asked as I forced my tense muscles to relax. I yet again regretted taking off all my weapons and stowing them neatly away in my closet of all things sharp, pointy, and explode-y. If surprise demons were going to become a regular thing, then I needed to get in the habit of walking around armed all the time. But then again, if they were a common occurrence, they could hardly be 'surprise demons', now could they? Perhaps 'annoying demons'? No, not strong enough. How about fu—

"We need to talk," Meridiana repeated, not moving from her slumped position as she interrupted my thoughts. I carefully evaluated her again. She didn't look like she presented much of a threat at the moment, but I didn't want to take risks.

"Meridiana, it's been a rough couple weeks for both of us and I'll be honest, trust is running a little low. The combination of vampires and an unexpected demon attack will do that to a girl," I said, still not moving further into the room.

Meridiana jerked her head up. "Demon attack? What demon?"

"Red guy, about this tall." I stretched my hand over my head to show his height. "Sharp claws, horns, rear end of a goat. Didn't seem terribly smart, because he couldn't dodge a fence that was standing right in front of him. But what do I know about demon intelligence? It's not like we chatted over coffee or anything."

Meridiana furrowed her brow. "I know him. That doesn't sound like an accident."

I nodded, finally coming fully into the apartment and locking the door behind me. "That's the conclusion I came to as well. I think he's tracking me somehow. Hang on a second." I moved past her swiftly and into my bedroom. I shut the door firmly behind me and turned to my closet. Most girls keep an overabundance of trendy clothes, shoes, scarves, and accessories in their closets, most of which they'll wear only once before donating to the local thrift store. Not me. My closet was full of something much better.

Weapons.

Swiftly, I grabbed my sheathed karambits and strapped them to my lower back, tugging my shirt back into place to cover them. Being armed instantly made me feel more secure. I kneeled and pried loose the floorboards, revealing an iron floor safe. When I opened it, there were only two things inside. I ignored the elaborately decorated egg-shaped artifact. I'd stolen it when I'd gotten wrapped up in a situation involving an ancient master thief, a nest of angry vampires, and a god. It was best for my survival that no one knew I had it locked away in my apartment. Hell, I wasn't even going to take it out of the safe if I could help it. The vampire leader of New Orleans would just kill me and reclaim his property if he ever found out that I had it. Being a fan of living, I had no intention of letting that happen.

I reached past the artifact for the other item. The small scroll had been my payment for doing the aforementioned god a favor. It was a magical sigil keyed to track three souls that had escaped the Abyss during a dark ritual gone wrong on Halloween. The demon following me around town was one of those souls. If he could track me, the least I could do was even the playing field. Satisfied, I relocked the safe and laid the floorboards back in place before returning to the kitchen.

"Razgothan," Meridiana said as I re-entered the room.

"Sorry, what?" I asked, confused.

"I think that's the demon who attacked you. The description fits at least."

"Razgothan?" I asked, testing out the strange name. It felt malevolent on my tongue. I flicked on the kettle and pulled two mugs down from my shelf, popping in a couple of tea bags while I waited for the water to boil.

Meridiana waved a hand dismissively. "It's the closest approximation in English. You wouldn't be able to pronounce his real name," she said, letting loose a truly horrendous collection of screeches, clacks, and snorts that I assumed was the demon's name. "But why is he interested in you?"

I shrugged helplessly. "The first time I saw him, I'd just figured out that this necklace might link my mom with a djinn," I said, holding up the gold charm for her inspection.

"Djinn!" Meridiana exclaimed. "That thing connects you to a *djinn*?!"

I held up my hands in protest and took a step back. "Well, maybe. Let's not go jumping to any conclusions. Right now, Barqan is just some voice on the other end of a magical phone. There is no way to prove that he is or isn't what he claims to be."

"Barqan the djinn *king*? He's the one on the other end of your mother's charm?" Meridiana shrieked.

"What do you mean, 'djinn *king*'?" I demanded. Other than some unsubstantiated articles on the internet, this was the closest I'd come to confirmation on Barqan's past.

"Barqan is one of the seven famous djinn kings who vanished centuries ago," Meridiana sputtered. "I think he was the one in charge of magic or something like that. Are you sure it's that Barqan and not some other guy using the name?"

"Maybe. Maybe not. I don't know. It's not like anyone around here is giving me any definite answers," I said, glaring at her pointedly before pouring boiling water into the waiting mugs on the counter.

She took a deep breath and then another. "You're right. I haven't told you very much, but in my defense, I didn't know your mother was talking with any of the djinn, let alone a djinn king. I mean, how did she even...?

When did she..." The demoness' voice trailed off as she stared into the middle distance, a worried crease forming between her brows.

I looked down at my necklace. "So, you think this guy Barqan really is a djinn king? Can you tell me more about the djinn? Or him? I've done some research online, but you know those fantasy sites can be hit-or-miss. And more importantly, why was my mom wrapped up with them?" I asked in a rush. I toed a chair out of the way as I sat across from her and slid her tea over. The hunger to uncover some of my mysterious history swelled within me and I leaned forward, drumming my fingers on the tabletop.

Meridiana scrubbed a hand over her face and then winced as she pressed too hard on a prominent bruise on her forehead. "Taking those one at a time. Yes, I think we need to assume that there is a higher-than-average chance that the man on the other end of your necklace is the djinn king, Barqan. Djinn are powerful Supes, but the kings are on the same supernatural tier as angels and demons. As for how your mother was connected to them, I have no idea."

"What the hell!" I exclaimed. My research hadn't turned up that. "You're telling me I have a hotline to an angel or demon or whatever hanging around my neck?" I grabbed at the charm, eyeing it with concern.

"You fear a charm when a succubus is sitting at your kitchen table?" Meridiana's voice was dry.

I glared at her. "You're not... I mean, you are. But not like... Look! I know you! I don't know this guy. Djinn! Possible king! Whatever! Wait. How can he be on the same level as angels and demons, but not one? Isn't it kind of a black and white system?"

Meridiana tsked at me. "There are always shades of gray, Cam."

I shook my head slowly. "No, pretty sure this one is clear. Light versus dark. Good versus evil. Angels versus demons. The plot of every superhero movie ever."

"And am I evil?"

I shut my mouth with a click. Was she evil? Sure, she was a demoness. But truly, heinously, fry-forever-in-the-fiery-pits *evil*? I didn't think so.

Meridiana's smile was wry and pained, as if she'd read my mind. She held out an outstretched hand and waggled it back and forth in a kinda-sorta gesture. "See? Shades of gray," she said. "Djinn aren't angels, but neither are they demons. They possess a certain amount of free will and lack of oversight where their, shall we call them cousins?" the demoness asked. I shrugged noncommittally, and she continued. "Very well, their cousins do not. That power level combined with free-will made the djinn immensely dangerous."

"So, why haven't I heard of the djinn before now? I mean, other than the wish-fulfilling genies, of course."

Meridiana lifted a slim shoulder. "Genies, while they do exist, are not always benevolent. Nor are they the only type of djinn. As the different djinn tribes multiplied, powerful beings deemed them too dangerous to be allowed to survive. That level of power, plus free will? It's a luxury and a crushing burden."

"With great freedom comes great responsibility," I murmured softly, parodying the famous line from a favorite superhero movie.

Meridiana clicked her tongue in agreement and shook her head in a world-weary gesture before continuing. "It was too late to eradicate them all, but something could be done to staunch their power. In an almost unheard-of alliance, the archangels and archdemons banded together with a powerful human sorcerer named Solomon to imprison the most powerful of the djinn. The seven kings. The djinn that survived the battle fled, taking up refuge in the remote corners of the world's deserts."

"What about these other djinn? The ones other than the kings. You said they aren't all genies?" I asked curiously, my mind flitting back to my internet research on the djinn.

"Not in the big, blue, show-tune singing, goateed way you are probably imagining. Lower-level djinn still exist today, including wish-granting genies, malevolent ifrit, and shapeshifting sila. Norms usually blame them for all the mischief or things that go wrong. Secretly, I believe that some of them still hold to the old ways. That they use their gift of free will to make helpful choices and hurtful ones. That they find balance.

My brethren disagree with me, but what can I say? I'm a romantic." Meridiana shrugged, seemingly content with her place in the world.

"How do you know all this?" I asked.

Meridiana met my eyes, holding them with her serious gaze. "It's one of the horror stories demons tell each other late at night around the gathering fires in the Abyss. That one day, the djinn kings will rise again and join with the angels to destroy us once and for all," she said, looking around like she was searching for ghosts. "Or vice versa. If we could convince them to join our side in the ultimate battle."

I swallowed hard past the sudden tightness constricting my throat. "And you demons are already planning for this battle?"

Meridiana shrugged. "Aren't we all? I mean, the book of Revelations, Ragnarök, the four Horsemen of the Apocalypse, Gotterdammerung, Doomsday, Armageddon. It all amounts to the same thing."

"Judgement day," I said in a hushed voice.

Meridiana nodded seriously. "But all this talk of djinn aside for the moment. What are you going to do about Razgothan? If he knows you are connected to a long-lost djinn king, he might try to kidnap or kill you. Get you to the Abyss and use you for leverage. No one has seen or heard from the djinn kings in a very long time. If one could be found and freed?" The demoness shuddered.

"That bad?" I asked.

"Razgothan could barter that information to many powerful beings in the Abyss. All of whom would come hunting you." She pushed to her feet and started pacing.

"That would be difficult," I replied, picking apart the important information as I watched her agitated pacing. She always appeared calm and in control. This new side of the demoness was unsettling. "Unless you demons can write or have telepathy, along with your host of other freaky powers."

"Doubtful on all counts in Razgothan's case. Why?" Meridiana turned to face me, interest lighting her face.

"Because I cut out his tongue," I said. It had been accidental, but Meridiana didn't need to know that. What can I say? Badass points are important to me. "And when I ran into him today, he could barely form an incoherent roar, let alone a word."

Meridiana tsked at me. "Demons can heal most anything. We might have a few days, if we are lucky," she said, resuming her pacing.

"To do what, precisely?" I asked, already knowing that I wouldn't like the answer.

"To figure out how to permanently kill a demon, of course."

Chapter 5

My jaw dropped. I fiddled instinctively with my necklace. I didn't want to mess with Razgothan again anytime soon. To be honest, I'd much prefer to hand the demon off to the Collective to deal with. If that turned out not to be an option, I wouldn't mess with him intentionally until I had a sword in my hand and a pack of werewolves at my back. However, if Meridiana could be believed, there wasn't time for lengthy negotiations. I'd have to convince either the Collective or the Pack to take action. Now. Luckily, I already had a meeting on the books with the latter.

I sighed, placing my hands on the table and pushing to my feet. "Right, let me get my sword," I said.

Meridiana whirled to face me. "What the heaven! Do you have a blessed blade you haven't told me about? Or worse, holy weapons?" She shuddered as she spat out the last sentence like it burned her mouth just to utter it.

I shook my head. "No. I don't think so at least."

"Trust me, you'd know if you had something like that in your possession, Cameron. One does not lightly forget a holy hand grenade."

I shrugged. "I heard those are only good against rabbits. Besides, I did just fine against this Razgothan with my karambits before and a piece of wood the second time. Although, I prefer the knives." The small, curved karambits were my favorites. The wicked blades could tear, slice, or rip into opponents with deadly efficiency, and the safety rings that looped over my fingers meant it was almost impossible to be disarmed, which was always a tremendous advantage in any fight.

Meridiana shook her head in frustration. "No. You don't understand. You can't just kill him on this plane with a mundane weapon. He'll just re-manifest in the Abyss. It might delay the information about your connection with the djinn king from spreading through the Necrocracy slightly, but we need to plug the leak. Permanently." The demoness' eyes flashed darkly.

I slowly lowered myself back into my chair. "I understood about half of what you said. Why don't you break it down for me? Re-manifesting in the Abyss? The Necrocracy? Why can't we kill the demon? I'm pretty sure that demon hunters do it every day. Why can't we?"

Meridiana sighed and marched back to the table. She sat down with a wince and folded her hands in front of her. She met my eyes directly.

"If you tell anyone I told you this, they will force me to eat your heart while you watch. If anyone asks how you know, blame it on Razgothan. After we kill him, of course," she said seriously.

I suppressed a shudder. Barely. "Ok, I guess. Why?" I asked.

"Because in the Abyss, there are rules and then there are guidelines. The rules are few and far between, but also non-negotiable. Talking about this openly with a mortal is a rule I'd rather not get caught breaking."

"Fair enough. Razgothan told me everything. Got it," I said, shooting a finger gun in her direction.

Meridiana nodded grimly, "Like you know, the Abyss is a catchall term for our side of the afterlife. There are so many variations of hell or the fiery pits of torture afterlife that we lumped them all together for ease of conversation. If you are talking about a specific place, you just say that. But all of it? It's the Abyss. Besides, it makes things so much clearer."

"How?" I asked, sipping my tea again. I loved a good story. This had all the earmarks of an excellent one.

"Well, if you mention hell, do you mean the Christian afterlife or hel, the Norse afterlife or Hel, capital H, the ruler of the Norse afterlife? It's confusing and has led to more than one debacle. The same thing applies to Hades. The word is both a person and a place. Calling it the Abyss on this side of the veil makes things easier. Besides, when demons cross over, we can travel between one afterlife and the next. Think of them like apartment buildings in the same city."

I nodded slowly, still trying to familiarize myself with the concept that all the world's afterlives were all crammed into the same metaphysical neighborhood. I sipped at my tea again to give myself a moment.

Meridiana continued. "Demons don't die. At least, not in how humans do. Unless you kill a demon with a holy weapon, something like a blessed blade or bullets dipped in holy water or something, it'll simply re-manifest in its home territory in the Abyss if its body here is destroyed."

"And if they're killed with a holy weapon?"

"They'll disintegrate, much like vampires do in the sun. Poof. No more Razgothan. No more problems," Meridiana winked, sounding more like the saucy demoness I knew.

"All right," I nodded, slowly digesting everything she'd shared. "What's the Necrocracy?" I asked.

Meridiana waved a hand, showing off her chipped manicure. "Oh, they're the officials of the Abyss. More or less elected, depending on the century. They enforce the rules, track down runaway spirits, relegate visits between realms. Generally, they run a tight ship, but it truly depends on who's in power."

"And who's in charge at the moment?" I asked, curiously.

Meridiana's gaze snagged on her ruined nails. She grimaced and started chipping away at her ruined manicure as she spoke. "Last I checked, Thanatos sat on the Necrocracy. Persephone usually lends a hand when she's around. If I remember correctly, Apophis replaced Anubis a while back. Oh, and Maman Brigitte currently leads the Necrocracy. She's the consort of Baron Samedi and kind of a big deal here in New Orleans, you know," Meridiana said matter-of-factly, her face impassive.

I nodded along, struggling to remember all the names she threw out except for one. Last month, I'd played a game of poker with Maman Brigitte. I'd been hired to steal from her. It hadn't quite worked out that way. She'd *let* me win the magical bottle of hot pepper infused rum and I'd never figured out why. Now that I knew she was the head of the Necrocracy, I was hesitant to do any sort of questioning. The woman who essentially ran the Abyss was not someone I wanted to end up on the wrong side of. I filed away the rest of the names I could remember for later research. I didn't want to send Meridiana off on a tangent by asking about them before I got the answers I truly wanted and, apparently, needed.

"Right. All jokes aside, how can I kill this demon? I don't have any holy weaponry, hand grenades or otherwise," I asked, setting down my mug of tea because it had gone cold. Not because my hands were shaking from the turn our conversation had taken. Nope. Not at all.

"Like I said, it's difficult to kill a demon permanently, but not impossible. You could kill him on this plane with your mundane weapons and then track him to the Abyss and kill him again there."

"One, I'm going to ignore the fact you just low-key insulted my knives," I said. "Two, going to the Abyss to kill a demon sounds like a horrible vacation. Is there any other option to deal with him?"

Meridiana shrugged. "A powerful magician can seal away demons. Most often in rings or gemstones. King Solomon was the most famous demon collector. He's also the sorcerer responsible for locking the djinn kings away, by the way. His seals are legendary." She shivered as a pensive cloud darkened her features.

"Great. Let's do that. Where can we find him?" I spoke.

Meridiana's gaze snapped back to me, and her smile didn't quite reach her eyes. "Solomon is long gone from this realm. Other than a long-dead king, do you know of any massively powerful magicians just hanging out in the swamplands of Louisiana?" The demoness' words were sharp.

I frowned at her tone and shook my head. "No. Fine. What do *you* suggest, then?"

"I can use my powers to bind him to this plane for a short amount of time. Hopefully, it is long enough for you to kill him."

"But you said he would just re-materialize in the Abyss if I killed him here," I said, confused.

Meridiana smirked. "I have a contact. Someone who might bless your blades for you. Kill him with one of those, and he won't be re-materializing anywhere."

"Who do you know who can bless things? And why didn't you lead with that?" I looked at her skeptically.

She brushed aside my query with a flick of her fingers. "Demons and those who give blessings are two sides of the same coin. The fact is that I can get some blessed weapons in your hands quickly."

I tipped my head, a chill creeping up my spine that had nothing to do with the temperature. "What do you want in return for this favor?"

"Ironically, it's the reason I came to visit you. Do you remember when we sat at this very table before and I told you I was being observed?" the demoness asked.

I folded my arms over my chest. "Sure. You couldn't say much about my mom or my past because of this mysterious watcher."

"Correct." Meridiana paused, closing her eyes and seeming to gather her nerve before speaking. "The watcher wants to be seen. To come in from the shadows, so to speak. She'd like to meet with you. This afternoon, ideally."

"Wow. That's awfully short notice, especially given this Razgothan situation," I observed.

Meridiana shrugged a thin shoulder. "I didn't know he was here. Regardless, she's not the kind of person to take disappointment well. If I can secure a permanently blessed blade that can destroy a demon on any plane, would you meet with her? Today?"

I considered my options. On the one hand, I could sit back and wait, hoping that either the Collective or the Pack would deal with the demon. However, if Meridiana's fears were accurate, I didn't have time to sit on my hands, waiting for someone else to save me. Even if I accepted her offer and went to fight the demon with a blessed sword, I wasn't confident I couldn't take him on by myself.

"So, the plan is, meet your mysterious watcher, get myself a blessed blade, and then what?"

Meridiana's bright smile looked a touch manic to me. "Why, you go pick a fight with a demon, my dear. The sooner the better."

"This seems like an epically poor life choice," I muttered.

"Time is against us. We need to dispatch Razgothan as fast as possible. Preferably before he grows his tongue back. Do you see another way?" the demoness asked.

I let my head fall back and let out a soul deep sigh, "Fine. I'll meet with this mysterious person today in exchange for a blessed blade capable of killing a demon, but I've got somewhere to be first. Could your enigmatic boss meet me at one o'clock in Jackson Square?" I picked the popular tourist destination on purpose. It would probably limit any overt supernatural activity, which would likely play in my favor if someone powerful enough to be Meridiana's boss wanted a meeting.

"What could be more important than hunting down Razgothan as quickly as possible?" Meridiana asked incredulously.

"Who says I'm not? I've already got a meeting set with the local werewolves today. Do you think they'd help me kill a demon if I bought them a pizza?"

Chapter 6

I pulled up to the Forge on my Rebel twenty-seven minutes after I gently but firmly kicked Meridiana out of my apartment, with my favorite sword and karambits in hand, ready to receive this mysterious blessing. I'd yanked on my fighting leathers, added some regular knives to my ensemble to compensate for the missing karambits, and thrown together a bag from my closet that likely would've gotten me arrested if an officer from the NOPD had seen what was inside. I slung the saddlebag off the motorcycle and over my shoulder, lugging it into the bar. No sense in leaving this kind of arsenal where anyone could grab it.

This early in the morning, the bar was almost empty. I glanced around, searching for the werewolves, but I must've beat them here. Rudolph, the wood elf bartender who often worked the opening shift at the Forge, waved at me as I entered. Despite the tension creeping up my spine, I waved back. Rudolph crafted some of the best beer I had ever tasted, and that was saying something. I'd had some heavenly beers in the past. That wasn't just hyperbole either. Beers literally crafted by gods.

The slender wood elf left his mid-morning inventory work and hurried over as I approached. "You're in early, Cameron. Sloane isn't here yet. She was up late dealing with some belligerent patrons who wanted to keep drinking past closing time."

I waved my free hand. "Don't worry, Rudolph. I'm here to meet the Pack for a job, anyway."

The wood elf nodded but didn't pry. Rudolph was accustomed to the unspoken nature of my freelance work. More often than not, it fell on the wrong side of the law. It didn't do to advertise that fact too openly.

"Can I get you a round of something? Your favorite beer perhaps?" the wood elf asked. Rudolph kept a stock of chunky unlabeled bottles containing his homemade brew for me behind the bar. It was tempting, but I shook my head regretfully.

"Better not. How about you bring us a couple of pizzas and some sodas instead?" I said.

"Sure," he said, grabbing a pen and jotting down a note for the kitchen staff. "What kind do you want?"

I crooked a grin at him. "Given that it's werewolves, better make them meat lovers."

Rudolph nodded and hurried off to tell the kitchen as I claimed one of the larger tables. It wasn't like I had to fight anyone for the prime table space. No one else was in the Forge this early, but I knew it would fill up later. Sloane's bar was a popular place with the Supes of New Orleans.

Four people walked in about ten minutes later. I recognized three of them instantly. Will was a wiry African American man with curly hair that was neatly styled. He was also Damon's beta or second in command. Julius strode in after Will. He was built like a brick house and hit just as hard. I should know. I'd been on the receiving end of those heavy fists a time or two before the Pack and I made nice.

Trailing Julius and Will into the bar was a woman who looked vaguely familiar. I probably met her in passing, but never had learned her name. She was taller than I, not that meant much. Her long hair was so blonde it was almost white. She wore it braided tightly down her back. Her eyes were a piercing Nordic blue. She was ripped and looked like she trained with Julius eight days a week. Yes, I know it isn't possible, but if you saw her, you'd know what I mean. Her cotton tank top showed off her well-earned muscular arms and upper back. Tight black yoga pants clung to heavily muscled quadriceps. I wondered briefly if werewolves' clothes were dramatically shredded every time they shifted or if they faded into the wolf's pelt. I'd heard it both ways, but had never seen the process firsthand.

I probably would today.

I stood to greet the wolves as they walked up to my table, and I caught my breath as I got a good look at the last member of the party. Magnus.

Of course it was. I don't know why I'd expected anyone else, but seeing the handsome werewolf looking all fierce and gorgeous momentarily took my breath away.

Magnus and I had kinda had a thing. Sort of. Maybe. Damn it! I don't know! It was confusing. He'd played me to help the Pack track down a missing magical relic. He'd also tried to kiss me, and, in full disclosure, I'd wanted to kiss the handsome man back. Badly. Hell, I wanted to do more than kiss, if I was being fully honest with myself. However, when I'd found out he'd lied to me about who he was, I'd shut down those feelings. Hard.

Hadn't I?

The only problem was, I knew in my heart, that was a lie. There was something about Magnus that drew me in. He ignited feelings and emotions I'd kept long buried. If I was being truly honest with myself, I was simultaneously curious and terrified of what it would mean if I took those feelings out and examined them in the full light of day. It didn't help me sort out my emotions when Magnus had handled the situation so, well, *nicely*. He'd owned his lies, apologized for how he'd made me feel without resorting to excuses, and then given me space to sort out my own feelings on the matter.

The considerate jerk.

I craned my neck as the door swung closed, but couldn't see Damon behind the four werewolves.

Huh. That was weird.

Will strode up to the table and offered his hand. I shook it formally, noting the beta's cool and business-like gaze. Not a glimmer of warmth lit the depths of his dark eyes when we shook. On the other hand, Julius pulled me into a bear hug, a giant smile creasing his face. I grinned into the muscles on top of his muscles and pounded his back affectionately. Although we hadn't had many encounters, I instinctively liked the big man.

Will introduced the female. "Cameron Blaze, this is Parker. And you know Magnus, of course," he said, gesturing to the other two werewolves behind him.

"Pleased to meet you," the woman said with an amiable smile. She extended a hand, and I returned the firm grip with one of my own. I met her eyes steadily. After a moment of sizing each other up, we exchanged a nod. I knew we'd get along just fine.

I turned to the handsome werewolf behind her. "Magnus," I said simply. I noticed his tight t-shirt showed off his lean, muscled shoulders and chest and his worn jeans were slung low on his hips. A flutter started in my stomach, and I looked away quickly.

"Cameron," he returned in exactly the same tone. Then he lowered his voice in an effort to be discrete. It was probably a futile attempt, given the rest were werewolves with supernaturally good hearing, but I appreciated the effort. "Are you ok? That phone call..." he trailed off.

I nodded. "Don't worry about me," I said with a smile imbued with more confidence than the situation deserved. "I'm ok and I've got a plan."

Magnus considered me thoughtfully and then nodded without saying another word. He made no move beyond that, letting me take the lead. I was grateful. I still wasn't sure how I felt about the big man. Besides intense attraction.

Down, girl. Now's not the time.

Will cleared his throat. He gestured to the table. "Shall we?" he asked, but the authority in his voice showed me he was the one in charge.

Where was Damon?

We all sat. Rudolph hurried over with some cups, pitchers of soda, and an extra pitcher of water for the table. A server followed him, carrying three gigantic, steaming meat lover's pizzas.

Rudolph winked at me when the server wedged the extra pizza on the table. "When you said werewolves, I upped the order. Hope you don't mind."

I chuckled. "Thanks, Rudolph." I turned to the wolves. "I figured you guys for carnivores. Hope I guessed right."

"Yes! I knew I liked you," Julius said with a small fist pump. He grabbed plates and passed them out.

"Thanks for that, Cam. Very considerate," Will said, finally sending a smile my way as he accepted his plate from Julius.

"Anytime," I responded cheerfully, helping myself to a slice.

By the time I looked up, Parker had devoured half of her first slice. A second already waited on her plate. She gave me a thumbs up around a mouthful of cheesy deliciousness. Magnus glanced at Will, who hadn't reached for the pizza yet. He accepted his plate from Julius with a small nod of thanks, but reached for his water instead of the pizza, keeping an eye on Will.

Will selected a slice piled high with a variety of spicy meats. He placed it on his plate without taking a bite. He delicately lifted one chunk of sausage and popped it in his mouth before carefully wiping the residual grease from his fingertips off on a napkin. Only then did Magnus take a piece for himself, tearing into it like he hadn't eaten in days.

Odd. Why the power play? I thought they were all Pack.

I realized then that I'd never really seen Magnus interact with the Pack. Not in a normal, everyday setting, at least. I raised an eyebrow at Will while Magnus' head was bent over his food. The beta met my gaze stoically, refusing to say anything. The only sound around the table for the next few minutes was the contented smacking of lips as the werewolves filled their bellies.

Will finally cleared his throat when the last slice had been devoured, bringing everyone's attention back to him.

"Damon sent us because he said you needed some immediate back-up and he's tied up in a meeting with the Collective. Tell us what you need, and I'll let you know how we can help," Will said, introducing the topic of our meeting.

My curiosity got the better of me. "What's Damon doing with the Collective? Does it have to do with the demon? Are they going to take care of it?" That thought scared me. Even though I'd wanted just that less than an hour earlier, if the Collective killed Razgothan and sent him back to the Abyss, that could cause some pretty serious problems for me.

Julius chuckled, "Damon's the Alpha. He's got shit to do. We don't question what he does or why. But one thing about Damon is that he honors his agreements. Always. Which is why we're here. Think of us as Damon without the disapproving dad vibe."

A rueful grin curved a corner of my mouth. I wondered what sort of business was more important to the Alpha and the Collective than a demon on the streets of New Orleans. I'd have to ask him next time I saw him, but there was nothing to be done about it now. Besides, there were four capable werewolves sitting right in front of me. Surely, I could take down a demon with their help, right?

As quickly as possible, I explained the situation. "I need help to kill a demon who has decided he wants to take up permanent residence in New Orleans. I disagree with the relocation proposal. But the trick is we can't just kill his mortal shell. We must kill him so he can't ever come back to this realm or any other, so I have to kill him with this magically blessed blade or the entire operation is worthless. Oh, and I have a demoness who is going to help, but she's injured. And I need it done today. Should be a good time!" I said, giving them a double thumbs up and wiggling my hands with an exaggerated grin on my face.

Will met my eyes and blinked slowly. Julius threw his head back and laughed. The bigger man chortled, wiping at his eyes. "I knew from the moment I met you that you wouldn't be boring! Count me in," the big man said when he had finally regained control.

"Didn't we meet in the alleyway of a club right before I knocked you unconscious?" I asked, grinning in response. Julius' mirth was contagious.

"My point exactly," he replied, shooting a finger gun my way.

Parker tossed her long blonde braid over a shoulder. "Julius said you were crazy, but this is a step above what I was expecting." She shrugged, "What the hell? Count me in."

Will spoke up. "Happy to lend a hand, Cam, but we need to approach this cautiously."

My gaze swung to Magnus. He was drumming his fingers on his worn jeans as he tipped back in his chair, making it creak. The silence stretched. He glanced up at Will. "I don't like it, but do I have a choice?" his voice was soft, but calm.

The beta wolf shook his head, his gaze turning steely.

"Sounds like a great way to get killed, then. Looking forward to it." The sarcasm ran deep in Magnus' voice. I wondered what was going on with him, but now didn't seem like a good time to pry into Pack dynamics. There were bigger demons to fry.

"Tell us the set-up, please, Cameron." Will's voice drew me back to the present.

"Ok. We need an area that is open enough to give us space to maneuver, but where you guys can also stay hidden until I draw the demon out of hiding," I said.

"How are you going to do that?" Parker interrupted curiously, leaning both elbows on the table and resting her chin on her fists. Her forearms rippled with muscles.

I reached under the table and dug the scroll out of the bag at my feet. "With this," I said, waving it at her. I unfurled the scroll and placed it on the table where everyone could see the sigil I'd gotten from Manannan Mac Lir, the Irish god of the sea. I pricked the pad of my right thumb with one of my knives and pressed the drop of blood firmly to the empty circle in the middle of the ornate compass while muttering the Irish command word Manannan had taught me. A brilliant cinnamon-colored flare of light shot out of the page, and I covered my eyes with my free hand. When I looked back at the paper, the sigil had vanished.

Confused, I looked around. Manannan had told me that the ink would glow to show me where the spirits were. How could it glow if it had disappeared entirely?

Out of the corner of my eye, I noticed something unfamiliar on the inside of my right wrist. Cautiously, I turned my hand palm upwards to examine the mark. A symbol similar to the sigil, but much simpler. The cinnamon-colored design pulsed faintly in time with my heartbeat on the inside of my wrist. There were two lines forming an 'x' in the most simplistic of compass patterns. Each line was tipped with an arrow on one end and a small dot sat on the other end. The letter 'N' sat squarely between the two arrows, and three dots appeared faintly around the perimeter. One was orange, another was blue, and the third was red.

I ran my thumb over the simplified compass symbol. It looked like a tattoo. The ink didn't move under my thumb, but I saw a slight change as I shifted positions. Curious, I stood and turned around in a full circle. The compass on my wrist spun with me, the arrows keeping the 'N' fixed firmly north no matter how I rotated.

Despite my years being immersed in the supernatural realm, it still surprised me what some beings could do with their extra gifts.

"Magic is so cool," I murmured under my breath as I spun around once more, admiring the complex simplicity of the spell. The spell linking me to a demon. Suddenly, the magic sigil didn't seem so cool anymore.

"What's that?" Will's voice broke through my admiration of the spell.

"A tracking spell," I said, showing him the compass. "It links me to the demon. Now I can find him."

"But if it links you, doesn't that mean he can track you too?" Magnus asked, a worried frown darkening his handsome face. "You should've waited to activate that."

I shrugged, trying to play it cool. "He's already tracking me. I'm pretty sure that's how he found me earlier today. I just evened the playing field."

Parker leaned over for a better look. "If this is supposed to track the demon, why are there three dots, then?"

I squirmed in my chair. I hadn't wanted to admit to the other escaped souls, not when I'd worked so hard to skirt the issue with the Collective. However, it wasn't like I could hide it now. "The magic users that created it didn't have enough information to lock onto just one soul, so they had to track all three souls that escaped the Abyss on Halloween."

"So, a demon can track you now, plus two other souls crazy enough to break out of hell?" Magnus asked sharply.

"Not Hell exactly. The Abyss." It was a pedantic redirection, and I knew it. However, what was done was done. "Let's take care of the demon first and then worry about the rest, shall we?"

Magnus looked like he wanted to snap a retort back at me, but Julius interrupted with his typical good humor. "Just tell me when and where.

I can't wait to beat down a demon," he said excitedly. "First time for everything!"

Will leaned back in his chair and crossed his arms. "We also need a place that will be free of Norms. Collateral damage is unacceptable. I have strict instructions to keep a low profile. No fireworks." He met my gaze significantly, and I winced. Apparently, Damon was still cranky with me. Great. He was probably only agreeing to this because he owed me a favor.

How did you make things up to a werewolf? Was this a bottle of whisky or big juicy bone kind of situation?

"In New Orleans? That's difficult unless we head into the bayou," I said, running through options in my head.

"The bayou doesn't make for great fighting terrain unless we can scout the entire area first. There are too many hidden obstacles and the footing sucks. Are you sure we have to do this tonight? The short timeframe complicates matters further," Will said.

"If I don't handle soon, things are going to get a lot more complicated, trust me," I replied.

Magnus spoke up, "What about City Park? There is a model airplane field surrounded by trees. Perfect combination of open space and hiding places." I stared at him in mild surprise. It was a good idea, but I didn't know that he knew the area that well. The werewolves must have been sniffing out their new domain in the past few weeks.

"No good. Too many Norms," countered Julius.

Magnus countered, "Not after sunset. The park closes then. If we get some official-looking IDs, I bet we could clear out the area on some pretense or another. And if we stay in human form, we might disguise our scent from the demon long enough to get into a flanking position."

Parker nodded slowly, fingering the end of her braid. "Isn't there a lookout point there? We could use the high ground to monitor Cam until she lures this demon out into the open."

Magnus spoke up again, surprising me. "LaBorde Lookout, but the tree cover is too dense. You can't see shit from up there. We'll have to be scattered in the trees closer to the airfield, but far enough away that the demon can't catch our scents right away."

I stared at him in surprise. "How do you know all this?"

He shrugged, meeting my eyes. "I like to get to know the neighborhood," he said simply, which told me a grand total of jack squat.

A frown tugged my brows together, but before I could respond, Julius interjected, "Anyone else got any other bright plans?" The big man looked around the table expectantly. No one said anything.

Will let out a long sigh. "Looks like that might be our best option on short notice. I need some time to fabricate the ID's. Let's meet up, say, an hour before sunset? That should allow us enough time to sweep the area and evacuate the Norms quietly before Cam summons this demon. Julius and Parker, you're with me. We'll work as a Pack to take down the demon."

"But don't kill him," I interrupted. I didn't want an overzealous wolf sending the demon back to the Abyss prematurely and giving him a free pass to share what he knew about me. "When the time comes, that's my job." The wolves nodded their agreement.

Magnus raised a finger. "What about me?"

Will looked over at him, keeping his face carefully neutral. "Watch Cam's back," he ordered. "Don't let her do anything stupid. Watch her back trail. With that tracker on, who knows what's coming after her now?"

Parker spoke up. "Do you think one wolf will be enough? Shouldn't we have more on Cameron-guard-duty?"

Will eyed Magnus coolly. "Do you need help, or can you handle it?"

Magnus clenched his jaw, making it bulge, and a vein popped out on his temple. "I can handle it."

Whoa! What the hell was going on here?

Julius snorted. "Good luck with that, man," he said, clapping Magnus on the shoulder.

I shot the big man a dirty look, but Will spoke over my sputtered indignation. "Take the rest of the day to get what you need. If I know Cam at all, expect the unexpected. And explosions. They seem to follow this girl like stink on a skunk."

"Hey!" I protested. But that was all I had because he wasn't wrong.

Chapter 7

There wasn't much more to talk about with the werewolves. They headed out to make whatever arrangements they thought prudent after inhaling their pizza. I knew from experience that they were competent. None of them needed my interference in their planning or Pack dynamic. In fact, I'd probably mess things up if I tried to be too controlling. I was happy enough to let Will take the lead, although it irked me that Damon had delegated the repayment of his favor to the beta of the Pack. Nothing for it now, though.

As the werewolves filed out of the Forge, I pushed back from the table and grabbed the empty pitchers, taking them up to the bar. Rudolph met me there and nodded his thanks as he accepted the empties and stuck them into the sink to be washed later.

"Hey Rudolph, I know Sloane is probably still asleep, but will you tell her to check her messages when you see her, please?" I waggled my phone at him.

He gave me a thumbs up. "Sure thing. Anything else she needs to know?"

"I'll send her the details. If you could follow up to make sure she checks her messages, that'd be great. It's kind of time-sensitive."

"Sure thing."

"Thanks!" I waved at him with the phone. He lifted a hand in farewell before turning to tidy up the remains of the werewolf pizza demolition.

My thumbs flew across the small screen as I recapped the meeting for Sloane, sketching out the situation as succinctly as possible. I didn't expect help. In reality, I didn't want her anywhere near City Park tonight. I had the utmost confidence in the werewolves' abilities, but I knew Sloane. She liked to be kept in the loop. She got pissy when she was left out. I could deal with a pissy Sloane if I had to. What I couldn't deal with was the owner of the Forge getting upset enough to ban me from the bar, especially tonight. I had a feeling I was going to need a stiff drink before this was done.

I walked slowly across the bar as I typed and leaned a shoulder into the door as I pressed 'send' on my text. Email. Small thesis. Whatever.

"What took you so long?" a gruff voice behind me asked.

I whirled, almost dropping my phone as my hands flashed behind me for the knives at the small of my back. I wished for a moment that they were my trust karambits, but those were with Meridiana still. A split second later, I recognized the speaker.

Magnus stood leaning a shoulder against the wall of the Forge with his arms crossed. He wore dark aviator sunglasses, but I could feel the intensity of his stare. The fluttering in my stomach flared to life again.

I consciously forced my fingers to uncurl. "What the hell! Don't sneak up on someone like that!"

"To be fair, I wasn't sneaking. I was standing and waiting."

"For what?" I demanded.

"Will said to watch your back. I can't do that if I don't know where you are," Magnus said, a sexy smirk curling the corner of his mouth.

I crossed my arms over my chest, not sure how I felt at this turn of events. "He meant tonight. I don't need a babysitter all day."

Magnus shoved himself upright and closed the distance between us. "Now, that is up for debate, especially given your escapades over the past few weeks. First, you upset the werewolves, then you take on the vampires, and now a demon. I'm worried about you. How do you attract so much trouble?" He stared down at me, looking impassive behind the polarized glasses.

Heat rushed up my cheeks, and my lips flattened into a thin line. "Look, I appreciate the assist tonight. But I've got things to do before then. Besides, don't you have a tech company to run or were you lying about that too?"

"No, I run a tech company. A small one, but it's mine."

"Great. Can we use some of that modern-day magic against a demon?" I asked.

Magnus shook his head. "Bad idea. I don't think it's been tried before. I don't want to take any unnecessary risks against a demon, do you?"

I didn't. I shook my head and frowned. "Well, don't they need you at your company? Don't you need to captain the office or something?"

"That's the great thing about tech. You can do it from anywhere."

I waved my hand, shooing him away. "Hop to it then."

His grin widened. "Wolves don't hop and I'm right where I need to be." He exuded an air of stubborn calm, like a mountain: noticing the wind, but standing firm despite how hard it blew.

"Did you put Will up to this so you could follow me around?"

"Nope. I'm not mad about the assignment, though."

I narrowed my eyes at Magnus. He didn't twitch. With a huff of exasperation, I spun on my heel and strode quickly to my Rebel, shoving my helmet over my long hair. I heard the rumble of a powerful engine roar to life behind me. I snuck a look over my elbow as I swung a leg over my Rebel.

Instead of his Jeep Wrangler, Magnus sat astride what looked like a custom motorcycle. It looked like the meaner, more dangerous cousin to the Harley. There were absolutely no frills on the all-black bike. Just a sleek body polished to a high shine and a sexy as hell engine from the sound of it. It was something you could ride all night and want to keep going in the morning.

The bike, I mean.

Magnus revved the engine at me. Shit. He had caught me staring. Annoyed, I flicked a wrist. My engine roared to life. I wasn't sure exactly how I felt about the handsome werewolf, which was even more annoying, all things considered. Feeling out of sorts, I tore out of the parking lot and heard Magnus' bike follow me down the road. I swear I heard a deep chuckle over the rumble of the engines as we raced down the street.

I tried to find the line between ditching my werewolf tail and not getting pulled over. However, I had hours to kill before heading over to the park and I still had that meeting with Meridiana's contact soon. I didn't want to drive aimlessly around New Orleans and I definitely didn't want to bring Magnus back to my house for a game of fetch or whatever werewolves did to kill time. An idea sprang to the front of my mind. When the demon had found me, I'd just come from Mama's. If he was tracking me, he might be able to track me to her house. An icy fist of dread grabbed me by the throat and *squeezed.* Why hadn't I thought of this before? I turned my bike towards Mama's and gunned the engine.

My thoughts churned as I raced down the quiet mid-morning streets of New Orleans. Ben and Mama were probably fine, right? I mean, they'd survived in the supernatural world for a long time now. Nevertheless, a demon wasn't anything to mess around with.

By the time I rumbled to a stop at the back gate of Mama's house, I knew for a fact that Magnus knew his way around a bike. He rode the beast between his knees like it was grafted to him.

Wiggling my helmet loose, I finger combed my long waves as I waited for the werewolf to park. Helmet hair was not a good look on anyone, especially me, as I had learned the hard way. I eyed his ride appreciatively again as he walked up.

"Nice bike. What is it?" I asked.

"A Type 6 Samurai Chopper from Zero Engineering. Think East meets West. A Japanese company takes old school American muscle, strips out all the frills, blacks out everything but the chrome, and raises the bars to create that beautiful piece of machinery. I like the work you've had done on the Rebel," Magnus said, casting an appraising eye at my bike.

"Thanks. I did it myself." Pride rang in my voice. When I purchased the second-hand bike, even the worst rusted out junker would have looked down its engine at my Rebel. It had taken some long hours, but now she was a smooth-riding, finely tuned piece of engineering.

I started walking toward the cheerful yellow house and Magnus matched my stride. His tone shifted subtly. "Look, Cam, as much as I enjoy chasing you all over town, when are we going to talk about us?"

I sighed. "Later? I don't know how I feel about, well, everything. My life seems to have spiraled out of control and I need to have some calm before I can figure out how I feel about you. But if you're going to follow me around all day, we need some ground rules." I turned at the gate and held up a finger. "Rule one. This house belongs to a very nice old couple. Don't embarrass me by trying to mark your territory every which way to Sunday."

Magnus chuckled and raised his hands, acquiescing. "Don't worry. I'm house trained," he said.

"Fine. Rule two. I don't know if the demon can track me or if he just got lucky last time. Either way, if he shows up, get Mama and Ben to safety first. I can hold my own until they're out of harm's way."

He frowned. I put a little more steel into my glare. Getting Mama and Ben away from the demon was as much a tactical move as it was an emotional one. Magnus wasn't dumb. He understood and gave me a grudging nod, but I could tell he didn't like it.

"Rule three, and this is the most important." I narrowed my eyes as I looked up at him. "There will be snacks inside. They're not Scooby snacks. No fair snarfling them all down, even if you are part canine."

He rolled his eyes. "I'm a wolf, not a dog."

Only time would tell if that was true.

Chapter 8

Magnus followed me into the back courtyard that warmly embraced all visitors crossing into Mama Atli's domain. The comfy wicker chairs practically begged me to come and spend a lazy afternoon chatting under the shade of an ancient oak tree. Brightly colored scarves and rustic lights decorated the limbs of the tree, providing a cozy ambiance to anyone lucky enough to visit the old couple who lived here.

Mama looked up as we entered. She wore a pink and teal gardening apron protecting her brightly colored skirt and held a small trowel in one gloved hand. Her white teeth flashed in contrast to her coffee bean colored skin as she smiled up at me from an altitude that probably had its own set of rules for how oxygen behaved. I bent down to give her a kiss on the cheek as she opened her arms wide.

"Cameron! What a lovely surprise! It's so nice to see you again so soon, child." Mama turned her head and exclaimed over her shoulder. "Ben! Look who came to visit!"

The lanky necromancer popped up from behind the oak tree, wild white hair dotted with leaves and small twigs. He precariously balanced a large plastic bag full of leaves in his arms. It looked like he had just finished sweeping up.

I lifted a hand, "Hi Ben!"

"Cam! Twice in one day! What a pleasant surprise!" Ben exclaimed, heading in my direction too confidently. The large bag in his arms obstructed his view of his feet, which meant he didn't see the bristles of the broom he stepped on or the handle come flying up to hit the black plastic bag. Leaves exploded out into the air, covering Ben in a riot of oranges and browns before drifting back down to litter the courtyard. I winced and tried to hide a smile.

"Dangnabit!" Ben exclaimed, kicking at the leaves and almost tripping over the broom, which was lying in wait under the leaves to attack the clumsy necromancer once more.

"Here, sir, let me help you with that," Magnus said, hurrying over to support Ben's elbow until the old man's feet were free of both leaves and broom-y-traps.

Mama jerked her chin at Magnus. "Who's that then?" she whispered to me.

"My guard dog for the day. Call him Magnus," I said.

"I'll call him whatever he wants me to call him," Mama said under her breath. She eyed the werewolf appreciatively as he bent over to help Ben lift handfuls of leaves back into the plastic bag.

"Mama!" I swatted at her playfully, missing on purpose. It wasn't hard. All I had to do was swing my arm at shoulder height and there was no way I could make contact with the older lady, even if she was on tiptoes.

"What? I can appreciate a fine-looking man when he wanders into my home. Speaking of wandering in, the witch from down the street brought in a couple of bushels of late season apples yesterday. You inspired me and so I'm whipping up some more treats to send over to the shelter. I have some fresh apple fritters with a sweet vanilla glaze if you're hungry."

I winced, forgetting that I hadn't told her about the fate of her previous offering. "Look, Mama, we've got to talk. Somewhere private."

Mama read the serious expression on my face and immediately slid the gardening gloves and apron off. "Well, come on in then. I'll put the tea on."

I took a glance over my shoulder before following Mama into the house. Magnus was busy sweeping the mess of leaves into a neat pile as Ben tried to help him, but the old necromancer ended up scattering more leaves around the otherwise pristine courtyard in a chaotic whirlwind. I thought I saw the werewolf's shoulders shake in silent laughter of as he bent to re-do his work from a moment before. I suppressed a chuckle of my own and followed my nose into Mama's warm and welcoming kitchen.

Mama placed a large plate on the table piled high with gorgeous apple fritters generously drizzled with icing and dusted with a fine spray of powdered sugar. She slid a mug of hot cinnamon tea large enough to swim in over to me. I inhaled the fragrant steam and let out a soul-deep sigh of contentment. Sitting at Mama's kitchen table was one of the happiest places I knew.

"Tell me what's going on, child," Mama said, settling in with her own cup of cinnamon tea.

Rather than prevaricate, I jumped right in and told her everything. The demon and the Danishes. The djinn king. Meridiana, and her mysterious boss. The plan to go demon-hunting with the werewolves, the magical sigil, and some blessed blades I didn't actually have in hand yet. All of it.

"You see," I said as I concluded my story. "I'm worried this demon is tracking me. Through the sigil now, if nothing else. Which means there's a chance he could track me back here. You need to be ready. Maybe leave town for a bit?"

Mama nodded seriously. "Thank you kindly for the warning. I appreciate it. I'll tell Ben we're battening down the hatches until this mess with the demon blows over. We've got enough wards around the property to keep out most evil, and the local witches are kind enough to top up the magic when the wards run low."

I sighed in relief. I hadn't realized Mama's defenses were so solid, but it was reassuring to know.

Mama took a deep breath and exhaled slowly. "When it comes to stirring up trouble, you don't mess around."

"I didn't stir up anything! This all landed on my doorstep, whether or not I liked it!" I protested.

Mama leveled me with a mom-look hyped up on disapproving steroids over the top of her tea mug. A tiny part of me withered and returned to its room with no dinner. "You didn't have to agree to the

Collective's deal. Besides, you can still hand the demon issue over to them. From what you said, Damon is trying to work on that angle for you."

"I'm not sure he can convince them to take action fast enough on the demon front," I protested. "Besides, they didn't give me a much of a choice in hunting the rogue spirit, which might be the demon after all. To be fair, I'm running out of time on that front as well and the clock has sped up now that I've activated the sigil. It will continue to draw me towards the spirits and vice versa until I can send them back across the veil."

"Or they send you over," Mama pointed out.

"I'd rather that not happen," I said sincerely.

"Me too." Mama leaned back in her chair. "You acted rashly, activating the sigil before you set the battle ground, that's for sure."

I frowned at her. "I thought he was tracking me! I wanted a way to see where he is and now I can," I said, flashing the inside of my wrist at her. A sigh of relief escaped me as I looked at the magical tattoo. The colored dots were nowhere near me, thank all the gods.

"But he is also being drawn to you now. Hasty mistakes are often confused for decisive action in the heat of the moment." Mama's tone was cool and logical, but I still bristled.

"What was I supposed to do? Just sit around and wait for him?" I demanded.

Mama folded her hands on the table and met my eyes directly. "Child, if you are going to insist on going after creatures older, meaner, and more dangerous than you, you are going to have to use every weapon in your arsenal. And, no, I don't just mean guns and swords. You need to think ten steps ahead, consider all the angles, and bend the situation to fit your strengths while emphasizing your enemies' weaknesses."

"Well, I found out one of the demon's weaknesses is a kid's swing to the head," I said, trying to lighten the mood.

"This isn't some low-level vampire or an uppity witch. You cannot afford to take this lightly or you will *not* be walking away from it," Mama said sternly.

She wasn't wrong. I sighed. "I hear you, Mama. Do you have any tips for fighting a demon?"

Mama continued, "Like I said, you could try force, but I don't think you have enough might to make this situation right. Trickery is always an option, but my best advice? You need to be clever. Find the demon's linchpin as quickly as you can and pull with every fiber of your being."

"I didn't follow that last part. What do you mean?" I asked.

"You need to search for your enemies' weaknesses and unabashedly exploit them," she said seriously.

"Minimum effort, maximum results?" I asked.

"Something like that. Although, I would recommend maximum effort and catastrophic results. For your enemies, that is."

"I don't know, Mama. I don't think I'd look good in red spandex," I said with a small smirk as I thought of the irreverent, but hilarious pseudo-superhero movie.

"As long as your enemies wear their brown pants, you're fine wearing whatever you want, child," Mama said with a wink.

I choked on my tea. Who would've thought a kindly old lady who loved to bake could also quote the most foul-mouthed merce-nary-slash-superhero ever to grace the silver screen?

Thankfully, Ben's loud voice echoed through the entryway to the kitchen, giving me a moment to collect myself. The old necromancer bustled in, a whirlwind of disaster. Magnus followed close on his heels, barely saving Ben from a disastrous headfirst collision with a giant pumpkin. I dove to save the apple fritters, because, well, priorities.

Goliath, the lanky necromancer's reanimated familiar, appeared from under Ben's mop of wild white hair and leaped onto the table as the old man regained his balance. I swear the little mouse shrugged at me as if to say, "What can you do?" before curling up on a napkin and tucking his nose under his tail.

It was hubbub and chaos for a few minutes in the kitchen until Mama got everyone settled with cups of tea and fresh plates. Mama and Ben asked Magnus the normal, getting-to-know-you questions. Magnus batted them away easily and with charming cordiality. After about ten minutes of friendly banter that uncovered nothing terribly significant about his past, Magnus excused himself with a wave of his phone, saying he needed to check in with the Pack. He walked out into the courtyard to make his calls.

As soon as the kitchen door latched quietly behind the departing werewolf, Ben jerked a thumb over his shoulder. "I like him. He would be good for you."

I shook my head in bemusement. "I thought we kept you from hitting your head! Getting into a relationship right now is not my idea of a good time. Demon first. Dating later." I glanced at the tattoo again. All three dots were on near the outer ring of the compass, far away from me, which was a good thing for the time being.

"I'm just sayin'! That werewolf? Now, he's a handsome feller. You're a purty girl. Sometimes you have to say screw the timin' and just go for it!"

"Ben!" Mama said, putting her hands on her hips. "We've talked about this! The last time you tried to set someone up, it was with a ghost!" She turned to me, cupped the wrong side of her mouth and loudly stage whispered. "Don't mind him, now. He means well. I find smiling and nodding works wonders."

I pasted on an overly bright fake smile and nodded like a bobble head at Ben. He glowered at us both and grumbled as he collected the used dishes, clattering them into the soapy water in the sink. "One time! It was one time and now I can't be trusted with anything woman related..." He continued muttering, but the sloshing water made it impossible to understand him.

Mama grinned lovingly at the old necromancer before returning her gaze back to me. She rescued a brown paper package from Ben's splashing and handed it to me.

"What's this, Mama?" I asked, fingering the string tied tightly around the parcel.

"Oh, this and that from my medicine cupboard. If you are intent on confronting demons, I've always found that it is best to have an extra line of defense. Even if it is just ointments and the like."

"That's so kind of you. Thanks! But how did you know to make up a bag?" I asked as I tucked the precious package of healing unguents and poultices under an arm as I stood. Mama was legendary in this region for her healing concoctions. Her thoughtfulness was touching. Hopefully, I wouldn't have to use them.

"I had a feeling," Mama said with a soft smile as she walked with me. She pushed the door open. "Now, go make that demon regret he didn't wear his brown pants today." She winked at me, but I could see the tension that added to the crinkles next to her eyes. She was nervous for me.

I was nervous for me.

But I didn't own brown pants and never would. Red spandex all the way, baby.

Chapter 9

Magnus watched me from where he lounged in one of the comfy wicker chairs in the courtyard as I said my goodbyes to Mama. I tipped my head towards the gate and Magnus followed me outside, watching carefully as I tucked the package of Mama's healing supplies into the Rebel's saddlebags.

"What's that?" Magnus asked, jutting his chin towards the disappearing parcel.

"How was your call?" I countered, noticing the lack of a phone in his hand.

The wolf shrugged. "Fine. Damon is still tied up with the Collective. Will is all set to meet us later tonight. Besides, I thought you might like some privacy with your friends," he said, slanting his eyes back towards the cheerful yellow house. Mama and Ben had already disappeared inside. "They seem like a really lovely couple."

"Yes, they are," I agreed quietly. My phone rang, interrupting my thoughts. I dug the phone out of a pocket and glanced at the caller ID. Logan, my job broker. I saw a series of missed texts from him. I must not have heard the notifications on my bike. If he was this insistent on getting in touch, it couldn't be good. I sucked in a deep breath and exhaled noisily. When it rained, it didn't just pour. It rained cats and dogs. No, scratch that, it was more like tigers and hyenas. Magnus raised an eyebrow. I held up a finger, silently asking for a moment as I thumbed open the call.

"Yes, Logan. How can I help you this fine morning?" I said brightly.

"Cameron. Tell me you aren't going after a *demon*." He nearly spat out the last word.

"Good news travels fast, I see. Wait. How do *you* know about it, anyway?"

"The wolves. That Julius is a talker. Apparently, he was bragging to one of my agents about it."

I scrubbed a hand over my face. I hadn't told the wolves to keep our activities a secret, but I hadn't known word would travel this fast.

Logan's voice echoed over the phone as he raised his voice. "What are you thinking? You're already contracted with the Collective to take down an escaped spirit. And time is fast running out on that job. Do you really think you should add anything else to your plate right now?"

"You sound worried, Logan. I'm touched. It's unnecessary though. I'm handling everything. Don't stress." I tucked my free arm under my elbow and casually strolled away from Magnus in hopes of a semblance of privacy. I figured the werewolf could probably overhear my end of the conversation easily, but I wasn't sure I wanted him to hear Logan's side, too. Thankfully, the werewolf stayed where he was.

"I know you may not believe me, but I care about you. I don't want to lose an agent. You're spreading yourself too thin by trying to take on both fights. It's too much. Even for you. Ask the Collective for help with the demon, if nothing else. I don't want the next rumor I hear to be about your death." Logan's voice shook a little. A small smile spread across my lips as I shook my head. I hadn't expected the reaction from my stoic job broker.

"You don't have to worry. I promise," I said, attempting to reassure him while giving nothing away to the werewolf behind me.

"Really?" Logan's tone brightened. "What have you got planned?"

"Oh, this and that," I said breezily. "I'll fill you in later. However, you don't need to worry. I've got this, Logan."

Logan was astute. He stopped pressing the point. He must have finally realized I wasn't alone. "Fine. But I still think you've bitten off more than you can chew," Logan grumbled.

"Thanks for the input. I'm sorry, but I've got to run. Let's talk later, shall we?" I said cheerfully. He mumbled a farewell before disconnecting. I tucked the phone away before returning the few paces to Magnus and my Rebel.

"He's not wrong, you know. Whoever he was," Magnus said as I approached.

"It's not nice to eavesdrop," I said, frowning at the wolf.

He shrugged, obviously not bothered by my lackluster scowl. "You could play this another way. Leave the demon alone, stay in your lane, and let the Collective handle this while you figure out whatever you've got going on with the spirit your friend mentioned."

"What, and just leave this demon to roam around New Orleans? To terrorize everyone, including my friends? No thanks. Not my style. Besides, the demon might be the spirit they want me to take care of, anyway."

Magnus considered me carefully. "Do you really believe that?"

I didn't, but also didn't want to admit it. My silence spoke for me, though.

Magnus shook his head. "I'm not trying to belittle you, Cam. There's more than one way to solve a problem. More than likely, someone will take the demon out. Eventually. Why does it have to be you? Or today, for that matter?"

I thought about what he said. He had a point. I could take a risk and ignore the demon threat. Maybe there was still time. Or the demon didn't care that I had a connection to the djinn. However, if Meridiana was right, the demon would blab to someone in the Abyss. Someone who was no doubt bigger and badder. Then I could really be up the river Styx without a paddle. Or even a boat.

I rubbed my eyes with both hands, giving myself a break from the intensity of Magnus' polarized gaze from behind his sunglasses. If I didn't act to take out the demon soon, he'd probably end up making a mess in New Orleans. Trashing the town, hurting innocents, destroying pastries, not replacing the roll when he used the last part of toilet paper, and generally messing up people's day. Besides, I wasn't one to just sit around and wait. I'd much rather wade into a fight with my eyes wide open and my fists swinging. I returned my gaze to Magnus'.

"Come on then. We've got us a demon to kill. And then you'd better suit up, Ray, because we're busting ghosts after that."

"Who's Ray?" Magnus asked.

I rolled my eyes. If he wasn't into watching classics from the 80s, there might really be no hope for him. "Look, I've got a stop to make before heading to City Park. If you want to just meet me—"

"Not a chance," Magnus interrupted. "I'm not leaving you on your own today."

I shrugged casually, but part of me was really glad to have the werewolf watch my back. A sudden thought occurred to me. What would Meridiana, the succubus, say when I turned up for our meeting with a handsome wolf in tow?

Chapter 10

Against my express wishes, Magnus insisted on walking me to the middle of Jackson Square. But the werewolf came with some benefits. Like a lockable storage compartment on his bike. I stowed my bag of weapons and the package from Mama, thankful that I didn't have to lug either through the middle of tourist-central New Orleans. I fished out a small satchel and tucked an extra pair of knives inside. I'd taken Mama's warning to heart. I needed to outmaneuver my opponents rather than waiting and reacting.

It didn't take us long to reach the center of the small square. We stood facing the triple spires of the iconic St. Louis Cathedral with the statue of Andrew Jackson riding his bronze stallion behind us. I adjusted the strap on my satchel to a more comfortable position as I looked around for Meridiana. The demoness was nowhere to be seen. I glanced up at the towering white church. I always thought that it looked like it could've been the inspiration for any of the cartoon princess castles. Magnus looked out of place as he stood with his arms folded over his gray t-shirt and low-key glowered at anyone who stared at us for too long as they hurried by the beautiful old building.

After shooting him pointed glances that he just as pointedly ignored whenever his glare sent a tourist scurrying away, I cleared my throat. "Hey Magnus? Stop scaring the Norms before you draw the wrong kind of attention."

He swiveled his head, monitoring the crowd from behind his sunglasses. "It doesn't matter. Norms are always uneasy around me unless I play up the charming. It's an instinctive thing. And I don't have the energy for it today. Not with a demon on the loose and able to lock onto your location."

"You could try smiling," I said, turning to look up at him.

He bared his teeth in a grotesque semblance of a smile. "Like this?" he asked through the forced expression that contorted his handsome face into a ridiculous caricature.

I rolled my eyes, smiling despite myself. A woman cleared her throat behind me, and I nearly jumped out of my skin. I whirled to see Meridiana. The demoness didn't look much better than the last time I saw her. The difference was she hid it better behind a large black straw hat, oversized dark sunglasses, and a slouchy pullover paired with skinny black pants and boots. She looked like she could've been a movie star incognito. As we approached, it was the bruises under her skillfully applied makeup that gave her away.

"I'm glad you made it. I was worried Razgothan might've tracked you down again," Meridiana said, eyeing me up and down.

"Not yet," I said. I flashed the compass tattoo at her. "Besides, now I can track him back and he's not close by."

"For the moment," Magnus growled.

I ignored him. As quickly as I could, I filled Meridiana in on the plan the werewolves and I had cobbled together.

She considered it thoughtfully and then nodded. "It should work. If Razgothan shows up, that is. I'll be there. An hour before sunset? Hopefully, if you stay in one place long enough, it will draw him in."

"Yes. But the plan only works if you got those blades blessed. Did you?" I asked Meridiana.

She nodded and handed me a tube that looked like it might hold a rolled-up painting. "Blessed and ready to dispatch any demon you might have a quarrel with." I popped the top off and peeked inside. My sword looked normal, as did my karambits. I'd have to take her word for it that the blessing had stuck. The word of a demon. That thought made me suddenly very nervous, even though Meridiana had never done anything to hurt me.

Moving as quickly as I could to avoid drawing the gazes of the tourists, I swapped the sheathed and blessed karambits for the knives I currently carried at the small of my back. Those went into my satchel. I toyed with the sword again, considering the pros and cons of carrying it through the heart of New Orleans in what was essentially a long plastic tube.

The demoness cleared her throat. "If you don't mind tucking that away, I'd appreciate it," she said, shifting ever so slightly away from the open tube.

"Oh, right. Demon killing weapons probably make you uncomfortable," I said, replacing the cap on the tube. "They're not my favorite," Meridiana allowed. "Now that piece of business is taken care of, shall I make introductions? Your host is waiting for you in that restaurant, on the corner or St. Ann and Chartres." Meridiana waved a hand towards the brick building.

"You mean Muriel's? You could've just said that from the get-go. It's an icon!" I slung the strap of the tube with the blessed sword over my shoulder and started walking. Magnus fell in behind me. Meridiana cleared her throat. I turned to face her, confused.

"Lose the wolf," Meridiana said, folding her arms over her chest.

Magnus let out a low growl. Before things could escalate, I stepped in. "You remember Magnus, right? He's my bodyguard until this thing with Razgothan is finished. Not that I want the protection, but you try arguing with werewolves. Stubborn a-holes, the lot of them." I didn't want to get into the whole werewolf fiasco in the middle of the street.

Meridiana shook her head. "I never took you for a bodyguard kind of girl. Besides, your host won't appreciate the extra company."

Magnus curled a lip, showing a sharp canine to the demoness.

"Why are you here, wolf? Sniffing around?" Meridiana shot back.

Magnus tightened a fist at his side and took a step forward, jaw clenching. Meridiana grinned invitingly, taking a step forward to meet the werewolf. Before relations could disintegrate further, I wedged myself in between them. They both stopped, although they continued to glare at each other.

"Stop it," I hissed. "You're scaring the kids." I pointed a finger at a prim woman who pointed pushed her toddler's stroller off her original trajectory, giving us a wide berth. The little tyke stared at us and sucked his thumb harder as his mom pushed him around the corner.

Meridiana and Magnus ignored me. They continued to glower at each other. I lightly tugged on Magnus' shirt. "Will told you to watch me. That doesn't mean you have to stay glued to my side. Here." I dug in a pocket and pulled out a wrinkled five-dollar bill. "Go buy yourself an ice cream and scowl from over there." I waved towards a local confectionary shop across the small square. It still did a brisk business with the tourists, despite the cooling weather. "We'll be right there," I said, nodding at the pricey bistro on the corner.

"Fine," growled Magnus. He ignored the money in my hand, wheeled on his heel, and strode toward the shop across the square. He leaned against the wall of the building, making sure we both knew he wasn't going anywhere and planned to keep watch.

Meridiana rolled her eyes and led me across the street towards the two-story reddish building with the lacey wrought-iron balcony.

"What gives?" I whispered to her. "I thought you were a succubus and would be all about throwing me at the nearest eligible man."

Meridiana smirked as she held open the door for me. "Oh, I am. But timing is everything. And now is not the time."

"What are you talking about?" I whispered as Meridiana led me into the restaurant and up to the second-floor balcony. There was a single table on the otherwise empty balcony. A woman in a dress of vibrant green and purple sat with her back to us, sipping from a tumbler of something dark. I caught a whiff of heavy spices on the breeze. A bottle of the same stuff sat at her elbow along with a pitcher of water.

I did a double take because I recognized the bottle. Which was weird. But I only recognized it because I'd been contracted to steal it. It should've been a straightforward job, but then there was this thing with an illegal poker game and a rooster. Cocked everything up for me.

The woman at the table turned to face us as we approached. My stomach dropped as I recognized the woman. "Thank you for bringing her to me, Meridiana. You may go about your business as you see fit," the woman said. I felt more than saw the demoness bob her head and back slowly away from the goddess sitting on the balcony, sipping rum.

Maman Brigitte favored me with a brilliant smile. "It is good to see you again, Cameron. Please sit. We have much to discuss and far too little time, I'm afraid." The goddess waved a hand at the empty chair across from her. In a daze, I sat as she poured some of her hot pepper infused rum into a spare glass and slid it across to me. Brigitte nodded at the glass. "Drink up, it looks like you damned well need it."

I didn't hesitate. I threw it back because when a goddess tells you to drink, you *drink.*

Chapter 11

I coughed and my eyes watered as the burn from the alcohol was magnified tenfold by the hot peppers.

"Give it a second," Maman Brigitte advised, sipping her own rum calmly as she splashed some water from a bottle into my glass. I sipped, hoping the water would dissipate the burn as I tried to sort out what was going on.

Maman Brigitte was Meridiana's secret, mysterious watcher? Her boss? What did that mean? More precisely, what did that mean for me?

I scrambled to recall the research I'd done on Maman Brigitte over a month ago. She was a loa, a local deity. Probably the best way to describe her was to put her on a par with the minor gods and goddess of the Greek or Roman pantheons. She was like the god of vegetation or the goddess of incredibly impractical shoes, but the Louisiana version, which meant a lot more spice. And, according to Meridiana, also led the Necrocracy, which kind of made sense. Brigitte watched over cemeteries, helped to ferry the dead to the afterlife, and was rumored to be a fierce protectress, particularly of women. Oh, and she loved rum, swearing like a sailor, and roosters. I'd have made a juvenile joke if she hadn't been a goddess of death. Shit! The rooster! He'd clawed me up badly last time. I looked around cautiously for the animal.

"You don't need to worry. He's not here," Maman Brigitte said, casually looking out at the milling tourists on the street below us.

"Umm, what?" I asked, not following her meaning and probably sounding incredibly stupid to the goddess.

"Cluck Norris. He's not here. After your brief run in at the poker game, I decided not to bring him. I hope your hand has healed," she said, turning to face me fully.

Looking down, I opened and closed my fingers. I had injured my hand last month. There was still some stiffness, but I'd been lucky that I hadn't suffered more permanent damage. "Yeah. I mean, yes, it has. Thanks." My tongue felt awkward and clumsy as it tried to form words in my mouth, even though I'd been doing the speaking thing for well over two decades.

Brigitte ignored my stumbling and looked back out at the teeming bustle of Jackson Square. "It's a beautiful town, isn't it? No place at all for that flaming fart-monger of demon. What was his name? Twinkleshit?"

I snorted and barely held back a laugh. "I don't think that's it," I said, not sure I trusted myself to handle more than monosyllables at the moment.

"Do you know why I asked you here?" Brigitte said, changing topics so abruptly that I answered on instinct rather than giving my words the due diligence they deserved.

"I don't know. You like making mortals dance?" *Shit. Probably shouldn't have said that to a deity.*

Brigitte winked at me. "Glad to see you are feeling more like your old self. Another shot?" She held up the bottle of rum. "I've found it to have the most rejuvenating properties when one has had an epically shitty day."

A laugh escaped me at the vulgarity. I leaned back in my chair, feeling a little more at ease. "I'm not sure I should. I should probably keep my wits about me if I'm going to take on Twinkleshit later."

She jiggled the bottle at me. "Are you sure? This isn't your normal, over-the-counter rum. I make it myself. Not only does it warm you up from the inside out, but it also has significant healing properties."

I eyed the bottle skeptically. "You made a hot pepper infused healing rum? Isn't that, I don't know, slightly contradictory?"

Brigitte smirked. "I'm a goddess and I do what I like. I'm a woman who enjoys protecting people. And drinking." She shook the bottle again. "This is the very definition of multitasking! Oh, and the bottle magically refills! Double win! Or is that a triple by now?"

I didn't really want to quibble with the goddess, so I slid my glass over to her. She splashed a healthy pour of amber liquid into it and I tossed it back. This time, I felt the burn radiate from the pit of my stomach and morph into a soothing warmth. Not at all in the light-headed way alcohol usually hit me. This was the same feeling as curling up on a snowy winter night in front of a crackling fire with a big mug of hot cocoa. Plus hot peppers, of course. Brigitte smiled knowingly at me.

I coughed to get the burn of the peppers out of my throat before I spoke. "So, are you going to tell me why you've been keeping tabs on me? Like why you allowed me to take a bottle of rum off you last month," I said, tipping my glass towards the magically refilling bottle between us as she topped me up, but set down a completely full bottle.

"Straight to the point, I like it." Brigitte splashed a little more of the dark liquor in our glasses and clinked hers against mine. We sipped. She set her glass on the table and nodded at the bottle. "Call it an introduction. I wanted to see how you operated and, might I say, you were fucking impressive."

"Thanks." I gathered my nerve and addressed the loa head on. "Look, I don't mean to be rude, but why did you call this meeting? Why have you been watching me? I mean, what do you want from me? I'm no one special."

"Oh, I don't believe that for a godsdamned second," Brigitte said with a smile. Her smile faded, and she lowered her voice. "Meridiana told me you were looking into the djinn kings. That you might have a way to contact one."

I froze, unsure of how to play this. Was Brigitte pro-djinn or anti-djinn? Which was I? I tried to play nonchalant. "Sure, I was. Academic exercise."

Brigitte pursed her lips and tipped her head to the side, shooting me a knowing look. "We both know that's not true," she scoffed lightly.

"Maybe. Maybe not."

"What about the rumor that your mother might have actually been in contact with one of the kings? That she had a way of talking to one of the missing kings?" Brigitte asked.

Shit.

I answered carefully, keeping my face a studiously blank mask. "My mom had a lot of different interests, but she didn't get the chance to tell me about all of them before she died. I'm just trying to unravel some mysteries she left behind. Are you suggesting I walk away without even trying to solve them?"

Brigitte squinted at me and then closed her eyes, letting her head fall back. "No. Maybe. I don't know. Damn! This is one of those times I wish I'd qualified for the omniscient upgrade!" She exclaimed to no one in particular. She opened her eyes and stared at me. "Cards on the table? All I know is that you've made my job simultaneously easy as shit and hard as fuck, which is a stupidly confusing sentence."

"What do you mean?" I asked.

"I'm mixing curses and it's muddying my meaning," the goddess said.

"No, about me helping you out and getting in your way," I explained, trying hard to keep from chuckling at the vulgar loa.

"Oh. Right. You seem to have a habit of saving people while putting yourself in deadly situations, which is great for everybody else but shit for you. Take that bastard Kingsley. Octavian and his screwed-up nest of vampires also spring to mind. Both times, you were acting to save someone else while putting your life on the line. Both times, you eradicated a threat to my city, but were injured doing so."

I rubbed my shoulder where a vampire had dug its fangs in during the aforementioned conflict, not quite knowing what to say. I suddenly realized the dull ache that had been annoying me for days was gone. Wow! Maybe the rum really was what she said it was. "I don't know. Just part of the job, I guess."

"Oh? And what job is that? Free-lance jill-of-all-trades? 'Saving the city' falls under your job description, does it?" I squirmed under her direct gaze. Brigitte sighed and fiddled with her tumbler. "I feel like I should damn well hire you to work on my team," she muttered. "I think you'd do a damn sight more for this city than those stinking shitweasels on the Collective. They can all go get stucking fuffed, the lot of them."

I chuckled and rubbed my forehead. "That'd be a hell of a thing to put on a resume. Can you imagine the next job interview? 'Yes. My last job was working for a goddess. Would you like a reference? Sure, I'll get her to email that over to you right away'. They'd think I was nuts!"

"To be fair, *I* think you are nuts." Brigitte smiled warmly at me, taking any sting out of her words. "But you're right. Working for me as your full-time job probably wouldn't fly. Perhaps you'll consider freelancing someday?"

I sipped the spicy rum, feeling like I was moving back onto familiar conversational turf. Was this all one big negotiation? "As long as the pay was right. Speaking of, you still haven't told me why you wanted to meet," I reminded her.

"Well, keep it in mind," Brigitte said seriously. "But it looks like you've got some other things on your plate right now," she said, pointing with her lips towards the sigil tattoo on my wrist.

I looked down and ran my thumb over the magical design. "Yeah, I'm kind of in the middle of something."

"Well then, until you are free from prior engagements, consider this a warning combined with a free drink and sprinkled with the tantalization of potential employment, should you ever want a new, life-threating adventure."

"So, let me get this straight. You're telling me to stay away from the dangerous djinn, drink even more rum, and risk my life working for you," I summarized.

Brigitte raised her glass in response. "No, I'm telling you to switch up your swear words now and then. It keeps them potent. For example, call someone a piece of fuck. Tell them to go shit themselves. Keep the magic alive." She winked at me. "But yes, more so the djinn, rum, and work things."

"No offense, but you're a weird fucking goddess. Shitting goddess? Hell, now I'm all confused about what's an insult and what's a compliment!"

"No offense, but you're my kind of people," Brigitte said with a wicked smile.

I furrowed my brows. "I'm not sure if I should thank you or be offended."

"If you don't know, then my work here is done!" The redheaded goddess pushed back from the table. "If I could offer you one piece of advice before I go?"

"Sure," I shrugged.

"The djinn are not to be trifled with. But if you can't leave well enough alone, always leave yourself a loophole." She tipped her head towards the street. "I'd offer the same advice about werewolves, but I don't think you'll listen."

I looked down to see Magnus leaning against the fence across the street and staring up at our balcony intently. When I looked back, Brigitte was halfway through the door leading back into the restaurant. She looked over her shoulder.

"Be careful, Cameron. I'm good at my job. But I don't think that even I can keep up with protecting you."

"Hey," I called after her. "You forgot your bottle." I lifted the dark rum off the table.

She held up a hand in farewell. "You keep it. Consider it me doing my part for the community. And don't forget about that job offer."

"I'll think about it," I said.

"That's all I ask." The loa gave me a little mock salute and disappeared inside.

I considered my glass of rum. "My life is shitting weird," I muttered and then shook my head firmly. "Nope. That felt wrong on so many levels." I slammed back the rest of my drink, letting it warm me deliciously from the inside out. Then I snatched up the still full bottle before heading down to smooth any fur that might have been ruffled.

Chapter 12

Magnus pushed away from his lean against the fence as I exited the bistro, shoving the bottle of rum into my satchel and adjusting the tube holding the sword so it lay diagonally across my back. The werewolf dug into his jacket pocket and pulled out a small brown paper bag, offering it to me.

"What's that?" I asked suspiciously, eyeing the wrinkled bag in his hand without reaching for it.

"Fudge. The owner of the shop said it's their best seller."

"When... scratch that. *Why* did you buy fudge?"

He shrugged and smiled. The smile transformed his face back into the genial, handsome man I'd first met. "You were right, that confectionary shop has a great selection. You've had a rough day. Let's be honest, chocolate always makes everything better."

You could have knocked me over with a feather. This werewolf was full of surprises.

I grabbed the bag and popped a piece of fudge into my mouth. The smooth chocolate confection melted deliciously on my tongue, making me feel instantly better. Magnus was right. It hadn't been a great day. No, week. Make that month. It had been a hell of a month. No matter what I did, it felt like powerful forces were conspiring against me to make things as difficult as possible. Somehow, the fudge cut through all the noise. The gooey cocoa and sugar helped ground me in reality, if only just for a moment.

I swallowed and took a deep breath. I had a feeling that things were going to get worse before they got better. Carefully, I re-wrapped the fudge and shoved it into my pocket for later. Emergency chocolate was never something to ignore. Especially when it was this good.

A movement on my wrist caught my eye, and I flipped my hand over, examining the tattoo. The brilliant orange dot pulsed in time with my heartbeat, a hair's breadth from the center of the compass.

I licked the sweet, sticky residue from my fingertips as I swung my arm from side to side. "Well, that's interesting," I murmured.

"What?" Magnus asked.

I took off without responding, weaving through tourists milling on the corner and started walking briskly down Chartres Street, putting Muriel's and the iconic, immaculate St. Louis Cathedral with its triple spires soaring majestically into the bright blue sky behind me.

"Cameron! Stop!" Magnus growled.

"Can't!" I shouted over my shoulder as I broke into a trot. "I've got a spirit in my sights and I'm not letting this be the one that got away."

I heard Magnus following close on my heels, but I ignored him as I dodged babies in strollers and oblivious tourists all the way down Chartres Street. The orange dot drifted to the left, so when I reached Dumaine Street, I turned that way. I hurried between the brick buildings housing a bike rental on one corner and an art gallery on the other. Luckily, Dumaine wasn't terribly crowded, and I could increase my speed.

I rushed down the street, alternating between looking at my wrist and watching for potential collisions with milling tourists. The tubular sword case thumped awkwardly against my back. A small shop with rose-colored doors selling "authentic" voodoo items caught my eye as I hurried down Dumaine. Recognizing the proprietor, I raised a hand in greeting. Nigel was a witch. He did a brisk business entertaining the tourists, but also used the store to traffic in powerful occult items for Supes as well. I'd used his services more than once. We were friendly, but I didn't have time to chat. Instead, I shot him a quick smile as I hurried past. Nigel waved at me in return and then I was past him and rushing towards an escaped spirit as a werewolf pounded after me down Dumaine.

Probably for the best. Some things were just not meant to be explained over afternoon small talk.

Another block, and I pulled to a stop so suddenly that Magnus swerved to the side to keep from knocking me over. I ignored the muttered curses from the annoyed werewolf as I looked up at the three-story building in front of me.

Balconies covered with potted plants stretched across the entire front of the building on the upper two floors of the brick building. Someone had painted the front a sandy beige color, but the paint stopped abruptly on the exposed, worn bricks on the side of the building. A carved wooden sign hung above the sidewalk, proclaiming that it housed ancient and mysterious voodoo artifacts inside the small museum.

And the little orange dot told me somewhere, inside the building, a ghost was hiding.

"Suddenly needed to see some shrunken heads?" Magnus asked drily.

"If I needed to see a tiny head, I'd just look at you," I replied, cupping my hands around my eyes to peer through the glass on the door to examine the cramped collection inside.

"Hey!"

I turned my head to look at him, pasting a wide-eyed innocent look on my face. "You're right. That was out of line. Your head is colossal. Some might even call it ginormous. Why, I do declare, it is the biggest head in all of N'awlins!" I thickened up my accent to a syrupy sweetness that Scarlett O'Hara would have been proud of.

Magnus lifted the corner of his lip in a silent snarl, but the twinkle in his eyes betrayed him. "Are you sure you want to poke at the wolf?"

I grinned unapologetically. "Seems like a good way to spend the afternoon." Wow! What was in that chocolate? Or was it the rum? Regardless, any residual aches and pains from the past few weeks had faded to a mere memory, making the banter even more enjoyable.

"What are we doing here?" Magnus asked, putting his hands on his lean hips and examining the voodoo museum.

Deciding I'd better stop tugging his tail, I flashed the tattoo on my inner wrist at him.

"Remember how I told you that this thing linked me to the escaped spirits? Well, either we got lucky or the magic in the tattoo is pulling the spirits towards me. Either way, one of them is in that museum." I pointed at the open museum door.

Magnus dug into his pocket for his phone. "It might be the demon. I'll call Lykaios and tell him…"

It took me a moment to realize he meant Damon. I took two quick steps forward and slapped my hand down over the phone's screen.

"If there was a demon in there, don't you think we'd hear screaming or something? No, I think it's one of the others. I don't need the Fur-eign Legion on this one. All I need is to get in there, find the spirit, trap it, and get out. One down, two to go."

Magnus raised an eyebrow. "Oh yeah? How're you gonna do that? Sweet talk it into holding your hand and going to the school dance?"

I held up a finger, a sharp retort tickling my tongue. But he wasn't wrong. I tipped my head to the side, tapping my finger lightly against my lips. "That is a… fair point. Hmm. Give me ten minutes."

Magnus didn't answer, but tucked his phone back into his pocket.

I smiled up at him. "Great. I'll be back in two shakes of a wolf's tail." I took off, returning the way we had come.

"What am I supposed to do?" Magnus said, at my retreating back.

I turned, walking backwards a couple of paces as I shouted, "What all good doggies do. Sit and stay!"

"The dog jokes have got to stop at some point!" he called after me.

"Oh, I'm just getting started!" I spun and increased my speed as the werewolf's growl chased me down the street.

Magnus trailed me down the street. I shouldn't have expected anything different. He even followed me into Nigel's shop and tried to look inconspicuous in the cramped space. He failed miserably.

When I finally got what I needed and started trotting back up Dumaine a few minutes later, Magnus fell into step beside me. He lowered his glasses and peered over the rims as I held up the heart-shaped glass jar with a small cork stopper aloft for his inspection.

"What's that?" he asked curiously.

"Oh this? This is magic!" I held up the heart-shaped jar in triumph.

"Great. Are you going to tell me that's Love Potion Number 9, like from the song?" he asked skeptically.

"Not unless you are gonna go kiss a cop on Thirty-fourth and Vine because I would love to see how that turns out for you." I waggled my eyebrows suggestively. Magnus shoved his sunglasses higher on his nose and gave me the polarized stare of death. I was fast developing an immunity to his glower and continued unperturbed. "It's not for you. It's for the spirit. I have an acquaintance who has a shop down the road and deals in occult items. Real ones, not the ones for tourists. Nigel swears that this will suck any rogue ghosts up like a vacuum."

"You know, I always thought I'd be good at ghost hunting if ever given the opportunity."

I checked my tattoo. The orange dot still glowed brightly near the center of the simple compass as we approached the museum. "Great. Now's your chance. In and out, easy-peasey."

Magnus held the door wide for me as I marched into the voodoo museum, the ghost catcher clutched firmly in my hand. The werewolf slid a couple of crisp bills across the front desk to the dark-haired, pale teen dressed all in black who sat behind the counter. Her phone entirely engrossed her attention. She barely glanced up as we entered. Her black tipped thumbs never stopped flying across the screen as she slid two tickets and a rumpled brochure across the counter to us. I murmured my thanks, but the girl was already lost in her digital wonderland.

We wandered through the cramped museum, taking in the bizarre objects stuffed into every nook and cranny. A skeleton stood in one corner, wearing a top hat cocked at a jaunty angle. Next to him was a strange scarecrow decorated in shamanistic paraphernalia with a crocodile's skull perched precariously on its stuffed shoulders. The sightless eyeholes of the croc's skull seemed to track us as we picked our way through painted masks, carved statues, and innumerable voodoo dolls. Luckily, it seemed like we were the only visitors for the time being. Well, the only corporeal ones, anyway.

I shivered. "This looks like a place that could've spawned Chucky."

"Who?" Magnus asked.

"You know? The terrifying-murder-doll?"

"Who's afraid of a doll?"

I eyed him skeptically. "Um, everybody in their right mind?"

"I think we have very different definitions of the word 'scary'. For example, you're scared of a doll but are actively pursuing a demon. Seems like it should be the other way around," Magnus observed mildly as he turned to examine a cracked oil painting of a voodoo priestess on the wall. "How are you going to find this spirit, anyway?" He asked as he peered at the next painting depicting a grave-looking bishop caught in the moment of giving a blessing to something below him. Someone had thoughtfully staged a large wooden statue of a well-endowed monkey fondling himself just below the portrait, making it look like the priest had the oddest holy ability ever.

"Wow, that George really is curious," I said under my breath.

"Sorry, I missed that. What'd you say?" Magnus asked over his shoulder as he inspected another painting, this time of a tall man draped in purple and black robes waving a wand.

I raised my voice. "I said, 'we'll have to search the mysterious'. You know, poke through all these hoodoo-voodoo-thingamajigs until we find the spirit."

Magnus slowly took his sunglasses off and tucked them through the collar of his shirt, leaving them hang against his chest. "You don't know how to find this ghost, do you?"

"Other than using the sigil, not a clue. But that's never stopped me before."

"I can believe that," Magnus said drily before resuming his inspection of the paintings on the wall.

I ignored him and flipped my wrist over so I could see the tattoo. With my eyes glued to the glowing dot, I spun in a slow circle, hoping for something to happen. Nothing did. The orange dot sat squarely in the middle of the crossed arrows, pulsing in time with my heartbeat.

"C'mon, is this thing on?" I said, tapping the tattoo with my forefinger. Remembering what Manannan told me about the magnetic properties of the magic, I closed my eyes and turned around again with my arm held outstretched in front of me. I tried to stretch out with my other senses, including my magic.

There! Was that a tiny pull?

I opened my eyes to see a small door draped in colored beads leading towards the back of the museum. I glanced over my shoulder. Magnus had drifted along the side wall and was examining a skull with a half-smoked cigar clenched in its teeth. I peered into the darkened doorway. It wasn't like the museum was a big place. If I needed help, Magnus could be through this door in faster than a roadrunner with a rocket. Besides, I didn't want him to think of me as incompetent.

Damn it, focus! I did not need feelings for the werewolf to get in the way of catching this ghost!

Pushing my thoughts of my handsome werewolf companion to the side, I moved toward the beaded doorway, my upraised wrist leading the way.

The deeper into the cramped museum I went, the stronger the force pulling at my wrist became. I turned a corner and halted abruptly in front of the back wall. It was painted a disgusting mint green and lined with mismatched cases stuffed full of bizarre items. I swung my arm back and forth like a ghostly metal detector. The magic pulled me to the right. The only thing on that wall was a locked glass curio cabinet. Following the tattoo, I brushed dust from the glass door and peered inside.

Cracked clay jars of all shapes and sizes dotted the shelves. Interspersed between the earthenware vessels were small, warped wooden chests inlaid with mother-of-pearl and ornately painted miniature boxes that one might have used to hold jewelry. There was even a dented lockbox on the bottom shelf that looked like it was more rust than metal.

"Find something?" Magnus' voice rang out behind me.

"I don't... wait!" I had half-turned to answer him when a flicker of orange caught my eye. Slowly, I swiveled my head back around, tracking the pulsing glow as it settled on the lock of the curio cabinet. The handle of the glass door gave a little shake. Suddenly, the spirit was inside the curio cabinet. It floated down and settled on a small blue glass bottle corked with purplish wax. Someone had tucked the bottle at the back of the cabinet, almost hidden from view, behind a large clay vase. The spirit slid over the smooth blue surface as if searching for a way in.

I sucked in a breath. I didn't know that spirits could affect the physical plane. To be fair, what I didn't know about spirits would've filled an encyclopedia and then some. What I did know was that the Collective hadn't wanted to deal with at least one of these escaped souls. That's why they'd subcontracted the job out to me. I just hoped this was the one they wanted, but I figured between it and the demon, I had a two-thirds chance of getting the right one. I'd assumed it was going to be difficult or dangerous to catch the soul, but this looked like it was going to be easier than I expected. As I uncorked the heart-shaped glass ghost vacuum, I was already imagining how I would spend the reward money.

Which means I wasn't focused.

I should've known better.

Chapter 13

A forceful thrust surprised me when the cork on the ghost catcher popped free. It felt like I was holding a supernatural firehose that had just been turned on full force. I stumbled back a pace at the unexpected jolt, just to have the magic reverse course. Instead of pushing out, it sucked back into the small bottle I held gripped in my hands. Off balance already, I staggered forward, almost cracking my head on the curio cabinet.

I saw a flicker of orange as the spell sucked the spirit out of the minuscule crack between the curio cabinet door and the frame, towards the heart-shaped bottle. With obvious effort, the spirit strained and broke away from the magical pull, zipping towards the ceiling as I crashed into the curio cabinet, pulled off balance by the magical tug-of-war. Thankfully, the glass door supported my weight, but the sword case on my back made it difficult to regain my balance. I scrambled for footing and banged my elbow painfully against the metal frame. The impact jarred the glass bottle out of my grip. I watched in horror as the bottle spun in slow motion before crashing onto the hardwood floor. It shattered into dust before burning up in a cold, brilliant burst. I looked away, raising a hand to protect my eyes. As soon as it had appeared, the flash of light was gone, as was any evidence of the broken bottle.

The orange spirit zoomed back down to circle the curio cabinet and me before zipped out the door just as the goth teen who'd sold us our tickets came rushing in.

"Like, what was that? You're not supposed to touch anything!" The girl looked around the back room wildly under her heavy eyeliner.

"I stumbled," I said by way of explanation, rubbing at my arm and screwing up my brow to emphasize how much pain I was in. To be fair, it was already fading, but the teenager didn't need to know that.

Magnus was suddenly at my side. "I said you were doing too much!" He exclaimed, looking for all the world like a concerned boyfriend. He cupped my good elbow and wrapped a hand around my hips, steadying me. "She had surgery on her knee a month ago, but still insists bed rest is for wimps." Magnus spoke to the girl, but kept his eyes fixed on me, telling me to play along.

"Yeah. Wimps." I gritted out, clutching my elbow and leaning into him with an affected limp.

The teen ran a hand through her asymmetrical cut black hair, looking around the room wildly. "I heard something break. Oh, my boss is gonna *kill* me if you guys broke one of his private collection. He's, like, super possessive about all his stuff back here. He won't even let me clean in here or anything."

Magnus looked around the room with an overly concerned air. "I don't see anything that's broken. Do you?"

Of course, he didn't. The magic ghost bottle had *poofed* out of existence.

The goth girl bent at the waist, peering under the curio cabinet in case we had kicked the mysterious broken item into an impromptu hiding place. "You shouldn't be back here. This is where the boss keeps, like, the oldest junk in this place. Visitors aren't allowed. You'd better go before he gets back." She pushed to a standing position, apparently satisfied that we hadn't broken anything after all, and she'd be off the hook for letting visitors explore where they weren't meant to go.

"Sure. Probably for the best, anyway. You look like you could use a rest, honey," Magnus said to me, playing the role of oblivious-tourist-slash-protective-boyfriend to a tee.

"You're probably right, babe," I said, leaning on him heavily as we walked towards the front of the museum.

Magnus paused at the door, addressing the girl as if something had just occurred to him. "Why does your boss have phylacteries, anyway? I thought those were an Egyptian thing," he said, waving a hand towards a placard on the wall that I had missed. It labeled the contents of the curio cabinet as 'Phylacteries: Various.'

The goth girl followed us towards the door, hands outstretched like she was shooing pigeons away before they could crap all over everything.

"They are, but other cultures use them too. It's not like the Egyptians get dibs on all the cool stuff," she said, waving her hands towards the front door.

"Oh? What are they used for?" Magnus asked as we began our awkward shuffle again.

The girl seemed happy enough to talk as long as we kept moving towards the exit. "From what my boss says, mostly rituals and stuff. Storing dead people's hearts and brains and whatever. Some practitioners who believe in the magical arts even think you can even store a soul inside one of those things. You know, like a genie in a lamp?"

I sucked in a breath at the mention of a branch of the djinn. Why were they cropping up everywhere in my life lately?

Magnus held open the front door for me as he gave a little chuckle. He smiled warmly at the girl, and I saw a blush creep up her pale, powdered cheeks. "What? Like the wish granting genie from Aladdin?"

She shook her head seriously, putting a hand on the door to keep it open as Magnus 'helped' me hobble outside. "No, the souls that get locked up in phylacteries aren't nice. They're more of, like, the suck-your-face-off-and-eat-your-soul type of things. At least, that's what the boss says." She finished with a shrug, watching Magnus shyly from under her heavy eyeliner.

"Ah, I see. Well, I hope that you have a good day, and sorry again if we caused you any problems." Magnus said with a cheery wave before turn solicitously to me. He helped me limp away from the museum, prattling all the way. "Now, you need to get back to the hotel and put your leg up before you do any more damage. You know what the doctor said..." He stopped the rambling dialogue as soon as we were out of earshot.

I glanced up at him as I straightened. "You're scarily good at playing a part."

"I've got a musical theater background," he said, deadpan.

I stopped in the middle of the sidewalk, letting the sparse foot traffic flow around us. "No way! What role? Is there video evidence?"

"You are never, *ever* going to find that out," he said seriously. He let go of my elbow and wedged his sunglasses back in place. "We really should get out of here and lie low until we're due to meet up with the Pack. What do you say about ordering some Chinese food and binge watching 'I Love Lucy' or something until we need to go?"

I shook my head. "I love me some Lucy, but there's no way I'm walking away from this. Not now, not when I almost caught that spirit. We've got to follow it." If I could catch this spirit today, it might fulfill my lingering obligation to the Collective. I'd earn my ten thousand dollar fee and get out from under their collective thumb, pun intended. The possibility was tantalizing. After all, Nigel's spell had almost worked. If I hadn't dropped the bottle, like a noob, it might have.

Nigel! I saw his shop and ducked in on the off chance that the witch had another ghost trap. Magnus waited for me on the street, keeping a careful eye out. I'd say one thing about the werewolf. He didn't get distracted from his bodyguard duty and he made body guarding look damn sexy.

Fine. Those were two things, but both were equally worthy of note. I was glad I could hide my blush from the werewolf in the dim interior of the shop.

Chapter 14

I tucked the second ghost catcher in my satchel, nestling it carefully next to the bottle of rum as I stepped out onto Dumaine. I readjusted the tube with the blessed sword across my back again. Magnus pushed out of his apparently casual, but hyper observant, lean as I hurried down the street. I noticed he followed me at a discrete distance, but I paid more attention to the magic tattoo on my wrist than I did to my werewolf bodyguard. The orange dot was now hovering northwest of our location. It looked like it had stopped after the initial burst of speed.

Magnus cleared his throat as I paused on the corner of the street, considering my next move.

"What's the play?" he asked.

"I don't know. The ghost flew off and is now somewhere to the northwest," I said, waving my arm in his direction. I glanced at the tattoo again. "He's moving fast. Although, there's a second orange dot now. Looks like it's back at the voodoo museum. Huh. That's weird."

"Cam, we have no business tracking down anything, let alone something potentially old and dangerous that escaped the Abyss. Not when we have a date with a demon on the cards for this evening."

"The demon is nowhere close to us right now," I said, showing him the tattoo where the red and blue dots hovered faintly around the edges of the circle. "Besides, I see a way we might keep up with this runaway ghost." I jerked a thumb at the shop on the corner behind me. It was a bike rental place, nestled in the heart of the tourist district.

"No. Just no." Stubbornness crept into his tone.

"Why not?" I asked, surprised.

"I don't like bikes. Let's do the takeaway and crap TV plan instead. Hell, I'll even spring for a proper dinner in a fancy restaurant after we take care of the demon if you come now," Magnus said, rubbing a hand through his hair.

Tempting.

I shook my head and focused on the werewolf instead of losing myself in daydreams of dates with the handsome man. "Out of curiosity, how are you going to stop me? It's not like you can shift in the middle of the day in downtown New Orleans. You'll scare the kiddies," I said. "And because I feel bad for you, I won't make a joke about dogs and bikes."

Magnus curled his lip at me. "Fine. We can go after the ghost. If we're fast and you keep an eye on that tattoo for the demon," he muttered eventually.

"Great. I'll be right back. Keep an eye out."

"Why? Did you see something?" He looked around wildly.

"No, because if you don't, you'll be an unaware-wolf." I articulated the final words clearly.

Magnus growled and took a step forward, but I grinned and darted into the bike shop before he could lay his paws on me.

In less than ten minutes, a stocky young man helped me wheel two bikes to the front of the shop. I thanked him for his help and swung a leg over my sporty black and green ten-speed.

Magnus looked at the other bike. It was a glittery bubblegum pink with matching tassels hanging from the handlebars, and a white wicker basket attached to the front. "No freaking way," the werewolf said.

I shrugged. "What can I say? There were no other bikes available."

He eyed the shop's display window, which was full of a variety of bikes. "Really," he said drily.

I shook my head sadly. "All booked up, I'm afraid. If it's any consolation, the guy who helped me said it rides like a dream. A glittery fairy dream."

"I'll walk."

"Suit yourself, but you'd better keep up. Think of what Will would say if you let me out of your sight. And after he gave you a direct order, too." I tsked in feigned regret at him before shoving off the sidewalk and pedaling down Dumaine.

"In this case, he'd understand," Magnus shouted at my departing back.

"Would he though? He doesn't strike me as the type," I shouted back. Then I refocused on pumping my legs. I sped down Dumaine, but it wasn't long before the growl of an angry werewolf drifted up behind me. I grinned and tried to coax more speed out of the borrowed bike.

Using the tattoo on my wrist as a guide, I led the way through the twisting confusion of one-way streets that peppered the tourist district. Finally, about ten minutes later, I pulled up in front of the Tulane Medical Center. I was digging into my satchel as Magnus wheeled up beside me a moment later. He glared at me and then up at the brick buildings of the medical center sprawling across two city blocks.

I made the most of his distraction to snap a picture of him on his ridiculous bicycle with my phone. Blackmail photos are never a bad thing to have in your back pocket. I chuckled and tucked my phone away just as an alarm from inside the hospital blared loudly enough to be heard through the sliding doors leading into the ER. My good humor vanished instantly. I threw a leg over my bike and kicked the stand down, hurrying through the sliding doors with Magnus close on my heels.

Inside, the reception area swarmed with harried nurses and flustered administration staff. Confused patients sat or stood in the waiting area, taking in the rushing hospital staff with growing consternation.

I emphasized my supposed limp once more when I entered the waiting room. I drifted toward the reception desk, where a serious-looking nurse dressed in teal scrubs whispered urgently to a sharply dressed member of hospital administration.

"... six patients! Six! That is no coincidence. Six patients coding within five minutes of each other just doesn't happen." My hearing wasn't as good as a werewolf's, but it was better than a Norm's. I easily picked up the nurse's concerned hiss from the other end of the desk. I grabbed a pen and a clipboard and pretended to fill in the form as I continued to eavesdrop.

The hospital administrator ran a finger around his crisply starched collar. "Things happen, Maude. Sometimes, it's just bad luck. How many did you save?"

"None of them!" Maude spat out. "That's what I'm telling you. This is no coincidence."

Sweat broke out on the administrator's balding brow. "What are you saying? A gas leak?" His voice dropped further. "A bio-weapons attack?"

Maude snorted, "Whatever it is, you'd better figure it out fast. In the meantime, I need more staff down here with fully stocked crash carts. Just in case..." The two walked purposefully toward the restricted area of the ER, the heavy magnetic door cutting off the rest of their conversation.

I put the clipboard down, looking at Magnus significantly. He raised an eyebrow over his sunglasses.

"What are you implying?" he asked. "This is an emergency room. Without being cracked about it, people die in emergency rooms. Sometimes multiple people at a time." He folded his arms. The nurse behind the desk caught the last part of his statement and glared at him. Magnus hurried to add, "Although, of course, we'd prefer it to be otherwise." The nurse sniffed disdainfully and moved to help an overwhelmed father with a screaming infant.

I rolled my eyes at his response. Out of the corner of my eye, I caught sight of a strange figure slinking towards the front of the ER. The person wore the same teal pants that Nurse Maude had worn, but paired them with a bulky, dark gray sweatshirt with the hood raised. It didn't look remotely like a hospital approved uniform. Strange.

I ignored Magnus and watched the curious figure pause, waiting for the sliding doors to whisper open. The hood swiveled, looking around the waiting room. My breath caught in my throat. Underneath the hood, a stark white skull with glowing orange eye sockets peered around furtively. Its gaze locked on mine. The skull gave me a creepy orange wink before dashing out the sliding door.

I grabbed Magnus' arm, digging in my nails to get his immediate attention.

"What? What is it?" The werewolf's head whipped around, looking for potential danger.

"Things just went from bad to terrifying," I whispered, forcefully dragging him out of the waiting room. As soon as we hit daylight, I spun around in a slow circle, searching for the skeletal specter.

Nothing.

"What do you mean?" Magnus asked, finally freeing himself from my claws.

"You know that spirit we've been tracking? I don't think it's just a spirit anymore."

"More details. Please." He gritted out the last word, looking like he was struggling to keep his cool.

"Somehow, what was a ghost has turned corporeal. I'd bet you ten bucks that it's responsible for the mayhem in there." I jerked a thumb back at the ER while still scanning for the skeleton in scrubs.

"OK." He dragged out the word, looking thoughtful. "Wouldn't having a body make it easier to kill? Wait, why would it choose *now* to go all body-snatcher? Didn't it escape weeks ago?"

"Yes," I said slowly, trying to put the pieces together.

"So, what changed to make him want to shift so suddenly from a bobbing orb of light to a walking skeleton?"

"I'm not sure," I murmured. I flipped my wrist over, hoping I could get a quick lock on the orange-eyed-skeleton. Dread seeped into my bones as I saw one orange dot fading from the center of the compass at a ridiculous speed while the other orange dot pulsed slightly behind us. There was no way we could catch this thing on rent-a-bikes. I groaned as I put the pieces together and smacked the heel of my hand against my head.

"What?" Magnus asked.

"You asked what changed? This!" I thrust my wrist with the magical tattoo at him. "The ghost must've realized that I can track him somehow. Maybe it's the magical pull of the spell. I don't know! It's the only thing that makes sense, though."

"Then why are there two orange dots now?"

"I don't know! I don't even know what that thing is or how there could be two of them now?" Trying to remember if a fourth soul had escaped, I cast my memory back to Halloween. I didn't think so, but it had been a crazy night. Was it possible I missed one?

"Right. First, we need to find out what it is. How do we do that?" the werewolf asked, scanning the area intently, looking like he was ready to shift in an instant if he saw even the hint of orange. He dug into his pocket for his phone. "I can search on the supernatural dark-web, but I'm not sure how much I can turn up on 'creepy, orange-eyed skeleton' though, you know?"

My eyes lit on the glass building across the street with the ornate decorative metal facade coating the windowed exterior from the second floor upwards. I smiled grimly, not liking the option, but knowing it was the fastest way to get definitive answers.

"As much as I'd like nothing more than to hunt this thing down as quickly as possible, I think you're right. Knowledge is power in this case. But it is going to take more than your techy skills and googling random keywords to get the answers we need. Where is the best place to do research?" I answered my own question, pointing across the street at the New Orleans Public Library. "At the library, of course. Just don't talk too loudly, or the Librarian might take your head off. Literally."

Magnus shoved his phone back in his pocket. "If I've learned anything about you in the past day, it's to not take anything you say literally."

"No, you really should take this completely literally," I said seriously, folding my arms across my chest.

"Sure," he drawled with a heavy Southern affectation.

I stared at him for a moment. Then I shook my head and silently led the way into the library. If he wouldn't take the warning seriously, then it was on his head. Which would be on the floor if he pissed off the goddess who lived in this wing of the library.

Could werewolves heal from decapitation?

If Magnus annoyed the Librarian, we were going to find out.

Chapter 15

I led Magnus through the winding stacks to the back of the second floor of the library without a word. We swiftly wove our way through shelves, around heavy carts full of books waiting to be re-shelved, and past innumerable tables tucked against windows for the devoted readers of New Orleans.

A small desk reared up out of the gloom along the back wall, as far away from the windows as one could conceivably retreat. As soon as I saw who was sitting behind it, I grimaced. I'd hoped it wouldn't be her. Pasting on what I hoped looked like a genuine smile, I raised a hand in greeting to the matronly old woman. Unfortunately, I'd had more than my fair share of run-ins with Petunia, the witch who currently manned the reference desk at the public library in our fair city. Somehow, I always left feeling a little smaller than I had when I entered.

Petunia's iron-gray bun pulled so tightly on her scalp that it lifted her wrinkles temporarily higher. She peered at us warily over the tops of her bifocals with flinty gray eyes. When she recognized me, her scowl seemed to drop the temperature of the entire wing.

I'll admit, I didn't always follow the library's rules. Actually, there'd been this one time when I'd been on a bounty that I'd completely ignored them all together. The job was tracking down some escaped imps for a client. It wasn't my fault they used Petunia's precious books to build a fortress from which they launched a literary barrage in the form of torn and crumpled pages. The corners of Petunia's eyes tightened as if she was reliving the entire event. My shoulders drooped.

Yeah, I wasn't getting off her shit list soon.

She looked down her nose at us from her seat behind the reference desk as we approached.

"Good afternoon, Book-Destroyer. Have you come to wreak havoc across our peaceful pages yet again? I must warn you; I am better prepared to defend the sanctity of this place from the likes of you," her flinty gaze flicked to Magnus, "and your companions."

The smile I pasted on was my most charming one. "Good afternoon, Petunia. Nice to see you again. Allow me to introduce Magnus. He's part of the new werewolf Pack who've just moved to town. We'd like to access the restricted section, please."

Petunia snorted, leaning to peer around me at Magnus. She gave him one derisive sniff before returning her attention to me. "Who are you pursuing today? Fire-breathing dragons, perhaps? Intent on scorching all my lovely books beyond recognition or repair? Or are you leading a horde of goblins this way and encouraging them to slime the entire library from top to bottom?" Her voice rose to a whispered screech at the end of her diatribe.

I held out my hands in protest. "No one, I swear. We just need to do a little research."

Petunia sniffed disdainfully, but before she could answer, a gaggle of tween girls pushed their leader towards the reference desk. The girl mumbled, "Where'stheromancesection, please?"

Suddenly, Petunia was so full of grandmotherly warmth that it oozed right out of her tightly wrapped bun.

"It's right over there, dearies. On the left, about five aisles down. I believe you'll find something especially captivating on the second shelf." The elderly witch smiled beatifically down at the teens as they tripped over their thanks and ran off giggling.

Petunia's smile dripped off her wrinkled face once the girls were out of sight. I raised an eyebrow when she finally refocused on us.

"What was that? Sending kids after romance books?" I asked, jerking my chin after the fading giggles.

"That is where we store the Waldo books, which, at their age, equates to the same thing," Petunia said primly.

Magnus coughed into a fist, poorly disguising a surprised snort of laughter. I nodded sagely and tried to hide my smile. It was too bad that Petunia had placed me on her permanent shit list. I would have been happy to take a masterclass in snark at the feet of a woman so experienced in sass.

Instead, I focused on the task at hand. "The restricted section, please?" I asked politely.

"I heard you the first time. I'm old, not deaf," Petunia groused.

She grabbed a massive key ring from behind the desk. The old witch pushed to her feet with a massive sigh, letting us know the extreme inconvenience we were in her life. Petunia's back was ramrod straight as she led us to a plain wall at the back of the second floor behind some tightly packed shelves filled with dusty tomes.

Petunia laid her hand on a bare portion of the wall near the back corner of the library overlooking the parking lot outside. The wall shimmered and faded to reveal a white door with the word "Restricted" stenciled in large red letters across it. I heard Magnus let out a soft grunt of surprise behind me. Petunia whirled on us before he could voice a question.

"Remember the rules, you miscreants!" Petunia hissed. "If you or that mutt puts a toe out of line, I will make sure that the Librarian's door is closed to you for a year and a day. By that time, you might have done us all a favor and accepted the symbolic death as an actual severance from this realm. Failing that, you could at least realize that you are not welcome here and never return."

"Wait. You're not the Librarian?" Magnus asked.

"I? I would never dream of claiming such a lofty title. No, no, I am simply the Gatekeeper." The way she said it, I imagined a giant, glowing capital 'G', formed of entirely unnecessary flourishes.

"Right," Magnus said, widening his eyes with faux sincerity. "No lofty titles for you."

Petunia sniffed through her long, slightly hooked nose. She shoved a key in a lock that burst out of the middle of the door in a flare of honey-colored light. As she twisted the heavy key with obvious effort, the door in front of us faded, revealing a wavering view of a reader's paradise. However, it was as if we were looking at the room through distorted glass rather than an open doorway.

Petunia grabbed my arm with more strength in her clawed hand than I would have expected from the elderly witch.

"Give me an excuse, *please*. I beg of you. I cannot wait to throw you out of this sacred establishment on your ear and ban you from returning once and for all." A sneer transformed Petunia's aged face into something ugly.

I gently, but firmly, peeled her fingers off my arm. "As always, Petunia, it has been a pleasure. What did I tell you?" I said to Magnus as I removed the witch's talons from my arm.

Magnus nodded sagely. "It's just as you said. Her charm is, indeed, legendary."

Petunia sputtered for a moment up into our smiling faces. Unable to find the words to address the apparent compliment, she whirled abruptly on her low, blocky heels and marched away. The witch trailed affronted indigence like a noxious perfume in her wake. I smiled.

Kindness really is its own reward.

Chapter 16

I pushed through the magical threshold, which felt like wading through jelly. My ears popped and then I was through of the magical barrier. Magnus appeared a moment behind me, scraping at his arms to brush away the ephemeral heavy, stickiness of the threshold. He spun around slowly, taking in the room.

"Cameron?" he asked quietly.

"Yeah?" I asked distractedly, as I craned my neck to find the Librarian.

"Umm. Where'd the door go?"

I glanced at the blank wall behind us and smiled. I'd had the same reaction the first time I'd entered the restricted section. "Well, you can't expect it to hang around all day, can you? Not with Norms on the other side of this wall."

"Right. Naturally. Why didn't I think of that?" Sarcasm ran strong in the werewolf. "Where are we exactly?" he asked.

I waved an arm grandly at the interior of the library. Stone walls punctuated by large windows to let in the sun embraced the room. Rows of shelves filled with books of all shapes and colors towered over me. I knew from experience that someone set the shelves strategically to create cozy reading nooks. Each was littered with over-sized, comfy leather armchairs perfect for snuggling in with a good book and the occasional heavy table. The configuration allowed for either comfortably private browsing or serious research on demand.

"Welcome to the Supernatural New Orleans Public Library," I said in a hushed tone.

"You set up a library in a library?" he asked, sounding like he thought I was playing a practical joke.

"Well, not me specifically, but yes, the Collective spearheaded the collaborative effort when the Librarian came to town."

"Spearheaded? That doesn't sound like the same Collective the Alpha talks about."

"Spearheaded, coerced, bullied. It all amounts to the same thing. The rumors are that ages ago, before I moved here, the Librarian came to New Orleans. She had been unhoused and was looking for a place to settle. Rather than lose a valuable asset by infighting, that iteration of the Collective created this." I waved again at the impressive trove of books spread out before us.

"How do the Norms in this city not notice a giant supernatural wing in their public library?" Magnus asked.

"Magic," I said, waggling my fingers in a mysterious gesture. He raised a brow at me. I acquiesced and elaborated. "All those circles, whorls, and patterns on the side of the wall next to the parking lot aren't just abstract decorations. They're really spells. And those are only the ones you can see. The witches, wizards, mages, and all other local magic users re-up the magical juice and maintain the spells as a kind of magical community service. They created this invisible, warded pocket dimension anchored to the public library. Once it was stable, the Librarian moved right in and added her own brand of magic to the mix, creating a pocket dimension that is almost like a mini realm within New Orleans."

"Like Vatican City in Rome?"

I snapped my fingers and pointed at him. "I've never heard it put like that, but it's a great example."

"I never knew something like this was even possible," Magnus said, running his hand over the wall carefully.

"Well, Supes aren't the most altruistic or cooperative beings. Most Supes I know would rather hoard knowledge than share it. Everyone usually hates working with other types of Supes unless absolutely necessary. Just look at the Collective for a prime example," I said.

"That's been my experience, too. Even before I moved to New Orleans," Magnus said in a hushed tone, brushing invisible dust from his hands after his brief inspection of the library's architecture.

I led him deeper into the Supernatural Library of New Orleans as we talked, weaving my way towards one of the window alcoves where perpetual sunlight filtered through the leaded panes despite the time of day. A stone statue of a leopard lounged in the alcove as if it were an actual cat, soaking up the afternoon sun.

"What are these rules, then? I'd hate to upset anyone called the Gatekeeper. Somehow, it seems like I'm already on her bad side, which can hardly be my fault," the werewolf said mildly, his tone implying what he was too much of a gentleman to say. I was to blame for Petunia hating both of us.

"Yeah, Petunia's sides are grouchy, grumpy, and gruff, with a side of grumbling. At least with me. She blames me for what she calls the Infamous Imp Imbroglio, which was only partially my fault. Petunia always seems to be the witch on duty when I need to access the library, so I've learned to err on the side of polite until she is out of earshot. And to always obey the rules."

"Rules? What rules?" prompted the werewolf.

"They're your standard library rules, mostly. No eating, drinking, or fire near the books. Never doodle in the margins. Leave the re-shelving to the professionals. That type of thing."

Before he could comment, I turned to the leopard statue in front of us and spoke loudly and clearly. "I am searching for information regarding escaped spirits, skeleton resurrection, skeleton reanimation cross-referenced with orange glowing eyes, ghosts, and phylacteries, please."

The stone leopard pushed to its feet, stretched languidly, and padded off deeper into the library.

Magnus shook his head, eyes wide. "What was that?"

"One perk of having a supernatural library is the help. Now, we wait and see what the cat can turn up."

Magnus followed me through the stacks of books to a set of four of armchairs nestled around a low table. I plopped in one and folded my hands over my stomach with a small sigh of contentment. Magnus sat across from me. "You said 'mostly standard rules'. What are you leaving out?"

I grinned at him. "If you ever meet her, try not to hit on the Librarian."

"Why not?"

"She doesn't have the same qualms about getting blood on the books that Petunia does."

Chapter 17

The stone leopard returned a few minutes later, harnessed to a small cart precariously filled with books, scrolls, and tablets. The animated statue shook itself, dissolving whatever magical binding connected it to the cart and padded away without a second glance at us.

Magnus eyed the cart curiously. "What's this then?"

I groaned. "It looks like a needle in a haystack, or in a cart in this case. The animated library constructs like the leopard will retrieve anything you ask for. Think of them like the supernatural database for the supe-r restricted section of your local library," I said.

"I see what you did there," Magnus said, pointing a finger gun my way with a smirk. "So, these constructs play fetch for you, but what if your keyword search was too broad?" he asked, gesturing towards the cart filled with reading material.

I scrubbed my hands through my hair. "There's only so much the constructs can do. Their brains are pebbles. Literally." Magnus let loose a hearty groan at the terrible pun. I grabbed a book from the top of the pile. "Rock jokes aside, we'll be here for days if we can't narrow our search."

"Perhaps I can help?" A new voice intruded on our conversation.

I scrambled to my feet, recognizing the voice instantly. I performed a little bow. Magnus followed my lead. The slim woman standing in front of us was slightly taller than me. Her nutmeg-colored skin glowed with health and vitality, belying the fact that she spent most of her time in a magically locked library. She wore a leopard print dress, belted with a knotted golden cord at the waist. Her dark eyes were heavily lined and brimmed with the knowledge of the ages. Long, straight black hair fell to her waist, held in place by a thin band of gold emblazoned with a seven-pointed star that rested in the middle of her forehead.

"Cameron, how lovely to see you again after all this time. And who is your companion?" The dark-haired woman eyed the werewolf curiously.

"This is Magnus. He's new to the area," I said.

"Ah, you must be a member of the new werewolf Pack. Of course. Be welcome in my home, the both of you," the woman said graciously, extending a delicate, long-fingered hand that looked more suited to playing piano than turning pages.

Magnus shook her hand once. "So, you're the mysterious Librarian?"

She laughed, the gentle sound washing over us like a babbling brook. "Mysterious? No. But I am now known as the Librarian."

The werewolf nodded. "And what's your real name?" I shot him a wide-eyed look of urgency, leaning around her shoulder to make sure he saw me. Magnus cleared his throat. "f you don't mind me asking. I don't wish to be rude, but I feel a little funny just calling you 'the Librarian.'"

"Of course, I do not mind. It is so rare to have new visitors to my humble home that I feel as if your presence is a boon that must be honored. A simple request for knowledge is hardly something I can deny. I am Seshat, but my people have also used the name Sothis. I am the Mistress of the House of Books. However, that is more of a mouthful than I expect my visitors to attempt. 'The Librarian' suits me nicely, especially in this modern age, when people are in a rush to shorten everything as much as possible. In truth, what sort of offense did vowels commit in order to be erased almost entirely from the vernacular?"

"You must hate texting," I said, hiding a smile. The corners of Seshat's mouth turned down.

Magnus was nodding, obviously searching his memory. He spoke before the Librarian could. "Seshat. So, your people were the ancient Egyptians?"

"Very good, dear boy. Yes, I found a home in Heliopolis and then in Alexandria, minding the scrolls, teaching the people how to read and write, enjoying the sun. However, book burnings and city sackings are not my ideal activities, in any century." Seshat let out a regretful sigh.

"Understandable," Magnus said.

"Indeed. Which is why I find myself here, in New Orleans, of all places. The community here has been so welcoming and one can hardly quibble about the accommodations, especially when they are magically bespoke. However, you have me at a disadvantage. You know who I am, but I have yet to meet you properly." Seshat arched a brow in Magnus' direction.

"Magnus," he said, dipping his head in the Librarian's direction again. "Maverick Magnus Donovan. It's a pleasure." My head whipped around towards him at the inclusion of the unfamiliar name? Title? Nickname? Call sign? He ignored me.

"It is indeed. A pleasure to meet you, Maverick Magnus Donovan." Seshat clapped her hands. "Now that formal introductions are finished, let's have a seat. You can tell me what you are seeking today and perhaps I can be of assistance." She settled herself delicately on the seat of an armchair, crossing her legs at the ankles, and folding her long-fingered hands in her lap expectantly.

I held up my hand, dropping a finger to point at the werewolf. "Wait just a minute. What's with this Maverick thing? Do you fly planes or something in your spare time?"

Magnus' lips twitched upward. "Not exactly."

Seshat raised a single elegant finger. "If I may?" Magnus dipped his head in acquiescence. Seshat continued, "The title 'Maverick' is a status more than a rank amongst werewolves. It is a rather obscure bit of lore that one rarely witnesses firsthand. It shows a werewolf is no longer Rogue but has formally applied to join a Pack. However, he has not yet been accepted into full Pack membership or rejected and sent on his way."

"And a Maverick is always male?" I asked, picking up on Seshat's pronoun choice.

"Usually. Females are rare among werewolves and fiercely protected by a Pack. If a female wants to join a Pack, she won't be a Maverick long, if at all," Seshat explained. The Librarian turned towards the werewolf, tipping her head curiously to the side. "Have I described your current title accurately?"

Magnus nodded once. "Usually, a wolf won't stay a Maverick for long, regardless of gender. They'll be accepted to the Pack or relegated to Rogue based on combat skills or Pack numbers," he explained.

"So, what's your deal, then? It's been, what? At least a month? Why are you still lugging around this Maverick title?" I asked.

"It's complicated," he said.

I waited for Magnus to elaborate, but he seemed content with the terse response.

Seshat covered the silence smoothly. "Other than meeting one of the newest Supes in town, can I provide some assistance today? You seem to be a touch overwhelmed by the wide net you've cast with the library constructs," she said, gesturing towards the cart on the brink of overflowing with tomes.

I smiled. "Well, now that you mention it..."

Chapter 18

I settled into the chair across from Seshat. Magnus lounged in another, content to let me do the talking. I fingered my tattoo as I weighed my words, trying to decide how much to share in my quest for answers. Finally, I flipped my wrist over and showed Seshat the simple compass with its glowing dots, explaining its purpose.

"Fascinating!" The Librarian exclaimed, scooting forward to trace a delicate fingertip over the design. "The Tuatha de Danann's approach to enacting magic in this realm is usually subtle and not easily detected unless you know what to look for."

"Who?" Magnus asked.

"The Tuatha de Danann. The Irish pantheon of immortals and gods. They do so fascinate me. Their magic, at its core, simply binds two entities together, but how they choose to enact their workings is elegantly complex. To share this magic with an uninitiated outsider is very rare indeed. How did you garner such a favor?"

I brushed my free hand through the air dismissively. "Irrelevant. What is important is that we find the spirits linked to this spell. Fast. I've got a feeling one is bad news. Really bad news."

"Oh? What makes you so certain?"

"I'm pretty sure that it killed six people today to get a body. Well, not a body precisely. More of a walking skeleton with glowing orange eyes."

Seshat leaned forward, grasping my arm urgently. "Are you confident this is what you saw? A sentient skeleton moving independently and of its own volition?"

"Yes. One hundred percent. The soul flew into the ER. According to a nurse, six people unexpectedly died. Then a skeleton in scrubs walked out the front door."

"Can you remember anything else? The smallest detail may hold the utmost significance." Seshat looked at me earnestly.

Magnus drummed his fingers against the armrest, drawing our attention. "When it was still a wispy ghost, the spirit flew into the voodoo museum on Dumaine. It focused on a cabinet full of phylacteries. It seemed to be drawn to a blue glass bottle."

I nodded my agreement. "After that, there were two glowing orange dots on my arm." I held out the tattoo again for proof.

Seshat tapped her lips thoughtfully. "Yes, I believe I might know what type of creature this is." She rose to her feet gracefully, gesturing towards the cart of books beside us. "You won't find the answers you seek in those pages. Give me a moment and I shall return with a better resource. A second person account, admittedly, but finding a first-person resource in this case would be nearly impossible. Still..." Seshat glided away as she spoke, disappearing behind the shelves forming our nook as her soft voice faded like a whisper of a turning page.

"You didn't tell me there was a goddess living in the library," Magnus said, focusing intently on me.

"You didn't tell me you weren't officially Pack," I shot back.

"Fair point."

I glared at him. "What's with all the lies?"

"Omissions," he said.

I snorted. "It amounts to the same thing."

Magnus shook his head. "Not precisely. Not in this case, at least."

"We've got a little time to kill. Besides, we are literally in the best place for stories. Indulge me. How did you become a Maverick in the New Orleans Pack, or wherever they lived, before they officially moved to town?"

He sighed and opened his eyes, staring at the ceiling. "You will not let this go, are you?"

"Nope," I said cheerfully. "I love a good story."

"I'm not sure this qualifies as good."

"Doesn't matter. I'm here for it. Get talking, wolf-boy."

Magnus shot me a dirty look. Then he sighed and answered my questions tersely. "My Pack dissolved a while back. It happens. I drifted for a bit, seeing the country, you know? Eventually, I got the itch to find a Pack again."

I waited a beat, but when he didn't elaborate further, I pursed my lips. "No offense, but you need to work on your delivery."

"I don't know what you mean. It was succinct and to the point. What more could you want?"

Before I could formulate a response, Seshat swept around the corner of the shelving unit, waving a heavy tone triumphantly.

"I found it!" she cried, thumping the large book bound in red leather on the table and patting it gently.

I craned my neck to read the gold leaf on the spine. "The Necrocracy and the Order of the Undead," I read out loud.

"Precisely. Are you sure you wish to continue? Knowledge, once learned, cannot be unlearned, only adapted to. If I tell you the pertinent information found within this book, it will shape your worldview, but perhaps not for the better, I'm afraid. Do you still wish to proceed?" Seshat laid her hand flat on the leather cover, meeting my eyes seriously.

My throat was suddenly dry. "Yes," I croaked.

"Very well then. I believe the creature you seek is called a lich." The way she said it, it rhymed with 'witch'. Seshat widened her eyes significantly and gave the book a small push towards me.

I glanced at the large, heavy book and then back to the Librarian. "It's an enormous book, Seshat. Can you give me a quick summary?"

The goddess sniffed, straightening her already ramrod straight spine in indignation. "Magical tomes do not come equipped with Cliff's notes for those too lazy to go searching for enlightenment."

I made a show of wincing as I rubbed at my knee. That fake injury was getting a lot of use today. "Please? It's been a rough day. I got attacked by a demon once already and he's likely going to come after me again, but for now, he's out there. Just wandering around the streets of New Orleans. And now there's this lich thing? I could really use a hand." I let out a long-suffering sigh.

"I'm not sure that absolves you from the need to conduct your own research, but I see your point that time is of the essence." Seshat inhaled deeply before speaking again, this time with a formal inflection to her voice. "I consider it a great service to the community that you choose to stand between the people of New Orleans and the evil walking the streets. To aid you in this quest, I will provide you with a summary of that book." Seshat pointed at the tome resting on the table between us. Personally, I didn't think that summarizing some ancient text was on par with killing a demon or hunting down a lich, but I wasn't about to argue with a goddess in her own domain, especially when she was willing to help me.

Seshat cleared her throat delicately, as her eyes glazed over like she was reading from a page only she could see. "A lich is a necromantic sorcerer who possesses a terrible combination of dark power and un-limited ambition. A lich will use this power to drain the life force from others and transfer it to his or her own body. This can happen even after death as liches maintain their powers beyond the grave by placing their souls in magical container, such as a gem or phylactery or other storage item capable of prolonged exposure to magic. Once imbued with a soul, they call this item as a soul jar, regardless of its actual jar-like properties. As long as his soul jar remains intact, a lich will maintain his immortality and can siphon magic from Supernatural beings to bolster his own power. With enough energy, he can even reassemble his body if it's destroyed."

"Sounds terrifying," Magnus observed. He was leaning forward in his chair, looking simultaneously intrigued and disgusted by the lich lore.

"They are, to be sure. There is a reason the living monitor those with necromantic tendencies with equal parts fear and trepidation. A lich can wreak unimaginable harm over decades, perhaps even centuries."

"Great. A lich resurrecting in my town is the cherry on top of the dysfunctional mess this month has been. Any idea how to deal with it?" I asked Seshat with little hope.

"Actually, yes. The literature is quite clear on the matter. Much like other undead Supernatural beings, liches are most vulnerable to weapons made of fire, light, or holy materials. However, their reconstructed bodies can be damaged by other weapons. I should note that they will eventually heal themselves regardless of the weapon inflicting the damage, provided that their soul jar is unbroken and a supernatural power source is easily accessible."

"What kind of power source? Life magic?" Magnus asked. I raised an eyebrow. "What? I just want to be clear about the details if I'm going to have to follow you into a harebrained scheme to attack a zombie sorcerer. You are going after it, aren't you?"

I refused to acknowledge his accurate assessment of the situation, returning my attention back to Seshat as she cleared her throat, gently recapturing our attention.

"To answer your question, yes, life magic. Like I mentioned, a lich can drain supernaturals of their magic, much like a vampire drains his or her victim of blood. It can also drain the life-force from Norms or even animals with diminishing returns. However, it is a time-consuming process, according to the literature. It's a coincidence that you mention zombies, for liches can cast vast amounts of necromantic spells, including summoning or raising the dead."

My eyes bugged out of my head, searching for any sign that she was exaggerating her claim. "Like calling ghosts or making zombies?" I asked incredulously. I knew familiars were a thing, but they were pretty benign in my experience. Goliath was a prime example. Besides, I'd never seen a real-life zombie before. Or was that an un-life zombie?

"Skeletons, ghosts, and yes, all manner of zombies," Seshat confirmed.

Motherless son of a fart-eating shitweasel!

I was a little shocked as the thought popped into my head. Brigitte must be rubbing off on me.

I didn't want to ask, but I had to. "There's more than one kind of zombie?"

Seshat smiled brightly at me. "Oh yes, there are three! Plague, revenant, and voodoo zombies, to be precise."

I closed my eyes, knowing already I wouldn't like the answer to my next question. "What are the differences between the zombies, Seshat?"

"I'm so glad you asked!" Seshat clapped her hands and bounced a little in her chair. She started ticking off fingers as she spoke. "Let's see, plague zombies are brainless, vile creatures who feast on the living and their bite spreads the infection, turning more people into plague zombies. They are the creatures that Hollywood loves to vilify."

"You find time to watch movies with all these books around?" Magnus asked curiously.

"Of course! What are movies except the digital age's version of the oldest form of entertainment; storytelling? Now, let's see. Revenant zombies are also resurrected corpses, but are sapient and self-directed. They often fixate on violently redressing past wrongs and will kill anything that interferes with their agenda, including the one that raised them," Seshat said, ticking off another finger.

"Charming," I said, drily.

"Not even remotely. I would recommend avoiding revenant zombies at all costs." Seshat obviously needed to study up on sarcasm.

"What about voodoo zombies?" asked Magnus. "I've never even heard of them. Are they like a necromancer's familiar?"

"Oh, I highly doubt you would have, and no, they differ vastly from a familiar. Familiars have given permission to be raised. Don't ask me how, that's a question for the necromancers. Voodoo zombies are inevitably enslaved minions, somewhere between a plague and a revenant zombie. They are hard to raise from the dead correctly. Think of voodoo zombies like the perfect soufflé. If you pull them out too early, they will collapse into the plague category and become mindless killing machines. However, if you wait too long, they will harden into a revenant and prove to be a useless minion. No, a voodoo zombie must bake to perfection. Then the necromancer can use it as the ultimate, intelligent, submissive thrall."

I leaned back heavily in my chair. "This is getting worse by the minute. I've suddenly lost all interest in soufflés. Zombies might come to town.

What's next?" I clasped my hands together tightly in my lap. Despite my flippant response, the thought of zombies shambling through New Orleans in search of brains gave me the heebie jeebies. "Do you have any good advice?" I asked.

Seshat tapped a long finger against her lips, seriously contemplating my query before speaking. "Avoid fried, empty carbs. They never make you feel as good as they promise to. Also, I would highly recommend never interfering with the inner workings of one's soul as it will inevitably lead to a spine-chilling punishment from a chthonic god."

"Great. Thanks for the pep talk," I said dryly.

"Anytime! Now, are there any good books I can help you find?" Seshat said brightly, still oblivious to my sarcasm.

Magnus glanced at me before clearing his throat. "Do you have any How-To-Kill-A-Zombie-For-Dummies books?"

Seshat tipped her head to the side and her eyes whirred in her head like she was some sort of demonic slot machine. Finally, her spinning eyes slowed, and she refocused on us. "No, I am sorry, that book is checked out at the moment."

Of course it was.

Chapter 19

The sun was on its descent back towards the horizon, spilling bright golden beams across New Orleans by the time we extricated ourselves from the library. Petunia glared at us for leaving after hours and forcing her to stay late. I gave the grumpy witch a cheeky wave as we hurried out of the library.

Seshat had insisted I borrow the tome on the Necrocracy. It sat heavily in my bag and thumped solidly against the tubular case holding my blessed sword. I'd have to dedicate some time to study up on liches and the Necrocracy as soon as possible. I tried to balance my awkward load as I navigated the rental bike back down Dumaine. We needed to hurry if we were going to make our meeting with the werewolves at City Park. Magnus followed me on his glitter-tastic-cycle without speaking, which I appreciated. It gave me time to think.

My thoughts whirled as my legs churned the pedals around and around. It was just my luck that one spirit the sigil linked me to was a lich. Part of me hoped it wasn't the spirit the Collective wanted me to take care of, but I doubted it. It would be just my luck to deal with an immortal necromancer who could raise zombies. I was in over my head, and I knew it. I was going to need help dealing with something as major as a lich. At least I had the Collective's backing to draft any Supe I needed in order to deal with the escaped spirit. The only problem was, I wasn't sure who to call up to the Major Zombie League.

I still hadn't reached a definitive solution by the time we pulled up to the rental shop. Luckily, we just in time to hand the bikes over to the owner before he closed. Magnus handled the niceties while I stood outside and stewed on the lich problem, hugging the heavy book Seshat had lent me like a life-preserver.

The werewolf exited the bike shop and evaluated my stance carefully. Finally breaking the silence, he said, "You look worn out. Are you sure it's a good idea to bait a demon into attacking you tonight?"

I nodded and opened my mouth to reply. Before I could get the words out, blue and red flashing lights whizzed us down Dumaine towards the voodoo museum.

My stomach sank. I doubted that a police presence in this area today was a coincidence. I took off running in pursuit as fast as the tubular sword case, the heavy book, and my rum-filled satchel allowed. Magnus followed, catching up to me easily with his longer legs.

A small crowd stood on the sidewalk opposite the voodoo museum, which was sporting a broken door. Two police cars and good sense held the onlookers back from approaching the building. A short guy with a beer belly and sweat stains darkening his too small t-shirt was grumbling to the taller man standing beside him.

"... he shoved me out of the way. Well, threw me, more like and I'm not a small guy," Shorty said, patting his protruding gut for emphasis. I sidled closer.

"What'd you say he looked like?" his friend asked.

Shorty puffed up his chest, obviously happy to have an engaged audience. "Some low-life druggie. He had on a hoodie, and this crazy ass up Halloween mask. Looked like a skeleton face and even had some LED lights glowing in the eye sockets. Someone should tell him Halloween was last month." Shorty chuckled loudly, and then wheezed at the exertion. He looked like he hadn't done much of a workout in a few years, aside from beer bicep curls.

"Did he say what he wanted?" the tall guy asked.

"Didn't say a thing. He just sorta growled at me and tossed me outta the way before breaking the door on my shop in some drug rage or something. Man, I don't know. I'm not stupid or nothing. I'm not gonna go chasing some druggie. Those people are unpredictable, am I right?" Shorty looked proud of himself to have thought of a word with over three syllables.

His friend nodded. "Good idea. He could've had a gun or something. You never know these days, do you?"

Shorty took an aggressive step forward. "Hey! Are you saying I was scared? Because I ain't scared of nothing or nobody, 'specially not some low-life in a mask!"

Before things could escalate, a policeman in uniform ducked through the doorway of the museum, searching the faces of the crowd. When he saw Shorty, he gave a two fingered point and beckoned him over.

"He'd better not have broken my stuff or I'm gonna hunt him down," Shorty muttered loudly as he hauled himself across the street.

A hand touched my shoulder, and I jumped, heart racing. I kept my voice low. "Someone broke in. Someone in a skeleton mask with glowing orange eyes." I widened my own significantly.

Magnus' lips tightened, but he caught my meaning. We needed to avoid saying anything related to the supernatural community where we might be overheard by Norms. "I heard. That's unfortunate. I hope everyone is ok. Does this change what you wanted to do tonight? What's the plan?" he asked. He kept his words and tone purposefully casual.

I shook my head slightly, refocusing on the building across the road. "There's nothing that us normal folk can do. Besides, the police look like they've got the situation under control." I tried to match his nonchalance. It must've worked because the rest of the small crowd ignored us completely as the cop I saw before exited the building with Shorty in tow.

The irate owner was shouting at the officer. "Nothing you can do? Like hell! My taxes pay your salary. I'm basically your boss! So, when someone breaks into my place of business, you'd damn well better do something!"

The officer paused, closed his eyes, and took a deep breath. When he turned around, his face was an impassive mask. He whipped out a small notebook with a deadly efficiency that screamed, 'I will eviscerate you with facts presented in the most professional way possible.' He read quietly from the pages, but the words carried easily to my ears. "Perpetrator: male, average height and build, wearing a dark hoodie and a Halloween mask. Not on the premises when the police arrived. Broken: one cabinet. Missing: one small blue bottle. If you would like to register a complaint..."

My eyes widened. I ignored the rest of the small drama across the street as I grabbed at Magnus' arm. He looked down at me grimly and nodded tightly, confirming my suspicions silently. There was only one reason the lich would've returned to the voodoo museum and stolen the bottle in the middle of the day.

A lightbulb went off in my head. I looked at my wrist and then grabbed Magnus' arm. "We've got to go. Now." I hissed.

I dragged him away from the growing crowd and flashing lights in front of the voodoo museum, back the way we'd come.

"What's going on?" he asked in a low voice as we headed towards the bikes.

I rotated my arm so he could see the tattoo. The orange dot was moving swiftly away from the center point. And there was only one. "I think I know why the lich had to manifest his skeleton body so quickly. Once he figured out that I could track him, he knew it wasn't just his ghostly body the spell tracked. It also tracked his soul. That's why there were two dots."

"Whoa!"

"I know! All the gods below! If only I'd figured that out sooner, we could've smashed the damned thing and turned him mortal!" I kicked a stone as we hurried past the namesake statue in Jackson Square.

"But once he saw you there and realized he couldn't get to his phylactery as a ghost, he went and created himself a body so he could steal it," Magnus said.

"If only we figured that out earlier!"

"We didn't have all the pieces to the puzzle then," Magnus reminded me.

"Wait!" I said as we reached the motorcycles.

"What?"

"Why did this guy stay in ghost form for nearly a month when he obviously could've created a body any time he wanted to?" I hoped Magnus could see an obvious answer, that I was missing. He considered my words and then shook his head slowly.

"I don't know, but we've gotta go if we're going to make it to the park on time," he said, lifting his phone and showing me the time.

Damn it. He was right. The lich had just made a body for himself and retrieved his soul jar after choosing to live in New Orleans for almost a month as a ghost, and I had no idea why. And a demon was lurking somewhere out there, just waiting to take another swipe at me.

I grabbed my helmet. "One problem at a time. First, we kill this demon and then we go after the lich! Easy as pie!!" Despite my attempt at bravado, I knew in my heart it would be nothing of the kind.

Chapter 20

Magnus and I parked the motorcycles at a chain coffee shop close to the park and hurried towards the model airfield in the middle of the green space with our fighting gear, locking the rest away in Magnus' storage compartment. He'd given me a strange look when I'd included Brigitte's magical bottle of healing rum in the bag, but I figured she seemed to know me well enough by now. She wouldn't have given me a bottle that was easily breakable. Probably. However, I was sweating from carrying all the gear at a brisk trot by the time we made it to the airfield.

Will, Julius, and Parker stood waiting for us in the middle of the clearing. We exchanged terse nods of greeting before Will passed out the very official looking fake IDs and some oversized brown uniform jackets that each had an embroidered emblem of a black bug crossed out in red.

I eyed the ugly jacket dubiously. "What's this then?"

Will passed a large jacket over to Magnus. "We are temporarily members of the New Orleans Mosquito, Termite, and Rodent Control Board trying to contain an invasive pest species from spreading through the greater New Orleans area."

I bobbed my head, surprised. "Wow. That sounds almost real."

Will slanted his eyes in my direction. "That's because it is. Feel free to delve into biological control issues, but don't mention a specific pest. We don't want to cause a knee-jerk reaction from the city for rumors about a fictitious threat. Also, reassure anyone who asks that the chemical control agents will dissipate by morning, but it is not safe to be in the area without the proper protection. That should keep everyone away for the evening."

Parker dropped a bag to the ground. She yanked out some small yellow signs on wire frames, each printed with a black skull and crossbones symbol and a warning about chemicals being used in the area. She passed each of us a handful. "Here, place these around the perimeter and on the trails leading to the airfield. That should help keep the Norms out of the area."

I eyed the procured paraphernalia. "Do the Norms actually buy this? It all seems a bit too easy."

Julius wedged himself into his drab jacket. It looked like it was close to bursting at the seams. "Oh, sure. We do this all the time. Bugs are the easiest. All you have to say is 'harmful insect' and something vaguely Latin sounding. The Norms run for cover every time." The big man grinned unrepentantly at me. I couldn't help but smile back.

Will nodded in agreement as he shrugged into his jacket. "Exactly. Let's meet back here in forty-five minutes. Cam, make sure you monitor the tattoo and let us know if there is a demon incoming. Donovan, keep an eye on Cam. Remember wolves, no shifting. We don't want to tip our hand too early." All of us nodded, grabbed a handful of signs, and headed off to scare away the Norms with talk of imaginary bugs.

Despite my initial misgivings, the pest plan worked like a charm.

An hour later, I stood alone in the middle of the model airfield, armed to the teeth. The sun was just dipping below the horizon, but the glade was already dim. The surrounding trees blocked out the last rays of the day. Will appeared at the edge of the clearing. He gave me a quick thumbs up before disappearing again. Meridiana stepped out of her hiding place and gave me a little wave as well. It had surprised me when she'd shown up. She looked like more of a lover than a fighter, but then again, she was a demoness. So what did I know? The rest of the werewolves scattered in the trees, hiding in a rough circle around the open airfield. I crossed my fingers that the demon wouldn't stumble across them on his way into the clearing.

I took a deep breath, trying to center myself. The red dot had been dancing in an irregular arc between the southern and eastern points on the compass, but it hadn't come any further towards the center dot. The faint orange dot was doing a jittery dance to the west, and the blue dot remained stationary south and west of me. If the red dot was in fact Razgothan, I wondered what soul belonged to the blue dot. More importantly, given that the other two were a lich and a demon, how dangerous was the third soul?

Thirty minutes later, I was sitting on the ground, picking dirt out from under my fingernails with the tip of a knife. I'd given up checking my magical tattoo every ten seconds. The orange and blue dots were stationary now. The red dot wandered closer, but was still hovering on the edge of the compass' circle. Unfortunately, I had no way to gauge how far away that was.

"*Psst.*" The hissed summons carried clearly on the night breeze.

I pushed up on my elbows. Meridiana was beckoning to me from behind a tree. I rolled to my feet and jogged over, swinging my arms back and forth as I tried to keep my muscles loose in anticipation of a fight that looked like it wouldn't happen tonight.

"What's going on? Is Razgothan coming?" she hissed as I neared the edge of the clearing. I snuck a glance at my wrist again. Was there more substance to the red dot or was I squinting?

"I'm not sure," I said.

Meridiana's brows drew together, creasing furrows into her porcelain skin. "Cameron, we've got to take care of this. If he grows back his tongue and reaches out across the Abyss, that could spell disaster."

"I know, I know, but what do you want me to do?" I hissed back.

Meridiana raised a slim shoulder helplessly. "Give it another half hour, I guess. If he hasn't shown up by then, we need to come up with a Plan B. Quickly."

I pressed the heel of my palm into the ache building right behind my left eye. "Our Plan B had better be spectacular because it's looking like plan A was barely mediocre."

A low snuffle behind Meridiana caused my frayed nerves to draw even tighter. My head whipped around to the right in the sound's direction. "What was that?" I whispered, peering into the darkness.

A black wolf with silver highlights to his fur broke through the underbrush. He crept into the clearing with a low growl. My breath caught. I didn't recognize him. But the wolf had to be on my side, right? Maybe it was Will? Or Parker? Somehow, that didn't feel right. The black wolf wheeled and snapped his teeth at the forest behind him, flattening his ears and snarling low in his throat, bright blue eyes flashing around wildly.

My head jerked back in surprise. "Damon?" I asked. The wolf's coloring was almost the same as the Alpha's in human form. But why would Damon be here personally if he had already sent his beta to help me? Had he finished his business with the Collective and come to lend a hand?

Magnus stepped out from the undergrowth in human form. He held his hands out low and wide of his hips. He met the wolf's eyes directly. Although he kept his voice low, his words carried on the night wind to where I stood.

"Get out of here or your dad is going to be pissed," the man said, halting before he entered the clearing, but refusing to lower his commanding gaze from the wolf.

The black wolf snarled and snapped his teeth at the man. The wolf jerked forward in a feint that had me convinced he would attack. Magnus didn't flinch. He kept staring at the wolf, hands at his sides. He looked ready to retaliate but was hesitant to instigate anything with the strange wolf. The creature lowered his shoulders towards the ground, his powerful rear haunches tensing, readying for a spring.

I shook my head, Magnus' words finally registering as I examined the wolf again. He was the size of a large dog, but smaller than Julius had been when I'd seen him in wolf form. Admittedly, I had only seen Julius and only once, but seeing a human as a wolf sticks with you. That shit gets seared into your brain. But Magnus had said 'dad', which meant that this had to be Andrei.

The Alpha's son must have followed us here. He didn't look like he trusted Magnus, though. In fact, he looked ready to rip the man's throat out. Without intending to, I took a couple of steps forward. I knew I was too far away to intercept an attack at werewolf speed, but my subconscious told me to try. Before I could figure out how I'd intercept the angry werewolf teenager, Will stepped out of the woods behind Andrei. He whistled, low and commanding.

Andrei's head whipped around, and his tongue lolled out immediately at the sight of the beta. He let out a little doggie yelp and wagged his tail slightly. I smiled. Teenagers. From the brink of uncontrollable rage to hanging with a friend in zero-point-three seconds flat.

"Get your butt over here!" Will whisper-shouted. Andrei gave Magnus a frosty glare so full of disdain that only a teenager could manage before flicking his tail in dismissal and trotting over to the beta, his head held high. Will crouched down and put a hand on Andrei's neck. The beta leaned his head close and whispered urgently in the werewolf's furry ear, too softly for me to overhear.

"Well then," Meridiana said, sauntering up next to me.

"What's *he* doing here?" I said under my breath.

"It's not that bad. They were going to shift, anyway. So, one wolf got itchy paws? It shouldn't interfere with our plans. Besides, it doesn't look like Razgothan is going to show up anyway," the demoness sighed, crossing her arms over her chest.

I pointed at the wolf as Will dragged Andrei into the underbrush. "That's the Alpha's son. His precious baby boy."

A movement drew my eyes to a pulsing light on my outstretched wrist. I twisted my hand, rotating it to look at the inside of my wrist where a red dot was rushing towards the center of the compass in a confusing, jagged zigzag path.

Which meant I had a demon locked on my signal and heading on a collision course right this minute.

Why were these things never easy?

Meridiana hadn't noticed my attention shift to the glowing sigil on my wrist.

"Tell me everything. Is this kind of some teenage rebellion schtick but on werewolf level? What will the Alpha say? Speaking of the Alpha, I'll have to admit that Damon is a fine specimen. For a wolf, that is. Do you think they eat like a wolf when they are a wolf? Gnaw on bones and things? Ooh, speaking of, I'll bet that sexy Alpha has a massive, juicy..."

"Finish that sentence and there will be two demon slayings here tonight, not just one," I said tersely, my muscles knotting in anticipation as I watched the red dot ditch the evasion tactics, if that's what they were, and arrow towards the center of the compass.

Meridiana opened her mouth to respond, but I raised a finger in the air and cut her off. "He's coming. The demon is headed straight for us."

Chapter 21

Meridiana instantly dropped into a low crouch, her hands forming into claws as her head whipped back and forth, searching the trees for the demon. "Where?" she whispered.

"Ah, now thith ith intherething," a lisping voice said behind us.

I spun on a heel, crouching instinctively to match Meridiana's pose. A red-skinned demon walked towards the middle of the clearing. The same one who'd attacked me earlier. Razgothan. He reached the center of the open area and posed with his clawed hands on his hairy hips. His tongue flickered out of his mouth, tasting the air as he clopped towards us on his goat hooves. I noticed that his tongue was longer than the last time we met. I probably wouldn't have noticed his tongue at all if I hadn't cut it off, stepped on the severed member, and then stuffed the demon-tongue into my teacup.

Demon-tongue-tea probably tastes worse than it sounds.

"Shit," Meridiana swore softly next to me. "You said he hadn't grown it back yet!"

"I didn't think he had!"

"And you were obviously wrong, now weren't you!" she hissed.

"Sue me! I'm not a tongue expert!"

"Well, maybe you should put that on the top of your to-do list. After killing him, of course. Now shut your mouth and follow my lead!" she whispered.

I blinked at her in surprise from where I still crouched, ready for an impending fight.

Before I could react further, Meridiana waved an imperious hand at me, shouting, "Freeze, minion!"

I was already this far in. Trusting her now was like deciding to trust the parachute *after* you jumped out of the airplane. It might make you feel like you had control, but you were still hurtling towards the ground with only a piece of cloth between you and imminent death. Or, in my case, hurtling towards a demon fight with only a succubus to hang on to. I just hoped Meridiana had a hell of a ripcord. I froze in my half-crouch, my muscles already burning in anticipation of staying frozen in the awkward position. Meridiana sauntered towards the red demon. I caught a predatory smile on her lips, and then she was beyond my range of vision.

"Intherething," the red demon said. "Why in the Abyth are you here?"

I had a hard time understanding him until I activated the lisp filter in my brain. Trust me, it's a thing.

"Sorry? What was that?" Meridiana said, cupping an ear as she continued her slow stroll across the clearing towards the demon.

Razgothan huffed and tried to manipulate his mangled member to form the words. This time, I could understand him better. "What are you doing here? And with her?" he asked, pointing.

"If you must know, she is precisely my type. Powerful with more than a hint of crazy thrown in for flavor. But I could ask you the same thing. Illegally inhabiting the human world again, are we?" Meridiana said, continuing to saunter closer to him, hips swaying seductively. I imagined a sensual smile curving her red lips.

"You know how it ith. Pulling out entrailth and repeatedly jabbing lava lanceth into dead thoulth can get tediouth. I mean, you go to work and itth the thame old thing, day in and day out. Torture, torture, torture of the thame pathetic broken humanth every day. But being up here?" The red-skinned demon took a deep breath in, and I heard him exhale with gusto. "Invigorating! The humans don't know a demon walks among them. It is so easy to corrupt them. It's delectable to sample their hope and then destroy it repeatedly. I can't go back after I've experienced the sheer life of this place!"

Ruh-roh. With his speech getting noticeably better by the second, it didn't look like Razgothan was going gentle into that good night.

I snuck a glance through my thick lashes as the demon strode forward, cloven hooves tearing up the grass. His tongue flickered out again. It was forked this time. Which meant I was forked as well.

"I know!" Meridiana gushed, closing the distance between the two and placing her hand on Razgothan's broad, red chest. I saw her fingers spread over his pectoral muscle as she tipped her head back to look up into his scarred face. "It's almost heart-stopping, isn't it?"

Her hand flashed a brilliant scarlet. I saw her fingers curve and claw into his chest, gauging deep tears. Razgothan yowled in agony and batted her away with a thick arm. Meridiana's slight frame flew through the air, trailing blood, and crashed with a sickening crunch into the forest behind me.

The red demon pawed at the scratches in his chest as if he were trying to put out an invisible fire, roaring in pain each time his claws brushed against the torn flesh. Spears of brilliant red light shot out of the gouges in his chest and sank into the lush grass of the airfield before disappearing.

I took advantage of Razgothan's distraction to lunge towards him, grabbing for the blessed sword I had strapped over my shoulder. The muscles in my legs protested loudly as I shoved them forcefully out of their quivering freeze and into a dead sprint.

A blur of black fur emerging from the trees behind the demon's shoulder caught my eye as I charged the horned demon.

Andrei.

I spared a glance towards the racing wolf, estimating the distance in a single heartbeat. As fast as I was, I couldn't match a werewolf for speed. Andrei was on a collision course with the demon and there was little I could do to stop it.

A tawny, lean wolf sprinted out of the woods, followed closely by a massive multicolored beast and a wolf so pale she looked almost white. Will, Julius, and Parker wouldn't catch Andrei in time, either.

Crap.

The demon's tongue flickered out of his fanged mouth, tasting the air. He twitched his wicked horns in Andrei's direction. I saw a grim smile split his gruesome face. He tensed, crouching, readying to meet the werewolf's charge head on. Razgothan's entire attention was on the attacking werewolf, completely ignoring me for the moment.

How could I turn that to my advantage?

Andrei! What the hell? Don't you know to wait for your Pack, kid? I screamed at the teenage werewolf in my head.

The black wolf's tongue flapped as he raced towards the demon, all eagerness and drool. Razgothan spread his hands wide, claws clacking against each other as he waited for Andrei to close the distance.

My heart stuttered. I knew what I would do to an enemy racing towards me if I had the equivalent of razor-sharp knives attached to my hands. I'd wait for him to get airborne and then let him impale himself on my claws. Or my horns. Either way, Andrei would end up with more holes in him than was survivable.

Oh, *hell* no.

I put on an extra burst of speed and flung my yatagan, the sword Meridiana had had blessed for me, with all my might. Right into the charging werewolf's path.

Andrei stutter-stepped to the side, easily avoiding the launched projectile tumbling inelegantly through the air. He swiveled to glare icy blue eyes at me even as he stretched out his legs to regain the speed he lost.

It didn't matter. My desperate ploy had worked. Enough to save the impetuous werewolf from himself, at least.

My hands flashed back for my karambits as I launched myself up and at the demon's back. My curved blades bit deeply into the meaty red flesh of his shoulder. I sent up a silent prayer to the gods of bad plans and over-thinking that I'd added my karambits to the pile of weapons to be blessed. Let me tell you, they *worked.* The flesh around the blessed blades bubbled like the metal had been dipped in acid. A faint flicker of hope sprang to life within me. The blessing on the blades was doing incredible damage to the demon's shoulder. Now the only question was how to manipulate the situation to use the blessed knives most effectively?

Razgothan threw his head back and yowled even as the entire weight of my body crashed into him, sending him stumbling forward. I anchored myself via the blade to his body tightly just as Andrei collided with us. I groaned at the effort of holding onto a bucking demon as a werewolf tried to mount us both like we were the most misshapen horse in the universe.

Worst. Rodeo. Ever.

At least my desperate plan worked. I'd knocked the demon's claws out of line with Andrei's soft underbelly. Instead of ripping out the werewolf's entrails, the demon tumbled to the ground with me on top of him and Andrei scrabbling at my back in a mess of fangs, fur, claws, and blades.

I felt Andrei's teeth and claws tear into my back. I screamed. The teenager hadn't expected my insane attack on the demon. On his kill. Andrei was so intent on ripping the thing in front of him to shreds that it took him a moment to realize that the thing in front of him wasn't a demon.

It was fragile little me.

There wasn't much I could do, caught as I was in a werewolf-demon sandwich. I desperately tried to think of a way out. My mind flashed back to my training with Barqan. Could I do the smoke form thing? If there was any time to use it, it was now. I shut off the part of my brain that was screaming in terror and tried to focus, going through the steps that Barqan had taught me. Nothing. I tried again, focusing even harder. I just needed to...

I felt sharp teeth tearing at the back of my neck. The werewolf broke my concentration. I screamed again, hunching my shoulders to protect my neck as best I could without letting go of the karambits that held me attached to the roaring, murderous demon. For a moment, I felt the heat of the werewolf's breath on the back of my neck and drool spattered my hair. Then, Andrei drew back with a confused whine.

Razgothan took that moment of hesitation to throw the young werewolf off, sending him spinning into the oncoming wolves. A red-skinned arm snaked around me so fast that I couldn't focus on it through the haze clouding my vision. The pain of demon claws digging into my arm and side jolted me back to reality. I left a scream hanging over the demon's shoulder as he threw me to the ground right in front of Andrei.

The teenage wolf jumped back in surprise at the human projectile flying his way. I was momentarily weightless before crashing to the ground awkwardly. My leg gave way under me with a painful twist. I screamed again. The demon turned merciless, predatory eyes towards me.

"I'd rather bring you back alive, but I suppose killing you gets you to the Abyss quicker. My master won't be pleased, but he can't fault me for speed. Am I right?" A terrifying, leering grin split Razgothan's face.

His hooves dug into the grass, twisting up the dirt as the demon flexed his claws, readying for the fatal attack. I tried to bring my karambits to the front and shove to my feet, but a blinding lance of pain stabbed through my ankle. My arm and side, where Razgothan's claws had dug in, didn't feel any better. Andrei let out a small snarl behind me.

Shit.

Damon would never forgive me if I let his boy end up as a demon's dinner. I'd never forgive myself. Despite the pain, I tried to push to my elbows and then to my feet. After the combined damage by Andrei and the demon, my body vehemently told me it was in rebellion for the rest of the night, at the very least. I barely dragged myself a few inches with my one good arm and leg.

Desperately, I tried to dissolve my body into smoke again. Nothing. I reached for my shadows next, but couldn't even focus on pulling them around me. Not that it would have done much good to blur out of visibility if I couldn't physically move out of the way of the demon's deadly reach. A gasp escaped me and all I could do was lay in the damp grass and watch my damnation descend, claws gleaming wickedly in the moonlight.

I wished I could have one more drink with Sloane. Just one. To tell her she meant the world to me. That would be enough.

The errant thought surprised me, and a hot tear slid down my cheek. I tried to brush it away, but only managed a weak blink as the demon's claws descended.

So much for wishes.

I closed my eyes and waited for the end.

Chapter 22

Between one blink and the next, a gigantic silvery gray wolf appeared between me and the demon. The enormous wolf planted his forefeet over me, lowering himself protectively as he growled menacingly at the demon. Razgothan jerked back in shock at the sudden appearance of the werewolf. The fur of the wolf's belly tickled my exposed skin as he shifted slightly to keep the demon in front of him. I squeezed my eyes shut, trying not to sneeze as his fur brushed my cheek. The growl that rumbled out of his chest shook me to the bone. The gray wolf made Andrei look like the puppy he was. And he made me look like the weak human I was. Not that it bothered me at the moment. All I could think of was that I was thankful to have the chance to draw in a few more precious, painful breaths.

A tawny blur crashed into the demon's side, knocking him off balance before he could decide whether to attack the gray monster poised over my prone body. A flash of white zoomed behind Razgothan and blood spurted out the other side. The demon threw his head back with an angry roar, his back arching as his clawed hand attempted to hold together his torn hamstring.

Julius, in his multicolored wolf form, crashed into Razgothan with a horrible crunch and snarl. A snap of jaws and an angry bellow from the demon let me know Julius came out on top in their first encounter. The three wolves regrouped, herding the demon towards the center of the airfield, drawing him away from us.

The massive silvery gray wolf, who had to be Magnus, rotated to always keep the demon in front of him, but didn't withdraw from his protective crouch over me to assist the other wolves.

Andrei yipped behind me. I twisted painfully onto my back to see the young wolf take a couple of bounds toward the three wolves harrying the demon. Magnus let out a short, commanding bark. Andrei jerked to a stop as if he had run into an invisible fence. The teenage black wolf swiveled to look at the massive gray wolf, hackles rising. Magnus rose from his crouch over me, staring the younger wolf down. For a moment, I thought Andrei was going to attack. Or Magnus was. I didn't know how werewolves dealt with hierarchy in the Pack below the alpha-slash-beta levels. Was it an age thing? Seniority? Size? I didn't know. I held my breath, afraid of tipping them into a battle to the death by the merest whisper of an exhalation.

Andrei locked gazes with the bigger wolf. The young pup quivered in anticipation. Magnus stood solid, watching Andrei squirm. Finally, the teenager dropped his gaze and exposed his throat. Although I was new to the inner workings of Pack dynamics, even I could figure out that Andrei had just submitted to the larger wolf. I briefly wondered what that would mean for Magnus' standing with the Alpha, to have Damon's son submissive to the handsome man. A crash of bodies and a horrifying snarl drew my attention away from the domination games in front of me to the other conflict raging in the clearing.

It was hard to see past the long fur on Magnus' forelegs as he resumed his crouch, but it looked like the wolves were doing a good job driving the demon further away from where I lay. One by one, they tore at his unprotected flanks while the other Pack members distracted the red monster.

Incredibly, our plan was working.

On that deserted model airfield, I witnessed firsthand why wolves are apex predators. The precision of their attacks and the utmost faith and confidence with which they relied on each other made their coordinated assault terrifyingly beautiful. Working as a team, one would feint for his throat, drawing the demon's attention. Instantly, another wolf would spring for his hamstring or Achille's tendon. Working as a team, they tore into Razgothan easily, shredding him bit by bit and spreading the bloody demon pieces across the clearing without ever going for the kill. It was an exquisite, coordinated, deadly dance.

My hand scrabbled in the grass, convulsing in pain. Something hard brushed my fingertips. I glanced down. Somehow, I'd landed near my sword. Thank all the gods I hadn't landed on its razor-sharp blade and unintentionally added to my injuries. I gripped the hilt, trying to work out a way to get my battered body close enough to Razgothan to end this with the blessed sword.

Behind me, Meridiana's voice rang out through the clearing, the urgency cutting through the tension like one of my knives through silk. "Disengage! NOW!"

As if they had trained with her all their lives, the wolves wheeled with precise obedience, scattering as they dashed away from the demon at a full sprint. Razgothan flopped to the ground, an arm's length away from me. Magnus snarled low in his throat, but didn't move towards the demon. He stayed rock solid in his protective crouch over me.

Razgothan looked around, gasping and bleeding from multiple lacerations and missing chunks of muscle. "What...?" he said as he tried to drag himself towards me with one arm that was missing its biceps. I noticed the other arm was gone entirely.

A scarlet light built in a cage around the demon, starting on his chest where a Norm's heart would be and splitting off to encase him in bars of crimson. He looked down his mangled torso in surprise as he shone as brightly as a lighthouse in the darkened clearing. The wolves kept running, sprinting as far and as fast as they could, away from the demon. All except Magnus.

"Give me a name! Who did you tell about Cameron and the djinn king?" Meridiana's voice cracked like a whip through the air. She limped into view, and I saw that her hand was glowing with the same scarlet light.

"Go to heaven, you..." the demon started.

I gritted my teeth to clench back the scream that was building. I grabbed onto Magnus' fur, pulling myself upright as agony shredded my pain receptors. With a jerk that was more convulsion than a throw,

I launched my sword at the demon with all the strength left in me. I collapsed to the ground, completely spent. The blade flew through the short distance between us, cutting through the cage of scarlet light like it didn't exist and embedding itself in Razgothan's chest.

A lucky throw? For sure. But I wasn't willing to turn up my nose when the capricious Lady Luck favored me now and then.

The demon looked down in surprise at the sword in his chest and then up at me in horror a moment before he exploded. Scarlet light radiated out from his torso like he was the most gruesome disco ball ever. It expanded until there was nothing left of him but itty-bitty demon chunks drizzling down like fine ash.

I was suddenly doubly grateful for my wolf protector-slash-umbrella.

I heard Meridiana mutter, "Oblivion is much worse than heaven or hell. Trust me."

Sucking in a deep breath and preparing for the pain, I laid a gentle hand on Magnus's lower leg, gently pushing him aside. He glanced down and gave my hand a small snuffle, but moved out of the way. I shoved to my feet, disguising my gasp of pain as a small inhalation. Andrei appeared at my side, leaning his furry weight against my hip. I dug my fingers into his fur, thankful for the support.

"What. The. Hell. Was. That?" I said, gesturing at the demon fertilizer sprinkled all over the clearing. Julius and Parker trotted over in wolf form. It looked like they had avoided most of the demon detritus. Will was nowhere to be seen.

Meridiana shrugged. "I told you I could keep him here until you finished him."

"Aren't you a succubus? Isn't lust your jam?" I asked, confused. I hadn't expected the cage of magical light to emanate from the petite woman. Right. Demoness. I wouldn't be forgetting that point anytime soon.

"There are many forms of lust, Cameron. Once I understood his deepest desires, I could bind him here."

"Wait, you're telling me that? What? You killed him with kindness?"

Meridian tossed her long, red hair over a shoulder as she wiggled a hand back and forth. "Not in the literal sense. I kept him here with understanding. You killed him. Besides, there really is no way to view intentional demoncide as kindness. Except perhaps to the rest of the world." Meridiana tipped her head back and tapped a pale finger against her chin, contemplating this new angle of considering the world. "Ultimately, I suppose it depends on the demon, doesn't it?"

I snorted and winced as my everything hurt. "Well, however you did it, you did just help to kill one. An actual demon. Does that make you some sort of angel?"

"Realms below! Bite your tongue." The demoness looked scandalized. I knew that if she had pearls, Meridiana would have been clutching them.

I grinned at her. The demoness smiled back, but it faded quickly. She scanned me up and down, grimacing at my injuries. Luckily, she couldn't see the worst of them, but I could feel oozing blood down my side and back. The darkness, black leather, and position of my body obscured the worst of the damage from her prying eyes.

"I'm sorry to leave you, but I need to go. If he grew his tongue back already, he might have gossiped to the wrong people. I need to return to the Abyss and run damage control. Or at least see what sort of shitstorm is heading our way."

I nodded. "Anything I can do here?"

Meridiana nodded. "Don't talk to anyone else about your necklace until I get back." Was that fear I saw in her eyes?

"Understood," I said. Before I could think of anything else to say, Meridiana vanished in a flare of red light.

A movement caught my attention as I scanned the clearing for the disappearing demoness. Will stepped into the clearing from the woods wearing a pair of loose sweatpants and pulling on a t-shirt over his wiry frame. He tossed a bag of clothes towards Julius and Parker. They shifted, and I averted my eyes to give them a semblance of privacy as they dressed quickly.

Well, that answered one of my many werewolf questions. Clothes did not become fur. Got it.

"Right. We're done here. I need to report back to Damon immediately. We'll be in touch." The beta snapped his fingers. Andrei yelped at my side and leaped into the air. He lowered his head as Will stared him down. The young wolf whined and crept forward. I didn't know if the kid didn't shift because he couldn't or there wasn't a spare set of clothes for him. Regardless, I was glad I wasn't in his shoes at the moment. I wavered on my feet as my support slunk after the beta in wolf form. Will spun and started jogging away.

Julius adjusted his sweatpants, leaving his impressive torso bare as he bid me farewell. "Thanks for saving the young one. I'll make sure that Damon knows what you did for his son tonight. I hope you heal quickly."

I nodded weakly in acknowledgement. Julius shrugged into his t-shirt and jogged after Will and Andrei, his massive muscles bulging as he loped after the beta and the teenage wolf.

Parker walked up to me, her sports bra and yoga pants showing off her svelte physique.

"I'll make sure the pup gets trained, so he doesn't mess up in a combat situation again," she said, extending a hand with a wry grin.

"Don't be too hard on him. He was just trying to help," I said, shaking her hand briefly. The slight movement almost caused me to lose my balance.

"Well, he didn't. He screwed it up royally, in fact. Besides, we can all use a little obedience school now and then." Parker winked at me and then sprinted off to catch up with her Pack mates.

If anyone saw them running through the streets of New Orleans, they would assume that three fitness fanatics were out taking their enormous dog for a run. In the middle of the night. Half-naked and shoeless. Then, the confused observers would likely turn back to their drinks, order another round to numb the dichotomy, and forget the whole thing by morning.

Only in the Big Easy.

Chapter 23

I took a step towards where I stashed my gear and almost toppled over. A muscular arm caught me, hauling me roughly to my feet before I hit the grass. I sucked in a deep breath that was half surprise and half pain. I glanced up at Magnus, who was in human form and somehow fully clothed. Deep concern was written in his gray eyes. This close, I noticed they had flecks of deep blue in them.

"Thanks," I muttered, fighting the wooziness of blood loss that threatened to drag me into an unconscious stupor.

"Just doing my job," he said, worry creasing his brow. He looked like he wanted to scoop me up, but he stepped back as soon as he was sure I was steady on my feet.

"Will just told you to go. Shouldn't you be, I don't know, turning furry or something?" I had to focus on each syllable to not give into hissing out the words through gritted teeth. The gouges from the demon's claws in my side and arm hurt whenever I moved. Which meant it hurt to breathe. The sharp stabs of pain from my ankle made it painful to walk as well. It wouldn't surprise me if it turned out I had a concussion on top of all the rest of my injuries, but I was determined not to let Magnus see any weakness.

"Did he? It sounded like he had orders from the Alpha. I was told to watch out for you, not to go homeward bound like a good little puppy."

"You know that isn't what Will meant," I said, eyeing Magnus dubiously.

"Isn't it? I could have sworn he told me to watch your back."

"Yes, but..."

"But Will hasn't told me anything to countermand that order. That explicit order. Therefore, I am operating as instructed by the beta of the Pack." His grin was, well, wolfish.

I winced. "Fine. Do what you want. I, for one, am getting out of here before someone investigates what made that burst of hellish light," I said, resuming my staggering hobble. "Where's my rum?"

Magnus wrapped an arm around my waist and half carried me to where we'd stashed our gear. "Since when did you become a pirate?" he grunted.

"Not a pirate. I'll have you know its magically infused healing rum. I got it from a goddess," I gritted out through a clenched jaw.

"Sure, sure. That makes total sense. Are you positive you didn't indulge in a little sip or three before the fight?"

"Just get me the rum," I muttered as he lowered me to the ground.

Magnus glanced at his hand. The one that had been wrapped around my waist. It was stained with blood. "You're leaking." He pointed at my side and back where blood oozed from the cuts Andrei's teeth and Razgothan's claws had slashed open. "It looks like you've lost a lot of blood."

"I know. Give me the rum, please. Before I pass out."

He fished it out of my bag and passed it over. "Here. Are you sure that's a good i..."

I twisted the cap off with my good hand and started chugging. The burn of the hot pepper hit a moment later, making my eyes water, but I kept drinking until I couldn't take any more. I set the bottle down and wiped my mouth with the back of my hand.

Magnus stared at me and then the bottle, which was still somehow full. "Alrighty then. My apologies for doubting you and your magical bottle of rum," he said with complete sincerity.

A warm, soothing sensation welled up from the pit of my stomach, pushing back the pain of my injuries and bringing comforting darkness with it.

"Apology accepted," I said, an enormous yawn cracking my jaw. "You should have some too, you know. Watch out for the peppers, though. They get you every time." I tried to pass him the bottle, but almost knocked it over instead as heavy weights dragged at my eyelids. Magnus' snort was barely audible as I finally relinquished control and slid into the welcoming depths of pain-free unconsciousness.

Chapter 24

Awareness stole uncomfortably over me in the form of sticky, hot confinement. Something soft and heavy covered me. It wrapped around my body too tightly and was making me feel sweaty and cold simultaneously. Voices intruded, rousing me from my blissful oblivion. Awareness brought pain. I scrunched my eyes closed tighter and rolled my head to the side.

Strange.

The last thing I remembered was we were fighting a demon. I'd been hurt. Magnus got me some rum and then... nothing. But now I was definitely in a bed. And definitely nearly naked.

I took stock of my surroundings without opening my eyes. Crisp, clean sheets that smelled of lavender covered me. The faint metallic tang of blood also tickled my nose. Something wrapped around my torso, not tightly enough to put pressure on my rib cage, but soft and secure. I could feel the cloth caress my skin with every shallow breath.

Voices. Right. That was what had woken me. Keeping my eyes closed, I focused on the voices again. Two men were talking, trying to keep their voices low. Now that I was awake, I could hear every word.

"How is she?" The low rumble was cultured and precise. It sounded like Damon.

Damn it. I didn't want to pull the Alpha in to this after the debacle with his son attacking a demon. It wasn't my fault Andrei had been there, but would Damon see it that way? What was Magnus thinking?

Magnus' voice rumbled softly from across the room. "The demon did a number on her. She's got a possible concussion and a twisted ankle, but it might be sprained. Besides that, and some minor cuts and bruises, Mama said that the lacerations from the demon's claws on her side and arm were the worst. They're pretty deep, but the good news is that time will take care of them. At best, she'll wake up with a nasty headache, a sore ankle and, once those cuts heal over completely, minimal scarring."

Shit. Magnus had brought me to Mama's house? What if the lich tracked me here through the tattoo? At least the werewolves were here, and Mama had her wards. Would it be enough to bear up under an attack?

"And the worst case?" Damon demanded, interrupted my thoughts.

"Worst case is a bad sprain, or possibly even a fracture to her ankle. Mama said those types of spiral fractures can be hard to diagnose without an X-ray. At the very least, she'd need Cam to be awake and tell her what it feels like. There's a danger of infection in the cuts the demon gave her. No one is sure what bacteria or poison might have been on his claws. Based on how quickly I got her here, getting the wounds cleaned out and stitched up, and the healing properties of the rum, Mama hopes that she'll avoid any sort of demonic infection taking hold. But only time will tell."

There was a pause before Damon spoke again. "At least she can heal from some scrapes and a broken bone or two."

He wasn't wrong. Supes healed at a much faster rate than Norms, which was usually a fantastic attribute. Another pause. I tried to keep breathing in the slow, shallow way that sleepers do so as not to alert the werewolves that I was eavesdropping on their conversation. And to avoid angering, the dull ache throbbing in my ribs.

Damon spoke again, his voice cold. "You could have informed me of her diagnosis over the phone when you reported in. Explain. Why drag me down here?"

"You saw the cuts and bites on her back?" Magnus kept his voice low.

"Of course. They're too numerous to miss. A lot of superficial damage, but shallow. Mama did a good job of treating them. They're cleaned up and closing already. They seem to be the least of her worries." Damon's barely contained annoyance was obvious, even to me.

"The demon did not make those injuries." Magnus' voice was heavy with unspoken meaning.

A beat of silence. "Who?" Odd. Damon sounded worried.

Magnus didn't draw it out. "Andrei."

A growl rippled through the room and suddenly I wished I was back in the clearing, facing down Razgothan again. Almost anything was better than confronting an angry Alpha werewolf when the matter regarded his only son.

Damon's voice grated over my tense nerves. "Does she know?"

Wait. What?

"If she didn't, she does now. Based on her breathing, she woke up a few minutes ago and probably overheard our entire conversation."

Damn werewolves and their damn hearing.

I opened my eyes as I heard Damon stride over to the bed. There was no use keeping up the pretense of sleep now. I opened my eyes to see Mama's cheerfully decorated guest room. I was familiar with it after asking for Mama's healing help on more than one occasion.

Damon's voice was flat and emotionless, but fury burned in his blue eyes. "Cameron. How are you feeling?"

I pushed to my elbows, trying to rise to meet the angry Alpha. The blanket fell away from my torso, a cool breeze kissing my bare collarbones. I flinched and scrabbled to pull the fluffy white duvet back up to cover the bandages wrapped around my body from armpits to hips. "Look, Damon. I didn't know Andrei would be there. I did everything I could to keep him out of the fight and safe."

"She did." My eyes swung to Magnus. He leaned against the door frame, watching me intently. "Cam jumped on the back of a demon to keep your son from impaling himself. It was the bravest stupid thing I've seen in a while." Magnus said. His voice was calm, but his eyes gave him away. A roiling tumult of emotion swirled beneath his masked expression.

Damon's tone was deadly serious when he spoke. "I know you aren't responsible for Andrei's involvement in last night's fiasco. As a father,

I'm grateful beyond words that your actions kept my son from coming to harm. As a member of the Collective, please accept my thanks for protecting the city from a demon. I will ensure the rest of the Collective knows the role that you played in last night's drama."

"Great. Glad to hear it. Why do you look so upset, then?" I asked.

Damon sighed and ran a hand through his dark hair, that was liberally sprinkled with silver at the temples. He sat on the edge of the bed, causing it to creak ominously, and laced his fingers together, leaning his forearms on his knees.

"Because of the repercussions of my son's foolhardy actions." Damon met my eyes meaningfully.

Slowly, the implication dawned on me. My eyes widened as the hair rose on the back of my neck. The same place where Andrei had attacked me. Momentarily, to be sure, until he had gained control of himself. But I'd still been bitten. By a freaking werewolf.

"Your son bit me. A werewolf bit me!" I rubbed at the back of my neck with my free hand, like I could scrub the incident away. My guts clenched, and I twisted the downy blanket in my fists. "What does this mean? Does this mean I'm going to become a werewolf? How do you even turn someone into a werewolf? Is it possible for that to happen? I mean, it's not like he *bit* me, bit me. It was more an accidental collision between his teeth and my skin." The words tumbled out of me in a rush. I took a deep breath, trying to slow my heart rate, but I couldn't. Panic was setting in.

Magnus strode over to me and took my hand. "Deep breaths, Cam. Just focus on me. Good girl, that's it. Deep breaths. And another. Keep going, you're doing great." His gray eyes captured mine. I was lost in them, obeying the soft, comforting commands as I fought my body for control of my brain.

Slowly, I regained a semblance of control. "Thank you," I whispered to Magnus. He squeezed my hand gently and took a step back. I swung my head towards Damon. The panic rose in my chest again, but I firmly squashed it down. "Am I going to turn into a werewolf?" I asked the Alpha of New Orleans.

Damon sighed and shook his head, turning away to study the delicate floral pattern on the pristine wallpaper of Mama's guest room.

"I'm not sure exactly," he admitted.

"How can you not be sure?" I croaked through a throat that was suddenly too dry. Where was a glass of water when a girl needed one? Or another shot of rum?

"Because I'm not sure how strong your Supe blood is." Damon said, shaking his head and staring blindly at the wall. I waited for him to continue, but he lapsed into silence. Wildly, I looked around, meeting Magnus' intense gaze. I sent a pleading look his way, begging silently for more information. He shook his head slightly, letting me know I'd better address my questions to Damon.

"What do you mean?" I asked.

Damon sighed. "We can only create a new werewolf under certain circumstances. Namely, when a werewolf bites a human while in wolf form. The assumption is that something in the mix of blood and saliva initiates the change," he explained, his voice detached and clinical. "Most Supes are immune to lycanthropy, but there have been a few cases where a half-human Supe has shifted. In the case of an unprovoked werewolf attack against a human, Pack law dictates what will happen next. The wolf, Andrei, and the human, you, will submit to the Pack. The Pack will imprison both until the full moon, where the Pack will monitor your first shift."

"What?!" I shouted.

Damon continued, as if I hadn't spoken. "The problem is that the survival rate of lycanthropy is low. Even if you survive, you could turn feral. Wild. Out of your mind. In that case, it will force the Pack to kill you. If you are killed, Andrei will also be killed in recompense for causing your death. If you survive the initial shift and don't go mad, then there will be a trial to determine Andrei's fate."

"Apparently, I'm suffering from a concussion and I'm not sure I followed all of that. Break it down for me and use small words." I asked, my gut telling me I wouldn't like the answer.

Damon pursed his lips. "Best-case scenario? You survive the shift and Andrei's exiled. Worst-case? You die either during your first shift, must be put down, or demand satisfaction from Andrei for forcing an unwanted change on you. If any of those circumstances occur, Pack law states Andrei will be executed in retribution for his actions because it means he is essentially murdering a human by biting you without consent." Damon spoke simply, keeping his eyes locked on mine the entire time. While I was grateful to have the complete picture, it was a lot to process.

A wave of dizziness washed over me. I was glad I was half prone or I might have fallen over. "You are crap at delivering bad news," I groaned in Damon's general direction.

He shrugged. "You strike me as the type of woman who wants to meet her problems head on. No sense in tiptoeing around it."

I closed my eyes, trying to think, and then glanced back at Damon. A sour taste filled my mouth as a flutter of guilt danced against the inside of my ribcage, right above my heart. The backs of my eyes burned with unshed tears as I realized what he must be going through. The man just found out that he was going to lose his son. Exile or death amounted to the same thing for a father. Besides, Damon was Alpha. That meant he'd have to hand down the sentence. Perhaps even carry it out. My vision wavered as the tears welled and threatened to spill over. I knew the pain of losing the only family you had all too well. That type of hurt never went away and would rear up to stab you painfully in the heart for the rest of your life at the most unexpected times. But I couldn't imagine the anguish of being forced to kill your own child.

My brain scrambled for a solution. I couldn't let this family be torn apart because of a teenager's stupid mistake. Because of me. But no matter how I looked at the situation, I couldn't find a way out. The wolves had refined Pack law over centuries to set boundaries for a society populated by savage monsters, despite any veneer of gentile behavior. The rules were simultaneously honorable, but ruthless; fair, but coldhearted. I knew without asking that, in New Orleans, Pack law would be fully upheld by the Collective as well. How could I buck both organizations?

Think, Cam, think! Or Andrei is as good as dead.

Chapter 25

Damon exhaled a shaky breath and spoke flatly, refusing to meet my eyes. "Cameron Blaze, I am placing you under the protection of the Pack until the next full moon, at which time your fate will be determined. You will come with me now. We will deal with your attacker as required by Pack law."

"No," I said immediately.

I felt Magnus' eyes burn into my back as I twisted painfully to face Damon. Damon's shoulders slumped. His head fell forward. He stared at the floor. "Please. Don't make this harder than it already is, Cameron," the Alpha whispered. He sounded like he was near to breaking down.

I reached out a hand, hesitating a moment before letting it fall back to the bed helplessly. We sat there in silence until Damon finally turned his head to meet my eyes. He pressed his lips into a flat line, and his blue gaze was flinty as he tried to suppress the pain mounting in his heart. As soon as I saw his eyes, I knew I would do whatever I could to keep the Alpha's family together.

An idea sparked in my head. I'd gotten into a friendly tussle with a werewolf when I was on a job up in Kentucky a few years back. To be fair, I'd thought it was just a large dog at the time. It wasn't until much later that I'd realized he'd been a werewolf. The incident had happened so long ago, I'd almost forgotten. I'd been scratched. Was it from his teeth or claws? I couldn't remember. I shook my head. That wasn't the important part right now. The important part was that I hadn't shifted.

Whether it was because of my Supe blood or dumb luck, but I didn't care. I wasn't a werewolf. That was all the mattered.

I wasn't sure Damon would agree with my conclusions, but something was better than nothing at this point. "I won't go with you because Pack law does not apply in my case. I've tangled with a werewolf before and am none the worse for wear," I said, infusing more confidence than I felt into my voice.

"It doesn't matter. Pack law is clear. Until we are positive you aren't a threat to yourself or others, you'll come with us. Please don't fight me on this." Damon's voice was husky.

I felt a painful lump build in my throat. I pushed it aside and spoke as calmly as I could. "How would Pack law address this situation if I were a vampire or a leprechaun or an elf?" I asked.

A flare of something resembling hope flared in Damon's eyes, but he shook his head, extinguishing it before resuming his silent examination of the floral wallpaper.

Magnus spoke from behind me. "Most Supes are inherently immune to contamination by lycanthropy. The situation would deescalate to either a trial instigated by the aggrieved party to be judged by the Pack or, more usually, a physical confrontation between the werewolf and the other Supe."

The tightness in my chest released marginally as I saw a glimmer of hope for both Andrei and me. Grandly, I brushed my hands together like I was wiping dust from my palms. "There you go. Problem solved. I'm a Supe and I'm not challenging your son or bringing him to a trial before the Pack."

Damon shook his head, grim determination creasing his rugged face. "Your origins are unknown."

"Not true!" I countered. "My mother was a mage."

"Are you?" Damon shot back. "And what about your father?" My mouth opened and closed like a fish gasping its last breath as it flopped helplessly on the riverbank. Damon shook his head. "You could have human blood in your past that you don't even know about. That makes you vulnerable to contamination from the bite and, therefore, a threat to the wider population of New Orleans! I will remand you into Pack custody until this matter can be resolved. Until we know you aren't a threat."

My gaze grew steely. "Sorry, Damon. I don't have time to be locked in a room while your wolves stare at me like a zoo exhibit. I'm telling you I am a Supe. An independent Supe, and therefore not subject to your Pack law. You have no jurisdiction over me in this matter. Push me on this and I will bring you before the Collective." I spoke forcefully, threatening him with the only thing I could think of. The Collective hated being forced to work together, but I had a feeling I could sway them to my side in this case. If nothing else, the Collective had the reputation of always adhering to the letter of the law, not the spirit. And, in this case, the letter of the law was on my side.

Damon shook his head again. "Pack law is clear. I must take you into Pack custody."

"Yes, if I were human. Which I'm not." I tried to meet his eyes without flinching. It took all my willpower.

"No! For the greater good!" Damon's authoritative tone cracked through the room, and I flinched back. He raised his hands in apology and lowered his voice. "I cannot risk a new werewolf who is not in control of her powers running wild through New Orleans. Think of the damage you could do, Cameron."

I thrust my arm out at him, showing him the tattoo. "There is a lich tracking me. An undead, nearly unkillable necromancer who can create zombies and he's got a homing beacon locked on me. You put me in a cell and you're painting a target on your Pack's house. Not to mention offering me up to the lich on a silver platter. At least Mama has this place warded from here to kingdom come! Can you say the same?" I wasn't one hundred percent confident that Mama's wards would keep a lich out, but Damon didn't need to know that.

"Wards can be arranged," Damon growled.

"You are assuming I will shift. Maybe I won't. I've tangled with werewolves before and never shifted." I rushed on to avoid any follow-up questions on that point. "Regardless, I do not submit to your custody. Period." I stubbornly crossed my arms over the bandages wrapped around my rib cage and tried not to wince at the stab of pain from the deep cuts in my side.

Magnus cleared his throat. Damon and I both turned at the unexpected noise. The man raised a single finger, silently asking for our attention. "What if I monitor her? Just until the full moon. Then she's not in custody but also not a danger to the wider population. And you know I can take care of the situation if things turn hairy." He addressed his comments solely to the Alpha, ignoring me entirely.

I rolled my eyes and glared at the handsome werewolf, letting my eyes communicate my displeasure as loudly as they could. After a moment's thought, I softened my gaze. Even though I didn't like the idea of the two men deciding on a babysitter for me, it was better than the alternative of being locked in a werewolf proof cell. Magnus was trying to help. I couldn't hold that against him. Apparently, the idea held merit for the Alpha as well. Damon seriously considered the proposal. I bit my tongue, sensing anything I said now wouldn't help. Silence stretched as the Alpha weighed the options. Finally, he nodded shortly and pushed to his feet, meeting my eyes directly. When he spoke, his tone was formal and his words almost ritualistic.

"This is an unusual situation and therefore, I am enacting my rights as Alpha of New Orleans. In this matter, my word is final. Given that she isn't fully human, it's my ruling that Cameron falls outside of Pack law, but we must still put preventative measures in place. Maverick Magnus, you'll be Cameron's protector until we can determine whether she has become a lycanthrope. You are within your rights to act as you see fit if the shift takes her and you deem her to be a threat. We will take the offending werewolf into custody. Cameron, you may bring a grievance against your attacker before the Pack within the next month."

I opened my mouth to speak, not really sure of what I was going to say. I wanted to protest Damon's apparently cruel dismissal of his son. The Alpha hadn't even said Andrei's name as he uttered the sentence against the young werewolf. A motion caught my eye, halting any words before I could form them. Magnus made the swift slicing motion through the air with a hand again, out of Damon's line of sight. I swallowed back my words.

Damon gave me a curt nod and wheeled on a heel, striding from the room. He eased the door closed behind him without another word. I waited until the thumping of Damon's footsteps faded away before turning to face Magnus, brows furrowing. "What the actual hell just happened?"

Magnus blew out a long, low whistle. "I'll be honest, that was impressive. I didn't see it coming and I don't think the Alpha did either." He picked up the chair tucked neatly under a small desk in the corner near the window and brought it over to my bed.

"What do you mean?" I asked.

He shrugged and sank into the chair, resting his arms on his thighs. "The loophole. You saw it and acted decisively, which probably saved the kid's life. For now, at least."

"I don't enjoy ripping families apart," I muttered.

Magnus gave me a thoughtful look. When I didn't elaborate further, he filled the silence. "Well, it looks like we get to spend the day together, for better or worse. So, what should we do? Still up for that 'I Love Lucy' marathon?"

I snorted. "Nice try, but I don't need a babysitter and I keep telling you, this isn't a date."

Magnus shook his head. "As much as we both know I'd like nothing more than a second chance to make a first impression, that's not what's happening here." He waved a hand back and forth between us and then added a smile. "Not today, at least. Today, I can either be a bodyguard, babysitter, or creepy guy in the shadows, but I'm not letting you out of my sight. Alpha's orders. Fair warning, if you try to give me the slip, you won't get too far before I'd track you down. Trust me." He tapped the side of his nose meaningfully.

I flopped back on the pillows and promptly groaned as several stabs of varying degrees of agony informed me that my body wasn't ready for sudden movements. I rolled my head to look at Magnus. "Tell me about you and the Alpha. It seemed a little frosty between you." I asked, curiosity distracting me from my injuries for the moment.

"Caught that, did you?" he asked, running a hand through his hair. "Lykaios is being standoffish until my status within the Pack is official."

I changed tactics. "So, you were on your own before you joined this Pack. What happened there?" I asked.

Magnus shook his head. "That's a story for another time." His tone was light, but I could sense steel shutters slamming down behind those cool gray eyes.

The door swung wide and Mama bustled in with Ben close on her heels. He carried a tray carefully, his tongue poking out between his lips as he concentrated on setting his load down without spilling it. I heard him sigh in relief once it was on the nightstand before turning to me.

"Cam!" the old necromancer exclaimed. "You're awake!"

"And she shouldn't be," Mama said with a frown. "She needs food and rest, not to be pestered all day by the likes of us." She gently, but firmly, reached up and tucked her hand in the crook of Magnus' arm. The werewolf had to stoop over to accommodate their height difference. "If you don't mind, dearie, a load of pumpkins were just dropped by the house and I need some help putting them somewhere more sensible than the middle of the kitchen floor."

The tiny woman was a force of nature when she wanted to be. The werewolf didn't stand a chance. He shot me a bemused look over her head as she gently dragged him out of the room.

Ben fussed with the corner of the blanket and then awkwardly patted my foot. "You have a good sleep now, you hear? It'll do you a world of good." He moved towards the door.

I stretched out an arm to stop him. "Wait!"

He turned and raised his bushy brows in surprise. "You want somethin' else? I can go get Mama if you want."

"No, it's just…" I paused, trying to put my thoughts in order. Ben sat on the edge of the bed, waiting patiently for me. I rubbed at my forehead and leaned back against the pillow. "It's just a lot. You know? First the demon. Then a lich materializes in town. Now this werewolf thing? It's too much!"

Ben nodded sympathetically. "Magnus told us bits and pieces. We sorta filled in the rest. That Alpha is a loud feller when he's mad."

"He's just concerned for his son," I whispered.

"As am I. But I'm also concerned about you. How are you holdin' up?"

I lifted a shoulder. "About as well as can be expected, I guess." I traced a finger over the tattoo on my wrist. Only the blue and the orange dot glowed up at me now. A sudden thought occurred to me. "Ben!"

"Yes ma'am," he replied.

"You're a necromancer!"

A small smile tugged at his mouth. "That's what they tell me, but I'm not sure if I should believe 'em or not." Goliath stuck his head out of Ben's wild, white mane of hair, looked around, and then promptly disappeared again.

"No. I know you are. It's just… I mean, you've got to know something about liches, right?"

Ben stroked his chin. "I know as much as the next feller, I guess. They're power mad, the lot of them. Always wantin' what the other guy's got and meaner than a wet panther."

I showed him my wrist and pointed to the orange dot. "So, what's he doing here, just hanging out in New Orleans? He's been floating around as a ghost until Magnus and I stumbled across his soul jar. Now, he's running around town as a walking skeleton. Why?"

Ben pondered my questions seriously. When he finally spoke, his voice was low and serious. "I wish I had those answers for you. I truly do. Maybe then we could make a plan to stop him before he causes an almighty ruckus."

"Well, he's obviously waiting for something. What do you think his end game is?"

"Power," Ben answered immediately. "He must've been a fair sight better than your average magician, even before the durned fool tore his soul outta his body and shoved it in a jar. When most people get to that level, they'll do just about anythin' and everythin' to claw a little bit more power out of this world for themselves. Never does anybody a lick o' good, but do people like that learn? Not a chance."

"So, what do we do? Just sit around and wait?" I asked, desperation flooding up from my stomach.

Ben patted my foot again. "Nobody's just sittin' around, honey. We sent word to the Collective that we suspect there's a lich in town. The werewolves are out on patrol. Mama's warned the magic community to be on high alert and you," he shook his finger at me sternly. "Your job is to rest and recuperate. Sleep. Leave the lich to the likes of us for the time being."

As soon as he mentioned sleep, fatigue clawed at the backs of my eyes, making them feel gritty and dry. Ben pushed off the bed with a creak of springs and started for the door.

The thought of being alone with a lich out there made my eyes flare wide despite my exhaustion. "Ben?" I called out, a little louder than I'd intended. He turned at the door, looking concerned. I swallowed hard. "Will you stay with me? Just for a little while?"

A soft smile creased the old necromancer's face. "Of course, darlin'." He tugged the chair Magnus had vacated closer to the bed and reached out to hold my hand. "I'll stay as long as you like."

A lump formed in my throat, and I squeezed his fingers in thanks. The last thing I remember before surrendering fully to the darkness was the gentle brush of soft white fur on my cheek as Goliath settled on my pillow and the comforting warmth of Ben's hand holding mine.

Chapter 26

It was three days before Mama let me get out of bed unassisted and another two before she trusted me with something as tricky as stairs. I used the time to study the book on the Necrocracy that Seshat had given me and have long discussions with Ben about undead creatures. Both were fascinating.

On the positive side of things, my ankle had been merely twisted, not sprained. It was almost fully healed, and the lacerations were mending nicely. To top it off, I hadn't turned into a werewolf yet, so everything was looking good. Except for the lich in town, of course.

I also had lots of visitors. Sloane came to see me almost every day. The werewolves stopped by as well. Even Logan made a brief appearance, which surprised me. The one person who came nowhere near the house while I was recuperating was the lich. I only knew because I checked my wrist more often than a teenage girl with her first crush checked her phone. The orange dot pulsed faintly to the northwest. Although I didn't know what the lich was up to, the unexpected lull me twitchy.

By the fifth night I'd spent shut up inside Mama's home, I was so on edge that I decided to call Alessandro, the leader of the New Orleans vampires and the head of the Collective. I wanted to ferret out some information. I was so shocked when he actually picked up the phone that I had to sit down.

"What is it, Ms. Blaze?" he barked.

The abrupt greeting took aback me. Alessandro was normally genteel to a fault. Besides, I hadn't really expected him to answer. It was early evening. I'd assumed he'd still be asleep or whatever it was vampires did during the daylight hours. "Umm, hello to you, too. What gives?"

"What gives is the fact that I am still dealing with the rooting out the corruption the little weasel of a rebel, Octavian, left in his wake. Apparently, his rot was far more widespread and insidious than could have possibly been imagined for one of his," Alessandro sniffed, "caliber. You are calling at the most inopportune time!"

"Well, sorry!" I dragged out the word. "But you said that I could ask for any back-up or resources I needed while going after this rogue soul. I need information. From you. So, unless you want to break that oath..." I trailed off significantly.

He huffed out a sigh. "No. Fine. This one is dead now anyway, so I've got a few minutes." I heard the heavy thump of something that might have been a head hit the ground in the background. "What is of such urgency that you insist upon interrupting my hunt for rebel scum?"

In that moment, I thought it was in my best interest not to point out how much the vamp sounded like Darth Vader. Instead, I focused on the more pressing matters. "Have you heard there is a lich in town?"

"Yes."

"And what are you going to do about it?" I demanded.

"I'm busy."

"Aren't you the head of the Collective? It's your *job* to make sure threats like this are neutralized. Do your job."

Alessandro's voice was icy, reminding me not to go criticizing the most powerful vampire in the city. Not where he could hear me, at least. "My *job* is to ensure that Norms remain blissfully unaware of the supernatural presence in our fair city, which I am doing quelling a vampire rebellion before it can spill out of basements and back alleys into the streets and across the front page of the news. At the moment, is this lich actively threatening to expose the supernatural world to the humans?"

"Well, no, I don't think–" I started.

Alessandro cut me off. "And has he openly attacked anyone, supernatural or human?"

I gritted my teeth. "No, but you can't just sit there and do nothing."

"I'm not. I hired someone to take care of the problem already."

"Really? Who?"

"You. Do *your* job, Ms. Blaze. And, by my calculations, your time to complete said job is dangerously close to running out." His voice was low, but the chastising tone burned like acid.

I swallowed hard. I didn't want to piss him off, at least, not any further than I already had, but I knew when I was punching above my weight. If I was going to take on the lich, I needed help and I wasn't sure the werewolves were going to be enough. When I spoke, I tried to make it as professional as I could. "I need back up and would appreciate it if you could send some vampires to help until we can track the lich down and take care of him.

"Not an option," Alessandro said instantly. "I need all those loyal to me to handle this rebel issue. Which is stirring up again," he said, sounding like he was twisting away from the phone as he watched something. I heard a feral snarl over the phone and the meaty sound of flesh hitting flesh.

"What am I supposed to do?" I said urgently. "I can't take him on my own."

"I heard the fae have bolstered their ranks. Call them," Alessandro said. I heard a blood-curdling shriek on the other end, and then the line went dead.

I stared at the black screen of the phone in shock. Magnus walked up behind me. The werewolf had taken his Alpha's orders to heart and hadn't left Mama's house the entire time I'd been convalescing. "What's up?" he asked softly.

I held up the phone. "Alessandro. He says he's too busy to help with the lich. That it's my problem to deal with, and I should talk to the fae if I need reinforcements."

"Do you think they could help?" Magnus asked.

"Maybe? He seemed to think they've increased their numbers, perhaps in response to rumors of the lich in town? I supposed I could head over to the Embassy and ask Letitia." I looked up at him. "Would you be willing to drive me?"

Magnus folded his arms over his chest. "Why do you need to go anywhere? You can ask for her help just as well over the phone as you could in person."

I ran a hand through my hair. "Honestly, I'm going a little stir-crazy. I should be out there, hunting him down. Doing something. Doing anything! But I'm stuck in here."

"Are you sure that this isn't a side-effect of the magic in that tattoo?" Magnus asked.

"No! Well, maybe. That's a fair point, actually. But the fae Embassy isn't that far away. I'm sure I'd be as safe there as I am here, especially with you acting as an escort." Ok, I was laying it on a little thick, but the anxiety that was building from being cooped up was playing against my better judgement.

Magnus considered my words. Finally, he said, "Fine. I'll drive you." I let out a little squeal of surprised joy. I hadn't expected it to be that easy. Magnus held up a finger, cutting my celebration short. "But only if you get Mama's permission first."

Ok, so not that easy.

It took me thirty minutes of wheedling to convince Mama and Ben that they healed enough for me to let me leave the house. Several trips up and down the stairs proved my ankle was almost fully mended. It surprised me that it had healed faster than the lacerations from the demon's claws. Maybe it was Mama's healing magic, maybe it was Brigitte's rum, but I wasn't about to go whining about any good fortune that came my way.

After that, it took me another ten minutes to convince Mama that I'd be perfectly safe with Magnus on the short ride to the fae Embassy. Once we were there, we'd be surrounded by fae guards. I'd met some of them. Even sparred somewhat regularly with a half-ogre named Hank. If all the fae guards were like him, they were competent and had a mean uppercut. I had no doubt we'd be fine.

At least, that's what I kept telling myself the entire car ride there until Magnus screeched to a halt in front of the Embassy gates. Or rather, what was left of them. Something had blasted through the faux-wrought iron like it was a pinata at a kids' birthday party, but instead of a stick, they'd brought a bazooka, leaving a veritable barricade of splintered debris blocking the entrance to the Embassy.

I was out of the car and sprinting up the drive before Magnus had even switched off the ignition.

Chapter 27

I heard a car door slam and the sound of feet pounding up the pavement behind me. Magnus was on his way. Good. I bent my head and focused on keeping my gait steady and smooth so as not to roll my ankle. It felt much better, but the last thing I needed was twisting it again or I'd be worse than useless.

I sucked in a breath as I neared the front of the house, crouching low behind some shrubs that were part of the immaculately kept land-scaping. Magnus crawled up next to me. "You should have waited for... wait! What the hell! When did you bring your sword?" He stared at the weapon in my hand in shock.

"I'm sneaky, but not an idiot. There's a lich somewhere out there. I wasn't about to leave the house unarmed," I whispered back.

I unsheathed my yatagan in a fierce, sharp move, tossing the useless sheath into the lush grass that surrounded the impressive Southern mansion. Normally, I would've attached the short sheath to my back, but in my hasty exit from the car, that'd been impossible. I wasn't about to waste time and do it now. I could always reclaim it from the fae later. If I survived the next few minutes.

I peered around the edge of the shrub. A flare of orange light lit up the front of the mansion. The flash illuminated three dark figures facing the Embassy. Suddenly, a shield of crackling orange magic snapped to life. Thin projectiles flared upon contact with the shield. Arrows. At least that meant that the fae were putting up some sort of defense. I used the distraction to dart forward, hiding behind the next bush as I considered my next move. Magnus joined me a moment later.

The lich stood in front of the grand entryway to the fae Embassy in only its stolen scrub pants. A thin layer of skin covered his torso, but he looked emaciated beneath his newly grown epidermis. The shield of orange magic snapped and popped as more arrows struck it. In the flashes of light, I saw that the two figures standing on either side of him looked beaten to hell. One was missing an arm and the other's neck was bent at an impossible angle.

My mouth went dry. Zombies.

The lich shouted, "Turn the ambassador over and I'll leave peacefully!"

Why did he want Letitia?

A powerful voice rang out from inside the Embassy. "Not a chance. Go back to hell, you bastard!" That sounded like Hank.

The lich roared, dropping the shield and hurling bolts of crackling orange magic at the house. The zombies rushed forward in a shambling run, heading straight up the stairs towards the front door. A rain of arrows knocked them backwards, pinning them in place on the front lawn.

I capitalized on the distraction and slid forward with Magnus close on my heels, closing the distance between us and the lich. A flicker of movement caught the corner of my eye. I whipped my head around, fearing there was another zombie out there that I'd missed.

My breath caught in my chest until a flash of orange light lit up the man's face. He was wearing the uniform of a fae guard and looked very much alive from my angle. He was also slinking through the manicured lawn to flank the undead sorcerer. The guard must've been stationed near the front of the property. He was closer than Magnus and I were to the lich. Maybe he could take down the undead sorcerer. I held my breath as the fae continued to inch closer on silent feet.

Letitia, the interim ambassador to Fae, appeared in the grand entryway to the mansion, flanked on either side by guards, each of whom held a nocked bow. The beautiful fae woman took in the scene at a glance, eyes sweeping over the lich and the guard creeping up behind him, her face giving nothing away. Not that I was surprised. Before the debacle last month, she'd carefully cultivated a party girl persona, playing the ditzy role perfectly in order to monitor her uncle for the powers that be in the Fae realms. I'll admit, she'd even fooled me with her party girl act. However, it wasn't a role she played anymore. Now, she was a badass in her own right, stepping into her uncle's role on the Collective and now playing decoy in front of a lich. I'll admit it. I admired her. The woman had balls.

"It is too late in the day to entertain visitors, expected or otherwise. Please come back in the morning if you wish to arrange a meeting. Good night," Letitia said coolly, completely ignoring the evidence of the magical battlefield as she folded her hands calmly in front of her like she was on the cover of a local socialite magazine instead of facing down a powerful necromantic sorcerer.

"Interesting," the lich muttered to himself, but I heard him clearly enough from where I stood. The lich raised his voice. "I have a matter to address regarding the fae delegation here in New Orleans. Who is in charge?"

Letitia tucked her arms behind her, widening her stance as she stared down at the skeleton on her front lawn. "I am," she said confidently.

Although I couldn't see his face, I heard the smile in the lich's voice.

"Perfect," the undead bastard chuckled. And then all hell broke loose.

The lich dropped his shield of crackling orange energy and sent a barrage of magic lightning spiraling at the Embassy faster than I could blink. Some magical bolts struck the pinioned zombies, making them scream and writhe helplessly on the ground from the unexpected attack.

Apparently, Letitia had been ready where the zombies had not. She whipped her hands out from behind her back, and they were glowing bright green with stored magic. Letitia's magic shot out of her fingertips and into the plants surrounding the Embassy, creating an explosion of growth. Shrubbery, flowers, and bushes grew at an inconceivable rate, forming a living shield around the Embassy. Letitia's formidable foliage intercepted some of the lich's magical bolts, but not all. I saw both guards stumble, their arrows whizzing off harmlessly into the night. I didn't have time to waste evaluating their wounds because I was already sprinting towards the lich.

The fae guard who'd been flanking the lich was faster and closer than I was. He sprang at the undead sorcerer with a sword in hand before the lich could release another barrage of deadly magic. The sorcerer whirled, a bony hand flying to his chest. He dug his fingers under the thin layer of skin and viciously tore a rib free with a resounding crack. The lich spun towards the guard even as the fae landed in a fighter's crouch.

The guard instantly swung his sword up at the sorcerer's midsection. He was obviously hoping to cut through the creature's thin middle and sever the spine, thus ending the fight quickly. Unfortunately, his plan didn't work. The lich diverted the blow to the side, catching the fae's sword arm as it slid past him. The sorcerer jerked the guard upright, pulling him in close. I could see the ghastly leer on the lich's thin face as he drove the broken rib into the guard's torso.

I heard Letitia let out a scream of rage and anguish as the impaled guard thrashed, driving the rib deeper into his own chest. The lich twisted the improvised bone spear. The guard gasped, rising erect in a spasm of pain and then slumped forward. I was close enough to see the light in his eyes dim and extinguish as he died.

I gripped my yatagan tightly, ready to attack and avenge the dead fae guard as I closed the distance between me and the lich. He couldn't get away with openly murdering people. That shit wouldn't fly. Not in my town. I pushed more power into my legs, readying them for a leap when a wall of furry muscle hit me like a freight train, knocking me sprawling into the soft grass of the Embassy lawn. Looking up, I saw a huge silver wolf standing over me, snarling down at me, and dripping drool down fearsome fangs.

Magnus.

"What the hell?" I grunted, getting some air back in my lungs as I shoved at his hairy leg. "I could have taken him!"

Magnus snorted and tipped his head towards the lich. From this angle, I could see the dead fae impaled on the rib and the other rib the lich held partially concealed by its body. I froze momentarily. If I'd continued my ill-conceived charge, I would have probably ended up just as dead as the guard. Magnus had just saved my life.

Orange light pulsed down the rib, crackling and snapping. The dead fae jerked like a fish on a string, spasming and flopping wildly. I looked on with horrified fascination as I pushed to my feet, holding the yatagan in a defensive stance, unsure of what was going on. I dug the fingers of my free hand into the ruff at the back of Magnus' neck, but didn't know if I was trying to hold the werewolf back or to draw strength from him.

Suddenly, the dead fae's eyes snapped open, glowing a wicked orange. I let out a little scream of surprise. The lich lowered his gaunt arm until the fae's feet were firmly on the ground. The guard lifted his hands to his chest and slowly pushed himself off the rib with a sickening, scraping slurp.

"Go! Kill the Ambassador!" commanded the lich, pointing a finger towards the Embassy.

The dead fae guard blinked his glowing orange eyes once, then twice. A snarl of rage creased his face, and he took off running in the opposite direction.

"Damn revenants! I'm off my game. That's what I get for being dead for so long," I heard the lich grumble. The sorcerer hurled another vicious blast of orange bolts towards the Embassy. I saw a group of fae guards had crept past the protective barrier of greenery and already decapitated both zombies. They dodged out of the way of the magical barrage. The lich cursed under his breath and then disappeared in a blaze of orange sparks.

I rubbed the back of my hand across my eyes, trying to get rid of the after images burned into my retinas. Blinking rapidly as I looked around, I saw no trace of the lich. I glanced at my wrist. The orange dot was already speeding away from the center point of the compass.

Damn it all to hell.

As much as I wanted to track down the lich immediately, I hadn't missed the fact that the dead guard had just come back to life or the lich's mention of a revenant. Which meant another zombie was on the loose. If Seshat was right, then the newly formed revenant zombie would be bent on violent retribution. For what, I didn't know, but he needed to be stopped. Fast.

Magnus let out a little whine, leaning hard against my side. I'd gotten so used to operating on my own that I'd almost forgotten about my werewolf bodyguard-slash-babysitter. And four legs could cover the ground a hell of a lot faster than two.

I pointed after the revenant. "Go! Track down the zombie. Kill it again if you can. If you can't, slow him down until I can catch up."

Magnus took off like he was an arrow and I'd just loosed the bowstring. He let out a bone chilling howl as he raced across the lawn in pursuit of the zombie. As much as I wanted to run after him immediately, I needed to check on the fae. Trusting Magnus to do his job, I whirled and ran toward the Embassy. Letitia's foliage shield was well over head height and still growing. A narrow corridor between the giant shrubberies remained, leading up to the entrance of the Embassy. I noticed with grim satisfaction that Letitia had purposely designed it to only allow one person passage at a time. A perfect choke point and easy for the defenders to hold.

Not wanting to fall victim to friendly foliage, I shouted to the guards as I approached, "I'm Cameron Blaze! I'm a friend! Don't attack!"

Letitia's voice came weakly from the other side of the dense overgrowth. "Cam? What are you doing here?"

"It's a long story. How are you doing?"

"Not good, but we're holding steady as long as there aren't any more attacks." Letitia's voice sounded thready. "What's it like out there?"

One guard answered her. "The sorcerer vanished, Madame Ambassador."

I chimed in, "Yeah, but there's still a zombie on the loose. Any reinforcements you have in there would be really useful right about now."

"A third zombie?" the guard asked in disbelief. "Those two were hard enough to kill. Just wouldn't go down."

"So don't waste time. Send back up to the eastern part of the estate. Oh, and tell them I've got a werewolf on my team. Don't kill him or Damon will be pissed!" I shouted, turning and sprinting away before I heard her answer. Although the situation wasn't great, it sounded like

Letitia had it under control for the moment. Which meant Magnus needed me more than the fae did.

I had to watch my step in the lush grass as I followed the sounds of fighting for fear I'd land wrong and hurt my ankle again. A fat lot of good it would do anyone if I couldn't walk, let alone dodge a vengeful zombie. By the time I reached Magnus, the zombie-Fae had nearly made it to the edge of the estate. My instincts kicked in and I evaluated the situation in a heartbeat.

The revenant couldn't be allowed off the property. We didn't know what sort of vengeance fantasy was driving the zombie-fae, but the population of New Orleans couldn't find out about fae, zombies, or werewolves. That would put the whole Supe community in a pile of shit that we didn't need and me in the Collective's crosshairs.

Gouges, cuts, and scrapes covered the zombie by the time I caught up. His blind race towards retribution had undoubtedly caused some as he crashed through the trees covering the estate, but I saw a few that were bite marks. Magnus had done a good job of harrying the zombie, then. However, the only obvious sign of blood loss came from the hole in the middle of his shirt. The werewolf leaped at the zombie, teeth flashing in the moonlight. The revenant let out a wordless guttural shout, crashing to the soft grass, and rolling over to protect his throat. Magnus bit and tore at any exposed flesh as the zombie fought to throw the wolf off. I pulled to a stop, holding my yatagan ready, but not wanting to hurt Magnus as the two rolled and snarled in front of me.

Finally, the zombie tucked his legs up under him and launched the werewolf through the air with a sick, tearing noise. Magnus twisted and landed with a yelp. He spat a chunk of something to side and yakked until the taste cleared his mouth. I realized with a start he'd just yanked off much of the zombie's biceps. I whipped my attention to the zombie as he scrambled to his feet again, looking unconcerned about the damage to his arm.

"Decapitation!" I shouted at Magnus, bracing myself. "Seshat said that's the quickest way to end zombies. And then we need to burn its corpse to ashes." Magnus gave a little snuffle of acknowledgement.

I raised my sword and attacked. The new skin of healing lacerations tugged with a dull ache on my arm and side, but I didn't have time for that now. I had a zombie to kill. Somewhere along the way, the zombie must have dropped his weapon because he countered with his bare arm. My blade sank into his flesh, clear to the bone. I whipped it out before he could pull the yatagan from my grasp, reversing and redirecting the sword straight into his torso. I tried to yank it loose quickly, but the zombie didn't have the same pain avoidance reflexes I was accustomed to in my opponents. He reached across his body and grabbed the double-edged blade with his bare hand, tugging on it fiercely even as it bit deeply into his palm. He snarled into my face, hot spittle flying to splatter my cheeks as I fought for control of the sword.

Magnus took advantage of the situation and darted into the fray. He tore at the creature's exposed hamstring, coming away with another mouthful of the former fae guard's uniform, which he promptly spat out. He started circling, searching for another opening as the zombie stumbled, but kept his feet under him. With the zombie's attention drawn to the wolf, I scrabbled for one of my karambits in its special sheath at the small of my back. Sliding my finger through the safety ring as I jerked it free, I tried to slash through the tendons on the zombie's wrist, but only scored a shallow cut. However, his grip on the yatagan momentarily slackened, and I twisted the blade out of his hand. I retreated, trying to buy myself some distance to make the most use of the sword's reach.

The zombie followed me swiftly, taking a wild swing at my head. I dodged and swung my yatagan to counter. The zombie leaned to the side and my blade whipped through thin air, sending me stumbling off balance. Magnus leaped at the zombie's unprotected legs again, aiming for the Achilles' tendon this time. The revenant was faster than I'd first imagined and dodged out of the way at the last moment.

It was slow, miserable work, but we whittled away at the enraged zombie. A tiny portion of my soul crumbled each time I struck out at the fae-guard-turned-zombie. After all, he'd just shown up at work this morning, assuming he'd get to go home and binge watch crap TV, hang out with his friends over a beer, or make a cup of tea and call it an early night. And then he got turned into a zombie. Life sucks.

Death sucks more, apparently.

However, letting a zombie roam around New Orleans wasn't an option, so Magnus and I kept hacking away at the zombie-fae with grim determination. It was a strange mix of relief and sorrow that welled up inside of me when I finally decapitated the zombie.

I slumped to the ground next to the corpse's corpse, waiting for reinforcements to arrive from the Embassy. The zombie's body needed to be burned, but I knew the fae would want to honor their deceased companion for his service, regardless of how he'd spent the last few minutes of his life. Or the first few minutes of his afterlife. Whatever.

Magnus came over and nuzzled my hand, snuffling wetly against my fingers and checking me over for injuries. I wasn't ready to talk yet, so I dug my fingertips into his warm fur and leaned my head against his massive shoulder. The werewolf sat, tail thumping lightly on the ground as we stared at the decimated body in silence, lost in our own thoughts.

Eventually, I heard the tromp of feet approaching. I sighed and patted Magnus' shoulder. "Thanks for that," I said. He nodded his head, understanding shining in his eyes. I pushed to my feet, brushing grass and twigs from my pants. "I'm assuming you don't want to shift right now. Do you have a change of clothes in the car?" I asked. He shook his massive head. "Ok. Stay close to me then. Although I told them you were on the same team, I don't want any misunderstandings with the fae. Tonight has been enough of a tragedy." My voice hitched slightly on the last word as I took one last look at the fae zombie. If it had been me, I would've wanted somebody to make sure I didn't mindlessly hurt others, but that didn't make this any easier.

Magnus must have sensed my mood, because he nosed my hand and expertly flipped it up, so it landed on his ruff. I smiled at the sheer doggy-ness of the move. I dug my fingers into the long, soft fur at the base of his neck again. He was warm, solid, and real, which helped to ground me as the contingent of fae guards approached cautiously.

The lead guard held a bow with an arrow loosely nocked. He spoke as the group approached. "Blaze? What's happened?"

I gestured at the remains scattered around us. "The sorcerer killed your friend and then turned him into a revenant. A zombie," I clarified when I saw the look of confusion shadow the leader's face. "You should collect all the remains, say your goodbyes, and then light the funeral pyre. Best burn the other two as well."

"Cremation is not our way," the lead fae said tightly.

I shrugged. "It's the only way to ensure he won't reanimate again, but if you want to risk a zombie popping out of the ground at some undetermined point in the future, that's on you. Where's the Ambassador?"

The guard pointed back towards the Embassy. "She was hit by one of those orange bolts the sorcerer was throwing around. She said you needed the help, and she'd only slow us down, so she stayed behind with the other wounded."

"How many?" I asked softly.

"Three dead. Some more of us got tagged by at least one of those bolts. No one is familiar with the magic, so until we get a healer from the local coven out to diagnose the injured, we don't know the extent of the damage," he responded, keeping his voice low.

"Right," I replied. Things were going from bad to worse. I waved at the walkie talkie on his belt. "Tell your people we're coming in and I need to talk to Letitia immediately. Oh, and remind them please the werewolf is a friendly. We don't need anyone else getting hurt today." I patted Magnus' shoulder to emphasize the point.

The fae nodded and grabbed his radio as we walked away. I kept my fingers buried in Magnus' fur, trying to ignore the wet, meaty thumps behind us of the remains of the unfortunate fae guard being readied for his final journey.

As the adrenaline faded, I felt the dull throb of my still healing cuts. I touched my side gingerly. My fingertips came away bloody. I must've popped some stitches. Mama wouldn't be thrilled with me, but it could've been worse. At least I'd held up long enough to deal with the lich and his minion. Hopefully, I could get stitched back up soon and the damage wasn't too bad.

The foliage almost engulfed the entire front of the mansion by the time we retraced our steps. I stopped well outside of the ferocious greenery and shouted, "Cameron Blaze and werewolf! We're friendlies and we're coming in!" The tunnel leading towards the entryway widened ever so slightly in unspoken welcome. We walked slowly through. It felt like we were walking into some sentient carnivorous plant's maw. I shivered. Being gnawed on by a meat-eating plant would be a sucky way to die.

Chaos reigned in the grand entryway of the Embassy. They'd stretched the injured out on makeshift pallets. I counted at least four bodies completely covered in white sheets. Letitia crouched by one of the injured guards, speaking in a low, comforting tone. When she saw us enter, she patted the man's shoulder gently and moved to meet us.

"We need to talk," she said tersely.

"Tell me about it. Can we go somewhere a little less public?" I asked.

"Yes, of course. Follow me," Letitia pivoted on a heel. I moved to follow her, but Magnus let out a little whine behind me.

"Uh, Letitia? Magnus wants to shift back but doesn't want to offend by walking around buck naked. Could you please lend him a set of clothes?" I asked.

"Certainly, how rude of me." Letitia raised her voice. "Geoffrey? Please arrange for a set of clothes for the werewolf as soon as possible."

I noticed I'd still entwined my fingers in Magnus' fur. Gently, I wiggled them loose. He nosed at my fingers gently. The impeccably dressed butler I'd called 'Jeeves' on my previous visits appeared out of nowhere. "As you wish," he said with a little bow. Magnus followed the butler out of the room while Letitia led me out of the entry hall towards the back of the house.

"Careful, you know that means Geoffrey loves you, right?" I said to her back, following her deeper into the Embassy.

Letitia snorted in a very unladylike way. "Doubtful. I'm neither a princess, a bride, nor his type."

She led me to what I recognized as Aldrich Kingsley's old office. She swung the door wide, ushering me into her newly decorated sanctum sanctorum. Gone were the heavy masculine furnishings and dark colors. Instead, clean white lines accented by soothing blues and greens greeted us. I looked around and whistled low. "You've been busy."

"Haven't we all?" Letitia settled herself on a cream and olive striped settee, gesturing for me to join her. She winced, hand flying to clutch at her side.

"Are you ok?" I asked.

"He grazed me, that's all. I'm fine," she said.

I looked at the light-colored upholstery and then at my dirty, blood-stained clothing. The soft seat looked inviting, but I didn't want to stain Letitia's new furniture.

"Don't worry," the Ambassador said, "it's spelled to be resistant to everything short of a nuclear disaster. I had a feeling that it was a wise precaution. I just hadn't expected to put the spell to use so soon."

With a sigh, I plopped on the couch. It was as comfortable as it looked. "It's a good thing you think ahead."

Letitia leaned forward, setting aside the banter for more pressing matters. "Not far enough ahead, obviously. What was that thing, Cam? I've never seen anything like it before."

I rubbed my wrist where my new tattoo lived self-consciously. "It's a lich."

She sucked in a breath. "The same one that has been rumored to be running around town?"

I nodded tiredly. "An undead sorcerer of immense power that can raise the dead. Speaking of, I know your people find it distasteful, but make sure you burn the guard the lich killed. He turned into a zombie after the lich shot him full of necromantic energy. Cremation is the only way to make sure that your man will rest peacefully."

Letitia nodded solemnly. "I will see to it."

"How are the rest of your people? How are you?" I asked.

"I'm managing," she said with a tight smile. "However, the same cannot be said for my people. There are currently four dead. Five with the addition of the guard this lich killed, but I believe that number will increase by morning's light if the witches can't do something. They're on their way, so we should have some answers soon."

"What do you mean?" Disquieting confusion welled up inside me. My gut was telling me I wouldn't like the answer.

Letitia grimaced and lifted her blouse, showing me her side. A dark splotch with a bright orange center defaced the creamy skin on her ribs. She dropped the fabric, clutching the injury with a gentle hand. "As far as I can guess, it's some sort of necrotic curse. Whatever the spell is, it spreads through the host's system. Those who suffered multiple hits of the sorcerer's magic succumbed quickly. Those of us with only one or two glancing blows are managing for now, but I don't know if our innate fae healing will be enough to counteract this curse. Hopefully, the coven can help."

I noticed she avoided stating what would happen if they couldn't. She and all her people would end up dead. Instead of focusing on something I couldn't change, I asked another question plaguing me. "Why did he come here? What did the lich want with you?"

Letitia shook her head. "How should I know? I've only been the interim ambassador for a short time. I've never even met the lich, nor did I know what he was fully capable of until this evening."

I nodded. That made two of us.

Letitia placed a hand on mine. "Thank you, Cameron, for coming to our aid. I shudder to think what would have happened if you hadn't been here to disrupt his plans, whatever they are. But how did you know to come at precisely the right moment?"

I grimaced. "I was actually coming for your help with tracking the lich down." She frowned as I showed her the magic compass on my inner wrist. "This allows me to track the spirits that escaped the night that your uncle tore a hole in the veil. The lich is one of those spirits, but he's made a body. It's a long story. Regardless, I think that this undead sorcerer dude is the one that the Collective told me to hunt down."

"Employed," Letitia corrected, absentmindedly.

I snorted. "Yes, I'm getting paid for the job, but employment suggests choice in the matter. I know you're a member now, but I don't lump you in with the rest of them. The Collective plotted, coerced, and blackmailed me to take care of this problem for them. I need to find out why."

Letitia shrugged. "I'm new to the Ambassador role and am the newest member of the Collective, even on an interim basis. We are sworn to the utmost secrecy regarding Collective business just as we are sworn never to harm one another."

I raised an eyebrow. That was a new tidbit of information but explained how the Collective could function even though it comprised members who fundamentally despised each other.

"Who do I need to pester into giving me answers?" I asked.

Letitia smiled grimly, flashing her teeth meaningfully at me. "I think you know."

I did. Alessandro Nicoletti. The leader of the local vampires and the head of the Collective. Unfortunately, he was busy putting out his own fires at the moment, given our last phone call.

I glanced out the window, trying to gauge the time, but dark green leaves completely covered it. Even if I could have made it over to

Alessandro's estate before the sun rose, I wasn't sure showing up unannounced and beaten half to hell would go over well. Besides, there was a chance he wasn't even at home if he hadn't rooted out all the rebels yet.

I turned back to the ambassador. "Look Letitia, as much as I'd love to track Alessandro down right now, this is the second fight I've had recently with a Supe that outclasses me in every sense of the word. We need a place to lie low and heal up for the night. I know you've got a lot on your plate, but..." I gestured towards the hallway leading to the makeshift infirmary, leaving the sentence floating between us.

"Think nothing of it, Cam. We've got plenty of space. The Embassy is fully equipped to handle surprise visitors. I'll ask Geoffrey to prepare rooms for you and the werewolf. I'll also ask the witches to come and check on you once they arrive. You should also know I intend to lock the Embassy down as soon as I can. No one will be able to enter or leave the Embassy until the morning."

I nodded. "That sounds perfect." And it did. I craved a night of protected rest after the shock of seeing how powerful the lich was. Anything that could help me regain a bit more strength was a gift more precious than diamonds right now.

Magnus returned and Geoffrey settled us in neighboring guest rooms just as a witch appeared to check us over. She muttered something under her breath as she stitched me back up before leaving. I was grateful for the help. The butler even offered magical dry-cleaning services should we require them. I gladly left my dirty and bloodied clothes in the hall for the laundry fairies to collect while I had a shower. Twenty minutes later, I felt like a new person. I pulled on the soft pajamas I found in the wardrobe and curled up in the enormous fourposter bed. My eyes were drifting closed when a knock sounded on the door. I sighed regretfully and went to answer it.

Magnus stood in the hallway, dark hair glistening from his own shower. His own borrowed pajamas emphasized the hard muscles in his shoulders and chest and the trim line of his waist. I could see his six-pack rippling under the tight t-shirt as he leaned against the doorframe. Suddenly self-conscious, I folded my arms over my chest.

"What's up?" I tried for casual, but was pretty sure it fell flat.

"Just checking to see you are ok. It's been a hell of a way to end the day," Magnus said, leaning against the wall next to my door. He eyed me speculatively.

"What? You mean the zombies? Yeah, you sure know how to show a girl a good time."

His eyes darkened. He leaned forward slightly. "Trust me, when I show you a good time, there will be neither zombies nor demons. All you have to do is ask me, Cameron."

The way he said it made my toes curl, but I didn't know what to say. My emotions about the handsome werewolf were so tangled up, and I hadn't had time to sort through them. Being constantly around him didn't help either. He was always just *there*. I hadn't realized I'd just been staring at him until the silence felt awkwardly oppressive. I shifted my weight, saying, "Well, I should really go..."

Magnus interrupted me. "Yeah, to bed. I know. But I thought you could use this, you know, to help you sleep. I may have snuck into the kitchen, so don't rat me out to the butler, ok?" He extended a white box covered in an embossed gold design to me. I took it on instinct, opening it up. Magnus watched as I unwrapped a thick square of fudge. "I've heard chocolate makes everything better," he said.

Butterflies sprang to life in my stomach at the unexpected kindness. "Thank you, Magnus," I mumbled, looking up at him.

The handsome werewolf reached out, hesitating just a moment before brushing a strand of my hair behind my ear. He cupped my cheek lightly, grazing the pad of his thumb along my skin. "Sleep well, Cam. And I'm just next door if you need protection from the big bad wolf."

I chuckled. "You *are* the big bad wolf."

A smile creased his face. "Exactly. I'm bigger and badder than anything out there." The humor drained from his eyes. "But seriously, I'm here if you need me."

My words got stuck in my throat and all I could do was nod. Magnus smiled down at me. He brushed his thumb along the curve of my cheek one more time. "Goodnight, Cam," he said before turning and padding on silent feet back to his room.

I leaned out of my room to watch the handsome werewolf slide into his room for the evening. Carefully, I tucked my head back into my room and shut my door as well. I leaned against the solid wood and popped a sliver of the delicious fudge into my mouth.

It had been a rough day.

And chocolate really did make it better.

Ah, fudge. I was falling for him, wasn't I?

Chapter 29

After the day I'd had, I expected sleep to take me quickly. Especially once I'd tested out the downy softness of the bed piled high with pillows and cozy blankets. However, I was wrong. I spent almost twenty minutes tossing and turning in the dark. Thoughts of liches and zombies ran through my head. I finally grabbed my phone and flicked it open. I pulled up a browser window and got to work searching up anything and everything I could find on liches. If I couldn't sleep, at least I could see if I could learn anything more about the lich. I rearranged the pillows and blankets, making a little reading nest for myself and set to work.

I skimmed through the articles, focusing on any details I could uncover. Apparently, fire did nasty things to them, but I already knew that from Seshat's book. After an hour, I'd discovered very little new information on liches. However, I had a wealth of new material to fuel my nightmares for the next year.

The one piece of positive information that I discovered was that, despite some similarities, liches were not Voldemort-like creatures. Liches couldn't split their souls multiple times and hide the pieces in objects, leaving them scattered around the world to corrupt the unknowing with horrendous nightmares and soul-rending rage. Thank all the gods for small mercies.

Liches could only separate their souls from their bodies, not fragment their souls. Once separated, the lich had to store their soul somewhere, usually in a gem or a phylactery. If you killed a lich's body, but didn't destroy the soul jar, he could reanimate eventually, given enough power. However, if you destroyed the soul jar and *then* killed the lich, well, he ain't coming back from that one. Not now, not ever.

Despite the interesting reading, I was grumpy and frustrated. I wanted to sleep but couldn't. I needed answers, but unfortunately, this wasn't as easy as a multiple-choice test. It felt more like one of those obscure math problems that's manically designed to trip you up.

A train is heading towards London at forty miles per hour, while another train is traveling to New York at thirty-five miles per hour. On each train is an abacus, mongoose, half of a watermelon, and a goat playing a harp. Given that the same company made the trains, what is the best type of pizza?

Umm. Hawaiian?

No, you fool! Who puts pineapple on pizza?? The answer to this question and indeed, the answer to all questions pertaining to life, the universe and everything is forty-two. Of course.

I shook my head and rubbed at a dull ache in my side absently. The witch had done a good job, but the stitches were pulling. I settled into a more comfortable position on the bed and started toying with the necklace at my throat. I had a lich on the loose in my city. What was my next logical move? If only I could discover a lich's weakness, their linchpin, as Mama called it. That would make this so much easier. But for someone to know that they'd have to be old and probably pretty powerful and... Wait! The Calling Charm!

My fingers flew to the back of my neck. I fiddled with the latch until the chain came loose. I held the charm in my hand and contemplated it. Maybe Barqan had come across a lich and had some handy-dandy guide on how to kill them. He was supposedly an ancient, magical being, after all. I snorted as an unbidden image of a sorcerer's bookshelf with DIY instructions floated across my mind's eye, but instead of a nice display for all things literary, this was a lot bloodier and murderier. Yes, I know that's not a word, Karen, but you understood it, which technically makes it a viable form of communication, so let's move on, shall we?

"What the hell?" I muttered. I grabbed one of my karambits from its sheath and pricked the back of my hand with the needle-sharp point.

Maybe Barqan would have something to add to my lich-y situation. I pinched the wound, forcing a droplet of blood to well up. "Here goes nothing," I whispered, rolling the charm in my blood. The blood sank into the grooves of the gold like water into a sponge.

I let out a small hiss of relief as a deep voice rang out the small charm. "Cameron, it's been a while."

"Yeah, I've been busy," I said, sucking the smeared blood off the back of my hand. Once clean, I pressed a finger over the wound, applying pressure to stop the bleeding.

"With what, pray tell," Barqan said, sounding slightly bored.

I matched his tone. "Oh, this and that. This demon, for one. I think I pissed him off or something and then there's this li—"

"Don't tell me this demon is still alive!" Barqan exclaimed, cutting me off and sounding decidedly less lackadaisical. "Demons hold a grudge like no other creature I've ever met. If it's still alive, it's coming after you. I can promise you that."

"No, no, he's very dead," I assured him.

"Dead or sent-back-to-the-Abyss dead?"

"No, he's dead-dead. There's no way he's coming back from bursting into a bunch of demon-sized confetti after I stabbed him with a blessed sword," I clarified.

"Oh. Well, good. Congratulations on killing your first demon then. It is your first, correct?" I grunted in acknowledgement. Barqan continued, "That is a feat to be celebrated, to be sure."

How did one celebrate the death of a demon? Was there cake involved? If there was, do you think it was angel cake? If so, I was totally there!

"Umm, thanks. But things got more complicated after I took care of the demon, which is why I'm calling."

Barqan paused before speaking. "I must admit, I am confused. How are things more complicated now that the demon is dead? Surely, the demon did not add comfort and ease to your existence. Now that he is dead, your life should be decidedly *less* complicated, should it not?" Confusion colored his tone.

"Well, that's kind of why I was calling. Have you ever heard of a lich?"

"Yes," Barqan rumbled, suspiciously. "They are necromantic sorcerers who have made unholy deals to extend their lives nigh unto immortality."

"Yeah, one may have escaped from the Abyss at the same time that the demon did."

"May have or did?" Barqan's voice was so cold that I wanted to dive back into the mountain of blankets on my bed and not come out for a long, *long* time.

"Did. A lich escaped. We think he's recovered his soul jar," I said.

A pregnant pause filled the silence before Barqan prompted me, "And?"

I sighed. "That's the problem. I don't know what he wants or has planned or anything. All I know is that he attacked the Fae Embassy out of nowhere. He also seems like he could use some anger management sessions."

"Hmm," Barqan mulled over my words before speaking again. "I do not understand what you think I can do to help you."

I ran a hand through my hair. "How do I destroy a lich's soul jar and, failing that, can I kill it any other way?"

"The creation of a soul jar and the powers it bestows on a lich are closely guarded secrets. I have never heard tell of someone who was not a lich having that information." Barqan paused. "At least, not someone who survived very long."

"Got it. Liches hate snitches and will give them stitches before they wind up in ditches. I'll just put a reminder in my phone in case I forget that one," I muttered.

"What's a phone?"

I stiffened at those words. Who didn't know what a phone was? My mind clicked into high gear. Only those ancient or powerful enough to ignore the advances of technology, that's who. Even though he'd told me he was a djinn and Meridiana had said he might be a djinn king who'd been locked away for centuries, I guess a little cynical part of me hadn't believed it. It was easier to imagine the guy on the other end of my necklace was some bored sorcerer than an ancient king of a powerful race of Supe. Wasn't it?

Barqan interrupted my thoughts. "Perhaps you will allow me to ask a question of my own. Is this a theoretical hypothesis or do you truly wish to kill the lich?"

"Oh no, not theoretical in the slightest." I assured him. "I literally want to kill the bastard who just attacked a peaceful embassy. Failing the literal killing him, I will settle for figurative, spiritual or, hell, even emotional right now. That is, until I figure out the literal part. Regardless, one way or another, this thing is ending up dead." I paused. "Again."

"Well, if that is your intent, I fear that the most I can offer is observations on the nature of powerful beings."

"No offense, Barqan, but I don't see how that's helpful. Now, if you had a wheelbarrow, that would be something!" I pushed faux enthusiasm into my words, using a line from one of my favorite movies.

Barqan ignored me. "Those who wish to possess immense power and pursue the lure of immortality either die or become masters of playing the long game. Their machinations are, at the heart, entirely self-serving. Their schemes may take years or even decades to bear fruit, but every action such beings take is a strategic move towards their goal."

"Meaning?" I asked, confused.

Barqan sounded like he was grinding his teeth. "If you can figure out what this lich wants, you will be that much closer to stopping him."

I scrubbed a hand through my hair. "Great. Like I hadn't figured that one out already. That's exactly the vague, sage advice that the wise, ancient sensei gives their young, naïve protégé in all the movies."

"Movies? What are movies?" he asked.

I bit the inside of my cheek, suddenly wary again. How old and far removed was this guy to not know about movies? And he hadn't known about phones either. That cynical part of me was slowly converting into a believer that legends lived, myths materialized, and the dude in my necklace really was a djinn. Possibly even one of the djinn kings.

My thoughts churned as I fingered the grooves of the charm. Finally, I said, "OK, let's do a little role play. Pretend that you are an ancient being set loose upon the world for the first time in years or even decades."

"One can only hope."

I ignored that eerie sentiment. "What's the first thing you do?"

"Consolidate power," he replied immediately. "Followed closely by eliminating any immediate threats, such as impudent protégés with more sass than sense." His tone held a whisper of a smirk.

"Yeah, well, you aren't the first one to have that opinion." I muttered.

"I am unsurprised by this," Barqan said, chuckling lightly.

I returned to the topic of lich-killing with all seriousness. "So, assuming you can't dispose of feisty protégés easily, what's your Achilles' heel? What's your weakness?"

"I don't know who Achilles is or why you are so concerned about his feet, but..."

"What?!" I exclaimed.

Barqan continued on as if I hadn't interrupted. "But based on context, I should know who this man is, which is precisely the answer to your question. In your hypothetical quandary, my weakness would be modernity. How can I counteract what I cannot fathom existing?"

Excellent point.

"Fine, you've passed the first question. On to the second. All liches have soul jars which allow them to steal their immortality. However, if you can destroy the soul jar, you can destroy the lich." I drew in a breath, readying myself for the big question. "So, if you're a lich, where do you hide a soul jar?"

"Somewhere it will never be found," Barqan answered promptly.

I let my head fall back on the chair and exhaled noisily. "Yeah. I got that much. Thanks, Captain Obvious. But what if you know someone can track the location of the soul jar?" I traced the tattoo on my wrist as I spoke.

"General."

"What?" The statement threw me.

"I was a general, not a captain. I don't appreciate the demotion, even if it is only a part of a hypothetical."

"Fine. *General* Obvious, where would you stash your priceless vessel of immortality if you had one, and you knew someone could find it?"

"That depends on how much time I've had. Do I have a secure base of operations? Or am I on the run? If it is the former, I would lock the soul jar up, hiding it among my well-guarded treasures. Possibly, I'd even create an ambush or a trap for those in pursuit of my soul jar. If it is the latter, it would force me to keep the soul jar on my person until I could find a place to secure it. Now, it's my turn for a question. Were you able to manifest your smoke form during your fight with the demon?"

"What does that got to do with anything?" I asked, scratching at my temple in confusion at the return to the demon topic.

"It has everything to do with everything," he said, biting off his words. I heard the frustration rise in his voice. "Did you or did you not use your smoke form?"

I rolled my eyes. "No, I could not change into smoke. I was a little distracted between the werewolves, the demon, the other demon, and the teenage werewolf who mistook me for a juicy bone. It was a busy day. I tried, but the smoke thing didn't work."

Barqan ignored my rant. "In summation, you did not create a smoke form. Is that correct?"

"Dude! Werewolves! Demons! Cut me some slack!"

"And do you think this lich will be the cutter of slack for you?" Barqan's tone was sharp.

I sucked on a tooth, loath to give him the answer we both knew to be true.

Barqan eventually filled in the silence. "I assume you have a time limit for addressing your lich issue?"

"Why would you assume that?" It came out more belligerently than I'd intended, but I was still smarting from the last verbal punch he'd landed.

"Because it seems like trouble finds you. One thing I have learned about trouble is that it always escalates."

"Yeah, well, what do you suggest I do about it?" I asked, trying to muffle a yawn that had crept up on me unexpectedly.

"I suggest you reconnect with me in six hours."

"And why would I do that?" I asked.

"Because I think I have a way to help, but I need some time to make the arrangements." I imagined Barqan stroking his beard, or tapping his chin if he didn't have a face rug. "Yes, six hours should be sufficient. Don't be late." And with that, the magic call ended.

I don't know how I knew he'd disconnected. It wasn't like he could slam a receiver down or anything. After a few half-hearted attempts to reconnect, I gave up and put the necklace on the bedside table. A jaw cracking yawn overtook me as I reached for my phone and set an alarm for six hours, putting my wake-up call during the ungodly hour that only bartenders and roosters ever saw. I curled up on the bed, worrying at the problem of the lich like a sore tooth as I waited for sleep to take me.

Chapter 30

A cheerful tinkling tune woke me. I moaned as I fought my way back from what felt like a partial coma mixed with the worst pre-hangover ever. The type of feeling where you know the storm is on the horizon and there's nothing you can do to avoid it. The best thing to do is grab the water and the aspirin to at least minimize the damage. I let loose a soul-deep groan as the jingling phone increased in volume. The sheer *happiness* of the alarm made me want to hurl it across the room. If only I could find the damned thing buried in the pile of blankets. I rubbed at my eyes with the back of one hand while searching for the offending noise maker with the other. My eyes felt gritty and swollen, adding to my overall crankiness. Finally, my questing fingers grazed the smooth, hard screen. I flicked the obnoxiously cheery alarm off.

Barqan. Liches. Right.

I pushed myself upright and sleepily reached for my karambit. A full-bodied yawn nearly incapacitated me as I pricked the back of my hand, but I managed not to stab myself. I grabbed the charm and smeared it in the droplet of blood.

As I spoke to the charm, I rubbed my bleary eyes. "Barqan? Are you there? Because if this was all some prank and you made me wake up at this ungodly hour, I am going to kill you."

"Never make a threat unless you plan on following through with it," Barqan's voice rumbled. It sounded closer than it had the night before. Like he was in the room with me.

"Yeah, right, I'll just…" I finally cracked open my eyes to see that I wasn't in the plush bedroom at the Embassy anymore. Not even close. I felt like a reverse-Dorothy. Instead of waking up in a technicolor land of munchkins and magic, a monochromatic world of swirling mist and smoke filled my sightline.

"There you are. We need to talk," the deep voice rumbled again. Knowing there was no point in faking it any longer, I opened my eyes and sat up in bed. No, on *shadows*. A shifting, roiling cloud of shadow morphed to adapt to my body, striving valiantly to form a chair as I spun around in the ever-shifting mist. I tensed. The man-like creature across from me sat in his own chair of churning darkness, watching me intently, but he made no threatening move my way. His dark skin rippled with swirls of all the imaginable shades of black. A thick beard covered his jawline and curled down to his chest. Twin ebony horns curved from his temples, ending in wickedly sharp points a foot above his bald head. Solid black eyes peered out at me, lit with faint flickers of indigo that were only apparent because the rest of his eyes were virtually without color. Long, loose robes that looked like they were made of wood smoke, complete with the snapping embers, drifted around his massive frame.

I didn't know much, but a gut feeling told me something big was happening here and I wasn't about to relax until I figured out who, where, and *why*. And that was just for starters.

"Barqan?" I asked, trying to sound calm, but it came out more like a squeak.

"Indeed. Whom did you expect, may I ask?" Barqan's lips curled in a devilish smile, revealing a sharp set of incisors.

"You're really a djinn?!" I'd started to believe it after our conversations, but seeing the djinn king with my own eyes was another thing entirely.

"Yes, I believe I told you that, did I not?"

"So, that's the who and the what. We're off to a great start. Now, where and why," I said, attempting to stand in the roiling cloud of smoke. To my surprise, it dispersed as I brushed a hand through the air, behaving like, well, smoke. But if it was smoke or shadows or whatever, how could I have been sitting on it a moment before?

Clawed hands tightened on the armrests of the shadowy chair across from me. Barqan's upper lip lifted in a silent snarl, showing more of his razor-sharp teeth. I tensed, preparing to throw myself out of the way if he attacked. He closed his eyes and took a deep breath through his nose, blowing it out past his beard. Finally, he spoke with great effort. "I do not have the time nor the desire to get into the finer points of astral projection. But for all intents and purposes, the simplest explanation is that your body is still wherever you left it. Safe in bed, I hope, or you may experience a nasty lump when you return. Your spirit, on the other hand, is now in the ether."

"Ether? What's the ether?" I echoed stupidly.

Barqan raised a clawed hand, waving at the smokey darkness surrounding us. "This is the ether. It is a space between, a place apart. The ether surrounds all the realms but is not a part of any. It exists but doesn't. It simultaneously depends on the realms and is independent of them. A location impossible to find unless you've been there before. A place of paradoxes."

"Sounds downright confusing," I grumbled.

"Ah, so you are familiar, then."

I kneaded the back of my neck where I felt a tension headache forming. "Yeah, I'm going to need a teensy bit more information than that."

Barqan squinted an eye closed and wavered his head back and forth, trying to find a way to explain. "Think of it like an advanced form of telepathy. Through that charm," he pointed a clawed finger at my chest, "we can communicate, but with enough time and resources, I can also form a tenuous connection with you. One that is strong enough to pull your consciousness here. Your body is still on Earth, but your spirit is here, having a conversation with me."

"And where is here exactly?"

"As I've told you, the ether. The spell has a limited duration. We have one hour, perhaps two, before the magic fades. Once it does, I cannot contact you again for some time. The magic must have time to regenerate. Now, are you going to waste the precious time we've stolen, or can we get down to business?"

Although a million questions swirled around my brain, Barqan's urgency was seeping into my bones. I gestured with a wave of my upturned hand in a 'go ahead' motion rather than risk opening my mouth and letting loose a torrent of tangential but ultimately irrelevant questions.

"You must develop your shadow magic. The parlor tricks you've described will not win out against a sorcerer of a lich's magnitude," Barqan said seriously.

"I wouldn't call them parlor tricks," I muttered, waving a hand through the smoke again like I was trying to catch the wind by sticking my hand out the window of a moving car.

"Stop. Wasting. My. *Time.*" Barqan hissed through bared teeth. Teeth that were extremely sharp. I shut my mouth, dropped my hand, and listened. "Try going up against a lich with your mundane weapons and your paltry grasp of shadow magic and he will kill you. You need more. You need to learn how to make shadow blades."

I spread my hands wide. "Great. I'm all ears. Teach away."

A crafty smile curled the corner of his mouth, revealing a long, sharp incisor. "I'd be happy to. For a trade."

A coil of unease clenched around my chest. "What kind of trade?" I asked, past a suddenly dry mouth.

Barqan waved a hand through the smoke, laying his flattened palm between us. "Ancient knowledge for ancient knowledge." He placed his other hand next to the first and made a balancing gesture. "I will teach you how to call and command a shadow blade at will. In return, I want you to find a scroll and bring it to me."

I narrowed my eyes at him. "What kind of scroll?"

Barqan leaned forward, smoke swirling around him. "One belonging to Solomon."

I frowned. "Solomon, like King Solomon? From the Bible?"

Barqan snorted. "And history, but yes. That Solomon."

"Why do you want this scroll?" I asked.

Barqan sat back in his chair and tapped his fingers on the armrests. "That is unimportant for our negotiation. All that matters is that I have information that could help you survive confronting a lich. In return, all I ask for is one little scroll. Your life for an old, scribbled parchment.

Surely, not too much to ask?" His tone took on a syrupy quality. My eyelids felt heavy, and I felt my head start to bob.

I shook myself. "What was that?" I asked, slapping my cheek lightly.

Barqan glowered, looking around at the shadows like they offended him. "The ether is... unpredictable. I suggest you make your decision quickly before I lose my grasp on the magic."

Thoughts swirled through my mind. If it was just an old scroll Barqan wanted, I could probably track it down, given enough time. Between my supernatural contacts and Seshat, I stood a fairly good chance of locating the thing. The problem was, I wasn't sure what the scroll might contain or whether Barqan should have it. I swallowed hard. "What if I don't agree?"

Barqan shrugged nonchalantly, like he'd expected the question. "Then you head into battle with an extremely dangerous sorcerer ill-equipped to survive. I wish you all the best, but I have a feeling that this will be our last conversation. Calling Charms do not work for the dead. No blood, you see."

I bit my lip, thinking through the various repercussions of both choices. What to do? Lives hung in the balance. If the lich wasn't dealt with soon, then more of the fae would die. Hell, if I went after the lich without knowing this magic, I might die. That is, if Barqan could be trusted. Could he? Or was he just capitalizing on an opportunity? I rubbed a hand over my face.

Barqan's crafty smirk peeled his lips back, revealing his sharp teeth once more. "Tick-tock. This spell will only last so long, and shadow blades can be tricky to manifest."

I pressed my forehead to the knuckles of one fist, but I already knew in my heart that I was going after the lich. I wanted, no, *needed*, to be as ready as possible to take him out. If that meant making a deal with this devil, so be it. I'd just have to make it as favorable as I could.

I exhaled a slow breath, weighing my words before meeting the djinn's dark eyes. "Fine. In return for you teaching me how to make shadow blades, I will attempt to locate King Solomon's missing scroll for you." I stuck out my hand.

Barqan snorted softly. "I'm no fool. An attempted search is not a fair trade for the knowledge I'm offering."

I gritted my teeth and let my hand drop, annoyed that he'd seen through my ruse, but not really surprised. "Fine. Teach me the spell. After I deal with the lich and I've had time to catch my breath, I will track down the missing scroll you desire or find its last known location if it was destroyed." I figured that gave me at least a little wiggle room if my search turned up nothing.

Barqan held up a clawed finger. "And deliver it to me upon its discovery."

I bit the inside of my cheek. Another loophole foiled. Finally, I nodded. "Agreed." I stuck out my hand again. He gripped it tightly, but was careful not to scratch my skin with his claws. A *whoomp* reverberated through my chest, making vibrations dance down my arm. When I met his eyes, the self-satisfied gleam in them made me wonder if I'd made the right choice.

Barqan glided smoothly out of his chair and started pacing in front of me. His tone took on that of a lecturer. "To make a shadow blade, you must first envision the shadows in your mind. Your mind is both forge and fire." I closed my eyes, listening to his voice and trying to visualize the images in my head. "Pull the shadows to you. Good, like that." Barqan's voice was warm and soothing. I lost myself in the rough cadence of his words. It felt strangely like meditation. "Now, press down on your shadows with your mind. You do not need to heat, fold, hammer, or sharpen your shadow blade. Just focus on what you want it to be, and it will appear. Good. I can see it now."

I moved to crack an eyelid to see what was forming in my outstretched hands.

"No!" His voice cracked through the air. "Don't lose focus now. You are almost there. Only one step more."

I closed my eyes completely again and allowed my mind to go blank as Barqan's voice guided me. "Now comes the hardest part. You must infuse the blade with your will to bring it fully into existence."

"How do I do that?" I heard myself ask, as if from a great distance.

"Belief. Believe that your will is stronger than the shadow. That the blade you hold in your mind's eye exists in the real world, in your hand. Believe it with every fiber of your being, every ounce of your soul. Believe it until anything else seems like a laughable implausibility."

I drifted on his words until I found myself in a void in my mind, staring at a sword of darkness floating in front of me. It was beautifully dangerous. An elegant instrument of death. My breath caught. I reached out a hand, grasping it by the hilt. The grip seemed to morph and shift under the skin of my palm, refashioning itself to fit my hand perfectly.

I gasped. I *felt* the blade. Not with my mind, but in my hand. My eyes flew open. I saw an elegant short sword made of dark metal gripped tightly in my fist.

"Well done," Barqan said, sitting back in his chair with a knowing smile as I experimented in slow motion with the shadow blade I'd created. It was perfectly balanced and looked deadly enough to give me shivers. I tested the edge carefully with my thumb. A small smile of appreciation curved my lips as a droplet of blood fell from the shallow cut on the pad of my thumb. I stuck the injured digit in my mouth and sucked the blood away. Barqan's knowing smile caught my eye.

"And our deal?" he asked.

"Yeah, yeah," I muttered. "After I deal with this lich. By the way, any leads on how to go about tracking this scroll down?" I asked.

"I've heard of a famous library. In a place called Alexandria. Perhaps you should start there. Mastering more elements of djinn magic will undoubtedly prove useful in your quest."

"Hold up. *Djinn* magic?" I asked.

"Yes," Barqan replied. He spread his arms wide. "I am a djinn sorcerer who is teaching you magic. I believe I told you this already."

"Sure. I mean, you did. I just thought you were teaching me shadow magic," I said.

He tipped his horned head to the side. "They are one and the same. Didn't you know?"

"No! I didn't know! I just thought..." I trailed off. I'd made assumptions about my magic. Namely, that it had come from a witch or a wizard or some other human magic user. I knew hadn't inherited my magic from my mother. She'd been an elemental mage. If I could use djinn magic, that meant my father must've been a djinn.

Barqan dipped his head, silently confirming the unvoiced realization he read in my eyes. I opened my mouth to unleash a torrent of questions when my shoulder started jerking back and forth, seemingly of its own volition. I looked down, shocked at the sensation. It felt like a hand was gripping me tightly, but I couldn't see anything.

I glanced at Barqan in surprise. He lunged at me, trying to catch the hand I reached out to him, but Barqan fell straight through me. Like I was a ghost. Or he was. I shuddered and dropped the sword. Instead of clattering to the ground, it fell apart into swishing curls of smoke as my concentration fractured.

"No!" I cried. "Wait! Who is my..." The smoke and shadows swallowed the rest of my words.

I blinked, my eyelids feeling suddenly heavy. "... father?" I slurred. My tongue suddenly felt leaden in my mouth. My eyes drooped closed, and my chin hit my chest. I shook my head wearily, trying to clear the fog threatening to drown me. When I opened my eyes, I was staring straight into the teeth of a werewolf.

Chapter 31

I stuffed a fist in my mouth to keep from screaming in Magnus' face. My heart raced wildly, pounding like a horserace was hammering through my chest. It took a few moments of focused breathing before I could speak.

Reaching behind me, I grabbed one of the downy pillows and smacked it against the werewolf's hard, muscled torso as he pushed himself upright.

"Never, *ever*, wake me up like that again," I ground out through gritted teeth.

"If you would have woken up when I had knocked, or called your name, or tapped your leg, then there would have been no need to get all up in your face," Magnus said, concern lighting his eyes. "Are you ok? Why were you talking about your dad?"

I rubbed at my eyes with the heels of my hands, not ready to explain my trip to the ether, the djinn, or Barqan. "Yeah. Mornings and I have never really gotten along. My mind must've been elsewhere."

"Lost in space, thinking deep thoughts?" Magnus asked as he settled himself on the foot of the bed. I tucked my feet up under me to make room for him.

"Something like that." I smothered an unflattering yawn behind a hand. "What time is it, anyway?"

"Nearly eight. I would've let you sleep longer, but Lykaios is here. He's claiming that the lich's attack complicates the situation."

I threw my hands in the air, confused by the loss of time and the Alpha's sudden appearance. How could over three hours have passed without me realizing it? I let my hands drop to my hair at an utter loss. "How? How could Andrei biting me and the lich possibly be connected?"

"The Alpha claims that 'the emotional upheaval of dealing with unprecedented stress could trigger an unexpected shift.'" Magnus bobbed his fingers in the air, making invisible quotation marks.

"Is that even a thing?" I asked.

"Unfortunately for you, yes. He's also not thrilled that you are magically connected to the lich." Magnus jerked his chin at my wrist. "He's worried the spell will cause one of you to do something stupid. Which would cause you stress and potentially trigger a shift."

I groaned. "How come things are never easy with you wolves? First a bomb. Then a demon. Now the Pack wants to lock me up."

"It sounds more than mildly dysfunctional, if you ask me. And to be fair, the demon was your fault, not ours," Magnus observed calmly.

I squinted up at him. "Logic somewhere else, please. Any ideas on how I can wiggle out of this?"

"Besides hightailing it out of here?" He jerked a thumb over his shoulder towards the windows, partially encasing an upholstered bench piled high with decorative pillows.

"Wait, is that really an option?"

Magnus snorted and tapped the side of his nose meaningfully. "Not really. They'd track you down before you got very far. Besides, why would you want to run? Wouldn't being under the protection of werewolves until you knew you were going to shift safely or not shift at all be the smarter choice? Especially with a lich on the loose?"

"That's precisely why I don't want to go with Damon. I'm gonna be a hell of a lot better to everyone out there than I will be locked in a room waiting to see if I sprout fur." I pointed out the window where the sun was desperately trying to pierce through the morning clouds to dance with the dust motes in my room. The new stitches tugged at my side with a dull throb and I winced. I caught Magnus smiling at me, even though he tried to hide it.

"What?" I asked, my jaw tightening.

"Nothing. It's just that people who are going through hell and still focus on looking out for everyone else are my favorite kind of badass."

Wait. What?

I shook my head, trying to catch up to the abrupt turn when Magnus held up his hands in apology. "I'm sorry. My mother trained me better than this. I should've knocked and brought you coffee or something at a decent hour rather than waking you up by barging into your room and calling you a badass."

I chuckled. "You know what? I think that is the perfect way to wake up. I can't think of a single woman I know who secretly wouldn't love to be told she was a badass first thing in the morning. But, also yes to the coffee. And maybe some more of that rum."

Magnus pretended to scribble on an invisible notebook. "Coffee. Rum. Badass. Got it." I shook my head at his antics as he tucked the imaginary pen behind his ear. "Today, you might have to forgo the coffee for clothes." A wry expression flitted across his face. Just a tightening of his lips under his dark stubble and a slight, regretful shake of the head before he continued. "I hear werewolves always go for the throat, so a turtleneck might be in order for the day," Magnus said, grabbing a neatly folded pile of clothes from the end of the bed and handing them to me. I looked at them in surprise. The black leather hadn't been what I'd worn to the Embassy last night.

A small envelope sat on top of the pile. Someone had written on the front in an elegant script. "What's this?" I asked, taking the pile and ripping open the card.

"It was at your door when I came in," Magnus said.

I pulled out the note and read it.

Cameron, I hope I'm not overstepping. Geoffry informed me your clothes were not salvageable after last night's fiasco. I trust you will find these to be suitable replacements. -Letitia

The leather felt cool and supple under my fingers. I'd never tried on fae clothes before, mostly because they were beautifully crafted and horrendously expensive. This was an unexpected treat that more than made up for the lack of morning caffeine.

I tucked the bundle of clothes under an arm and wriggled out from under the covers, snatching up the necklace from the nightstand as I passed. I hurried into the ensuite bathroom, leaving the door slightly ajar so I could continue talking with Magnus while I got ready. When I glimpsed myself in the mirror, most of the superficial damage from the demon attack had healed, but the long lacerations on my arm were the shiny, angry red of newly forming scars. Bruises covered my hands and arms from the fight with the lich. I wasn't too worried about them, though. They'd heal in a day or two. A shallow scratch I didn't remember incurring from last night sliced up my cheek. It looked days old instead of hours. I prodded at it with a tentative fingertip. I wouldn't be winning beauty pageants any time soon.

I sighed and splashed water on my face. I really wanted to practice making another shadow blade, but this wasn't the time. Not with the Alpha waiting downstairs. As I tugged on the new clothes, I shouted out the door to Magnus. "So, tell me, oh wise protector and knower of all wolf-y things..."

"That is a horrible title," he said from somewhere in the other room, his voice slightly muffled by the partially closed door.

I continued, as if he hadn't spoken. "How do I get out of this werewolf fiasco?"

"You can't."

"Helpful! Oh, so helpful," I shouted back, sarcasm dripping from every syllable as I struggled into the tight leather outfit. It stretched and molded itself to my body. The vest was similar to my typical fighting gear, covered in sheaths designed for throwing knives. Except this one was of much better quality. The pants fit like a second skin, allowing me to move easily without the sticky sweat that wearing leather usually created. I noticed there were panels dotting the clothes along my most vulnerable bits. I examined one of these panels closely. It looked like the tiniest, most dense chain mail I'd ever seen, but moved like silk under my fingertips. My breath caught. The fae craftspeople deserved their legendary reputation.

"You know what isn't helpful? Lying to assuage your ego," Magnus pointed out logically from the other room. "And I told you the truth.

I don't see how you can get out of this conflict. Lykaios can push his agenda based on your half-human side."

"My mom was a mage," I said, tugging the shirt down before sliding my feet into my enchanted boots. At least those hadn't been ruined.

"Nevertheless, technically a human," he countered.

"Well, if he can use technicalities, then so can I. What if I use an impartial third-party judge to act as a mediator?" I asked.

"You could, but you know the Collective's laws as well as I do. If you go down that path, you'll be bound by the decision just as much as Lykaios will be. Do you really want to take the risk that this judge will side with the Alpha?"

My mind churned through possibilities as I ran a brush through my hair. I tied it back in a long braid, letting my fingers fly through the repetitive motions almost like a meditative practice. "What if we come at this from another angle? What would it take to get Andrei off the hook? Can I just forgive him? You know, let bite-gones be bite-gones."

"That was a horrible pun. But the answer to your question is no. The only thing that could alter his fate is if someone has a prior claim on him that supersedes this issue, but whatever it is, it has to be incredibly serious to the Pack, the Collective or to the Alpha personally to take precedence."

My fingers froze mid-twist, and I stuck my head out of the bathroom. "I don't understand. Walk me through it. Use small words, though, because you forgot my caffeine," I said, my fingers resuming their weaving as my brain danced through a web of complications.

"Well, you'd need to invoke the trial. Then, it's kind of like all those wedding rom-com movies where they ask if someone has an objection and inevitably the ex stands up and proclaims their love for the main character."

"You watch rom-coms?" I asked incredulously.

He snorted. "I've had girlfriends."

A part of me twisted inside at the thought, but I shoved that aside. Of course, he'd had girlfriends before. But somehow, the idea of him with someone else bothered me. "Right. Not the point." I said quickly, "So, someone objects?" I prompted.

"A second claim is laid and then the claims are weighed. The person judged to have the higher claim is awarded the right to satisfaction."

"What happens to the secondary claim?" I asked.

"It's voided," Magnus said instantly.

"Just like that?" I asked, sensing a glimmer of hope for the first time.

"Just like that," Magnus confirmed. "These things usually end in death, so there's never really been a point to include a contingency plan for the runner-up. It's more about who gets to do the deed."

I grinned, rubbing my hands together like a caped villain in every good-bad movie.

"Perfect."

I would've chuckled, but that seemed a step too far.

Chapter 32

I descended the grand staircase like the worst debutante in the history of the South. Black leather and weapons do not a lady make. But they do make an impression. A hush fell over the crowd of Supes gathered in the foyer of the Fae Embassy as I thumped down the staircase. I knew it wasn't just because of my leather fighting gear. I had opted not to cover my multitude of bruises with makeup. Mostly because I didn't have any, but also to make a point.

It was a *don't mess with me if you want to keep breathing* kind of day.

Someone had moved the injured fae elsewhere, but the foyer still showed evidence of its hasty repurposing. Soiled bandages and rumpled blankets were strewn about haphazardly. Geoffrey was attempting to direct his staff to tidy the area as unobtrusively as possible. With the number of people jammed into the entryway, it looked like an effort in futility. I counted five werewolves, and the Ambassador amid the frantic clean-up endeavor. Letitia looked drawn and on edge. Hank, the half-ogre bodyguard, stood behind her, shooting wary looks at anything that moved. Julius whistled low as I reached the bottom of the stairs, Magnus padding along silently behind me. "Whoa," Julius breathed, drawing the word out over three syllables. "What happened to you?"

I shrugged, "Lately? A nest of vampires, a demon, a zombie, an undead sorcerer, and a partridge in a pear tree. Guess who's got two thumbs and is still breathing?" I waggled my thumbs at the huge werewolf and then jerked them towards my chest with a wide grin.

Julius whistled again, this time in appreciation. "Remind me to never get on your bad side."

I winked at him before schooling my face and turning to stare the rest of the werewolves down. Will had a firm grip on Andrei's upper arm. The beta nodded in my direction, but the teenager kept his eyes stoically fixed on the floor. Parker wiggled her fingers in greeting from behind Andrei's head. However, it was Damon who captured my attention. The Alpha stood at rigid attention in his starched three-piece suit with his hands clasped behind his back. His eyes were two chips of ice that focused on a spot above my head.

"Cameron Blaze, we are here to..." the Alpha's voice echoed through the suddenly still entryway.

I interrupted him, gushing enough to make a 1950s housewife proud, "Damon, how nice to see you again! I simply must thank you for all the help your Pack provided. Perhaps you would allow me to express my gratitude over a nice cup of tea?" I made a show of patting down my skintight leather ensemble. "Good Lord! It seems as if I've misplaced my tea set. Lady Letitia, would it be an incredible imposition if I requested to use yours? Perhaps we could even find a more appropriate place to have a pleasant visit with our werewolf friends?"

Letitia, ever the gracious hostess, jumped at the opportunity to move the confrontation behind closed doors. "Yes, of course. It would be my absolute pleasure. Geoffrey, would you be so kind as to arrange for a tea tray to be brought to my study?" The butler jerked to attention when he heard his name. The man actually clicked the heels of his highly polished shoes together and whirled to make it so.

Letitia turned back to us. "Please, follow me." She spun on a heel and set off at a stately trot. The swish of her perfectly tailored morning dress parted the sea of activity in the foyer at a speed that would've rivaled Moses. Damon lifted a lip in a silent snarl in my direction. However, he couldn't be seen to be disrespectful to the leader of the New Orleans fae in her own home. Not with an attentive audience of servants hanging on every word and movement.

Letitia led us through the Embassy to her office, ushering us in with a welcoming smile plastered on her face. Damon paced in front of

Letitia's pristinely organized desk as Will and Andrei perched uneasily on the delicate furniture, looking uncomfortable in the tense silence. Julius gave the furniture a disdainful look and stood sentinel at the door, Parker mirroring his posture. Magnus leaned on the back wall, watching the entire situation with a studiously blank expression. At the door, Letitia dismissed her bodyguards. She waited until the pair had vanished into the depths of the Embassy and everyone was settled before she moved towards the door, saying, "Well, I will leave you in peace. Please let me know if I can be of further assistance."

I raised a hand, watching Damon even as I spoke to Letitia, "Please Ambassador, stay a moment more." Letitia paused, her hand on the handle of the door, caught by my use of her title. I gestured to Damon. "I believe you were about to issue a proclamation."

Damon glowered at me. "Cameron Blaze, we're here to take you into custody. Given the heightened tension caused by this undead sorcerer, the raising of multiple zombies, and the nature of the injuries inflicted upon you by that werewolf," he pointed at his son without looking at Andrei. I saw the Alpha's eyes glitter and his jaw clench before he continued, "We have deemed you and your situation a risk to the entirety of New Orleans. Therefore, until it can be determined that you pose no threat to the greater population of this city, you will immediately submit to the Pack's protection."

Protection? Imprisonment is more apt.

Although I'd planned what I was going to say, the fire of hurt and determination in Damon's eyes made me question myself for a moment. However, I couldn't see another acceptable option.

I kept my voice cool, striving for ice queen territory. "Like I told you before, no. I will not submit to your custody."

"You have no choice! It's Pack law!" Damon replied, narrowing his eyes under ferocious brows.

"I'm not human. Pack law doesn't apply," I said calmly, restating my argument from the night before. I stiffened my spine, refusing to wilt under the Alpha's glare.

"Then as a member of the Collective, I must enforce this decision. You are a Supe who is in danger of revealing our existence to the human world. I am well within my rights to ensure that you do not." He strode forward, invading my space.

I refused to back down, glaring up at him with all my might. Secretly, I was glad I had emptied my bladder before I came downstairs because *damn*. The Alpha had intimidating on lock. "Then, as a member of the supernatural community, I invoke the right of judgment by an impartial member of the Collective. Oh look," I said, turning in feigned surprise to look at Letitia, "we have such an individual in the room. How fortunate."

Letitia's eyes widened as she realized that when I'd asked her to stay, I must've intended this all along. I spoke formally before she could escape, "Lady Letitia, as a member of the Collective, I beg you to hear the disagreement between Damon Lykaios, Alpha of the Pack of New Orleans, and myself. I trust your impartial judgment to be fair and just in this matter and will submit to your decision. If the Alpha will consent as well."

Letitia focused her attention on Damon. He muttered something vaguely akin to agreement. He didn't really have a choice, though, given the circumstances. If there hadn't been witnesses present, I'm not sure I would've gotten away with the first step of my plan so easily. The Alpha had come here to do a distasteful job and was committed to the task. If I had to guess by the look in his eyes, he didn't like that the situation was spinning out of his control.

Letitia took a deep breath and exhaled slowly. "Very well, I agree to sit in judgment of your dispute and you both will be bound by my decision." She stared meaningfully at me.

I held up my hands, my innocently bland, "Of course."

"Fine," growled Damon.

There was a quick reshuffle of the furniture. Letitia settled herself behind the pristine desk while Damon and I were seated in front of her. The rest of the wolves ranged behind us. I ignored them. They were accessories to this little drama. I needed all my attention focused on Damon if I was going to get Andrei and myself out of this mess without bloodshed or spending a moment behind bars.

Letitia waved a hand gracefully. "Tell me the facts of the case, please."

Damon spoke first, "One of my werewolves attacked..."

I raised a finger, clarifying, "Accidentally attacked."

"One of my werewolves *accidentally* attacked Ms. Blaze. As is custom, I insist you place her under Pack surveillance in a location of our choosing. If she shifts, she won't be a danger to herself or others. If she doesn't shift, we will release her after the full moon."

Letitia nodded thoughtfully and swiveled to me. "Ms. Blaze, do you dispute the facts as Mr. Lykaios had explained them?"

"I do not."

Letitia looked startled at my lack of confrontation. "Well then, if there is no dispute, then my decision is simple. I find that…"

I interrupted the Ambassador, "It's my understanding that, as the injured party, I have the right to demand that my attacker be placed on trial before the full moon."

Letitia looked at Damon with a single raised brow. He nodded tightly. Letitia looked back at me. "I take it you wish to put the young werewolf on trial immediately and want me to sit in judgment of his case as well?" she asked.

"I do."

"Is this acceptable to you, Alpha?" she asked.

Damon shot me a sidelong look, unsure of what I was doing. A deep furrow formed between his brows as he tried to figure out my play. He knew I had a soft spot for the kid, and I'd just employed a piece of Pack law that it was unlikely I'd know on my own. Some inner sixth sense was likely telling the wily werewolf a deeper game at play, but he didn't know what it was. I'm sure it rankled him like fleas on a hot summer day. I gave him a brief nod and a *look*, willing him to trust me. The anger bled out of his countenance. A confused wariness replaced it. Placing Andrei on trial meant that, one way or another, the young wolf's fate would be sealed tonight.

Finally, Damon nodded, "It is."

I let out the breath I'd been holding slowly. A small wave of relief washed over me. We weren't out of the woods yet, but at least there was a glimmer of light in the darkness.

Letitia waved at Will. "Bring forward the accused."

Will led the teenager forward, positioning him to the side of the Ambassador's desk. Letitia spoke coolly, her formal tone that of a judge. "Andrei Lykaios, you stand accused of an unprovoked, albeit accidental, attack on one, Cameron Blaze. The penalty for which is death. How do you plead?"

Andrei shot his father a terrified look. Damon's stern gaze locked on his son's face for the first time I'd witnessed since they walked into the Embassy. The Alpha gave him a tight nod. I watched as unshed tears welled in the kid's eyes, but he nodded back, trusting his dad.

Andrei sniffed loudly, clearing his throat. "I plead guilty." His voice was clear, despite the obvious torrent of emotions rushing just below the surface.

Letitia nodded slowly. When she turned back to face me, I could see the seeds of resentment take root for what I was making her do. I schooled my face into a haughty mask. I needed her to continue, even if it meant her hating me.

"It is with a heavy heart that I must pass judgment on this case when it seems a shame to separate a father and son earlier than absolutely necessary." Letitia shot me a glance so venomous that I nearly withered. "However, the situation is beyond my control. Before I issue the sentence, I must ask if there are any objections?" Letitia made a show of looking around the room.

I raised a finger. "I object."

I heard Julius begin, "What the actual f..." before Parker elbowed him into silence.

Letitia sighed. "How can you object if you are the one who called for the trial? That can't be possible, can it?"

"It can and is because I have a prior claim on this young man. One that sentencing him to death would impede to my detriment."

There was a hitch in Damon's breathing next to me. I ignored him. I couldn't afford to get distracted. If I didn't play this precisely right, then Andrei would be executed immediately.

Curiosity bloomed in Letitia's eyes. "Explain."

I set my shoulders, picking my words carefully. "Last month, I saved that young man from certain death." I pointed clearly at Andrei. "In return, he swore a blood oath to save my life or serve me until I see fit to release him. I object to his execution because he hasn't yet repaid the blood debt."

The ambassador nodded slowly and then shook her head. "I'm not sure I follow."

I smiled, focusing solely on the woman across the desk. "It's up to you to decide which holds greater importance. Honoring a blood debt or punishment for, as the Alpha of the Pack himself termed it, an accidental attack."

Letitia tipped her head to the side in consideration. "Alpha Lykaios, could you clarify a point of Pack law for me, please? Once I rule on this dilemma, what becomes of the secondary charge?"

Damon spoke softly next to me. "They cannot simultaneously exist."

"Unless it's a Schrödinger's wolf situation," I said, unable to resist. Damon turned his frosty glare on once more. I held up my hands in acquiescence and mimed zipping my lips.

"As I was saying," the Alpha growled, "according to Pack law, whichever claim you deem to be of lesser importance will be permanently voided."

Understanding blossomed across Letitia's face as she finally unraveled my desperate ploy. "Well then, as the judge in this matter, I must side with the raised objection and instruct the accused to fulfill his blood debt. I conclude this matter!" She banged a glass paperweight on the desk for emphasis.

Damon leaped up and pulled his son into a bear hug, then snaked a long arm around me and yanked me in as well. There were tears, lots of them, but for the sake of manly pride, let's say they were all mine.

Chapter 33

The next few minutes were joyful chaos. Out of the corner of my eye, I noticed Magnus slip silently from the room. Then Julius was there, wrapping me up in a surprisingly gentle hug for the big man. Before the wolves left the Embassy, I pulled Andrei aside. Damon's eyes followed us like a magnetic force was attaching him to the boy. I didn't blame the Alpha. I'd never experienced the mix of emotions that came with being a parent, but I imagined that the thought of being forced to execute your own child was enough to drive anyone to the brink.

"Andrei, there's one more piece of business that we have to address," I spoke softly, aware that it was likely a useless precaution given the company we were in, but the semblance of privacy might make this easier on the kid.

"Thank you! I mean, seriously, thank you. Anything, anything you want, Cam. I owe you my life." Andrei grinned, giddily, "Again."

Good Lord, this kid is like a puppy.

"Focus!" I said, snapping my fingers. He blinked and tried to look serious, but I knew that if he were in wolf form, his tail would thump a rapid staccato on the floor.

I cleared my throat and spoke formally, "Andrei Lykaios, I release you from your blood debt because of the heroic way you engaged a demon on my behalf." I raised a finger as the kid's eyes widened. "On one condition."

"Name it!" he exclaimed.

"You get yourself some proper combat training with someone who won't just spar with you and be afraid of hurting the Alpha's son. If you're going to fight in the real world, you need to train to fight in the real world. The bad guys out there won't let you get a water break and a re-do if you mess it up the first time. They'll just kill you."

Andrei squirmed uncomfortably, but I stared him down until he nodded. I let out a silent breath as a weight lifted off my shoulders. He was a good kid, but I had too much on my plate for obedience school right now.

I leaned in close and discretely pointed over my shoulder. "I'd suggest Parker. She plays for keeps. She won't go easy on you, but that's not what you need right now, kid."

Andrei jerked upright, puffing out his chest. "I'm no kid! You're only a couple of years older than me anyway," he protested.

"No offense, Andrei, but it's not about years. I've been adulting for a lot longer and a lot harder than most people ten years older than me. I'm also not too proud to know my limits. You need to learn yours. I can't look after training you properly and manage my own shit. Sorry... kid." I winked at him as I drew out the last word and the teenager rolled his eyes.

"Seriously, though. Your dad's great and all, but he's got an honorable streak a mile wide. He won't teach you all the dirty fighting tactics because he's trying to build a safer world for you. One where you won't need all the tricks to survive. But I promise you, knowing how to play dirty, even if it is just so you can recognize it when others are messing with you, is going to keep you alive a lot longer than always being the white knight. Find someone who'll teach you that and learn as much as you can from them. Then make your decisions on what kind of man you're going to be."

Andrei weighed my words. He opened his mouth to respond when a heavy hand landed on his shoulder. Damon smiled down at his son.

"I trust I'm not interrupting?" the Alpha said. Andrei shook his head, smiling widely up at his dad. A pang shot through me at the obvious bond they shared. I thought my mom and I had shared a similar bond. However, having found out that she'd been keeping secrets from me that were more than just my dad's identity made me question a lot of my memories about my past.

The Alpha distracted me from diving too far down into that quagmire of emotional quicksand. "Andrei, the others are pulling the car around. Join them, will you? I want a private word with Cameron."

Andrei nodded, shooting me one more brilliant smile before jogging out the door. I noticed that the room was empty. Somewhere in the hugs, tears, and whispered conversations, everyone had disappeared.

"Cameron, I owe you..." Damon started.

I held up a hand, cutting him off. "Please. No more of that. I just got out of babysitting one werewolf. No offense, but I think you would be a lot harder work to manage than your son. He was tough enough."

Damon grinned. "I can't argue with that. Then let me just say 'thank you' to the newest Friend of the Pack." He extended his hand.

I gripped his hand on instinct as my eyes widened. Even I knew that was the highest honor that a non-Pack member could be granted. "I, uh..."

Damon's grin widened. "I'll take that as acceptance of this lofty title. Besides, I figured you used up your quota for formal speaking about five minutes ago," the Alpha said, winking at me. He tugged me into a massive hug, which caused a flare of pain to dance up my newly stitched side. He spoke so softly I almost missed it. "Thank you, Cameron."

I wriggled free of the powerful embrace carefully, to avoid any more tugging at my stitches. I patted him awkwardly on the back. "Glad to help."

Damon put his hands on my shoulders and spoke seriously, "Despite what just happened here, don't go getting too cocky. There is still the possibility that you shift into a wolf at the full moon. With Andrei acquitted, I cannot enforce Pack safety protocols, but please know that you can request them whenever you wish."

"Thanks, Damon. I appreciate the offer, but I've got business to handle that I can't do while I'm in a kennel."

The Alpha nodded once down at me, like he'd expected the answer. He gave my good shoulder a squeeze and then strode out of the room, leaving me alone with my thoughts for the moment.

I stared at the empty room for a moment before collapsing into a chair. Whoa. I needed just a minute. I hadn't been sure that things would play out the way I wanted them to. Mostly because I was more comfortable in a physical confrontation than a verbal one. My tongue usually got wrapped around my teeth and then everything got jumbled when I tried to word the words too wordy. At least I'd held it together long enough to smooth out this wolf nonsense.

After taking a deep breath, I headed upstairs to grab my sword. I eyed the bed and wished I had a few more hours to enjoy the downy comfort. Unfortunately, the lich was still on the loose. Every moment that spooky skeleton spent wandering around my city was one too many. I picked up my yatagan and was searching for my phone when I heard a soft knock on my door.

"Come in," I shouted, searching for my boot under the bed where I'd somehow kicked it.

Magnus backed into the room, holding two steaming mugs. He offered me one. I accepted it, sipping gratefully. Then I grimaced violently at the bitter coffee.

"What? You told me to bring coffee. Did I forget the milk or something? Are you a six sugars kind of girl?" Magnus asked, settling onto the window seat with his own mug cradled in his hands.

"No. This is fine," I said. He raised an eyebrow. "No, really. It's fine. See?" I took a loud sip and almost spit it back out because it was so strong.

"'Fine' is different from 'Oh Magnus, thank you so much for this divinely brewed cup of the elixir of the gods! The sun shines brighter, the birds chirp louder, the flowers smell sweeter because you have brought me a delicious coffee!'" He raised his voice an octave, mangling a heavy Southern accent.

I rolled my eyes and shook my head at his antics. Raising the mug in a small salute, I said, "For future reference, I prefer tea. But caffeine is caffeine and I'm going to need it today."

Magnus sipped at his bitter brew, eyeing me over the mug. "I've got to admit, watching you operate downstairs made me realize you are no Southern belle or damsel that needs rescuing. You figured out possibly the only solution to that Gordian Knot and manipulated the situation to make that solution the only viable outcome. But it makes me wonder, what game are you playing now?"

"Game?" I asked.

"The whole lone wolf thing you've got going on. You are friends with some powerful people. Like the Alpha and the Ambassador downstairs, for starters. From what I've seen, you also have some extraordinarily protective people in your corner. A feisty leprechaun springs to mind." He rubbed at the back of his head ruefully. I suddenly wondered what Sloane had said to him. She'd never mentioned any confrontation with the werewolf, but I wouldn't put it past her. Magnus continued, "And yet you're going after this lich sorcerer alone. You've gotta respect bravery even when it's fueled by stupidity." He waved his mug at me in a mocking semblance of a salute.

I bristled. "I don't have to explain myself to you!"

"Of course not," he said mildly, sipping from his mug.

"Damon just got his son back after he thought he was going to have to go all Abraham to Andrei's Isaac. I'm not dragging them back into the thick of it." My hackles were still up, and I wasn't exactly sure why.

"Like I said, my favorite kind of badass is a kind badass, but you can't handle this thing on your own."

How could he make me go from irritated and defensive to throwing out compliments in the same minute? It's enough to give a girl conversational whiplash.

I attempted to change the subject. "I notice you aren't going with the Pack. Doesn't the Pack have to follow the Alpha's orders?"

"Sure. That's exactly what I'm doing. The Alpha gave me orders to watch over you until the full moon."

"But the trial—"

Magnus interrupted. "Doesn't impact my orders in the slightest. Did you hear Lykaios walk them back?"

"Well, no, but..."

"Neither did I. And I wouldn't dare disregard an order when I'm still on Maverick status. Which means you're stuck with me for a while longer yet."

"It feels like a technicality," I complained.

"Hi Pot, I'm Kettle." Magnus smirked at me from behind his coffee mug.

"Fine. Come along if you must, but fair warning, I'm going to see a vampire. I hear they're a tad cranky in the morning."

"Do you think this vamp is going to let you in?" he asked.

"You're asking the wrong question. It's not about who's going to let me in. The real question is, who's going to stop me?"

Magnus muttered into his coffee, "Yeah, I'm getting that impression."

Chapter 34

I insisted we swing by Mama's house on the way to see the vampire to get the rest of my gear. If last night had taught me anything, it was not to underestimate the lich. I wasn't about to go running around the city under prepared when the undead sorcerer had the equivalent of a homing beacon locked on my location at all times. Neither Ben nor Mama were particularly pleased that I wasn't planning on lying low and letting my injuries heal. Ben wrapped me up in a tight hug before I got in the car. "You be careful now, you hear me? I don't wanna see anything bad happen to you," the old man murmured in my ear.

I patted his back. "Don't worry, Ben. I'm not doing this on my own. That's why we're going to Alessandro's. To ask for help."

"Good girl," Ben said gruffly. "Keep on makin' them smart choices now and don't go doin' anything stupid." When he pushed away, I saw a tear at the corner of his eye. He brushed it away brusquely and gave me a tight smile.

Mama wrapped her arms around me. "Come back safe, child."

I returned the hug. "I will, Mama."

Despite the stop, Magnus pulled up in front of Alessandro Nicoletti's mansion in record time. It was just past noon when we knocked on the vampire's front door. Robert, Alessandro's doddering butler, answered it. It took a few minutes to convince the old-timer that this was a matter of utmost importance and warranted waking his master from his rest. Vampires always slept during the day and had to fight against their nocturnal instincts to function during daylight hours. It was possible, especially for the older ones like Alessandro. Just incredibly difficult.

Robert slowly shuffled through the house, leading us to the vamp's study. The elderly manservant politely asked us to await his master's pleasure and carefully shut the door, leaving us in a pitch-black room. Even with my acute night vision, I needed at least a glimmer of light to see and there was no light source in the room.

Anxiety climbed from the pit of my stomach and up my spine to my brain stem as the inky darkness seemed to swell around us. I heard Magnus give a low growl. I reached out a hand, trying to find the werewolf. My fingers clutched his just as a warm glow spilled out of expensive wall sconces, illuminating the study. Magnus crouched next to me, his arms looking furrier than normal. He caught me looking at him strangely as he pushed fully upright once more. The fur faded before my eyes as he regained control.

Thirty minutes later, I'd given up examining the titles of the innumerable heavy tomes on the shelves in Alessandros's study and had settled into one of the plush reading chairs with a selection on vampire history. I even contemplated exploring the mansion to help Alessandro greet the morning. I was just about to go looking for him when the vampire lord of New Orleans finally flung the study door open with a bang, announcing his displeasure along with his entrance.

"What are you doing here at this ungodly hour?" Alessandro growled past gritted fangs. His milky red eyes flashed dangerously from behind his contact lens.

"It's nearly one," I said mildly, carefully shutting the book and placing it on the small table next to me.

"Precisely." Despite his outward grumps, not a hair was out of place on Alessandro's head, nor could I see a wrinkle on his pristine, dove gray morning suit.

"Who knew vamps needed their beauty sleep?" Magnus said from across the room, where he was examining the intricate curtain and shutter combination covering the windows. The window coverings were the only thing protecting Alessandro from the sun and death by illumination immolation.

Alessandro huffed out an annoyed breath. "Who's this?" the vampire asked, wrinkling his aquiline nose. "He smells like wet dog."

"Alessandro Nicoletti, meet Magnus Donovan." I left it at that, knowing there was little point in delving further into introductions.

"Wolf," Alessandro said, dipping his head fractionally. His voice was cool.

"Vamp," Magnus returned in the same tone, returning the slight bow.

It wasn't the warmest greeting, but I supposed it was too much to expect them to want to have a tea party and paint each other's nails. "Great," I said, clapping my hands and rubbing them briskly together as I tried to stifle a grin at the thought of the vampire and the wolf spending quality time together. "Now that introductions are finished, we need some help."

Alessandro shook his head resignedly. "With what? What couldn't have possibly waited until this evening?"

My good humor vanished as quickly as it had appeared. "A lich is in town raising zombies," I said seriously. "He attacked the fae at their embassy last night."

"Ah. I see."

If I hadn't been watching carefully, I might have missed Alessandro's pale skin drain of what little color was left in it. The vampire silently sat behind his desk, gesturing towards the two chairs in front of his massive workspace.

"Tell me everything," Alessandro said.

As quickly as I could, I recounted everything from the events leading up to the attack on the Embassy and the deadly toll it had taken on the fae delegation.

"You're positive the spirit you saw manifested into a skeleton with glowing orange eyes?" Alessandro asked.

I waved the tracking tattoo on my wrist at him. "Absolutely, and this thing confirms it."

"The Librarian confirmed what you saw was a lich?"

"To the best of her knowledge, yes."

"And you saw him raise a zombie?"

"Yes," I said with a little shudder. It wasn't something I ever wanted to see again. "The one thing I can't figure out is why the lich went after the fae. I mean, that seems like a pretty hard target."

Magnus spoke up. "But they aren't always. Didn't you say that they'd hired in more guards? Maybe the lich didn't know that and thought it would be an easy win for him."

"Yes, but to what purpose?" I asked.

Alessandro inhaled a completely unnecessary breath and pushed an intercom button on his desk. Robert's voice quavered over the small speaker a moment later.

"Yes, sir?" the butler murmured.

"Robert, please summon Janko immediately."

"He's back?" The old butler's voice rose half an octave. "Are you sure? He isn't very pleasant at the best of times."

"Yes, Robert. Immediately."

"Very well. I'll tell the staff to make themselves scarce."

"Please do." Alessandro released the button and interlaced his fingers, resting his chin on his hands, considering us. "Tell me what you know of the Collective," he commanded.

The turn in the conversation surprised me. "Why don't you tell me if you have any idea why the lich would attack the fae? Surely that's more important than a supernatural civics lesson?"

"Humor me," Alessandro said.

I rolled my eyes at the inane command, "The Collective is the ruling body of New Orleans. It includes representative members of every major supernatural power faction in the city. Together, the Collective ensures the secrecy of the supernatural world. Why are you messing around with quizzing me on answers you know I already know?"

Alessandro ignored my question. "How do you think we all get along despite our inclinations to the contrary?"

"Cut the crap. I hate guessing games and I would be shit at Jeopardy! Just tell us what you're getting at," I said, exasperation getting the better of my manners.

Alessandro eyed me intensely, but said nothing. His eyes widened like he was trying to speak through his strange milky red orbs instead of using his mouth. My mind flashed back to something Letitia had said in the Embassy. "Wait. Does the Collective use oaths? Magically binding oaths?" I ventured.

Alessandro's head dipped in what could've been a shift in position. Or a nod. He widened his eyes slightly, silently encouraging me onwards.

"Oaths that forbid you from hurting each other. Also, they likely bind you to secrecy, at least to some extent?" I guessed.

Another small nod greeted my words. "And, purely for the sake of argument, how many former Collective members that are still living in the region do you know? Members that have opted for peaceful retirement in the countryside?"

I stretched my memory, searching my history in New Orleans for any word of retired members.

"None?" I finally said, but my voice rose at the end, making it a question.

"Exactly. It's a lifetime membership. Former Collective members would be too powerful and privy to too much privileged information to just resume normal life here in New Orleans. Permanent exile or death are the only options and, if I'm being completely transparent, death is usually the preferred form of retirement."

"Great. I'm so happy that you have job security. Congratulations. Why are we talking about this?" I asked.

"Because a surviving former Collective member hasn't existed in decades. Until now."

It didn't take much to put the pieces together. "The lich was a member of the Collective?"

Alessandro spoke dispassionately, "Kroxius Vesak, a powerful necromancer. He sat on the Collective as the leader of the undead until his death fifty-seven years ago. Or should I say, supposed death? I wasn't aware that he had actually been successful in the conversion to a lich. It is an arduous process with a low survival rate, thank all the gods."

"What happened nearly sixty years ago?" I asked.

Alessandro leaned back in his chair, looking thoughtful. When he finally spoke, he chose his words carefully. "Kroxius represented a group of supernatural extremists. Although discontents have always agitated the relative peace we strive for here in New Orleans, they flourished under Kroxius. The faction grew so large that there were threats of a schism of power amongst the Collective. Threats we now know Kroxius actively encouraged."

"What sort of extremist faction are we talking about here?" Magnus asked.

Alessandro locked eyes with him. "The kind that always exists in our world. Kroxius' followers wanted to dominate, subjugate, and, eventually, eradicate or enslave the entire human population. They were convinced that Supes were the natural, more powerful next step in evolution. Far superior to our weaker human cousins. These extremists weren't content living in the shadows. Brawls in the middle of the streets between the extremist and more moderate Supes became everyday occurrences. Battle lines were being drawn. It was all the Collective could do to keep a lid on the bubbling pot, but it was bound to boil over, eventually."

"What happened?" I asked, drawn in by the vamp's story.

"Kroxius promised his followers a weapon of such destructive power that the humans and the Supes combined would face the choice between decimation or submission. Other than harrying his proxies, there was little that the Collective could do to stop him."

"Because of these oaths?" I asked.

Alessandro glared at me.

"Hypothetical oaths?" I amended quickly.

Alessandro nodded. "Theoretically, members of the Collective swear a magically binding oath to not cause intentional harm to fellow Collective members. Every time a new member joins, the oaths must be re-sworn. It's tedious but ensures a semblance of peace among neighbors with violent tendencies. All of this is theoretical, of course. I couldn't talk such oaths about in the open without serious repercussions."

I nodded my understanding. Alessandro was taking an enormous risk by telling us this much.

"Obviously, these are protection oaths, not privacy oaths, right?" Magnus asked.

Alessandro drummed his fingers on his desk and then said, "More like non-aggression oaths with an understanding of the need for secrecy, but essentially, yes."

"So, you can tell us what happened to this Kroxius guy?" Magnus asked.

Alessandro made an explosion gesture with his hands. "He vanished. One night, he proclaimed he would return with this weapon. It whipped his followers into a frenzy. That was the last anyone ever saw of him. Until today."

"How do you know this lich is Kroxius, the necromancer?" I asked.

"I knew Kroxius. His magic was a distinctive orange color. When you combine that with his quest for a magical weapon of mass destruction and the limited options for a necromancer to create such a weapon, the circumstances align too neatly to be a mere coincidence."

"Tenuous, but I can see your point," I said, rubbing at the tension creeping up my neck as I considered his words.

"This Kroxius guy vanishes, and you all, what? Just gave up?" Magnus asked.

Alessandro pursed his lips. "There was quite a lot to deal with regarding the leaderless extremists. They didn't go quietly, let me assure you. By the time we had the manpower to hunt down Kroxius, we found a ritual space that looked like a small nuclear explosion had occurred. We never found a body, but we assumed that his ritual had gone wrong, and he died. Not that there was anyone left alive in New Orleans to grieve his passing."

"So, what happened? How did he come back from the dead?" I asked.

Alessandro shrugged. "Much of this is conjecture, of course, but I now believe that he never really died. Somehow, he preserved a part of himself, a link to this world."

"A soul jar," I breathed.

"Precisely. My hypothesis is that he created his soul jar and ripped away a piece of his essence to ensure his immortality. Then, somehow, his body was destroyed, but the soul jar was left intact."

"He crossed over to the other side of the veil but was too weak to cross back from the Abyss into our world," I breathed.

Alessandro nodded at me. "Until that idiot, Aldrich Kingsley, tore a hole in the veil, and Kroxius, ever the opportunist, escaped."

"Why not hunt him down and take him out yourself?" Magnus asked.

Alessandro glared at Magnus. "If it was indeed Kroxius who escaped, no one who sat on the Collective at the same time would've been able to hurt him without catastrophic consequences. Theoretically, of course." I nodded in understanding. Magical oaths wreaked havoc on those who broke them. Alessandro continued. "Which is why we hired Ms. Blaze to be our intermediary until we could identify the escaped souls."

"Fine. Operating under the premise that Kroxius is this lich, how do we kill him?" I asked.

"Liches are created through necromantic magic. Therefore, the only way to kill a lich permanently is to kill the lich's current body and destroy its soul jar. However, no one knows where or what Kroxius' soul jar is. Without it, there is no hope of permanently dispatching him." Alessandro explained, rehashing information I'd already discovered, but it was good to have the situation confirmed.

Magnus looked at me, raising a single eyebrow. I nodded my agreement at his silent assessment. "I think we accidentally discovered his soul jar in a little touristy voodoo museum. A little blue glass bottle, but the skeleton stole it before we realized what it was."

"Do you know where it is right now?" Alessandro asked urgently, leaning forward.

I glanced at my inner wrist, hoping that there were two orange dots. One for skeleton Kroxius and one for the piece of his essence in the soul jar. No such luck. Only one faint orange dot off to the west pulsed faintly in time with my heartbeat. The blue dot was so light I could barely see it. I shook my head slowly.

Magnus interrupted my thoughts, "Out of curiosity, who was on the Collective fifty-seven years ago?"

Alessandro cleared his throat. "As I said before, sitting on the Collective is a lifetime membership. Supes are usually long lived unless they meet a violent end."

"Fine. So, who was sitting on the Collective when Kroxius was a member?" I asked, instantly seeing where Magnus was heading with his line of questioning.

"The members are the same, save three. Two of whom you are well acquainted with, Ms. Blaze."

I nodded. "The new interim ambassador to Fae, Letitia, and the werewolf Alpha, Damon Lykaios."

"Indeed. They won't have any ties inhibiting them from raining retribution down upon Kroxius' head because they have sworn no binding oaths to him or he to them. It would make sense that Kroxius would attack these three first, to divide and weaken the Collective while still allowing his powers to grow."

"You said three. Who is the third?" Magnus asked.

A knock on the heavy study door rang hollowly through the room.

Alessandro's smile was predatory. "Ah, I believe that is Janko now."

Chapter 35

Robert opened the door for a stocky man with the build of a professional boxer and the style of a mafioso from the early 70s. The newcomer had a jagged scar running from cheek to eyebrow. It nestled close to a nose that had been broken recently. The potential for violence rolled off him like ionization in the air that you can almost taste before a storm. The hair on the back of my neck prickled as his coldly calculating gaze crawled over my body from top to bottom and then slowly back up again, obviously lingering on its return journey.

Alessandro rose from behind his desk, nodding at the newcomer. "Janko, thank you for coming so swiftly. May I introduce Ms. Cameron Blaze? Cameron, this is Janko Ryba, the current leader of the undead faction in New Orleans."

The stocky man jutted his chin in my direction. "Nice to meet you, Blaze."

"Likewise." Curiosity got the better of me. I looked between the two of them. "Wait a minute. I thought Alessandro was in charge of the undead."

Janko brushed a hand through the air. "He's in charge of the vamps. There are too many of the damned bloodsuckers running around these parts to keep them in line and take care of the rest of the undead. That's where I come in."

Goosebumps crept up my arms. "Which makes you..." I trailed off, not sure I wanted to know the answer to my unasked question.

"A ghoul," Janko offered with a disturbing grin that revealed a gold tooth.

I paused, suppressing a shudder. Ghouls were nasty creatures. Cannibalistic skin walkers that didn't care if their food was alive or rotting. They could also take on the appearance of the last creature they ate. Terrifying A.F. Never, *ever*, mess with a ghoul. I wracked my brain, trying to remember if I'd seen Janko on the night I'd met with the Collective. I didn't think so, but I couldn't be sure. It'd been dark, and I'd been distracted. Besides, he could've looked like someone else. I shivered at the thought of wearing someone's skin to take on their appearance. Most. Disgusting. Suit. Ever.

Alessandro interrupted my thoughts as he gestured at Magnus. "And this is Ms. Blaze's companion, Magnus Donovan."

Magnus stood, folding his arms across his chest. "Ghoul," he acknowledged coldly.

Janko sniffed loudly, wrinkling his nose. "Ah, a werewolf," he returned. "I had one of your kind over for dinner once. Not very good eating. Too stringy." The ghoul made a show of picking his teeth with his fingernail as Magnus bristled beside me.

Alessandro raised a hand. "Now, now, gentlemen. We are all on the same team."

"Today," snorted Janko.

"Bring it. Anytime, anyplace," Magnus snarled.

"Be a good doggie, and sit down when your betters are talking," Janko sneered.

"Enough!" Alessandro's voice rang through the room, cutting off the conversation like a machete through a snake. The two men fell silent but continued to glower murderously at each other.

"Enough," repeated Alessandro, soft menace ringing through the single word. "Kill each other on your own time."

A thought popped into my head. "If you're the leader of the undead, don't spirits fall under your domain?" My mind flashed to Kroxius. Why wasn't Janko taking care of this issue? Surely, he was better equipped than I was in this matter.

Janko nodded. "Sure. Which is where I've been. A ghost up north at Myrtle's Plantation in Saint Francisville has been causing a ruckus. Apparently, Chloe got her panties in a twist because someone said she wasn't real. Then she just *had* to go and prove she was, didn't she? Not only that, but she found out she could upgrade from normal annoying ghost to poltergeist. Made my life a nightmare for the past couple of weeks, I'll tell you that for free."

So, he wasn't at the meeting before. If he'd been out of town, that explained why the Collective needed to hedge their bets by pressing me into service to take care of the lich.

Magnus furrowed his brow. "What's the difference between a ghost and a poltergeist?" he asked.

Janko snorted. "One is mildly irritating. The other is a gigantic pain in my ass. The most a ghost can do is thump on walls, bang doors, or give you an icy chill. A poltergeist can communicate with anyone stupid enough to conduct a séance. And, let's be honest, there's always a stupid someone. Once Chloe found out she could do that, she was out to get revenge on all the descendants of the people who'd killed her. It didn't matter to her this had all gone down a hundred and fifty years ago and these people's grandparents hadn't even been born yet. She started convincing those weak-minded, séance-loving fools to do all sorts. Long story short, there was a poltergeist-driven-murderer running around Louisiana and giving me one hell of a headache. But I took care of him and ol' Chloe, so all's good, baby." Janko smiled widely, flashing his gold tooth at me again.

I tried not to shiver. I didn't want to ask how he'd taken care of the problem. Some things were better left unknown. But at least that explained why he hadn't been around to deal with Kroxius. I glanced at Alessandro. "Does he know?"

Alessandro shook his head. "No, not yet. He's been devilishly hard to track down of late."

Janko snagged a chair and dragged it over to the side of the desk, plopping down and propping his dirty boots up on Alessandro's meticulously stacked papers. "What'd you mean? Know what?"

The vampire narrowed his eyes at the offending boots, glaring loudly at the ghoul. Janko sighed and cracked his neck before slowly dropping his boots to the carpeted floor. Straightening the mussed paperwork, Alessandro resumed his seat behind the desk.

"I *mean*, your predecessor's predecessor has returned," Alessandro said levelly.

Janko wiggled a finger in his ear, pretending to remove a blockage. "Sorry. Thought you just said that old Kroxius was back from the dead."

"Indeed," the vampire said.

"That's not possible," Janko said confidently.

"And yet, it appears to be true," Alessandro replied.

"Right, give me the down and dirty," the ghoul said, leaning back in his chair and looking like he was going to put his boots back on Alessandro's desk until the vampire shot him another withering look. The ghoul settled on stretching out his legs in front of him instead.

"If we are correct, the necromancer has successfully completed the transformation fifty-seven years in the making to become a lich."

"Fuck me sideways with a chainsaw," the ghoul breathed.

Alessandro's eyes tightened. To say the vampire disliked foul language was like saying Mount Everest was a small hill. Regardless, the vampire heeded his own advice and focused on the issue at hand. "If we are correct in our hypotheses, Kroxius has been trapped in the Abyss since he vanished. It separated him from his soul jar, which undoubtedly weakened him."

"I like the idea of a weak lich over a strong lich. Let's find this bastard's soul jar and smash the shit out of it before he can get his damn filthy hands on it," Janko said.

Alessandro gritted his teeth. "Unfortunately, things aren't so simple. Ms. Blaze and Mr. Donovan believe Kroxius is currently in possession of the soul jar. Beyond the description of 'small, blue glass bottle', no one but the two of them knows what it looks like."

"Fan-fucking-tastic. You've released a lich, lost the fucker and now you, what? Want me to come in and clean up your godsdamned messes?" Janko squinted at us and snorted derisively.

"If you won't exercise your vocabulary, at least make use of your brain, ghoul!" Alessandro snapped, his fangs descending. "As you well know, I cannot take direct action against a member of the Collective. Former or current."

"I told you those oaths were a bad idea," grumbled the ghoul.

"Those oaths were the only thing that kept you from eating poor Penelope when you first joined us," Alessandro pointed out.

"I know, and it was a shame. That little witch looked downright succulent, let me tell you." Janko leered at the vampire. "For the record, I still think those damn oaths are bad news."

"Noted. Moving on," snapped Alessandro. "That's not why I asked you here. Kroxius is an undead Supe, which falls under your jurisdiction. I suggest you take care of the matter before he comes after you."

Janko jerked upright, "Me? What the hell would he want to come after me for?"

Alessandro leaned back in his chair, smiling like a lion toying with a mouse. "Oh, I don't know, any number of reasons, really. He wants his old job back. He wants to throw the tenuous balance of power into disarray by killing off members of the Collective. Maybe he just doesn't like the way you smell."

"I don't blame him. I don't, either," said Magnus with a loud sniff.

Janko whipped his head around to glare at Magnus. The werewolf bared his teeth in a grim smile, refusing to break eye contact with the ghoul.

Stupid testosterone driven dominance games.

"Fine," gritted out the ghoul. "Any chance I can count on you for some backup?"

Alessandro shook his head. "You know why I can't interfere directly."

I perked up. "What about the magic users? You know, the local witches, wizards, and mages? Could they help?"

Alessandro shook his head, but Janko spoke first. "Nah. If old Fangy here can't lift a finger, that bunch can't wave their wands. Probably sat on them anyway. That's why they walk around like they have a stick up their ass. Besides, the magic users in this town operate more like a democracy. They have to meet and vote and re-vote and count the damn ballots and vote one more time for good measure. Me and my crew? They do what I tell 'em, like a dictator, you know?" Janko puffed out his chest.

Magnus muttered out of the corner of his mouth, "Not something to be proud of."

"What was that?" Janko demanded loudly.

"I said that you should probably open a history book sometime. Learn a thing or two," Magnus replied. I hid a smile as a flush crept up the ghoul's neck.

"You and me, wolf. Someday..."

"No one likes a tease. Why someday? Make it here and now," Magnus said, putting his hands on the armrests, looking like he was ready to spring for the ghoul's throat.

"Menstruating Pope on a pogo stick!" I shouted into the room, shattering the tension threading to build to a bloody crescendo. All three men looked at me in bewilderment. I took advantage of their stunned silence, barreling on, "Magnus, Janko, chill out. I don't have the energy for your dick measuring. You don't like each other? Fine. But can you please wait to kill each other until after we deal with this Kroxius guy?" They turned simultaneous glares at me. I rolled my eyes. "Screw you. Women perfected resting bitch face before it was a thing and then weaponized it while you were still in diapers. You think a little brow furrowing is going to intimidate me? Don't make me ask again, or I *will* unleash my womanly nuclear reserves all over your asses." I received grudging nods from both men, although they swiveled to glare at each other a moment later. Fine by me.

"Fabulous. Now, what's the plan?" I asked.

Janko spoke up. "I'll go after Kroxius. Track him down and kill him."

"You're going to want our help," I said, speaking quickly to cut off Magnus as he opened his mouth.

"Oh really? Why's that?" Janko sneered.

"Because the lich nearly took out the Fae Embassy by himself. Well, almost. He raised a revenant zombie, but it didn't really stick around for long."

Janko's head whipped towards me. "I haven't heard of a rogue revenant wandering the streets."

"That's because we killed it. I mean, it was already dead, but we killed it. Again."

"Did you burn the body?" Janko demanded.

"The fae weren't too happy about it, but yes, they burned the corpse."

Janko pinched the bridge of his nose. "Wait. Did you say that the lich took out the Fae Embassy? How?"

"He sent some sort of bolts of orange magic into the Embassy."

"Death magic," Janko breathed, turning to face Alessandro, who nodded grimly. "I'll send a necromancer over right away. Maybe he can slow it down."

"Slow what down?" I asked.

"Slow down the death magic poisoning your little fairy friends. Anyone who caught one of those bolts, no matter how small, is going to die. Death magic will spread like a necrotic plague through the host's system, destroying all the heathy tissue until there's nothing left."

"What?!" I exclaimed, thinking of all the Fae who were infected, who were *dying* because I hadn't stopped the lich's attack in time. My chest constricted. Letitia was one of the wounded, although she had seemed fine this morning.

Magnus put a warm hand on my arm. It helped to ground me as my thoughts swirled. "What can a necromancer do? Can he remove the death magic?"

Janko shook his head. "No, but he can slow the spread, which buys us time to deal with the lich. If we can kill the necromancer who cast the spell, the death magic will fizzle out. It's tied to his life force, or undeath force, or whatever fancy term the magic bastards call it."

"Will killing him reverse the damage done to the fae?" I asked.

Janko shook his head. "Nope, just stop it. Which is why we gotta deal with Kroxius fast. If the death magic eats too far into the host, there won't be anything that anyone can do even if we kill the bitch lich." Visions of Letitia being eaten from the inside out by magical death parasites played across my inner eye, and I shuddered.

"What's the plan?" asked Magnus, leaning forward with a deadly serious expression on his face.

I held up my arm, twisting my wrist to show off the magical tattoo with its single orange dot. "We use this to track down Kroxius as fast as possible. Before he stashes the soul jar."

Janko let out a low whistle. "That'll be helpful." He shot Alessandro a look. "Anyway, I can get some support here, fanger?"

The vampire grimaced, "Unfortunately, no. Daylight and vampires don't mix." He waved a hand towards the shuttered windows. "Kroxius is smart and will sequester himself somewhere safe during the evening hours, negating the effectiveness of my vampires. However, if he's foolish enough to attack after sunset, I suggest you try calling this number. I will ensure my lieutenant answers the phone. I, of course, can have nothing to do with these plans."

The ghoul snarled and looked at us. "How about you two? Do you have any bazookas or grenade launchers or something, I dunno, useful?"

"Damn, I left my bazooka in my other purse with my matching lipstick. You know how important it is for women to accessorize," I said, rolling my eyes.

"I can call the Pack. I'm not sure how fast they can get here, but I can try," offered Magnus.

Janko wrinkled his nose, but the wisdom in Magnus' offer was undeniable. "Fine. Call the wolves. Let the dogs out." He threw his head back and let out a gruff rhythmic, "Who, who, who, who, who?" He looked over at us, seeing if we appreciated his reference to the famous Baha Men single. When no one responded, Janko rolled his eyes and shook his head. "Fine. Grab your shit, Lewis and Clark, we've got a lich to track down."

"If I'm anyone in this scenario, I'm Sacajawea," I grumbled. "Leading the men to the right places and getting none of the credit."

"Don't you worry your pretty little head. If you lich-slap the shit out of this asshole guy, I'll give you all the credit," Janko said with a wink, taking refuge in the familiar dark banter that most fighters I'd ever encountered engaged in.

"Kroxius is a powerful sorcerer. I fear becoming a lich will have increased his power exponentially. This is a grave matter you're facing," Alessandro warned, stone faced.

"And he's being dead serious," Magnus said, keeping his expression blank. Alessandro glared, and Janko guffawed. I smiled at the gallows humor. Something about looking Death in the eye and laughing gave me courage.

I pushed to my feet. "I've got nothing else on my calendar today. Besides, I owe this Kroxius for what he did to the Fae. Trust me, I'm *dying* to repay the debt."

Janko snapped his fingers back and forth in a sassy manner. He pitched his voice higher in a horrendous impression of a valley girl, "You go, girl!"

I ignored him, looking at Magnus instead. "You don't have to come. I don't think your orders encompass this and you didn't sign up for fighting a lich today."

Magnus shook his head slightly, a ghost of a smile curving his lips. "Let's go show this Kroxius that liches get stitches."

Janko's dark chuckle sent shivers down my spine as our tiny strike team set out to assassinate an undead, zombie-raising sorcerer.

Chapter 36

In case you were wondering, magical compasses aren't made to navigate in a car, especially in the confusing urban sprawl of New Orleans. I'd have to tell Manannan to upgrade his sigil services to align with modern technology. By the time we escaped the concrete confines of downtown and I told Magnus to pull the car over, it was late afternoon.

I looked out of the car window at the empty stretch of bayou in front of us.

"Bug spray," I muttered to myself. "You forgot the damn bug spray. Idiot."

"What was that?" Janko said, extricating himself from the backseat of the car.

I raised my voice. "Nothing. Magnus, you'd better call Damon again and make sure he has these coordinates. I know he said he had to solidify defenses before coming out, but it's going to take a while to get here, and we don't know how long Kroxius is staying put."

Magnus nodded and stepped away; phone already pressed to his ear. I turned to Janko, crossing my arms over my chest.

"Tell me about you," I said, speaking over the incessant drone of insects emanating from the swampland.

"Whaddaya mean?" He scratched idly at an armpit while keeping half an eye on Magnus.

"Fighting style, things I should watch out for. I don't know how ghouls operate. Do you Hulk out and lose your shit? What do you bring to this party, other than a freaky diet?" I asked.

Janko's smile was unpleasant when he turned to face me fully. "Don't you worry about me. I won't eat you or your little boy toy over there. At least, not today. I've got this shit covered. You stay in the car like a good little girl. I'll take care of the lich. Then I'll let you buy me a drink to celebrate. Who knows? If you're lucky, I might even let you do more." He winked lasciviously at me.

I rolled my eyes, ignoring the ominous flash from his gold tooth in the afternoon sun. Janko strode off into the bayou without waiting for Magnus or me.

"Wait!" I called after the ghoul.

"I got this. Trust me," Janko shouted over his shoulder.

"I don't, that's the problem," I muttered, dashing towards the car and fumbling for the trunk's release button. I grabbed my sword from the bag. Luckily, I'd already strapped on my knives. I slammed the trunk before hurrying after the ghoul. Magnus turned at the sound. I pointed a finger into the bayou. I knew Magnus could track me by scent once he finished his call, but I wasn't so sure I could find the ghoul in the swampy murk of the bayou if I let him get too far ahead. Magnus nodded shortly in understanding.

I sloshed and clattered after the ghoul. My knee pulsed only slightly as I slipped on the uneven footing. Every time I slid, a twinge in my ankle let me know it wasn't happy with me for the swampland excursion. However, it felt better than it had the day before. Honestly, it was far better than what I deserved. The rest and the rum had done me good. I ran a tentative hand over my rib cage, pressing lightly. A slight ache greeted my probing instead of the flashes of agony from two days ago. By the feel of them, they were well on the way to healing, too.

I tried to move quietly through the wetlands, but cities were more my style. Between slapping at the swarm of bugs plaguing my every step, the splashing in the fetid water, and the unintentional cursing, I would not win any swamp-ninja awards.

I was distracted by swatting away mosquitoes the size of moths when an arm appeared out of nowhere and jerked me off my feet. I landed on my tailbone. Hard. Before I could get enough air to verbalize the curse on my lips, Janko's meaty hand slapped over my mouth.

"Shh," he whispered in my ear, his stale breath washing over me. "Look over there." He pointed a stubby finger past my head.

A small, ramshackle hut almost sinking into the bayou on a small island in front of us. Overgrowth partially obstructed it, which is why I'd missed it. A shallow span of water surrounded the raised island like a child had dug a moat around the place before getting distracted by something shiny. I wriggled angrily in Janko's hold, trying to decide if it was worth it to bite the ghoul's hand, when a flash of orange light flared between the hut's warped wooden slats.

"Kroxius?" I whispered as the ghoul peeled his fingers away from my face.

"In the flesh. Or bone. Depends on how much magic he's harvested," Janko confirmed, breath tickling my ear.

"Right. You stay here and keep watch. I'll go back and get Magnus. We can keep a lookout until the Pack arrives and then decide how to take him down," I murmured.

I felt Janko shake his head behind me. "No. You stay here. I handle this." He used my shoulder to lever himself upward and splashed confidently across the shallow expanse of muddy water surrounding the hut.

"Janko!" I hissed. He ignored me and kept walking. "Janko!" I tried again, louder this time.

Nothing.

I looked around wildly for Magnus, hoping he'd appear out of the shadows and keep the ghoul from calling out the lich. No such luck.

Janko planted his feet and shouted at the hut, "Kroxius! You're in my territory. Get out or get dead."

Silence descended over the bayou. I thought it had been quiet before, but even the chirping of birds vanished as Janko's voice chased the wind from the small clearing. The only sounds that remained were the ominous buzz of mosquitoes and my thundering pulse roaring in my ears. A droplet of cold sweat rolled down my spine. Let me tell you, when you can hear a bead of sweat drip, you know things are going from bad to worse.

A skeletal creature in torn hospital scrub pants appeared in the dilapidated doorway of the crumbling hut. My breath caught. He was *skeletal*, but not a *skeleton*. The lich had somehow regrown a thin layer of skin since the battle at the Embassy. It pulled tightly over his entire body. Orange and blue pulsed lightly under the thin, newly grown epidermis as magic visibly coursed along the lich's veins. Flaming orange eyes glowed ominously in the sunken sockets of the lich's emaciated face as Janko encroached on his private island.

"Haven't you heard? I'm already dead." Kroxius' voice sounded like velvet. If they made velvet of bone dust, ashes, and the tears of the children of a future apocalypse.

"Yeah, yeah, yeah. I use that line too," Janko said, unimpressed.

"Go away. I have no quarrel with you," the lich grated out.

"Oh, I think you do, old man. I'm the new and improved version of you. I'm not a fan of returning to the old ways. Onwards and upwards, baby," Janko sneered.

"Ah, I see," said Kroxius. He leaned against the doorframe and ran his blazing gaze over Janko. The sorcerer's gaze slipped past the ghoul to peer into the shady depths of the bayou. I hunkered lower, ignoring the muddy water seeping into my clothing. "Nicoletti sent his hired thug instead of coming to confront me himself."

"No one *sends* me anywhere," growled Janko belligerently. "Especially the vamp."

"Sent, sacrificed," the lich shrugged, ignoring the ghoul. "It amounts to the same thing. Alessandro is too scared of losing a portion of his precious power to attack me directly, so he has manipulated you into coming in his place. He is weak. He and his kind are a debilitating poison, sapping the strength of the supernatural community through their hesitancy to take action and desire for discretion."

"Are you sure we're talking about the same vamp?" Janko asked, stalking forward. "Alessandro is a motherfucking badass who takes no prisoners."

"As long as they are Supes or a meal. Throw humans in the mix and he is a weak as a three-day-old kitten." Kroxius waggled a bony finger at the ghoul. "Supes shouldn't be forced to hide in the shadows any longer. They must assume their rightful place as the dominate predators in this world."

"And where do you think that is?" Janko asked.

"Why, on a throne of human corpses and bones, naturally. Humans are frail, vacuous creatures who have reached the height of their evolutionary abilities. We must relegate them to their proper place in the new order so the superior, blossoming wave of highly evolved supernaturals can finally fully assume control." Kroxius spoke in the compelling manner of a master orator.

Janko snorted, flexing his fingers and cracking the joints as he tightened them into fists. "One problem, bub. Attack the humans openly and they will destroy us by sheer numbers, if nothing else. You may be old, but you aren't older than fucking math."

The lich sneered at the ghoul. "Ah yes, Alessandro held similar views. Which is why his removal has become a necessity for Supes to assume their natural position. We must excise his weakness from the region, like removing a snake's venom before healing can begin. Before the rightful order can be established." Kroxius tipped his head to the side, considering. "No, he and his kind are the stinking pus inside a boil. Like a boil, their infection must be lanced and drained. Starting with a stake right through Nicoletti's shriveled remains of a heart." A rasping rattle shook Kroxius' frame. It took a moment before I realized the skeletal sorcerer was laughing.

Janko cracked his neck twice, rolling his shoulders back. "You know, if I wanted to hear from an asshole, I'd just fart. Enough of this, and enough of *you*!" The ghoul raised an arm and flung it forward as he charged Kroxius. The lich's eyes flamed and crackled with orange magic. Although Janko was built like a boxer and no doubt a vicious fighter, I suddenly doubted his chances against the murderous lich.

A small army of undead rose, eerily silent, from the bayou. Ghosts, skeletons, and vaguely humanoid creatures sprang from the murky shadows. For a moment, I thought they were on Kroxius' side. My heart thundered in my chest. There was no way we could take all of those on. However, a moment later, the horde started flooding towards the island and Kroxius.

I hissed out a silent sigh of relief. Janko must've called them. He was the leader of the undead, after all. Admittedly, there were less than I would have liked, but beggars can't be choosers.

A crackling, snapping sound drew my attention back to the small island. Kroxius held a bone knife with a wavy white blade in one hand and a ball of crackling orange magic in the other. He flung the ball at Janko, forcing the ghoul to break off his headlong attack and dive to the side. Kroxius called up another smaller, snapping ball of death magic and smashed it into the bone blade. When he withdrew his hand, the blade pulsed with crackling orange magic that sparked and crackled menacingly when the lich waved it through the air.

"I have no quarrel with you, boy! Take your minions and leave this place before I destroy you all!" Kroxius roared, hurling bolts of magic at the oncoming rush. I held my breath, waiting for Janko's small army to collapse in agony. However, the orange magic sizzled through undead flesh and swished through the ghosts harmlessly.

Right. How can death magic harm the dead?

Janko snarled, flipping to his feet. "I don't take kindly to poachers sniffing around my territory. And I didn't swear an oath to you, bub, which means I get to really cut loose."

Janko's muscles rippled and bulged grotesquely, bubbling under his skin as his face elongated, features twisting into a monstrous form. His jaws cracked and widened, putting his long, strong teeth on full display. I watched in horror as he grew to half again his normal size, hunched over and corded with asymmetrical muscles.

Kroxius's eye sockets narrowed. "Fine. I could use a warm-up." He raised his arms and thrust them forward, bolts of paper-thin orange spiraling out like he was one of those plasma globes filled with radiating wavering beams of light to impress school children and prove that science was indeed *cool*. Except his magic was far from cool. Shit-your-pants *terrifying* was a better description.

I ducked, covering the back of my head with my hands and no longer caring about the swamp muck. I just didn't want to get tagged by one of those death bolts.

Nothing happened. I raised my head to see Janko's contingency of undead looking around, confused. None of Kroxius' second round of bolts had done any damage to them, either. I could see the moment when they all mentally shrugged and resumed their charge.

And then the swamp exploded into chaos.

Chapter 37

The lich raised his arms dramatically in the center of his tiny island as the rotting corpses of dead animals erupted from the muddy water, sending a noxious spray of silt rocketing into the air. I hid my face again and held my breath, trying not to inhale any of the rotting detritus raining down on me as animal zombies joined the fray.

One look around told me all I needed to know. The animal zombies weren't smart, strong, or fast, but they came in hordes, tearing at Janko's undead with stunning ferocity. Birds of all shapes and sizes flapped haphazardly on rotting wings to rip the ghosts to shreds of ephemeral spirit pieces. Dead river rats crawled up legs and gnawed on exposed, undead flesh. Emaciated raccoons scampered through the trees, leaping on anything like masked kamikaze paratroopers. The bony remains of a wild boar crashed through the undergrowth. Janko let out a curse as an unseen scaled tail swiped his legs out from under him. He rolled on the ground, trying to keep from being a zombie alligator's lunch.

I looked around at the melee. Janko's forces were stronger, but Kroxius' zombies outnumbered them badly. It didn't help that neither side could truly die in the conventional sense. The only way to stop the undead was to rip them apart. Torn bits of animals flew from the center of the clearing as Janko's undead exploited their size and strength. I watched in horrified fascination as the zombie boar charged through a pack of Janko's skeletons like a rotting bowling ball, sending bones flying. The boar twisted its head, looking for new prey. A skull rattled ominously on its tusk as it trotted off.

I searched for Janko in the gruesome brawl. As far as I knew, ghouls couldn't use magic, but somehow Janko had summoned all the undead to this place. Was it a perk of being on the Collective? Did he have a party line to all his minions whenever he needed them? If so, did that mean that he could take control of the animal zombies rising from the swamp? They were undead, after all.

I finally found Janko with his teeth sunk deep into the back of the zombie gator's neck. He flung his head back and spat a huge chunk of rotting flesh to the side before diving back in.

Okay then. Don't interrupt the ghoul. No need to tell me twice.

My eyes landed on the lich. Kroxius still stood in the middle of the clearing with his arms outstretched and head thrown back, looking like he was beseeching the weather gods for help. Even at this distance, I could see his arms and exposed torso trembling. His magic pulsed weakly, looking less vibrant. Raising all the decaying animals and re-animating them was draining Kroxius of his limited magical resources. I saw the semi-translucent skin pull tighter across his bones. Blue flashed under his thin skin as orange magic pulsed brightly for a moment before dimming again. Kroxius struggled with the demands of his spell. The newly formed epidermis drew in closer to the skeletal frame until it ruptured, revealing stark white bone as Kroxius used his life force to fuel his spell.

I sucked in a breath. The bone wasn't the only thing the magic drain revealed. As Kroxius turned, struggling to direct his zombie horde at the distracted ghoul, I saw a flash of blue sparkle beneath the scraps of remaining skin covering his ribcage.

Blue? Why blue when Kroxius' magic was orange?

Barqan's words rang through my head as I squinted through the shifting shadows to get a better look at the lich's ribcage. Could it be? Surely not. Kroxius wouldn't be that arrogant. Would he? I glanced at the compass on my wrist. There was only one orange dot in the center.

A primal roar of fury interrupted my thoughts as Janko leaned forward. The ghoul tore the zombie gator's lower jaw clean off, hurling it at the lich like a serrated boomerang.

Kroxius hissed in surprise and twisted out of the way, barely dodging the toothy projectile. He pointed at a large pelican corpse flapping aimlessly around the clearing with his bone knife and forced it to dive bomb the ghoul with his magic. Janko batted off the zombie bird's relentless attacks, finally latching on to a wing and wrestling it to the ground as the jawless gator waddled over to assist its avian counterpart.

As Kroxius stumbled off balance from the magical throw, the blue sparkle in his chest winked at me again through sparse, flapping scraps of remaining skin. As he whirled, searching for another zombie to send at Janko, I could easily see the glass phylactery glimmering within the bony cage. His soul jar.

I yanked hard on the shadows, using them to mask my movement as I rose silently to my feet. My yatagan's grip was slick in my hands. I crept through the shallow expanse of water, trying to move as quietly as I could. I was afraid the splashing foot would give me away, but the clamor of the undead host fighting the zombie animals covered any inadvertent noise I made as I crept up on the lich in the center of the small island.

I pressed my back to the corner of the hut, ignoring a dead raccoon as it zipped past me and scuttled across the island in search of new prey. Taking a deep breath, I made sure I held my shadows around me as tightly as I could and peeked around the corner, ducking my head back swiftly when I saw Kroxius was only half turned away. I took a deep breath and readjusted my grip on the yatagan. If I could destroy that phylactery he used as a soul jar, this would all be over. Kroxius would die. The zombies out there would drop. The magical death parasites would stop eating away at Letitia and her fae. Things could go back to normal. Well, as normal as New Orleans ever got.

All I needed to do was smash one small glass bottle.

I could do that.

No, I *had* to do that.

I took another deep breath and pushed off with my enchanted boots in a powerful leap, short sword ready to deliver a crushing blow.

I don't know how he heard me. Maybe it was some sixth sense. Regardless, Kroxius spun just as I raised my sword to strike at his exposed side, knocking my yatagan aside with his arm. The blade bit through the scraps of fragile skin dangling from the skeletal arm, causing no other damage. No look of pain crossed the lich's bony features as he watched me sail by.

Surprise locked my muscles momentarily as I tried to process the lack of injuries and simultaneously form a plan to incapacitate the lich in order to smash the soul jar. In that split second of surprise, the lich wrapped one bony hand around my blade and the other around my throat.

He twisted his hand, trying to snap the yatagan in half. If a uniquely gifted mage hadn't specially enchanted it for strength and durability it, he might have done it too. However, a horrifying screech of bone on metal reverberated up the blade and jarred my grip as the lich wrenched it out of my grasp. My hands clawed at the bony vice tightening around my throat. Kroxius used his grip to raise me up onto my tiptoes.

"Well, well, what have we here? A little witch?" He cocked his head, scanning me with his orange, flaming gaze. I struggled to breathe. I scrabbled desperately to loosen his hold. "No, not a witch. Something different, new. I've seen nothing like you before. How fascinating," he mused.

My vision darkened at the corners as I struggled to suck in a breath past his chokehold. My left hand shot to the small of my back for my karambit, but the lich knocked my weak, flailing arm wide.

"Unfortunately, our meeting is inopportune, and I do not have the time to delve into the mystery you present. Not in this life, at least. Perhaps we shall find more time in the next?" Kroxius winked one orange eye socket at me before ramming his bone knife into my side, death magic snapping up the wavy blade and into my flesh.

Chapter 38

Desperately, I flailed my body in an effort to escape the blow, but agony erupted from where the bone blade tore through my skin and glanced off my ribcage, letting me know I hadn't been successful. Searing heat blazed up my side, making me gasp and lose control of my higher functioning abilities. For a moment, all I could see was white hot pain. I fought for breath as the lich grunted in annoyance. He must've meant that to be a fatal strike, but my desperate dodge had been enough to turn the lethal blow into merely a glancing one. I forced my eyes to focus just as Kroxius tightened his grip on my throat once more and raised the bony blade for the final, fatal strike. I struggled weakly, but couldn't force my oxygen deprived brain to communicate with my muscles past the rictus of agony coursing through my nervous system.

"I'll see you on the other side, and then we'll have all the afterlife to explore what you were," whispered Kroxius through a grotesque smile.

The blade descended. I struggled to reach for my time-slowing magic. My smoke form. A shadow blade. Anything! Pain lanced through me as I struggled. I forced it into a little box, trying to focus on something, anything I could do to buy myself a few precious seconds more of sweet, sweet life.

A blur of silver flashed across my eyes. The wolf knocked into the lich with a ragged rattle and snarl. I fell on my side, letting out an unintentional shriek as I landed on the ragged tear in my side. Whatever magic Kroxius had imbued in that knife was really doing a number on me.

Either that, or he'd dug his knife in deeper than I'd first thought. Either way, I needed help. I rolled, pressing my hands to the wound, trying to staunch the blood as a large werewolf planted himself protectively over me.

"Magnus." I hadn't realized I'd whispered his name until the werewolf twitched an ear back at me. He rumbled low in his throat. I dug my bloody fingers into the fur of his flank desperately. "The jar. In his chest. Soul jar," I wheezed.

Magnus shot a look over his shoulder, obviously torn between protecting me and going after the lich.

Kroxius laughed a bone rattling chuckle. "Don't worry, wolf. When she is mine, I'll make sure she is well taken care of. I might even send her back to you one last time. After she kills you, both of you can serve me together for eternity."

I released my grip on Magnus' fur. I gave him a weak pat with my fingertips, leaving a bloody smear on his silver fur. "Sic him, boy."

Magnus dove forward before the whip of my words finished falling from my tongue. The werewolf was a whirl of snarling fangs and flashing claws as he drove the lich back. Kroxius lashed out with his crackling death magic blade, trying to score a hit, but Magnus was always just out of reach. The sorcerer and the werewolf circled each other as zombies and ghosts battled in the background. Despite the distractions and the agony from my wound, I focused on the fight in front of me. If Magnus could take Kroxius down and destroy the soul jar, then this could all be over.

The lich and the werewolf performed a deadly dance; circling, snapping, and swiping at each other, but neither landed a debilitating blow. It looked like it was a stalemate. I clawed at the muddy ground, trying to push past the injuries to be of some use. Perhaps I could fling myself at the lich, distract him enough that Magnus could take him down. But my legs wouldn't obey my commands. I scrabbled in the dirt, about as effective as a turtle caught on its back as Kroxius and Magnus clashed again and again.

I sucked in a breath as the lich drove at the werewolf with unexpected speed, knife at the ready. Magnus dodged at the last minute, but I saw a tuft of fur go flying.

That was too close.

A moment later, I understood. Magnus had *allowed* Kroxius the strike to get within the lich's guard. The werewolf locked his jaws on Kroxius' scrawny arm and wrenched his head to the side. If the lich's arm had all the normal tendons, muscles, and fat of a normal person, the damage might not have been so bad. As it was, the big werewolf's vicious attack snapped whatever magical binding held the lich's skeletal arm in place at the elbow. The bony hand fell apart in a rattling clatter as the magic was severed. Magnus tossed his head back in victory, powerful jaws snapping the brittle forearm bone to splinters.

The lich roared again, lurching toward me with his knife upraised, but Magnus was faster. His powerful haunches bunched. He leaped at Kroxius, knocking the lich off balance. The wolf crouched low in front of me. Magnus snarled. It rumbled out of his chest like ominous thunder, warning of an epic shitstorm waiting to be unleashed.

Kroxius took a quick look around. His zombie horde, while numerous, was dwindling in the face of the smarter, stronger undead under Janko's control. Through the haze of pain, I saw cold rationality chase anger across the lich's bony features.

"Another time," he sneered and snapped a faint orange whip of magic towards Magnus. The big werewolf dodged to the side, but the attack had been a distraction. Kroxius left the magic whip dancing mindlessly in midair as he whirled and sprinted deeper into the bayou.

Magnus looked anxiously back and forth between me and Kroxius, who was disappearing into the murky depths.

"Go," I gasped. "Get that son of a lich."

Magnus shook his head and whined. He avoided the snapping magical whip as it cracked at anything that came close. He snapped the heads off a couple of little zombie songbirds that might have been cute if they weren't, well, zombies. I winced as Kroxius escaped, but I was secretly glad Magnus hadn't deserted me.

The werewolf snuffled at my side gently. I patted him, trying not to hiss in pain as I released my hold on my side. My bloody fingers painted smeared, primal patterns on his gorgeous coat. I jerked my hand back, concerned about dirtying his fur. Magnus woofed out a low puff of air that I realized was a laugh in his wolf form. He was right. We were in the middle of a bayou fighting zombies. What did a little dirt and blood matter?

Magnus stayed by my side, snapping his jaws at anything that got too close. However, with Kroxius gone, the magic reanimating the zombies weakened considerably. Janko's crew dealt with them with savage efficiency, tearing them to shreds until all that remained of the zombie horde were flopping bits of bone, skin, and feathers.

The ghoul jogged over. He spoke to me with difficulty, past his massive teeth. The words came out a bit garbled, but mostly understandable. "What happened to you?"

I glared up at him. I clenched my jaw as I pushed myself to a sitting position. The world wavered. I was glad for the wall of fur that appeared at my side. I dug my fingers into Magnus' coat. Janko's eyes tracked the new smear of blood I left on the werewolf's fur down to my side, where my other hand still clutched at the knife wound.

The ghoul spoke over my head to the werewolf. "She needs help. I'll call a necromancer."

I felt Magnus shake his enormous head, so I interjected. "I know one," I panted through the pain. "Get me back to the car. I'll call Ben."

Janko nodded once. "If that's the case, I'm going after Kroxius. You got this?" He directed the question to Magnus again, ignoring me completely. This time, I felt Magnus nod. I couldn't even come up with a witty retort. Comebacks are hard when the world is spinning.

Janko nodded once at the werewolf and then took off at a dead run. The remnants of his horde of undead followed in his wake, stomping on zombie bits as they pursued the fleeing lich.

Magnus snuffled at me, urging me to stand. I flopped my arm over his broad shoulders and pushed on the heavy corded muscles under the soft fur. I finally convinced my body that upright was the correct formation for my torso and limbs. For about a split second. I don't know if it was the blood loss or the slippery muck under my feet, but one minute I was standing, leaning heavily on my werewolf bodyguard. The next minute, I was flat on my back, bloody mud oozing into my hair.

I grunted as the wind was half-knocked out of me. The fuzzy form of a concerned werewolf's face blocked my view of the clouds chasing each other across the blue Louisiana sky.

"This is *so* not my week," I groaned as blackness crept in at the sides of my vision. I blinked, enjoying the peaceful darkness.

No! That's not right! Open your eyes, you moron.

I forced my eyes open. Sleep was not my friend right now, not with the amount of blood loss I'd suffered. Somewhere deep in my brain, I knew that. I focused once more on Magnus' furry face. It was blurrier than it had been before. Maybe I just needed to refocus.

I blinked my heavy eyelids again.

And the darkness took me.

Chapter 39

I blinked again as something whipped past my head, whistling through the air and brushing by my cheek. I lurched to the side, scrambling to pull shadows around me, hiding from whatever was attacking me. My heart raced as I whipped my head back and forth, searching for my unseen attacker.

"Interesting," a calm voice said from behind me. "I hadn't predicted we'd meet again so soon. Strange. I shall have to keep a closer eye on you. I haven't met anyone this interesting in damn near three centuries."

Incrementally, I allowed the shadows to roll back until I recognized who was speaking. A familiar redheaded goddess smiled at me. Maman Brigitte wore a black lace dress with a fitted corset top and a flared skirt slashed artfully to reveal flashes of a deep amethyst underskirt. She waved a hand and a table and chair materialized out of the darkness.

"Brigitte?" I asked incredulously. "How did I get here? How did *you* get here? And, umm, where is here exactly?" I asked in a rush.

Maman Brigitte shoved a tumbler filled nearly to the brim with rum across the table to me as I sat down. I sniffed at it cautiously. The biting aroma of her favorite pepper infused drink assaulted my nose. I sneezed violently.

"Drink up. You're going to need it." I looked at the glass and then back at Brigitte, the blood loss making it hard for me to comprehend what she was telling me to do. When I didn't instantly move to comply, the loa leaned back in her chair and folded her arms. She pointedly raised a single eyebrow. I drank.

She nodded before speaking. "This is a place between. We're both here because of that," Brigitte said, pointing with her lips at my side.

I looked down at my side, noting the jagged wound with interest. The blood had slowed, but there was a blackness edging the ragged tear. An ever-widening darkness creeping up my side with irrevocable determination. I poked a finger at the blackened splotch curiously. It didn't hurt. In fact, I couldn't feel any pain when just a moment before I'd been screaming in agony. Hadn't I?

"That's weird. I can't feel anything," I said, continuing to poke at the wound.

Brigitte waved a hand around her head vaguely. "Like I said, this is a place between. Think of it like a train stop between life and the afterlife. Rules are different here. Time flows differently here." She eyed my side significantly. "Which is probably good for you. It looks like you don't have much of it left."

I sighed, "Yeah, I figured as much. From what I'm told, a lich's death magic is incurable."

Brigitte sipped from her tumbler of rum. "I find all power to be more of a spectrum than an absolute."

"Meaning?" I asked.

"Meaning a kitten might fear a dog, but a dog will lose its shit if it sees a hungry lioness."

"It may be the blood loss talking, but I don't understand," I said.

"Perhaps a poor analogy, but think of yourself as the kitten," she said.

"Hey!" I exclaimed.

Brigitte continued, ignoring my interruption. "And this lich as the dog."

"Who's the lioness then?"

She bared her teeth in a grim smile. "I am."

Looking at her, I could believe it. Understanding what she meant, on the other hand, was a whole different kettle of ball game. I shook my head. I meant, ball of fish. It was something like that. Wasn't it?

I swayed in my chair, nearly falling. Brigitte was at my side in an instant, holding me upright until I could sit on my own. She pressed the tumbler of rum into my weak hands. "Drink. Drink it all, Cam," the loa advised.

I sipped, then gulped, and finally guzzled until the glass was empty. The room snapped back into focus.

"Where's Magnus?" I asked, looking around. He'd been here just a moment before, hadn't he?

"He's still in the real world, looking after you while life still clings to your mortal form." Brigitte smiled softly. "You should forgive him the lie, you know. Call it extenuating circumstances if you need the excuse, but trust me when I say there is too little joy in this world as it is. Damn well listen to me. When you find your joy, you grab on to it and never let go. Even if it comes in werewolf form."

I snorted, but bobbed along to her words in unconscious agreement. A whistle sounded off in the distance. "What was that?" I asked, groggily.

All humor fled from Brigitte's face. "The long, black train is coming for you, Cam. But before it does, you have a choice to make."

A fog crept from the corners of my mind towards my awareness, bringing with it a woozy lack of equilibrium. "What do you mean?" I slurred.

"The lich may *use* death magic, but I *am* death magic," Brigitte said, throwing her head back as arcs of purple lightning shot out of her eyes. They illuminated her beautiful face, showing equal parts benevolent protectress and righteous judge. She lowered her gaze to meet mine. Purple lightning danced in solid black eyes, reminding me of... something...

She tapped on my fingers, which were clutching my side. I hadn't realized I'd been holding my wound again. I let go of my grip. Blood stained dark red, shot through with wriggling tendrils of black. Brigitte waved her hand. Iridescent purple magic pooled in her palm, forming a ball of violet lightning.

"The death magic he infected you with is damn nigh impossible to cure. For a mortal. Lucky for you, I'm not mortal."

"Great," I gritted out, watching one of the wriggling black tendrils grow until it split in half. Each half dove deeply back into my side, wiggling their way deeper into my wound. "Could you, uh, I dunno, do something about this?" I asked, gesturing at the death magic infused wound. "Please?" I added as an afterthought.

Brigitte shook her head ever so slightly. "Not even gods and goddesses who walk the Abyss can grant another chance at life. Not without a substantial cost." She eyed me seriously. "What are you willing to pay to avoid death this day?"

My breath caught. That was a loaded question, if I'd ever heard one. "That depends," I said carefully. "What kind of bargain are you offering?"

Brigitte chuckled. "Well, you aren't a moron, I'll give you that. Even in the face of imminent death."

I swayed in my chair slightly. Brigitte steadied me with a strength that belied her size. I blinked slowly, trying to focus my eyes. A sound tickled at the corner of my foggy awareness. Was the train whistle coming closer?

Brigitte's head jerked up as if she'd heard the same sound. She gripped my arm tightly. "Fuck! We don't have nearly enough time to do this right!" Brigitte reached up and gripped my chin, turning me to face her. I blinked until she came into focus.

"There's only one way that we can do this, Cam," Brigitte said seriously. "The lich's magic is potent. Unchecked, it will consume what's left of your life energy. I can counteract it, but only if you agree to serve me." She held up a finger. "Not as a fucking free-lancer either. You will be mine. Body and soul. Until I release you or you die, in which case you will continue to serve me in the afterlife."

I closed my eyes, running her words through my mind a second time. And then a third. "Hell of a bargain," I grunted.

"Comes with the territory," Brigitte said. I heard her wry smile in her voice.

I opened my eyes to study the loa. "And if I don't work for you?" I asked in a whisper.

A soft, warm smile lit her face. She dipped her head towards the oncoming train, now visibly chugging up through the darkness. "We will get on that train together. I'll personally escort you to your final destination. Your mom is waiting for you, you know. I don't think she expected you this soon, but she'll be so happy to see you again."

"Mom?" I whispered. My mind flashed to my memories of my mother. Playing cards games late at night. Reading in bed by the light of a flashlight. Baking cookies. Mom had tried so hard to be both a mother and a father to me. I hadn't understood that as I child. Hell, I barely understood it now, but my heart ached for her and how hard that must've been. Still, she did it all with an easy laugh and the biggest bear hugs you could ever imagine.

Then she used the last of her life's energy to fuel a protection spell for me. I still didn't have even half the answers I wanted. Why did she do it? Who was she protecting me from? What about me was so important that she felt like she had to give up her own life? Who was my father and how did he figure into everything? If I went with Brigitte now, I could see my mother, and pepper her with questions into eternity.

But I couldn't do anything with that knowledge because I'd be trapped in the Abyss.

Dead.

On the one hand, Brigitte was offering family, answers, and peace, but with the caveat of a choosing my final rest start right now.

On the other hand, Brigitte offered ambiguity, heartache, and pain. Images of Sloane, Mama Atli, and Ben danced across my mind's eye unbidden. Choosing to go with Brigitte now meant never seeing them again. Not helping them in their time of need when a freaking lich was messing with *my* city.

I rubbed a hand over my eyes, holding back tears. As much as I longed to see my mother again, I knew what I had to do. I whispered to her in my heart, "I'm sorry, Mom. Soon, I'll be there. I've just got some things to do here first."

It could have been the blood loss, but I could almost feel her wrap me up in one of her giant bear hugs and whisper, *It's ok, sweet girl. We have eternity waiting for us. Just keep following that beautiful heart of yours.*

A weight lifted from my shoulders and warmth swelled up from my soul, making me feel buoyant and loved. I opened my eyes and looked down at Brigitte. "I'll take the job," I said, past the tears clogging my throat.

She nodded, understanding what it cost me to say that. "Very well. Brace yourself, Cam. This won't be pleasant."

Brigitte slammed the magical ball of purple lightning into my side just as the black train whistled by us without stopping. I screamed. My shriek formed a discordant duet with the train's hellish whistle. They intertwined into a single, mournful sound that rose to a crescendo before crashing down into silent darkness. In the sudden silence, the purple lightning flickering up my side was the only sound.

And then there was nothing.

Chapter 40

I sat up with a gasp. My hand clutched my side. A small shriek sounded loud in the confined space. I looked around wildly, trying once again to figure out where I was. Soft pillows supported my back, and a warm blanket covered my legs. Familiarity and comfort stole into my subconscious before I realized where I was.

Home.

How did I get here?

Concerned faces met my eyes. Mama. Ben. Sloane. Magnus. I wondered how my little bedroom was holding so many people at once without bursting at the seams.

Sloane's gasp drew me back to the present. She pushed by Ben to grab my hand. "Cam! Can you hear me? Say something, anything!"

I wrinkled my eyes, coughing to get some moisture back into my dry throat. "Stop shouting, Sloane," I rasped. "I'm right here."

Sloane squeezed my hand and tears ran freely down her cheeks, making her luminous blue eyes glisten as she searched for words. Mama placed her hands gently on the petite leprechaun's shoulders, easing her out of the way. The tiny old lady laid her warm, wrinkled hands on my side, encouraging me to peel my fingers away. She sucked in a breath.

"Ben," Mama hissed, "Come look at this."

The lanky necromancer gently shifted Sloane to the side and bent to get a closer look at my side. His eyes widened. He twisted to glance at Mama. The look they shared was pregnant with significance.

"What? What is it?" I asked, worried that I'd just dreamed the strange encounter with Brigitte and was still being poisoned by Kroxius's death magic.

Ben brushed his hands together briskly. "Right. Mama 'n' me got a pile to do to heal this here girl up." He made shooing gestures at Sloane and Magnus. "Y'all get out there and make us some tea or some such." He ushered them out of my tiny bedroom and shut the door firmly behind them.

"Tell me what happened," Mama said firmly as she pulled various small pots and jars of healing unguents out of her bag. Ben stood at her elbow, acting as her assistant as she patched me up. I laid back in bed and let her work as I filled them in on the past few days.

Mama interrupted me to examine the sigil tattoo on my inner wrist, muttering darkly about gods sticking their noses in where they weren't wanted.

"There's also something you should know. About Barqan," I said.

"What's that, child?" Mama said distractedly.

"He's been teaching me magic, like how to make a shadow blade and, well, I think he might be my father." I whispered the last words.

Mama shook her head seriously. "If Barqan is a djinn king, there's no way he could be your daddy. He's been locked up for centuries!"

"But he did something called astral projection and the ether and I'm pretty sure I have djinn magic and—"

Mama put a hand on my shoulder. "You're rambling, child. Hush now and let me look at this tattoo. We'll sort the rest out in due course." Her fingers were gentle on my wrist. I closed my eyes, enjoying the sensation. Another, fainter... something... tickled at my inner wrist. I kept my eyes closed, trying to focus on the unfamiliar sensation. It felt like it was barely tugging at me, pulling me... somewhere. Was this the magnetic force that Manannan had warned me about? Would this magic inexorably pull Kroxius and me together until one of us died?

I shook my head, refocusing as Mama urged me to sit upright. She poked and prodded at my side and back, but there wasn't any pain. Maybe she'd given me some morphine or something?

"What do you see Mama?" I asked, hesitantly. Part of me needed to know the answer while another part dreaded hearing the death sentence fall from her lips.

Mama inched back around, eyeing me skeptically. "Nothing. What did you expect me to see?"

"There's no darkness? Nothing eating at the wound?" I asked incredulously.

Ben cleared his throat. "As a necromancer, I can guarantee you, there is no death magic in that there cut."

"Wow! I mean, I know you guys are good and all, but I didn't expect to fight my way back from this one," I exclaimed, twisting to get a look, which just caused a dull ache to rocket up my side.

Mama swatted at me. "What he means to say is that there isn't any more death magic in you *at all*, child. You were riddled with it when you came in and shouldn't have been able to survive the night. Now? It is simply gone. Vanished. As if it never plagued you in the first place. Not to mention that this cut looks days old instead of hours."

Ben sat on the foot of my bed. "Why do I get the feelin' that you're leavin' something out?" he asked kindly.

I sighed. "Because you know me too well?"

"Spill the beans, child," Mama said sternly.

And so I did. I told them everything that I had been holding back about Brigitte, the strange place between, the chance to see my mom, and taking a job working for the loa. Whatever that entailed. When I finished, I asked the old couple, "Just before I woke up, what did you see?"

"Nothing but you dyin' on this bed," Ben said, rubbing at his jaw thoughtfully.

"Why? What did *you* see?" Mama asked.

"A flash of purple light. Brigitte's magic flashed through me, burning away the death magic. Am I healed?"

Mama held up a cautionary finger. "You aren't dying, but you are very far from healed. However, you should make a full recovery, given enough time and rest." Her eyes were stern. I wilted.

"Yes, Mama." I hung my head.

Ben cleared his throat. Mama turned to look at him. "I've got this handled, Mama. Why don't you head back on over to the Embassy? I'm sure they'd welcome any help you can give shiftin' those poor folk across the portal."

"What do you mean?" I asked.

Mama started putting her things back in her bag, leaving a few pots and jars on the nightstand for me. "Letitia's people are moving their injured back across the border into Fae. There's usually a small burst of rejuvenation magic upon crossover into the Fae realm which will help slow the death magic. However, the primary goal is to get the injured to fae healers who might find a cure where we can't." She paused, clearing her throat loudly.

"And if they can't," Ben continued, "then switchin' realms may slow the lich's death curse long enough for the injured to say goodbye to their loved ones."

Mama nodded sharply and her voice was firm. "Yes. But it won't come to that."

I rubbed at my eyes. "Wait a second, don't fae who die get, I don't know, a second chance at life? Kingsley had mentioned something like that at least..." I trailed off, not sure of how to finish my thought without sounding heartless.

"Kinda," Ben said. "But the fae ain't cats. They don't have nine lives now, ya hear? They just get the one, just like you'n'me. But there's this here special ceremony that happens once every blue moon or somethin' where those that have passed on can make contact again, but only for a brief time before they get pulled back into that there Abyss."

Mama frowned at him sternly. "But we don't even need to think about that because we're going to find the evil lich who did this and reverse the curse."

I opened my mouth to tell Mama that wasn't possible when I caught Ben's eye. He shook his head just once, ever so slightly. My mouth snapped shut. Mama turned and pointed a finger at me. "And don't you think I forgot about you and that Barqan fella. We'll talk about that once I see to these poor fae."

"Okay," I said lamely.

Mama finished gathering her things and bustled out of my room, looking like she was off to save the world. Ben shut the door softly behind her.

"Thank you for that small kindness, truly. She don't need to know it's hopeless. Not just yet," Ben said, settling himself back on the end of my bed. Goliath, Ben's reanimated mouse familiar, poked his little pink nose out of the wild white nimbus of hair floating around the necromancer's shoulders and gravely shook his head at me.

"We really can't do anything to help them?" I asked, hesitantly.

"Oh, sure. We can help slow it down by keepin' that darn lich on his toes. The more time he spends runnin' all 'round town, the less power he can drum up, which means the less power gets poured into the active death curses. That's why everyone at the Embassy is schemin' and plottin' a way to make the lich dance to their tune, to buy those poor souls time to say goodbye to their families."

"We can't save them?" I asked, my voice loud in the room's quiet.

Ben shrugged, toying with a loose thread on the blanket covering my legs. "Only if we can destroy the soul jar. If we separate the lich from that there phylactery, he won't have enough magic to keep himself alive and still pour juice into his curse."

"He's carrying it in his rib cage! I saw it!" I exclaimed.

Ben pursed his lips and nodded at me. "Yep. Magnus told us. But I doubt it's still there. He'd have to be a special kind of stupid to carry it around with him all the time, especially after you saw him with it. Why, that makes him no better than the rest of us except his heart is a tiny glass bottle instead of a tiny pumping muscle. No, he's hidden it by now. You can mark my words. But that's not why I wanted to talk to you, Cam."

"What do you mean?" I asked, not sure where we were going, but positive the conversation had taken a turn.

Ben leaned an arm on the bed and caught my gaze. Gone was the klutzy old man. Staring at me was a necromancer who had survived decades of supernatural life to be here. In this room. At this moment. With me. I swallowed audibly.

"Cam, things are changin' for you, almost too fast to keep track of. When you came to this town, you were this scrawny little thing who was about as confused as a fart in a fan factory." I opened my mouth to protest, but Ben raised a finger, cutting me off. "Don't bullshit a bullshitter, kid. You didn't know whether to check your ass or scratch your watch and we all knew it. But you changed, adapted, grew into a lovely young woman. Why, you've almost been like a daughter to Mama 'n' me. We love you that dearly."

My eyes misted over at Ben's heartfelt words, but I kept my mouth closed. He obviously had something he wanted to get off his chest.

"Look Cam, like I said, things are changin' for you. Takin' on some pretty scary things, even for a Supe, mixin' with the Collective, hangin' out with a werewolf, drawin' on some ancient magics no one's seen or heard tell of in a century or more..."

I took a deep breath. "What are you getting at, Ben?"

He reached out and took my hand, patting it gently. "What I'm sayin' is that you need to do some soul-searchin', the sooner the better. You got a pile of folks out in your kitchen who are gonna be lookin' to you for answers, but before you go out there, you damned well better know what kind of Supe do you want to be? What kind of leader? What kind of person? You're spiralin' towards a crucible and if you don't have your course firmly set in your mind, you're gonna get sucked into a whirlpool and pulled under."

I opened my mouth and Ben held up his hands, palms outward in surrender, stopping me. "I know, I know," he said. "You're a grown woman who can make her choices, but I've been 'round the block a time or two. I've seen enough people that act as a fulcrum, tippin' the world towards good or bad to recognize another when I'm lookin' at her. And Cam? I'm lookin' at one right now," Ben said softly, staring into my eyes.

I swallowed hard. Ben smiled gently at me. "What kinda father figure would I be if I didn't look out for my little girl?"

My breath hitched on a little sob. I threw myself into his arms. I struggled not to cry as the ragged breathing tore at my side like a hot iron. The past month had been a *lot.* He was right. Things were spiraling. I felt like I was along for the ride, more than piloting of my own life. But how could I be expected to navigate all the crazy shit that had been thrown at me? Murderous fae, demons, liches, vampires, werewolves, djinn, just to name a few? Sure, I was a Supe, but there was a part of me that was still that barely grown girl who'd lost mother too early in life. I lived on the fringes, straddling the human and supernatural worlds. Somehow, my world had shifted on me, dumping me into the thick of it, and I was trying to keep my head from going under in the deep end of dark water while waves continually slapped me in the face.

Ben held me, stroking my hair and murmuring soft, comforting words into the side of my head. I felt like a little girl once more, which I rarely allowed myself the luxury to be. "What do I do, Ben? How do I keep my head above water?" I held on to him like I was holding onto a life preserver.

He chuckled, "The same way all of us folks do, Cam. We figure out who we are and what we want to be in this life. Findin' what makes you tick and goin' after that with all you've got in you, that's the real way to live a full life. Stay true to your course. If you do that, then you can bet your britches you'll be proud of the life you've lived when you get to be my age." He gently pushed me back and wiped a tear away from my cheek with his thumb.

I gave him a watery smile. "Thanks for the advice, Ben. And the shoulder."

He shrugged and smiled down at me. "We all need a safe place to break and re-make ourselves. I'm glad that I could be yours."

I chuckled and wiped at my eyes with the palms of my hands.

Ben sniffed loudly, and I looked at him through my fingers. "Cam, one more thing."

"What's that?"

"I'd recommend a shower before you head out there," he said, jerking a thumb at the closed bedroom door. "You stink to high heaven and look like you're a whisper away from hell."

Chapter 41

I took Ben's advice and contemplated my future as I washed the muck and blood off my body and hair. The shower felt glorious. The sluice of warm water helped me think through the situation even if I had to work to avoid getting the stitches on my side wet.

It might have been the idealist in me, but I did not want my legacy to be the way I'd been living. I'd been existing mostly for myself. Living from paycheck to paycheck. Bouncing from job to job. Doing whatever I could to make ends meet. Not that there was anything inherently wrong with that. I mean, a girl had to eat after all. And there was nothing wrong with wanting croissants instead of moldy day-old stale bread. Still, there was a part of me that wanted more. That wanted to do more. To be more. To contribute towards making my corner of the world a little better. And that was all on top of figuring out who my father was, my strange magic, and what role Barqan played in my mother's life.

I washed the last of the shampoo out of my hair. I watched the bubbles spiral down the drain. My thoughts spiraled as well.

I got out and wrapped a towel around my torso. I'd taken all the time I could afford at the moment, but I felt better. Like my feet were back on solid ground for the first time in longer than I cared to admit. And I knew the path I wanted to walk. Even if I didn't know where it was going to lead me.

As I towel dried my hair, I looked in the mirror. Mama had done an excellent job stitching up my side. The dark black thread snaked up my rib cage like the tail of an angry serpent, surrounded by inflamed red flesh. I shuddered. I'd seen wounds like this before, and I knew I shouldn't have been able to walk away from it. Brigitte's magic might have saved my life, but she left me a reminder of the cost of the bargain I'd made. I rubbed some of Mama's healing unguents over the stitches and slapped a large gauze adhesive bandage over the top to keep the stitches as clean and the pungent unguent from staining my clothes.

I rubbed absently at the tattoo on my wrist as I searched for some clothes that weren't covered in stinky swamp goo. I yanked on a soft sports bra, grimacing at anything with wires in my drawer. A lightweight sweater and some yoga pants completed my look. Comfort and nothing that could dig into Mama's neat row of stitches was the name of my fashion game.

Something brushed at my subconscious. I looked around the room, trying to figure out what was niggling at me. The bed was a mess, full of slime and blood. I'd have to wash everything before stains set in. Or just chalk it up as a loss and toss the whole mess.

I fingered the tattoo on my wrist again as I tried to place what was unsettling me and almost jumped as a strange buzzing sensation tickled at my fingertips. I looked down in curiosity.

The compass glowed up at me, a faint orange dot hovering somewhere to the South and East of me. Kroxius was still out there somewhere, no doubt plotting his next move. My eyes widened in confusion at the other soul the compass tracked. The blue dot that had always been on the fringes was now smack dab in the center of the compass.

I held my wrist out like a bizarre metal detector, sweeping my room like a child might look for hidden treasure on a beach. The tingling in the compass grew stronger when my arm spun toward the door.

I flung the bedroom door wide. Sloane sat alone at my kitchen table, fiddling with her phone. She stared at me with her jaw hanging open as I moved through the open room, wrist first. I held up a finger, asking for silence as I swept my arm through the air. I moved through the living room and into the kitchen. The buzzing sensation intensified as I approached the kitchen counter, but nothing was there. I crouched down, examining the floors in confusion. The buzzing grew into a full bone rattling vibration. My fingers shook as I swept a questing hand along the floorboards under the countertop. They bumped into a cool, round shape. I fished the item out and the buzzing in my fingers faded.

I held a silver ring up to the light. It had delicate, ornate swirls of metal holding a pink quartz stone in place. Flickers of azure blue danced in the depths of the stone. The same blue that decorated my wrist.

"What is it?" whispered Sloane, craning her neck to peer over my shoulder.

"It's the ring that I found with that relic Kingsley hired me to track down. It must've fallen down there. I forgot about it in the craziness of the last few weeks."

"What? And you just remembered it was there?"

I held up my wrist, showing the matching blue colors. "Not quite. The other soul that escaped the night that Kingsley ripped open the veil must've flown in here and got stuck or something." I twisted the ring, catching the light to inspect it.

"How do you get it out?" she asked, leaning in to get a better look.

"Magic?" I guessed. "Or you could probably smash it."

"Yeah, that'd probably work. Want me to get a hammer?"

I shook my head vehemently. "Not a chance. The other two things that slipped out of that tear were a demon and a genocidal maniac who's also an undead, unkillable necromancer. Who knows what sort of horror is in here?" I held up the ring for emphasis.

"It could be some nice old granny just wanting to say hello to her grandkids one last time," Sloane said optimistically.

"Yeah, if you believe that, I've got real estate on Mars to sell you," I said dryly. I took off my necklace and threaded the chain through the delicate ring. The ring nestled cozily next to the oblong gold charm. I considered it thoughtfully. Barqan said that the trip to the ether would drain him so much that communication would be impossible for a while, but he hadn't given me a specific time frame. I'd have to try calling continually until he responded if I wanted my answers.

Sloane interrupted my thoughts, "What now, Cam?" I realized then that I hadn't told her about Barqan. Or Brigitte. Or possibly trading work experience for my soul in a hasty bargain with the loa of death.

I shook my head. There wasn't time for all that now. Instead, I said, "Now, we deal with the lich. If we don't deal with him quickly, more people will die."

Sloane nodded seriously. "We reached the same conclusion, which is why both Mama and Ben left for the Embassy while you were in the shower. They are going to help where they can."

I sat down in the chair with a groan. My hand gripped my side as a dull ache radiated from there to my everywhere. Sloane popped up with spritely ease, steadying me gently in the chair.

"You're injured. You don't have to do this, Cam."

"Yes, yes, I do." I smiled at her, patting her shoulder as I released my hold on my side. "Now, pour me some of that rum on the counter and call in the wolves. We've got work to do."

Chapter 42

A half hour later, there was what seemed like a small army in my living room. My tiny apartment wasn't designed to hold so many large people. Given the age of the building, I was genuinely worried that the floor might collapse if Damon kept pacing the way he was. Will leaned against the kitchen counter with his arms folded. The beta paid attention to everyone in the room. Andrei lay sprawled on the sofa, his lanky teenage form dripping over the edges as he absently flicked through one of my many books. Magnus was nowhere to be seen. He must've been keeping watch outside with Julius and Parker.

What really surprised me was that Janko was sitting at my kitchen table. He was sipping a bottle of Rudolph's excellent beer he'd stolen from my fridge. I glared daggers at him when I noticed. He lifted the chunky brown bottle in a snarky salute.

"Ah, Cameron. Good. How are you feeling?" Damon said, striding over and placing his hands on my shoulders, peering down into my face with concern.

I bobbed my head in a vaguely reassuring manner. "I'll be better once we deal with this Kroxius problem."

Damon searched my face, his own lit by grim acceptance. He didn't need to say anything. He knew we were on a ticking clock. I might have been able to eradicate the death magic infecting my body by making a deal with Brigitte, but the fae who'd been injured by Kroxius hadn't.

The lich's death magic would consume them unless we dealt with him quickly.

I cleared my throat and spoke loudly, "So, what's the plan?"

Damon pulled out his phone as he led me to the kitchen table, tapping out a number. He set the phone in the middle of the table.

Letitia picked up on the first ring. "Damon," she said, her voice sounding tinny over speakerphone. "How's Cam?"

I leaned forward towards the phone. "I'm here, Letitia. Doing as well as can be expected. How about your people?"

"Not good, Cam. Not good at all. Ben and Mama are on their way to see if they can help, but we need to take care of this lich before his curse kills any more of my people."

Damon spoke up, "I agree, Ambassador. I've reached out to the rest of the Collective for aid, but their hands are tied for... various reasons." He shot me a look laden with significance. I nodded my understanding. "As the new kids on the block, it looks like we are going to have to take care of the problem ourselves. If we're going to have a battle, I want to pick the ground."

Janko put his bottle down. "Agreed. Kroxius is more powerful than I thought possible. His power is growing fast. The shitty stalemate of today won't happen again tomorrow. If he's allowed to live, the days after will be worse. I promise you that."

"I hope you have a plan," Letitia said. "My people are weak, injured, and dying. We can't handle this Kroxius on our own."

"I do, but it means we're going to have to work together. All of us." The Alpha glared across the table at the ghoul.

Janko raised his hands in self-defense. "I can play nice when I want to."

"You'd better," growled Damon. "My plan hinges on your *cooperation*." The last word hung in the air between the two men like a dueling glove thrown down on my kitchen table.

Janko glared at the wolf, jaw bunching and eyes tight. "Whatever you say, wolf. This time."

Damon nodded shortly. "The fae can't come to us, which means we need to go to their embassy. Janko, you and your undead will be the first line of defense. If Kroxius shows up, hold the zombies at bay. Take the lich out if you can. An elite team of wolves will assist you, but their primary focus will be to kill the lich. Hopefully, he tracks us down and is still cocky enough to carry his soul jar with him. However, I'm sending my best tracker, Will, to follow his back trail. Maybe we get lucky." Will nodded stoically from across the room while Damon continued, "The rest of the Pack will form a perimeter around the Embassy, protecting the injured inside from any flanking assault."

I cleared my throat. "What about me? I'm not staying here."

Damon shook his head. "Unfortunately, no. You are not. We need you to act as bait, to draw the lich in with the magic that connects you." He gestured to my wrist and the tattoo.

I'd expected more of a fight from the Alpha. "Good. I'll be with the wolves then, protecting the Embassy."

"No. You'll be *inside* the Embassy with the rest of the injured." Damon's voice was cool, dispassionate, but it hit me like a slap in the face.

"The hell I will..." I started.

Damon cut me off, his tone frosty. "In your current state, you are a liability. If you collapse in the middle of the battle, you will either be killed or drain our valuable resources as allies try to protect you."

I saw his point, but I didn't like it. Before I could protest, Letitia interrupted, "Sorry to spoil your plans, Damon, but I need to protect my people. I've just gotten notice from Ben that even with his necromantic powers, he cannot stop the death curse, only slow it. My people need more time."

"Exactly, which is what we are trying to buy you," Damon said, speaking loudly and leaning towards the speakerphone on the table.

"To what end? Hoping that the lich will show up? That you can find the phylactery in time to render him mortal and then kill him? I can't just sit here and hope. My people don't have that kind of time."

"What do you suggest then?" the Alpha asked coolly.

"We're moving the injured through the portal to Fae. There are healers in Fae that may be able to help. Regardless, it buys my people time."

"How so?" he asked.

"Time flows differently in Fae. If I can get the injured to a pocket where time runs slowly, we may extend their lives long enough to either kill the lich or find a healer who can help them. I am not leaving the fate of my people to luck," Letitia finished firmly.

Damon rubbed his jaw thoughtfully. "What do you suggest?"

"Do what you need to the Embassy or the grounds. Turn it into a kill-box for the undead for all I care! It's warded from human eyes, so you have nothing to worry about on that front. Short of a nuclear explosion, you could host an entire war on the grounds and the Norms would never know. I've already sent for reinforcements from the Courts. They should be here within a few days. In the meantime, I could use the Pack's aid in moving the injured to the portal. There are too many grievously wounded for the healthy fae to move them quickly by ourselves. Once the injured are clear, do what you whatever you want with the Embassy as long as you kill the lich. A building is a small price to pay for my people's lives."

I spoke up, "Make sure you cross over too. You need to get that injury looked at asap."

"I know," Letitia said. "But my people come first."

Damon nodded slowly. "Fine. We'd have to do it quickly, though. I don't know how long we have before he strikes. If Alessandro can be believed, Letitia, Janko, and myself are his targets. With our factions in disarray, Kroxius will be able to enact his ultimate goal, whatever that is. Regardless, I don't like the idea of being outmaneuvered when we are transporting the injured."

Letitia spoke again, "Agreed. We are stronger together, but us joining forces will inevitably draw him towards us."

"Unless he just waits for us to tire ourselves out," Janko pointed out. "Wouldn't that be smarter?"

"True. But with the fae injured, we cannot leave Letitia alone and in such a weakened position. And if we know she's vulnerable, so must he. If we plan this right, we can lure him into an ambush he can't escape," Damon replied.

"I see your point," Janko said as he scratched his cheek. "And I do like the idea of ambushing the bastard."

Letitia spoke up. "One rather important issue that I feel compelled to mention. The lich absolutely cannot be allowed to cross over to Fae. Once all the injured are through, I will close the portal from the Fae side until our reinforcements arrive. I cannot allow the lich to wander through our realm. Murder, magic, and mayhem are all games to my people. There are too many powerful things that would flock to his banner if he crossed over. Minions waiting for a master, and not the cute, yellow, overall-wearing kind either. Not to mention the festival we have when Autumn is in power. All the dead can revisit their living relatives. I don't even want to imagine the turmoil a lich could unleash that night!"

"Good to know. We need to keep the lich here and kill him as quickly as possible. It sounds like we have a plan, even if it is rough. Any other suggestions?" Damon asked, looking around the table.

Janko raised his bottle. "Get your gear and your people together. Pack for every eventuality. This isn't the time to play nice."

Andrei pushed up onto his elbows, joining the conversation for the first time. "What should we play, then?" His face was curious and questioning. Obviously, he hadn't been listening to the conversation. Only a teenager could ignore the threat of an imminent attack in favor of the promise of playing a game.

I hid a smile behind a hand. There were times I was convinced Andrei was a puppy masquerading as a werewolf.

Janko shook his head. "Dungeons and dragons, kid," he said dryly.

Andrei's face lit up. "Really? I've never played, but I hear vintage games are cool too."

"Totally," Janko deadpanned. "But you need to roll a combat bard. Preferably one who's trained in a marching band. It's the only class to play."

"Why?" the kid asked.

"Who else do you know who could take on a dragon power walking backwards and playing the tuba without asphyxiating?"

My estimation of the ghoul rose by plus twenty in that moment. But this wasn't the time for games or joking. This was the time to get ready for the fight of my lifetime.

And hope we all survived.

Chapter 43

I hurried into my bedroom to pack a bag. The wolves headed downstairs, talking strategy with Janko. I was determined not to be caught flatfooted when the lich struck, even if I was still recovering. My typical fighting gear was a no-go, but even if it hadn't been coated in blood and swamp muck, I doubted that I could have wriggled into it without opening up my stitches. I sighed, admitting to myself, if no one else, that Damon might have a point in benching me.

Sloane popped her head around the door as I stood in front of my open closet, considering my options. "What do you think you are doing?" the leprechaun demanded, putting her hands on her hips.

"Just doing what I'm told and preparing for every eventuality," I said, not taking my eyes off the arsenal in my closet.

"Since when do you do as you're told?" Sloane groused.

"When it suits me," I said with a shrug. "Get over here and help me strap on my karambits."

Sloane muttered some unladylike curses under her breath, but she grudgingly fastened the buckles, saving me some painful twisting. I slid into my jacket before looping the sheath of the yatagan over my shoulder, patting the strap into place to ensure it wasn't twisted.

"Got anything in there for me?" Sloane asked.

I raised an eyebrow, but moved to the side. "Sure, help yourself."

The tiny leprechaun selected my favorite matching handguns. She also strapped on a set of throwing knives. Sloane finished up by loading the pockets of her jacket with extra ammo as I slid my enchanted boots on. The smell from them made my nose wrinkle, and I gagged slightly. I wished there'd been time to clean them, but nicely scented footwear fell low on the priority list today. I just hoped no one thought it was actually *my* feet that reeked.

Something hit the window, jerking my thoughts back to the present.

"What was that?" Sloane asked, whirling towards the window.

"I don't know," I said, sidling along the wall to cautiously to look outside, holding my breath in case a zombie's decaying head popped into view. Nothing. The empty street looked positively normal. Except for the small gathering of Supes outside my front door. Damon looked like he was giving orders to his wolves as Janko jammed his hands in his pockets and headed towards his car.

"It must have been a bird," I said, continuing a casual scan of the street. Janko revved his engine, pulling away from the curb and roaring down the street. I thought I saw some misty figures materialize and chase after the ghoul. It must have been his ghosts or something.

Another loud *crack* snapped my attention back to the window, where a fine spiderweb of cracks crinkled out from the center of the pane.

"What the…" I trailed off as I searched for the hapless bird. I'd never heard of a Louisiana bird strong enough to crack glass. I mean, *maybe* a pelican or a larger bird of prey, but they usually avoided heavily populated areas. My eyes landed on my avian attacker, ragged scraps of skin and feathers fluttering around its wings as it dove at the same spot on the window again. More cracks spiraled up the glass as the zombie bird struck.

"We've gotta go!" I shouted at Sloane, shouldering the bag that I hadn't had time to fill completely. I gritted my teeth as I dashed through the empty apartment, Sloane hot on my heels.

I flung the door to the hallway wide, almost catching Magnus in the nose. The werewolf sprang back with unnatural grace, a snarl curling his lips as he took in our frantic exit. I tossed Sloane the keys. She caught them, spun, and locked the door behind us.

"What's happening?" Magnus said, panting and looking like he was trying hard not to shift.

"Kroxius found us! Go, go, go!" I said, grabbing Magnus' arm and thrusting him towards the stairs. Another thump sounded from inside the apartment, followed by the tinkle of breaking glass. The three of us clattered down the staircase and hit the street just as the zombie bird found a friend. The pair dive-bombed our heads. Magnus rolled out of the way of the first. I batted the second bird into the wall. Sloane leaped on the thing, stomping for all she was worth until the bird stopped its unnatural flapping.

"What was that?" Damon growled. He crouched low on the street, his hands outspread as he tracked the sky for incoming threats.

"Scouts," I said, my breath coming fast and shallow as I searched the sky as well. The remaining bird was flapping weakly away, heading towards the south. "We need to get to the Embassy. Now."

No one spoke as the Pack, Sloane, and I piled into the remaining cars. Everyone kept a tense eye on the sky, searching for any more zombie birds as we whipped through the darkened streets of New Orleans.

Sloane leaned over once we were underway and whispered, "How'd they find us?"

I held up my wrist, flashing the tattoo at her. "Pretty sure they are tracking this. If Kroxius is sending his zombies after me already, you can bet he's not far behind. We've got to get to the Embassy, or the people of New Orleans are going to see what a zombie apocalypse looks like firsthand."

"If anyone, the locals here could handle a zombie apocalypse," Sloane said with a dark chuckle.

"Oh, no doubt about it. But they shouldn't *have* to. That shit belongs in books and late-night movies. Not on the streets for everyone to see."

"And get bitten," Sloane added.

"Yeah. Let's avoid starting World War Zombie if we can help it."

"Amen." Sloane reached across with a fist. I tapped my knuckles on hers.

The wolves wove through the sparse traffic, looking like they were auditioning for yet another remake of the *Italian Job: The Supernatural Remix*.

By the time we reached the neighborhood where the Fae Embassy stood, I thought we were clear of the aerial attack. I'd even stopped checking the sky every other second. However, as soon as we turned onto the street in front of the Fae Embassy, that all changed. First one bird, then a second, and finally a handful started throwing their tiny, decaying bodies against the caravan of cars with unbelievable force. Luckily, the Pack's vehicles were better reinforced than my apartment window.

Someone must have called the Embassy because the newly repaired gates were already swinging wide as the small caravan of cars screeched onto the drive and flew up to the grand mansion. Damon was out and shouting orders before the cars even stopped.

He waved his arm frantically at me as Sloane and I ejected ourselves from the car.

"Get inside!" The Alpha shouted, easily batting a zombie bird out of the sky with a vicious slap before stomping on it and grinding it under a heel. These zombie minions were stronger than the normal bird, but nowhere near as smart.

He continued shouting orders as we sprinted past him, hands over our heads. "Magnus! You're with Cameron. Keep her safe. We need her alive to reel in the lich."

"Got it!" Magnus shouted, running after us. Somehow, he beat us up the steps, holding the door wide as his eyes alertly scanned behind us for any incoming zombie birds.

I heard the Alpha growl behind me. "Andrei! What are you doing here? I thought I told you to go home. Never mind. Get inside. Help the fae get their wounded to the portal."

"But I..." the teenage werewolf started.

"Now!" Damon roared as I rushed through the doorway into the Embassy's foyer. The usually pristine entryway was a mess of provisions and weapons. Sloane skidded up next to me and Andrei was only a breath behind. Magnus slammed the door shut behind us. He shouted for the wide-eyed fae staring at our abrupt entrance to barricade it closed. They leaped to follow his orders without hesitation.

Letitia's blonde head whipped up from where she was helping one of the injured guards to stand, her blue eyes flashing as she searched my face for answers to our hasty appearance. I nodded at her, my jaw set. Her eyes went steely. Her quiet voice rang out in the sudden hush that fell over the foyer.

"He's here."

Chapter 44

An unearthly howl sent shivers racing up and down my spine. The wolves were on the hunt. Part of me wanted to be out there with them, stalking down the sorcerer who was hurting my friends. Unexpectedly, Ben's words ripped through my mind.

What kind of person did I want to be? Not one that put her friends in danger, that's for sure.

Letitia interrupted my inner monologue. "We've got to get the injured to the portal and then seal it. That is of utmost importance. Oh, and we can't afford to let the lich cross over into Fae. The results would be..." Her voice trailed off as her eyes lost focus, imagining the worst.

"Bad?" I asked.

"Cataclysmic," Letitia responded seriously. Her already pale face drained to a chalky white.

"We'd better get a move on, then. Where is this portal?" I asked.

Letitia gestured towards the back of the house. "Through the gardens, there's a hedge maze. The portal is in the center of the maze."

"Of course it is," sniffed Sloane. "It's never easy with you, fae." Sloane had never really explained why she disliked the fae so much. However, now wasn't the time to go searching for answers.

Letitia's eyes flashed at the leprechaun, but didn't rise to the bait. Instead, she gestured at all the gear and the fae congregating in the foyer. "We need to get all of this across," she said. "Where they're going, they'll need the provisions and the weapons."

"Really?" I asked, surprised. "Why send them there then, if they'll need weapons?"

Letitia shouldered a heavy camping backpack, strapping the support belt around her waist. "Currently, time trumps all. We need to get my people to Fae as quickly as possible. Besides, it's not like this place is Fort Knox right now, anyway. I need to make sure that they have what they need to survive until help arrives." She winced as she tugged the belt tight, grasping her side and breathing deeply for a moment.

Right. Letitia had taken one of Kroxius's death curse bolts too. She needed to get to the area of slow time in Fae just as much as everyone else.

I looked at the gear, fingering my own stitches thoughtfully. Although I wanted to help, I doubted my magic could counter Kroxius' death curse. "We'll follow your lead, guard your backs," I said, infusing more steel into my voice than I felt.

Letitia nodded at me and raised her voice to be heard in the bustling foyer. "Anyone who can carry something, grab a bag or offer a shoulder to someone in need. Anyone who can hold a weapon, do so. We'll take all the injured across first and leave a guard at the portal entrance. The rest will return for any other gear we need. Remember to only take what you need. We will be back. All of us." Her brilliant blue gaze bore into every being in the foyer, making the promise personal.

Organized chaos erupted in the foyer as the fae jumped to do their ambassador's orders. As Letitia led her people towards the back of the house, Magnus sidled over to me. "Are you sure you can handle this?" he asked me softly as the last of the fae hurried past us.

In response, I unsheathed my yatagan. I met his eyes calmly. "I don't have a choice. These people need to get somewhere safe until we can get them help or until we kill Kroxius. I may not be at the top of my game, but I'm better equipped than some." I jutted my chin at a young woman leaning heavily on Geoffrey, the butler, an arm limp at her side. A large swath of dark magic crept from her wrist and disappeared under her sleeve.

"I take your point," Magnus said, eyeing the sword meaningfully.

I scowled up at him. "Is that a joke in the face of mortal danger?" I asked in surprise, pressing a hand to my chest in an overly dramatic impersonation of a Southern matron.

"It's been known to happen. I find it cuts the tension," Magnus said easily, scanning the departing fae with professional detachment.

I followed his gaze. My breath caught in my chest. A familiar wild white head bobbed above the crowd, wading against the tide of fae to get to me.

I threw off all semblance of dark humor as I waved an arm at the old necromancer. "Ben! What are you doing here?"

"What'd mean? We came to help!" Ben finally broke through the last of the fae ranks and hurried over towards us.

"We?" I demanded. "You mean Mama's here?"

"Not anymore. She ran along on home to get some more of her unguents and things. I stayed to put a halt on the death curses where I could."

"Thank the gods for small mercies," Sloane said beside me.

"You can say that again," Ben said, wrapping an arm around both of us. "I'm glad she got gone before this durned lich showed his ugly mug 'round here."

"How do you know he's ugly?" Sloane asked, grinning up at the lanky necromancer.

"Girl!" Ben exclaimed, turning and picking up the pace as we caught up with the tail end of the fae procession. "I don't need to see that durned lich to know he's ugly. He didn't get hit with the ugly stick. He got whopped with the whole danged forest!"

I chuckled and even saw a small smile flicker over Magnus' face before he jogged to catch up with the fae disappearing through the French doors opening into the back garden. He ducked around a corner and out of sight. A moment later, a large silver wolf loped around the flank of the fleeing fae, scanning the surrounding grounds for enemies.

I wiped a sweaty palm on my pants before re-gripping my sword. I saw Sloane held both of her guns pointed at the floor and Ben even held a small, flickering ball of magic in his palm as we hurried to catch up with the fae, tramping through the cultivated flower beds as carefully as we could.

"Did it work? Your magical block on the death curse, I mean?" I asked Ben, even as I kept my head on a swivel, watching for any incoming attacks.

Ben grimaced and shook his head slightly. "I couldn't heal them. When all's said and done, I'm not even close to the same league as that there lich. I bought them some time, that's all. A week maybe? Ten days at the long end." He shook his head angrily, "It's not enough. Not even close to enough. If only I was stronger." Ben held up his hand where a small ball of dark green magic flickered in and out of existence, as if to prove his point.

I reached up and laid my hand on his shoulder. "It's better than nothing, Ben."

Ben patted my hand. "I know. I just wish I could do more."

"Don't we all," muttered Sloane as we passed a small, above ground mausoleum and a wall of what looked like temporary housing for deceased fae. At least, I couldn't see any names carved into the stone plaques. I assumed that any fae who passed away in this realm would find temporary respite in the aboveground tombs before being returned to their families and laid to rest in Fae.

I shivered as we hurried past the small cemetery and entered the hedge maze at the back of the Embassy property. It might have been my nerves at the impending zombie attack, but between the unexpected cemetery and the sinister hedge maze, the grounds of the Embassy were more spooky than reassuring. Calling the towering, living walls of the maze a hedge was like calling a whale a minnow. Although the thick, green walls provided additional security, they also blocked my line of sight of any incoming enemies.

Ben took the lead, followed by Sloane. I brought up the rear, prowling through the maze on the lookout for any rogue zombies, even as I carefully mapped the path in my head. A tiny part of me twisted inside as I watched the lanky necromancer hurry along the path. As much as I appreciated what Ben had done for the fae, I didn't want the old man here, but where could he go safely with the lich attacking? At least Mama was out of harm's way. For now.

Until zombies overran the city.

I shivered at the unbidden thought. I glanced up at Ben, something suddenly occurring to me. "Ben, you're a necromancer, aren't you? Can you do anything about these zombies? Like, I don't know, wrestle control or something away from the lich?"

Ben shook his head even as he turned a corner, following the fae towards the center of the maze. "That Kroxius fella outclasses me by a few margins and then some. I might sway a sparrow to my side, but not much more," he said, kicking at a loose stone angrily as we hurried down the dirt path.

I spoke consolingly even as I scanned the sky, now paranoid about zombie sparrows. "Well, it's a good thing that you're here, anyway. You gave these people some extra time, and that's more than any of the rest of us could do."

"I suppose," the necromancer grumbled as we broke through the towering walls and into the center of the maze. A small fountain burbled at the entrance to the clearing in the center of the maze, bubbling unendingly into a small pool. Behind the fountain, a large, oblong tear in reality crackled with purple and green energy. Letitia stood at the edge of the portal, ushering her people through to Fae. Ben hurried over to the Ambassador, leaning his wild white head close to speak with her.

"Now, we've got to buy them just a little more time," I said, putting my back to the portal and planting my feet carefully on the grass slick from the mist kicked up by the fountain. I raised my yatagan, ready for any incoming attack.

"Or kill the lich," Sloane said, setting herself at my side, guns ready.

"Trust me, I wanna show that asshole my resting lich face," I muttered to her.

I saw a wry smile twist the corner of her mouth as she recognized my gallows humor as the coping mechanism it was. It had been too easy getting the fae to the portal. We both knew it. The storm was coming. I could feel it in my bones.

Chapter 45

A hissing noise caught my ear. I whirled, sword at the ready, searching for the source of the sound.

"No need for that, my dear," cooed a familiar voice. An image flickered faintly in the mist, rising from the burbling fountain before solidifying into the outline of a familiar red-haired demoness.

"Meridiana? What the hell?" I hissed.

"'Where', not 'what', my dear, but enough about me. We don't have the time. You've been devilishly hard to track down."

"What do you mean?" I asked.

Sloane looked at me funnily. "What does what mean? I didn't say anything."

Meridiana's watery image shook her head. "The leprechaun can't see or hear me."

I held up a finger, silently imploring Sloane to wait while widening my eyes at the demoness, encouraging her to continue.

Meridiana's image blew out a breath, the mist not fluttering an iota at the expelled sigh. "I mean, I've been trying to find you ever since I crossed over. I have news and not the good kind, I'm afraid."

An icy fist clenched in my guts. "Tell me."

"The demon we dispatched, Razgothan? Well, it seems he could communicate past that mangled excuse for a tongue."

A fist twisted my gut. "What does that mean?" I rasped.

"It means that news of a human with ties to a djinn king is spreading like a sulfur scented fart through the Abyss even as we speak. I wouldn't be surprised if word of your existence spreads to the djinn tribes soon. Please tell me you've found a way to harness your power completely."

"Not well enough," I said shortly, aware that I had an audience.

"Well, why ever not?" Meridiana exclaimed, a small wrinkle of irritation forming between her misty brows.

"I've been busy. There's a lich in town."

"Oh. Well, that complicates matters," Meridiana sounded annoyed.

"Yeah," I said grimly. An idea suddenly sparked, lit by the crackling portal behind me. "Wait! What if we opened a passage to the Abyss and shoved the lich through? He had a hard time fighting his way across the first time. Maybe this time it would stick?"

I heard Sloane suck in a breath behind me, but ignored her, focusing my attention on the wavering image of Meridiana in the fountain. She cocked her floating head to the side. "Perhaps. Is there anyone powerful enough to open the veil and close it again? Without someone able to do both, I'd advise against tearing a hole again. Isn't that what got you into this mess in the first place? No, it would be much better if you could find one of the official Ferrymen like Manannan, Thanatos, or Charon to help you."

"Someone like Maman Brigitte?" I asked, my mind racing to connect the dots. Maybe I could reach out to her somehow. She was kinda my boss, after all.

Meridiana didn't give me time to think. "Precisely. Failing that, you could always try to use one of the designated crossings. Be warned, the Necrocracy placed powerful wards on those to prevent escaping souls, so you need to ensure that you don't accidentally get pulled through."

"Why?" I asked.

"Like I said, they're guarded to prevent souls from escaping the Abyss. Even those who crossed over accidentally. However, those crossing points are difficult to find and even harder to activate and for good reason." Meridiana's flickering image glanced over her invisible shoulder. She leaned forward and whispered urgently. "You need to do whatever you can to get a grip on your powers, Cam, as fast as you can."

"Why? What's coming?" I asked, my stomach churning at the urgency in her misty eyes.

"Everything." Meridiana looked over her shoulder and then back at me, her eyes wide.

"Hurry, Cam, for both our sakes."

Her misty form winked out of existence. It left me staring blankly at a mundane, burbling garden fountain.

Sloane touched my elbow. "What's going on?" she asked softly.

I jerked my chin towards the fountain. "Meridiana just popping in for a visit," I said by way of explanation.

Sloane was well aware of my entanglements with the demoness and perhaps knew the redhead even better than I did, having unintentionally inherited the demoness' powers for a short time on a wild girl's night out.

"Did she say anything helpful?"

"Nope. Only vague, dire warnings about the future." Now wasn't the time to get into a long, complicated story involving demons, goddesses, a cryptic caller, and unusually powerful Supes.

"Typical," Sloane snorted. "Ignore her for the time being. We've got bigger things to handle right now."

I bobbed my head, but the icy fist on my guts hadn't loosened with the demoness' disappearance. If anything, it gripped even tighter.

Chapter 46

Ben hurried over to where Sloane and I stood, his long legs gobbling up the distance as Letitia tried to keep up.

"What's the plan?" I said, noting their arrival out of the corner of my eye, but keeping my attention focused on locating incoming zombies.

Letitia had her arm wrapped around her side and a faint sheen of sweat covered her brow. "We've got to get the last of the provisions from the Embassy back here. I've split our healthiest forces. Half are guarding the injured in Fae, the other half will help me finish transporting what we need."

I glanced over at her, suddenly glad that the rest of her coterie were out of earshot. I lowered my voice. "Not to undermine you, Ambassador, but you don't look like you could carry much of anything. Stay here and guard the portal. I'll make sure that your people get what they need and get back here safely."

Letitia opened her mouth to protest, letting go of her side to tell me off. She wavered and almost collapsed. Ben caught her as she clenched her arm back to her side. She spoke stiffly, falling back on comfortable formality in her current predicament. "I believe, given the circumstances, that is the best alternative. The fae thank you for your help."

I snorted at her overly formal tone. "No need to stand on ceremony. I'm pretty sure that's one of the top three rules of a zombie apocalypse.

One: Don't let anyone eat your brains. Two: There's no such thing as too many bullets. Three: Don't waste time on formal speaking."

Letitia grinned through the pain at me. I nodded tightly in return. We said all that needed saying in a millisecond. Letitia turned and raised her voice. "Fae! Follow Cam. Get what you need and get out. No unnecessary risks."

I took off at a trot, hurrying through the maze, the fae hot on my heels. We'd been lucky to avoid any sort of attack so far, but I knew that luck couldn't hold. Finally, I saw a gap through the towering hedge maze into the garden. I held up a hand for silence and crept forward, scouting ahead. Sounds of battle in the distance greeted me as soon as I broke through the dense cover of the maze. A blur of motion caught my eye as I neared the entrance. I froze and then relaxed just as quickly as I recognized the silvery mountain of fur.

Magnus.

He trotted over, snuffling at me. I ran my fingers down his ruff and dug them in to the soft fur underneath, drawing strength from the werewolf. "I'm ok," I whispered, squinting through the gloom at the gardens and the mansion beyond. "Is there anything out there?" Magnus shook his enormous head, snuffling softly.

A dark shape appeared on the veranda, stepping out from behind the pillars. I froze, my fingers tightening in Magnus' fur. The werewolf leaned his shoulder against me, tail thumping against my leg.

"What is it? A friend?" I asked, loosening my hold. Magnus bobbed his head in assent.

The figure on the veranda loped towards us, solidifying into a lean werewolf with fur so dark it looked entirely black in the dim light. I let out my breath as I recognized Andrei in wolf form. I squatted next to Magnus as Andrei raced towards us. The teenage wolf ducked his head as he approached us, eyeing the larger wolf with trepidation. Magnus didn't acknowledge the younger wolf, so I held out my hand in welcome.

Stupid werewolf domination games.

"Did you see anything in the house, Andrei?" I asked, running a hand along his shoulder. His coarse fur wasn't as thick or soft as Magnus'. The young wolf shook his head. I patted his side in silent thanks and slid back to the fae waiting behind me. Sloane held them back, giving me space to scout ahead uninterrupted, for which I was grateful. A wild white head bobbed up at the back of the group.

Ben?

That surprised me. I hadn't realized the necromancer had followed us back to the house. I would have preferred if he stayed with Letitia, but there was little I could do about it now.

As I outlined my plan to my followers, I kept my voice low. "The wolves say there's nothing out there. At least not yet. Andrei is going to scout ahead. Magnus, you watch our backs. Sloane, you stay on the porch and start shooting if you see any zombies coming around to flank us. Ben and I will go with the fae inside. Once we get to the house, get in and grab what you need. Then get out quickly and quietly." I made eye contact with each of the fae until they all nodded their understanding. "Good. Then we all make it back here as fast as we can. Got it?" Tight nods met my words again. Knowing we didn't have time to waste, I spun and led the way through the towering entrance of the maze and into the open gardens.

My nerves were singing on high alert as our little party rushed across the once pristine flower beds, grinding brilliant petals into the dirt as we rushed by on silent feet. The sounds of battle out front crescendoed, but we slipped into the back of the Embassy without being seen. I was thankful that the fae Letitia sent knew what they were doing. We were in and out in under five minutes, the entire party hurrying back towards the maze, loaded with precious provisions for the injured.

"I think we're gonna make it," Sloane whispered as she jogged alongside me at the back of the group.

"Don't jinx it," I said on instinct. Out of the corner of my eye, I saw a dark shape flit across the entrance of the maze. What were the chances it was as mundane as a bat? Luck, the capricious bitch, hadn't been turning my way lately. I doubted she would start smiling on me now, of all nights.

The snarling, roaring clamor of battle spilled around the corner of the mansion. A little part of me hoped that Letitia's wards were as good as she claimed. If they weren't, the Norms of New Orleans were in for one hell of an eye-opening ride tonight.

I raised an arm and yelled at my party, "Go, go, go! Get to the maze!"

The fae needed no additional encouragement. They raced for the entrance guarded by the towering hedges, disappearing into the dark greenery in a matter of moments with practiced ease. I skidded to a halt next to Sloane and Ben just inside the entrance a moment later, peering around the corner of the living green wall at the mayhem boiling towards us.

Janko strode through the battle, roaring orders at his undead horde. Ghosts swirled around his head, diving at the zombie horde. Skeletons clattered over the paving stones in a macabre game of follow the leader.

The werewolves harried slow moving zombies at every step, darting in and out with practiced ease, ripping and tearing away whatever they could before dancing out of arm's reach. It looked like the zombies were a mix of human and animal this time. They moved slower than the zombie animals in the bayou had done. As I watched, I saw one zombie take a swipe at an attacking werewolf. Instead of thoughtlessly pursuing the wolf and breaking ranks, the zombie looked over its shoulder, choosing to stay with the slow-moving pack as they pressed forward towards the gardens and the maze.

Shit. They were sentient.

I whistled, high and shrill, the sound cutting the encroaching battle noise to my allies' ears. "Listen up, everyone! Sloane, you get back to the portal as fast as you can and warn Letitia and her folks about what's coming. She needs to get that portal closed. Shoot at anything that moves, especially the birds. I don't want any scouts making it easier for that mess of zombies to get through the maze."

"Stumble," Ben said absently at my side.

"What?"

"A group of zombies is a stumble, not a mess."

I rolled my eyes. "Whatever. Sloane, get back there and warn the fae. And in those moments where you're not sure if the undead are really *dead* dead, don't get stingy with your bullets."

Sloane nodded at me, a grim, half-crazy smile lighting her face. "You've got it." She offered me a fist bump before sprinting off into the maze after the fae.

"Andrei, you and Ben hold the entrance. Don't let anything through if you can help it, but fall back before you get killed. We don't know if the lich can reanimate the dead in the middle of all this crazy, but I don't want to be forced to watch you die and then kill you a second time. You feel me?"

Andrei let out a low yip I took for agreement. Ben patted the young werewolf on the head. "You got it, Cam," the old necromancer met my eyes seriously. "Make sure you take your own advice now, you hear me?"

I smiled up at him. "I hear you." I wheeled on my heel, calling to Magnus. My voice was low and urgent. The silver wolf appeared out of the darkness, matching me stride for stride as we raced to intercept the stumble of zombies.

What a shit name for something so terrifying.

If we all lived through this, I was going to have to tell Ben that his nomenclature sucked. And then I had no more time for thinking, only slashing, stabbing, and striking at anything undead that came remotely close to me and my yatagan.

Chapter 47

What felt like hours but was likely mere minutes later, I fell back to the fringes of the fray, panting heavily and sweating profusely. These zombies weren't as fast as the ones from the bayou, but they were more coldly vicious because they applied rational logic to their attacks. We were also at a distinct disadvantage because we were mortal. Fatal wounds didn't slow the plodding progression of the zombies, but they drained our meager resources.

As I stepped back to catch my breath, Magnus filled the gap. He was deadly, efficient, and frighteningly beautiful as he drove the entire group of zombies stumbling backwards a few paces. I leaned over, hands on my knees. I used the precious few seconds he had bought me trying to catch my breath.

A garbled voice sounded next to me. "This isn't working."

I turned my head to see Janko panting next to me, drool dripping down from his jaws as his oversized teeth protruded grotesquely from his gaping mouth.

"No," I panted. "It's not. We can't win like this. We need to change the game."

"How?" the ghoul ground out past his massive chompers.

I looked around, my eyes lighting on the massive hedge maze behind us where Andrei and Ben were easily picking off the few, small zombie creatures that made it to them. Janko followed the direction I looked and then our gazes locked.

"Fire," we said in unison. Well, I said it. Janko's mouth moved in the grim approximation of the word.

I pointed at the mansion. "Find anything you can to douse those trees. We need to light them up as soon as we lose the zombies in the maze. Fire will kill them deader than we can. I'll get the wolves to fall back to the fae. Hopefully, we can hold them off until you can get the bonfire started."

Janko nodded once and sprinted for the mansion without a backwards glance. I let my head hang down as I sucked in another deep breath.

No more time to mess around. Time to go play bait for a bunch of zombies. Again.

I pushed upright and a movement on the fringe of my periphery snagged my attention. I spun, sword raised, but nothing was there, only the small mausoleum and temporary cemetery.

What had moved back there then? Friend or foe?

Without realizing it, I had already taken a couple of curious steps forward when I saw the orange magic flicker to life behind the small stone structure, sending shadows dancing ludicrously across the smooth stone face of the mausoleum.

No way in hell. Kroxius was hiding back there? But why?

My feet were carrying me towards the lich's hiding place as the logical part of my brain finally kicked into gear. Once I figured out the answer, I would have facepalmed myself if I hadn't been holding a sword. As it was, I let out a long, low groan followed by a high, shrill whistle I hoped against hope cut through the battle madness.

Kroxius was going to outflank us. He was going to raise anyone and anything in those temporary tombs to surprise my allies. They had enough on their plates, what with battling the sentient zombies across the Embassy's formerly pristine gardens. And he was going to create more zombies? Over my dead body.

Yeah, that was probably precisely his intention.

I poured more speed on as I raced towards the cemetery, unsure if Magnus had heard my signal. Someone else had, though. A dark blur sprinted at me. I juked to the side, afraid of what was rushing up from the darkness. A wild white blur bobbed up behind the dark, furry shape a moment later. Andrei and Ben.

I slammed on the brakes. "What are you doing here? I told you to guard the entrance!"

Andrei whined and lowered his belly to the dirt. Ben jogged up behind the young werewolf. "I don't know what to tell you, Cam. When he saw you runnin', he just took off like a bat outta hell."

I crouched next to Andrei and grabbed his snout, shaking him lightly. I infused my voice with the ring of command as I spoke to the young werewolf. "Pay attention. You need to get back to the fae. Track them by scent through the maze. Warn them that Kroxius is here. He's coming for us all. We're going to lure his zombies into the maze and then burn it down around their ears. The fae need to get to safety before we light the match. You tell them, Andrei, and then you get the hell out, you hear me?" My eyes bore into Andrei's until he bobbed his head with another small whimper. "Good. Go on now, get." I let go. The werewolf took off running like a shot from a crossbow.

I pushed to my feet, meeting Ben's eyes. His mouth turned downward, reading something in my face he didn't like. "What is it, Cam?"

"Kroxius is back behind by the mausoleum," I whispered.

"Butter my biscuits and call me a cactus. If he can git back to that graveyard and raise the dead, that'll be mighty bad for those folks scrappin' out there," Ben said, jerking his thumb over his shoulder.

"I know. We can't let him do that."

Ben met my eyes seriously. "Where you lead, I'll follow, even if it's to hell and back."

I smiled. I couldn't help it. There was something about Ben that just brought a little more joy to this dark world every time he opened his mouth and let loose a stream of incomprehensible Southern nonsense he called 'colorful language.'

I pointed to the far side of the mausoleum. "I'm going to slide around there. You go that way and distract him. Hopefully, I can sneak close enough to end this fast before he even realizes I'm there."

"Right." Ben looked around, wild white hair floating around his head in the evening's gloom. "How'd you want me to distract him again?"

"Anything you want!" I hissed. "Just make it loud!"

"Right," Ben repeated. He took a deep breath and strode off, long legs eating up the ground between us and the small stone building. I took off at a sprint, moving as quickly as I could, making no undue noise.

"Hey! You!" I heard Ben's voice ring out, bouncing off the stone and into the darkness.

Silence.

The old necromancer infused more gusto into his voice. "What? Are you givin' me the cold shoulder? Git it? Because you've barely got any skin covering them bones of yours." Ben gave a gigantic guffaw at his own joke. I heard the lich let loose a massive sigh as I crept closer, pressing my back against the cold stone wall of the mausoleum.

"Ben," Kroxius's rasp rang eerily through the air. "Why, I've been dying to see you again, old friend. How long has it been since we saw each other last?" A dry, throaty chuckle clacked out of the skeletal frame. "How is dear Noreen these days?"

I heard Ben's knuckles crack as I snuck closer. "Me 'n' you are gonna mix, Kroxius."

Wait, Ben knows Kroxius?

"Why would you say that? Last time I checked, we were on the same side."

"Yeah, once and once only. To my everlastin' shame. But then it was all about the craft, you know? Findin' the beauty in the magic despite the darkness. But you had to go off the deep end and start actin' all crazy. Huntin' down humans for sport and the like."

"That is all they are good for," Kroxius said with a throaty chuckle.

Anger rang in Ben's words. "You're a snake in the grass, Kroxius. Nothin' more than that. And what you're doin' here? It makes about as much sense as tits on a bull. You'd best git back to where you come from because your kind ain't wanted here."

"So you told me last time and look how that turned out. Your little pet human bleeding out in your arms. Me on the Collective and you running off to Tennessee with your tail between your legs."

I peeked around the corner of the mausoleum to see Ben's fist clenched and his flickering ball of magic spring to life again. "Boy, you're nothin' but an egg-suckin', low-down dog. You'd better give your heart to Jesus because your butt is mine!"

"Your tactics still lack flair and, dare I say, actual tactics," Kroxius sneered, an impressive ball of orange magic crackling to life in both of his upraised palms.

"We'll see about that," Ben said. He whipped his own small green ball of weak flickering magic at Kroxius and it splattered against the sorcerer's chest. Kroxius looked down at the remnants of the magical orb dying out in spurts against his chest. The lich dragged a bony finger through the residue. He shook his hand like he was trying to flick a piece of fecal matter from his fingertips.

I heard the smile in the lich's rasping voice even as I pushed away from the wall and launched myself at him. "Now, it's my turn."

Chapter 48

I swung my blade with all my might, aiming for the back of the lich's neck just as he sent both balls of orange magic screaming into the night. If I could end this with an ambush, I had no qualms about doing so. As far as I was concerned, if Kroxius wanted to produce the murderous play being shown in the theater of war that was sprawling across the Embassy grounds, he knew what he was signing up for. However, the lich stood, chuckling maniacally in front of me one moment and then collapsed to the ground, writhing in agony the next.

I stumbled, the force of my swing not connecting. It threw me off balance. I recovered after a couple of steps, whirling with my sword out, anticipating a counterattack.

Nothing.

Ben stood with his arms folded, shaking his head at Kroxius's collapsed form. "You never did take the time to learn, did you?"

Kroxius panted raggedly, pushing to his feet. "It is weak. *You are weak!*" he screamed at Ben.

"Life isn't weakness. Destruction isn't strength. You never wanted to admit it, but magic is always a double-edged blade."

"Meaning?" spat out the lich.

Ben reached up to stroke Goliath, the little mouse's beady red eyes peering out of the necromancer's wild white mane. "Meanin' that where there's death, there's also hope for new life."

Kroxius chuckled darkly, "We may not agree on much, but we can agree on that, old friend." I saw he had regrown an epidermis entirely over his skeletal frame. He wouldn't have passed for Normal, but he could've walked down Bourbon Street without getting too many strange looks. At least if the Norms didn't look into his blazing orange eyes.

A strange scrabbling sound drew my attention to the wall of temporary tombs. I squinted at the rows of stone plaques in confusion, leaning to peer behind the wall to see what was making the odd scraping noise. Nothing was back there. Which meant...

I realized what Kroxius had done just as two sets of decaying arms exploded the stone casing of the tombs outward, raining stone shrapnel down on all our heads. Fae zombies clawed their way out of what was supposed to be their ultimate resting places.

I whirled towards the nearest emerging zombie, hacking away at any exposed bits that poked out of the destroyed tomb. The other zombie slithered out of its stone cocoon in the worst rendition of an emerging butterfly I'd ever seen. The dead fae had gone in ugly and come out uglier. Like a reverse butterfly. Butter-bie? No. Zombie-fly.

I divided my energy, slicing off anything that moved, but the zombies were too strong. The zombie grabbed my yatagan and disarmed me with a vicious twist that would have torn some ligaments in my wrist had I not let go. He sent my sword spiraling off into the night. My hands flashed for my karambits, but even that split second delay allowed for the other zombie-fly to wriggle out and slide to the floor. Rather than wait for it to struggle to its feet, I rushed the stronger, more complete of the two undead monsters, my knives ready and reflecting the flickering orange magic lighting its eyes.

For what it's worth, no matter how sharp they are, knives are not a great weapon to bring to a zombie fight.

I thrust, slashed, and carved away at the zombie, using all the dirty tricks I'd ever learned. The tough thing? Those tricks worked against someone who had skin, muscles, and pain receptors. All things that the zombie lacked. Besides, the zombie was smart. After a couple of slashes carved away some of the remaining flesh dangling from his bones, he started to counter my blows. Effectively.

I cursed under my breath and flowed into a different fighting style. If my knives wouldn't cut it, then maybe I could bludgeon the thing into submission. I whipped the karambit out, spinning it in a flail on the retention ring around my index finger. The flashing movement made the zombie jump back, reacting instinctively from a lifetime of avoiding sharp and pointy objects flying at its face.

I used the split-second hesitation to drive my enchanted boot into the side of the zombie's knee. A splintering crack sounded like music to my ears. I danced back out of the way as the zombie roared and swiped at my head. It stumbled forward, off balance. I shoved it hard in the back, sending it sprawling to the ground. And then I enjoyed performing a macabre Riverdance impression on its legs, snapping brittle bones wherever I could. The zombie writhed and thrashed under me, impolitely refusing to be a sedentary stage for my dancing endeavors. Eventually, it sent me tumbling. I landed awkwardly, my arms only half catching me as the wind whooshed out of my lungs on impact.

Ignoring the pain, I flipped myself over and started scrabbling away in the worst imitation of a crab imaginable. The zombie snarled at me silently through scraps of rotting lips. It dragged itself after me, useless legs flopping behind it. I smashed the heel of my boot into the zombie's face once, twice, and then a third time, buying myself space to scramble to my feet.

Despite the cracked, distorted skull held together by the merest fragments of skin, the zombie shook itself once and then resumed its unnatural crawl towards me. I backed up a step or two and took a running start, not just kicking the zombie's head, but kicking *through* the zombie's head in a strike that would have made even the best soccer players jealous.

Maybe I'd get a soccer movie made after me too, but they'd title it something like *Bend it? Nah, Just Explode the Damn Thing.*

I spun my karambits on their retention rings as I searched the darkness for the other zombie I'd started taking apart earlier. A snarl floated on the wind off to my right and I saw a mountain of silvery fur glint in the moonlight. Magnus lifted his head, tossing what looked like a femur into the air. Then he dove back down, out of my line of sight. A horrible snapping sound crunched out of the darkness as the werewolf bore down with relentless ferocity.

A rasping, cackling laugh drew my attention away from the zombie dismemberment. Ben crouched on the ground, one hand flat on the crushed grass, bleeding heavily and breathing hard as Kroxius stood over him, spinning his bone knife crackling with orange magic.

"You never were strong enough to take me on and win. You should have known better," Kroxius cackled, grabbing Ben by the hair and forcing the necromancer to look up at him as he raised the knife overhead, angry orange sparks spitting off the twisted bone blade, readying it for the final, fatal strike.

I started running.

Goliath, that brave little mouse, darted up the lich's hand and bit down hard on the bony fingers. Kroxius screamed, releasing his hold on Ben's head and flinging the tiny familiar into the darkness.

I pushed myself faster. I had to get there in time. I *had* to.

Kroxius refocused on Ben, reaching out to grab at the fallen necromancer and raising his bone knife once more. In a sudden burst of unexpected speed, Ben blocked the lich's grasping hand, thrusting it to the side. The necromancer lunged awkwardly up, driving his hand into the lich's chest cavity, tearing through the fragile layer of skin Kroxius had rebuilt. A flare of Ben's flickering green magic sprang to life inside the lich's ribcage. The two locked eyes for an interminable moment.

The world froze. A horrible, oppressive silence descended, locking the combatants in their own fatal struggle. One mortal, one immortal, they held each other clasped tightly in a ghastly embrace, a deathly clinch from which only one would rise.

I saw Ben's jaw clench. Just once. And then he moved, breaking the spell. Sound flooded over me in a deafening cacophony. The world sped up to normal speed. I hit the ground hard, almost stumbling at the unexpected landing, but I couldn't take my eyes off the necromancer as he pulled his hand free of the lich's chest, an orb of his flickering magic surrounding his hand.

Kroxius screamed in rage. His bone knife slashed low and deep, orange magic crackling gleefully along the blade. Ben fell to his knees, hands clutching at his stomach as blood spurted out, painting the grass red.

"No!" The scream ripped through me. Kroxius whirled, eyes widening when he saw me closing the distance. Without so much as a backwards glance, the lich spun and darted towards the maze, disappearing into the tall wall of living greenery even as I fell to my knees in front of Ben, catching at the necromancer as he toppled over with a groan.

"Ben! Ben, talk to me!" I shouted, patting at him, trying to staunch the knife wound with my bare hands.

Ben coughed, groaning again as the movement jarred the tear in his abdomen. "Got him," the necromancer wheezed.

"What?" I asked, not comprehending.

Ben lifted his arm weakly, the orb of magic flickering once more before winking out of existence. In his palm lay a small blue glass bottle.

I looked at it and then at Ben incredulously.

"Hubris. Gits 'em every time." Ben coughed again, his fingers loosening on the phylactery. The small bottle tumbled to the grass.

I looked at it, but couldn't reach over without releasing my hold on Ben's wound. "You'll be ok, Ben! Just hold on a little while longer," I said.

Ben shook his head, a small moan escaping his lips. "That dog won't hunt, love. I know death when I feel it. The old Ferryman is comin' for me to take me on my last trip. I'm just sorry I couldn't take that son of a bitch with me."

A tear rolled down my cheek. "No, no, no. We've just got to get you some help." I looked around wildly, searching the darkness for anyone or anything, but everything around us was still and silent.

Ben stretched a hand up, brushing the tear away with his thumb. "Don't cry, darlin'. The Ferryman 'n' I made peace with each other years ago. Part of the job." Ben coughed again, wheezing slightly.

"Ben," I croaked, my heart seizing in my chest as the necromancer's blood spattered his chin.

He patted my hand weakly. "Do me a favor, will you?"

"Anything."

"Look after Goliath for me? He's got a fair bit left to him yet, even when I'm..." he coughed again, spitting up more blood.

"I will, I promise," I choked out, past a rising lump in my throat.

"And tell Mama I love her, will you? She'd like to hear that. One last time."

Tears streamed down my face, but I nodded.

"Ah, don't cry, darlin'. I've had a blessed life, filled with more love and laughter than you could shake a stick at. I had Mama and Sloane and you…"

A little hiccupping sob escaped me, but Ben's eyes were glazing over, looking past me into the darkness of the night.

"Still, I would've liked to have one last sweet treat and cup of tea with y'all. Just one last…" and then he was gone.

I don't know how long I sat there, tears streaming down my face as I held Ben's body and rocking him gently. Goliath appeared out of the darkness at one point. The little white mouse clambered up his master's side and pressed his tiny head against Ben's chest. Goliath just lay there for a moment, eyes closed.

I couldn't tell you if it was an eternity or a second later, but the mouse finally patted the necromancer with his tiny paw. The tiny creature opened his beady red eyes, looking up at me expectantly. Not really knowing what to do, I extended my hand to the small creature, palm up. Goliath clambered aboard, scampering up my arm and settling under my left ear. His favorite spot. A sob built in me, but I ruthlessly pressed it back down.

A soft whine caught my attention. Magnus padded up out of the darkness, eyeing me warily. The massive silver-gray werewolf sat on his haunches next to me. He threw his head back and let loose the most eerie, mournful howl imaginable. Shivers danced down my spine. I dug my fingers into his warm fur, leaning against his flank. The three of us sat there, honoring the old necromancer in our own ways.

But there wasn't time for anything more than a moment. Mourning Ben would have to wait. The lich was out there. Our people were still in danger.

I shoved to my feet, feeling Goliath shift and scramble at the unexpected motion. The little mouse latched onto a strand of my hair, tugging on it as he held himself in place. It wasn't painful per se. The gentle tugging was actually reassuring. Like I had part of Ben riding on my shoulder. I guess, in a way, I did.

Magnus looked up at me and let out another soft whine. I answered him like he'd really spoken aloud. "I know, but there isn't time to mourn. Not now. Not properly. Besides, he wouldn't want us crying over him while there were others in danger." I felt a small, mousey paw pat my ear in what I took for agreement.

Magnus bobbed his head. He let out a little bark, turning his head and snuffling in the darkness.

"Where'd Kroxius go?" I asked. The werewolf flicked his snout towards the towering greenery.

"He's in the maze?" I asked. Magnus dipped his head once in agreement. I flattened my lips into a grim line. "Good," I said, raising my foot and stomping down with all my might. The small glass bottle shattered under the sole of my boot and I ground the fragments of glass into the bloody mud. "And now's he's mortal."

Magnus bared his sharp teeth in a disturbing combination of anticipation and undirected violence. The part of me that might have found that expression unsettling had shriveled up and died with Ben. I grabbed my karambits from where they had fallen and spun them expertly, making the blades look like beautiful mandalas of death.

"Let's go hunting."

Magnus threw back his head and let loose a second bone-chilling howl as we sprinted into the maze.

Chapter 49

Magnus put his nose to the ground, picking up the lich's scent. He gave a little yip and took off at a trot. He was careful to keep a pace I could match on two legs. I ran after him, karambits held at the ready. Although I would've preferred the reach of the sword, I didn't want to waste time searching for my yatagan amid the shattered tombs and trampled flowers.

The bark of a gun thundered over the clash of the fight behind us as soon as we hit the maze. I skidded to a stop, looking at Magnus. He had his nose to the ground and was snuffling down the path to the right. He sneezed once and shook his shaggy head, trotting further down the path. I caught a faint whiff of gasoline. Janko must have already set the trap. If I could smell it, the noxious scent must be overpowering to Magnus. It was a wonder he could track Kroxius at all.

Magnus led me down a confusing number of turns, back tracking only once as the overwhelming smell of the accelerant intensified. We must've been near the edge of the maze for it to smell this strong. The hedges muted the sounds of battle and, aside from dispatching the occasional aerial zombie scout, it was eerily quiet.

Magnus stopped in at a crossroads and his head jerked up suddenly. He sniffed at the air twice before letting loose a massive sneeze. I prowled forward, but the werewolf let out a low, quiet bark. I turned to face him.

"What is it? Do you hear something?" I whispered. He lifted his nose into the air and mimed taking a big sniff.

I shook my head. "You know I can't smell as well as you," I protested.

Magnus growled, low in the back of his throat and mimed sniffing the air again. I rolled my eyes and took a deep whiff. Then another. There! I caught something on the faint breeze. Was that?

"Smoke?" I asked, my stomach dropping. Magnus dipped his head in the affirmative. "Shit. I was hoping we'd have more time."

A staccato rattle of gunfire rang out. Dread settled in my gut as I recognized the bark of my guns. Whatever Sloane was shooting at meant I didn't have the luxury to track Kroxius through the twisting maze, fire or not.

I looked down the left-hand path that led to the center of the maze. Sloane was down there, fighting. And she didn't know that her battleground was about to become an inferno. Magnus looked up at me, making little jerky motions towards the right-hand path. I groaned and knuckled my forehead with my fist, not liking what I was about to say. Revenge or my friend. It was a gut wrenchingly hard, yet simple choice.

"Magnus, track down Kroxius. I've got to get to Sloane. Janko's lit the match, and the hedge will go up quickly, so be careful. Don't get trapped in a dead end."

The enormous wolf nodded his shaggy head once. He disappeared into the maze before I could offer any warnings. I mentally shrugged. It wasn't like he needed them, anyway.

I clutched my karambits tightly as I ran down the other path as fast as I dared, checking around each corner for any undead monsters. Nothing popped out at me, but with every burst of gunfire, I cursed the necessary precautions and the valuable time they consumed. At least the sound of the guns helped me triangulate Sloane's position.

Cold sweat dripped down my spine and beaded on my temples as I finally peered around the corner of the towering wall of greenery into the center of the maze. Sloane stood in front of the open portal to Fae with her feet planted, guns at the ready, as she scanned the sky. A pair of humanoid corpses twitched limply on the ground in front of her. Small, dark blobs dotted the entire clearing. Before I could move, Sloane raised the guns, letting loose a deafening roar and two new feathery bits of darkness hit the ground. Zombie birds.

"Sloane," I called softly. "Don't shoot me, ok?"

"Cam?"

"Yep, it's me," I said as I crept around the corner.

"Good to see you." Sloane smiled at me before firing into the sky again. Another flutter of darkness dropped to the grass as one of her guns clicked empty.

I winced at the roar from the handgun as I neared, but there were more pressing matters than potential hearing loss. "Why the hell is that portal still open? What is Letitia doing?" I demanded.

"Letitia is getting her people to safety," a voice chimed from off to the side. I squinted, not having seen the Fae Ambassador in the darkness before. Letitia put her hands on her hips and nodded tightly at me. "Good to see you, Cam."

"We need to get out of here. Janko set the maze on fire and... wait. What's going on?" I asked, striding over to her. As I neared, I saw there was a body in the grass at her feet and Letitia herself bore several deep cuts on her arms and face. Faint wisps of smoke drifted up over the hedges and wafted down into the clearing. We didn't have much time.

Letitia crouched down, wedging her fingertips under the fae man's shoulders and hefting him towards the portal with a grunt. I tucked my karambits back in their sheaths, hurrying to lend a hand. Together, we managed to half-drag, half-carry him to the edge of the portal. Embers and sparks flew up in the air as the fire raged closer. I kept my attention focused on the task at hand.

"Zombies ambushed them," Letitia explained as we worked. Sloane kept a lookout for more zombie kamikaze birds. "Somehow, a group of zombies slipped into the maze and intercepted my people on their return."

"Did you get them all?" I asked, a grunt escaping me. The fae man was heavier than he looked.

Letitia shook her head. "There's one more out there. Andrei is keeping watch until I can get back."

Looking at Letitia, I bit back my instinctive response about leaving a teenage werewolf alone in the middle of a battleground. Given the circumstances, I might have made the same decision. Regardless, now was neither the time nor the place for analyzing tactics. We worked together to drag the man across the grass. As gently as we could, we pushed the unconscious man through the portal.

"Look out!" Sloane's shouted warning held an unexpected quaver, followed by another deafening rattle from her still loaded weapon.

I dove to the side as a sizzling bolt of orange magic zipped over my head. If it hadn't been for Sloane's warning, the spell would've caught me right in the middle of my unsuspecting back.

Sloane's gun clicked empty, but I was already running, my hands flying to the sheaths at my back.

"Cam?" Sloane asked, backing up as Kroxius strode into the clearing.

"I've got this! Help Letitia!" I shouted as I rushed past her.

Kroxius sent a ball of magic screaming at me. I expected the move. I threw myself forward, diving under the shot and rolling to my feet without losing my momentum. He tried lobbing another orb at me. I juked to the side and knocked his arm wide with my forearm, swinging for the ragged hole of skin covering his bony torso. The same place Ben had ripped the hidden soul jar from.

Ben.

My thoughts stuttered. Kroxius took advantage of my momentary distraction, knocking my blow wide and taking a step back. I followed closely, refocusing. No, I couldn't let him win. I needed to stay inside his guard. I couldn't afford to let him regroup to take potshots from a distance. Not when all I had were my knives. I swung and sliced at Kroxius, driving him back and to the side, but the lich was quick. I couldn't land a blow. The smell of smoke rose around us, clawing at my throat.

I heard a noise behind me. I sliced at Kroxius and then looped a foot around his ankle. He jumped back and tripped, buying me enough time to look over my shoulder. Sloane and Letitia were half-carrying a different, semi-conscious fae towards the portal. They needed to get this final one through and seal up the damn thing already.

A snapping rustle sounded off to my left, drawing my attention. A slow-moving, human-shaped zombie crashed through one of the smoking hedge walls. Its clothes were on fire, but it didn't seem to notice. Flaming bits of cloth fell to the ground as it plodded menacingly towards Letitia and Sloane. None of the embers ignited the dried leaves and twigs on the ground of the clearing, but it was only a matter of time.

Kroxius sprang to his feet, launching himself at me and interrupting my thoughts. He laughed maniacally as his zombie minion ignored us completely. It focused its complete attention on the women lugging the unconscious fae towards the portal.

I fell back a few paces, trying to keep both the zombie and the lich in front of me. Kroxius threw his head back, letting loose another rasping chortle. It sounded like he was gargling glass in his bony throat.

"Choices, choices," he mocked.

I opened my mouth to respond when a blur of dark fur smashed into the zombie with a snarling growl. Andrei ducked out of reach, dancing in again to tear at the flaming zombie's leg, mangling what little muscle the creature had left to it. Letitia and Sloane tried to increase their speed. They managed a shuffling stumble towards the rip in reality as Andrei darted back at the zombie.

I smiled, refocusing on Kroxius again. But he wasn't in front of me anymore. The slippery skeletal sorcerer had taken advantage of my distraction and was already three steps into a full sprint, racing towards the glowing portal.

Oh, no you don't.

I leaped forward, silently thanking my cobbler friend for the enchanted boots that gave me extra mileage on my jump. I flung myself at the lich in a full out football tackle, wrapping my arms around his waist and sending us both tumbling to the ground. One of my karambits spun on my finger and off into the darkness before I could close my fist on it. I tried stabbing with the other knife, but the lich was quick. Kroxius rolled over my arm, trapping my knife and arm under his body with me on top of him.

He grinned at me, the orange lights from his eye sockets glinting off his exposed bony cheekbones. "Well, I didn't expect to see you again so soon. You can't have much time left, not after our last encounter. Unfortunately, I'm going to have to cut that time even shorter."

A wicked-looking bone knife appeared his hand. Kroxius drove it up at my rib cage. Instantly, I rolled to the side. I fell off him and catching his wrist as I crashed onto my back to avoid the knife.

I grunted under his weight. Kroxius kept my arm pinned and bore down with his knife, trying to make the most of his advantage. Twisting my head to the side, I suddenly stopped resisting, allow the knife to slice past my face and get buried in the dirt next to my head. With Kroxius off balance at my shift in tactics, I bucked my hips, sending him tumbling to the side. I scrambled to my feet, intending to back up and place myself between him and the portal. Letitia and Sloane were almost there. I just needed to hold him here a little while longer.

Kroxius was quick. Quicker than I could've imagined. I was just pushing to my knees when he grabbed my ankle, yanking my leg out from under me. The lich swarmed up my back, grasping my hand that was still holding the karambit. He slammed it repeatedly into the ground until I finally let go of the knife, letting the retention ring slide off my finger into the dirt.

He grabbed the back of my head, gripping my long hair tightly in a bony fist and yanking me painfully to my feet. There was an extra tugging on my hair that surprised me. Goliath! I'd forgotten almost entirely about the little mouse! The reanimated familiar clambered up my hair to launch himself at the lich. I strained my head to see what happened.

Goliath landed on Kroxius' face and tore strips of thin flesh from the bone of the lich's skull. I tried to use the distraction to my advantage but couldn't pull free. Kroxius clawed at the small mouse, but Goliath darted away. The mouse scampered across the lich's face and head, scratching and biting the entire time. Finally, Kroxius grabbed hold of the brave little mouse and flung him away. I couldn't see where he landed.

"No!" I shouted, re-doubling my effort to escape. Kroxius twisted my head cruelly to the side, forcing me to submit once more. He dragged me towards the portal by my hair as I awkwardly stumbled along next to him, my scalp screaming at me the whole way, making it impossible to focus. With my mundane weapons gone, I had to rely on my magic.

I tried to call up a shadow blade, turn to my smoke form, or even pull my shadows to cloak my figure, but Kroxius interrupted me every time with sharp jerks to my hair.

Letitia and Sloane shoved the fae's feet through the portal just as Kroxius sent a ball of magic screaming their way. Letitia ducked, eyes wide and a warning cry resonating through the clearing, but Sloane's back was turned. She couldn't see the attack coming.

I watched in horror, terrified I was going to have to witness the death of a second friend at this monster's hand, when a dark blur crashed into the tiny leprechaun, sending her stumbling forwards and through the portal into Fae.

Thank all the gods! Andrei! At least they were both out of harm's way.

Kroxius growled and yanked me forward, readying another ball of magic in his free palm, aiming at Letitia again.

"Go!" I screamed at Letitia. The fae woman looked at me, hesitation written across her beautiful features. In that moment, I knew she was trying to weigh my life against those of her people. Part of me loved her for that because I hadn't expected that kind of loyalty from the former party girl, but she had to seal that portal before the lich could get across into Fae. She was the only one who could perform that magic.

The unbidden thought popped into my head, sparking a desperate plan.

"Just go!" I shouted again, one hand scrabbling blindly up my head for the sorcerer's bony grip on my hair. Doing what I could to mitigate the pain, I grabbed on to the lich's arm and wrenched my head out of his grip. I left a long strand of hair and a good portion of my scalp behind as I stumbled forward, almost falling on my face.

Letitia nodded at me once, a look of fleeting relief crossing her face as she dove through the portal, which slowly closed like someone was pulling a magical zipper from the top to the bottom of the tear. Except it was closing too slowly.

I whirled to face the lich, calling on the shadows to coalesce into a blade. I drove all my will fueled by rage into the shadows. They instantly solidified under my fingers into a short knife. It was the first time I'd tried it in the real world and it worked. Maybe I doubted my abilities or, more likely, I'd feared what using djinn magic meant. That I was part djinn. But that was something to consider when my life wasn't on the line.

The lich's eyes widened. "Fascinating. I've never seen anything quite like that. You intrigue me," Kroxius hissed, jerking his chin at my shadow blade. "But once again, you are standing between me and my goal."

Twin balls of crackling orange magic snapped to life in his clawed hands, blazing against the darkness and illuminating the scene in an eerie flickering light. Shadows danced between us in the ominous orange light. Light that reflected off his exposed bones. Light that showed me the silver mountain of fur that was suspended midair behind the lich.

Magnus crashed into Kroxius's back and his magic orbs fizzled as they fell from his hands. The lich lost his balance under the unexpected weight of the huge werewolf, and I couldn't move out of the way in time. Kroxius sprawled into me as Magnus tried to leap free. We were entangled in a moment of weightlessness. A trio of deadly combatants locked in a snarling, growling jumble of fangs and magic, struggling to be the one on top when we hit the ground.

Except the ground had moved. I fell for longer than I expected, finally freeing myself of the lich and looking around. But I was still falling. The portal glowed above me as I flailed my arms and legs through the empty air.

Wait, that's not right. How could the portal be above me?

Unless... Unless we had fallen straight through the last slice of the portal leading to Fae.

I flailed, trying to find some sense of equilibrium through the tangle of bone and fur as I spun in mid-air. My eyes locked on the sliver of portal overhead. I watched in horrified fascination as the oblong portal shrank and vanished with a little pop.

I was in Fae.

I barely had time for the thought to register before the back of my head hit something hard. Then all I knew was darkness.

Chapter 50

I groaned. It hurt to be alive. Where was I? Why did it hurt so much? I blinked my eyes open slowly as everything came crashing back to me.

Kroxius. Magnus. The portal closing.

Fae. I was in Fae. I groaned again, rubbing my hand over my face.

"She lives," a deep male voice rumbled next to me.

I blinked again and rolled my head to see Magnus in human form and fully clothed, sitting next to me. "What happened?" I said, sitting up slowly.

He offered a hand, helping me to sit fully upright. "Andrei tackled Sloane through the portal and then we crashed through with Kroxius. The fae weren't expecting it. Between them and the teenager, I couldn't get to Kroxius before he escaped." Magnus waved a hand towards a grassy meadow bordered by an ominous forest in the distance.

Sloane hovered nearby, looking anxious. "Cam? How are you? Can you see how many fingers I'm holding up?"

I glanced over at her and groaned at the movement. "It looks like three fingers and, wait, is that a mouse?"

"Goliath," Sloane clarified. "Somehow, he slipped through the portal before it closed."

I carefully rubbed a hand over the back of my head, feeling a tender lump. "How long have I been out?"

"Ten minutes or so. We were getting worried," Letitia answered, coming up and crouching next to me. "How do you feel?"

"Like I've been run through a meat grinder. How do I look?"

"About the same," Letitia said, smiling at me to take the sting out of her words.

I snorted. "Thanks."

"Give it a minute." Letitia advised. "The magic inherent in the realm speeds up your own natural abilities, including healing."

I blinked in surprise. "Does that mean that your people are safe now? That they'll heal?"

Letitia bit her lip and slowly shook her head. "It just means that we've bought ourselves some time. While the lich's death curse is active, it will continue to drain us."

"What's the plan?" Magnus asked. He looked twitchy. Like he wanted to be in wolf form, sniffing out the lich.

"I don't know about you, but I'm going after Kroxius," I said, the fleeting touch of a smile on Letitia's face vanishing before my grim words.

"Are you sure that's wise?" Letitia asked.

I clenched my jaw and nodded. "I've got a score to settle. Besides, we took care of his soul jar." I swallowed hard, thinking of the terrible price that Ben paid to accomplish it.

"You're sure he's mortal?" Magnus asked.

"For now," I said, nodding at the wolf.

"Can he make another one?" Letitia asked.

"I don't know, but I don't want to find out. Do you?" I met her eyes coolly.

"No. No, I do not." Letitia shook her head emphatically. She looked up and over my head. I twisted to see the party of fae loading the injured onto horse-drawn travois in preparation for travel.

Letitia cleared her throat. "Umm, Cam, I..."

I cut her off. "Your people need you. And you need to find that pocket of slow time you keep talking about."

"Yes. I need to get them somewhere safe and send word of our location to the healers. Perhaps they can help, perhaps not. Either way..."

she trailed off, glancing back at the people who were looking to her for leadership.

"Either way, you've got to go with them. And the best way to make sure you're all safe is for me to kill Kroxius as fast as possible."

"You'd do that?" Surprise and shock colored her voice.

I tried to appear nonchalant as I gave a little shrug.

Letitia shook her head slightly. "I want to help, really, but the best I can offer is supplies. Oh! And this." She plucked two small, white stones from the lush grass dotted with delicate flowers. She cupped them gently and held them close to her lips, whispering gently. A glow of purple sparked to life under her fingertips. When she was done, she held out one stone to me and kept the other for herself. Each throbbed faintly with purple magic.

"What's that?" I asked.

"Think of this like a magical walkie-talkie. When the stone is glowing, it can communicate with its twin." Letitia held up the stone in her hand. "Tap on yours three times and say my name. We'll be able to talk for a brief time. But be careful. The magic will fade with use, so only reach out in the most dire of circumstances."

"Thanks," I said, accepting the stone gratefully. I'd been so focused on tracking down the lich, enacting visions of revenge in my mind for what he had done to Ben, that I had forgotten that we were in an entirely different realm. It wasn't like I could kill the lich and then call an Uber to take me home.

Letitia closed my fingers over the daisy. "Be careful out there, Cam. Nothing in Fae is quite what you expect. If I could offer some advice?" I nodded at her. Her jaw set as she scanned the open area. "It's best to assume everything is trying to kill you."

I waved a hand at the beautiful meadow dotted with small blooming buds. "Even the flowers?" I teased.

"All of it," she said seriously.

I swallowed under the intensity of her stare. "Got it," I said. No more flippant jokes about flowers.

Letitia nodded once and turned to Magnus. "What about you?"

Magnus shrugged and pointed at me. "I'm with her."

"Me too," Sloane said.

"Are you sure?" Letitia asked.

At the same time, I protested, "You really don't have to."

"You're my best friend!" Sloane exclaimed.

"But you hate Fae," I pointed out.

"Hate is a strong word. Loathe is more like it. But I also spent a lot of time here when I was younger. I can help guide you." Sloane waggled a hand. "To a point. But it's better than you wandering around here on your own while you try to hunt down a lich."

"Thanks Sloane." I smiled at her. She really was one in a million. I glanced over at Magnus.

He shrugged again. "I've got my orders," he said simply.

I rolled my eyes, but before I could protest further, Andrei bounced up, wearing some borrowed clothes and a backpack. "I'm ready to go," he announced.

"No way," I said.

"Not a good idea," Sloane chimed in at the same time.

"I don't think so," Magnus added.

"Send him home, Letitia," I said.

The fae shook her head. "I can't. Once closed, we can't open this portal for a week. It's part of the safety protocols to prevent any unauthorized travel to Earth. My people don't have the time to babysit the young werewolf until the portal is ready again. We've got enough on our hands."

Andrei scowled. "I don't need babysitting! Besides, you told me to find someone who could give me combat training. Someone I trust who won't go easy on me. Someone like you," he said, pointing at me.

I glared at him. "I meant someone like Parker! I don't have the time to train you properly. Not while I'm tracking this murdering lich across a hostile environment!"

Andrei folded his arms across his chest. "If you don't take me with you, I'll just slip away when the fae aren't looking and track you down. Who knows what sort of evil monsters I might stumble across on the way?"

Magnus put a hand on my shoulder. "I know it's a pain in the ass, but it's probably better to know where the kid is than to have to rescue him later."

"Hey!" Andrei protested. Magnus shot him a cool look, locking gazes with the teenager. The kid withered under the older werewolf's stare and eventually looked away.

I shoved to my feet and cracked my neck loudly to break the tension. "Fine. I don't have the energy or the time to argue, not with Kroxius slipping away." I held my finger up as Andrei's eyes lit in excitement. "But you do what I say when I say how I say. Without question. Until we kill this thing, I can't be playing nursemaid to a spoiled pup. Got it?"

Andrei's eyes flashed once, but he nodded, "Understood, Teach."

I grimaced at the nickname, remembering when he had used it the first time in that grimy warehouse. The gods had a perverse sense of humor to make me someone's teacher. I mean, what kind of role model was I? An image of Ben's smiling face popped into the forefront of my mind. He'd been encouraging me to take control of my life, to focus on the legacy I wanted to leave behind instead of just following where the chaos leads. I wasn't sure pursuing a legacy as a teacher would benefit anyone, but protecting those weaker or less able? Now that I could do. Maybe going after Kroxius in an effort to save Letitia and her fae was the first step towards securing a legacy that would make Ben proud.

Taking advantage of my momentary silence, Letitia dashed off to gather supplies for us, pulling Andrei along with her. Sloane shot me a concerned look. I gave her a smile that held more confident bravado than I had any right to and gave her a small nod. She returned the gesture and followed along after Andrei and Letitia.

I turned to Magnus. "You really don't have to come," I said.

"Like I said, I'm just following orders," Magnus said swiftly.

"I doubt Damon meant for you to follow me to an entirely different realm," I scoffed lightly.

"I don't know what you mean," Magnus said, dropping a stony mask of impassivity over his features. His eyes gave him away, though. They glittered with laughter.

I narrowed my own eyes at the wolf. "I think you do. Your orders were to make sure I wasn't a threat. Well, I pose no threat to the people of New Orleans here, even if I were to shift, which we both know is highly unlikely. So, why'd you jump through the portal after me?"

"Like I said, I had my orders," Magnus said firmly.

I snorted. "You're grasping."

He shrugged and finally smiled, cracking the mask. "You figure it out then," he said simply.

From behind him, Andrei shouted at us. Heavy looking backpacks lay at the young werewolf's feet. Sloane was already shouldering hers. Once he'd gotten our attention, Andrei turned and started jogging towards the ominous forest in the distance, his own pack bouncing up and down as he ran. She shrugged helplessly at us. I saw her tuck Goliath into a pocket of her pack before taking off after the wolf.

"C'mon. The pup is outdistancing us. Unless you'd rather he explore this crazy new place on his own? I'm sure his dad would *love* that," Magnus said drily.

"Damon can never, ever know. As far as the Alpha goes, this was all one jolly holiday," I said seriously as I jogged over and shouldered one pack with Sloane's help.

Magnus chuckled, settling his own pack on his back as we took off after the teenage werewolf and the leprechaun.

My mind churned as we ran. Putting aside the pressing issue of dealing with Kroxius, the impromptu trip to Fae might be a blessing in disguise. If Letitia was right and time ran differently here, perhaps I would have enough time to get a handle on my powers and be able to use them with more control. If Meridiana's warning could be believed, I was going to need all the practice I could get, especially if things in the Abyss were looking into me, my connections with the djinn, or my unknown bloodline. I hoped they weren't, but knew better than most that hope was not an effective defense. On the positive side, at least I was going to be difficult to track down. I mean, who would come looking for me in the land of Fae?

Where even the flowers wanted to kill you.

Enjoy the book?

You can make a big difference.
Reviews are the most powerful tools in my arsenal when it comes to getting attention for my books. Much as I'd like to, I don't have the financial muscle of a New York publisher. I can't take out full page ads in the newspaper or put posters on the subway.
(Not yet, anyway).
But I do have something much more powerful and effective than that, and it's something that those publishers would kill to get their hands on.

A committed and loyal bunch of readers.

Honest reviews of my books help bring them to the attention of other readers.
It's easy to skip this step – I often did myself until I realized how much authors count on these reviews. If you've enjoyed this book, I would be very grateful if you could spend just five minutes leaving a review (it can be as short as you like) on the book's review page.
More reviews help other readers discover this series and, as I now realize, it helps your humble author enormously.
Thank you!

L.L. Gray

Don't forget! VIP's get early access to all sorts of book goodies, including signed copies, private giveaways, advance notice of future projects, and a FREE NOVELLA.
Click here to join: www.llgray.com

Don't forget, your FREE book is waiting!

A killer pair of shoes, a party of a lifetime, and a demon. What could possibly go wrong?

Cameron Blaze owes a demon a favor and what better way to pay off a debt than to have a girl's night out? The plan was simple. Find a killer pair of heels, go to a great bar, and party into the early hours of the morning. Cameron thinks that she has everything planned. The shoes on are, the drinks are poured, and the party is in full swing. She just forgot to account for one small thing. Magic going haywire.

Sign up here to get your free book!

https://www.subscribepage.com/llgray

Thank you!

Thank you for picking my book. If you enjoyed it, please consider adding a review. I would be grateful if you could spare a couple of minutes to leave a review. It need only be a line or two and it makes a massive difference. It's easy to skip this step – I often did myself until I realized how much authors count on these reviews. I'd be so grateful if you would take a moment to post a rating and a few words. More reviews help other readers discover this series and, as I now realize, it helps your humble author enormously.

Best wishes,

L. L. Gray

Turn the page to read a sample of **TEMPEST AND TREASON** - Smoke and Shadows Series Book 4

Tempest and Treason

An innate sixth sense dragged me out of my night-mares. Something was out there. In the dark. *Watching* me.

Magic sprang to life inside me before consciousness. The insubstantial form of my shadow blade slapped into my palm before I opened my eyes. Instinctively, I ran the shadowy form along the whetstone of my will. The blade sharpened from a wavering dream into a dark blade with a razor-sharp edge as I stood up. I scanned the darkness, careful to keep my eyes averted from the dying embers of the campfire so as not to affect my night vision, searching for the sound that had awakened me.

Nothing.

I looked at my companions to see if the noise had disturbed them. Both were still asleep on the hard-packed earth. I was wary of waking them, especially if it turned out there was nothing prowling through the night. Ever since we had crashed through the portal to Fae, everyone's nerves were stretched tight. Mine felt like discordant piano strings, jangling at every unfamiliar sound. I looked back at the slumbering forms. Sloane and Andrei needed their sleep. Unless something was coming to murder us in the night, I was determined not to wake them.

A low whistle caught my ear, and a whisper of movement snagged at the corner of my eye. A tall, lean man with dark hair and enough stubble to form the start of an impressive beard stepped briefly out of the sparse tree line, marking the end of the forest.

Magnus.

The werewolf raised a finger to his lips and made a circling gesture with the other hand before fading back into the foliage.

It hadn't been my imagination then. Something was out there. The werewolf had sensed it, too. I ghosted across the campsite and placed a hand on Andrei's shoulder and then Sloane's, waking them silently. It was a credit to the trials of the past week that they woke swiftly, reaching for weapons as soon as I touched them. I made the same circling gesture Magnus had. In unison, the three of us left our rumpled blankets on the ground around the campfire and faded into the tree line, waiting with bated breath.

We had been tracking Kroxius for the past week across the unfamiliar, and often murderous, land of Fae. As a lich, Kroxius had unbelievable powers over the dead and was virtually unkillable. Until my friend had given his life to destroy the lich's soul jar, making the undead sorcerer mortal again.

Ben.

My heart squeezed painfully as I crouched behind a small bush covered in a smattering of dying leaves. I scanned the darkness, but could see no movement. My mind drifted back to the events that had led me to this spot. Memories tore at my fragile heart. Ben had sacrificed himself to protect the unsuspecting people of New Orleans. In doing so, he'd given us this infinitesimal chance to kill Kroxius before the lich made himself another soul jar. It was a noble, selfless act of bravery. The old man was a hero. He'd also been one of my closest friends. A surrogate father to a fatherless girl.

I ruthlessly squashed down the wellspring of grief that sprang to life inside me until it was merely a trickle. A trickle I could ignore. I'd mourn Ben properly once I had killed the lich, burned his corpse, and danced a jig on the bastard's grave.

Soft rustling in the long grass off to the northwest caught my ear. I squinted through the darkness, tapping into my extraordinary night vision. There were benefits to being a Supe other than being able to make weapons out of shadows, although that was one of my cooler tricks. I squinted at the grass, which came nearly to chest height. The moon wasn't bright enough to illuminate the entire field. Another crunch and snap of dried grass sounded. It was closer this time.

I flexed my fingers against the hilt of my sword, waiting to glimpse whatever undead creature Kroxius had raised. The lich had escaped when we all unexpectedly tumbled through a portal into Fae. He knew we were tracking him across Fae and he was cunning. Kroxius had been using his powers to raise any creature he stumbled across and turn it into a zombie to distract, deter, or deadify our small party. He just needed to buy enough time to either give us the slip or make another soul jar.

We needed to keep him on the run and unable to have the time or energy to conduct the ritual to create a new soul jar until we could catch up with him. So far, we were at a stalemate, but something had to tip the balance one way or the other soon.

Another rustle whispered through the darkness. I saw a twitching ripple slither through the tall grass. My eyes widened. It was closer than I'd expected. That small shiver was all the warning I had. Three blurred shapes flung themselves out of the tall grasses on the opposite side of the recently vacated campsite. As one, the monstrosities viciously attacked the empty blankets strewn on the ground. In the glowing embers, spindly legs coated in bristling orange and black fur scuttled over the blankets. The legs supported a furry round body, about the size of a basketball, and a knobby head with too many eyes.

Spider-tigers? Huh. That's a new one, I thought.

Fae was filled with many things that storytellers left out of fairy tales. Things that would've sent all the good boys and girls screaming for their mommies. Danger in Fae didn't just come from the strange and horrible creatures like the spider-tigers murdering our blankets, either. Leaves were so sharp they could slice you into smithereens. Trees could move and liked to indulge in murder. Babbling brooks really talked and tried to lure you close enough for sylphs to drag you under the water. Faeries were not the only things that lived in Fae. Both creatures of myth and fae nightmares populated the realm. From what I'd seen, if you could imagine it, it lived in Fae. Hybrid monsters lived alongside their Earthly counterparts as if the laws of interspecies mating didn't hold true in this bizarre realm. We'd seen badger-deer, wasp-monkeys, and scorpion-otters. The latter were devilishly cute with a deadly sting to their tail.

I started inching through the sparse foliage to get in a better position to attack. Magnus was closer. He leaped out of the darkness in his massive silver wolf form. He was both beautiful and deadly. I was thankful he was on my side.

The werewolf snapped his powerful jaws around the base of the nearest spider-tiger's neck. Magnus threw his head back and forth, shaking the monster violently until the thing's neck cracked and the head popped off, revealing a host of maggots feasting on the internal organs of the undead creature.

This wasn't a chance attack. Kroxius *had* reanimated the fae spider-tigers and sent them to murder us in our sleep. The sooner we dealt with the lich, the better.

With a snort, Magnus tossed the body into the embers of the campfire. The bristly dead fur lit up like a Christmas tree in February. The fire popped and snapped as it greedily crawled up the zombie's dead-undead body. Magnus finished the job by shoving the thing's head into the fire with his nose.

Andrei followed Magnus's lead and charged into the fray. The younger werewolf snapped another spider-tiger's head off and tossed the body into the fire. The two wolves converged on the final spider, dispatching it in short order. Seeing that they had the situation under control, I stayed hidden just in case there were unseen threats still lurking in the night.

Andrei yipped at Magnus, who let out an answering rumble. They melted silently back into the darkness, working together as easily as if they'd been Pack for years instead of weeks. Magnus wasn't even officially part of the New Orleans Pack yet and Andrei was still a battle-green kid. However, I had to hand it to the teenager. Andrei had been so green that he was more of a detriment than an asset a week ago. However, between the frequent skirmishes with Kroxius's minions and the evening training sessions with Magnus or me, he was shaping up to be a quick student and a clever opponent. Even Sloane tried to help. She wasn't much of a fighter, but helped where she could in demonstrations or sparring. Hopefully, the kid would survive his adventure in Fae. If he didn't, I had a feeling his dad, the Alpha of the Pack of New Orleans, would make sure I didn't survive it either.

As the third and final spider head collapsed in on itself in a shower of angry orange sparks, Sloane crept into the camp from her hiding place in the darkness. I followed her, silently, scanning the darkness for any more movement. The charred smell of rotting flesh hit my nostrils and made me gag. I started breathing through my mouth to avoid the worst of it. Fire was an excellent way to deal with zombies, but I hated the resulting stench.

"Well, that was easy," the petite leprechaun commented as she gathered the blankets, pulling them away from the sparking fire before any embers could burn holes in the thin fabric.

"Almost too easy," I muttered. "Any idea what that was?"

Sloane shook her head. "I've never seen anything like it before. But that's Fae for you. It's always coming up with new and bizarre ways to kill you."

I chuckled in wry agreement, but kept my eyes on the gently swaying grass, just in case there were any more undead creatures out there. I waved my free hand at where the two wolves had disappeared.

"Once they finish scouting, let's move camp. No sense in staying put if Kroxius has already found us once," I said.

"Agreed," Sloane replied, shoving a blanket into one pack at random.

I let my shadow blade dissolve as I bent to help Sloane. I'd been practicing with my shadow magic whenever I found a spare moment since arriving in Fae. However, I still couldn't keep the blade corporeal if it wasn't directly in contact with me. It was annoying, but I was working to see if I could find a solution. I had to do it on my own because I hadn't been able to get in touch with Barqan, my mysterious magic tutor, since arriving. I didn't know if crossing over into Fae had disrupted the magic of my enchanted necklace or if he'd worn himself out by summoning me to meet him in the ether in a sort of out-of-body-astral-projection thing.

Not that I had a great deal of time for practice or magic lessons. I'd spent nearly every waking minute of the last week fighting, tracking, or trying to survive whatever Kroxius and the Fae realm threw at us.

Now wasn't the time to bemoan my lack of magical tutoring. We needed to get out of here as quickly as possible, in case Kroxius had more surprises heading our way. Working efficiently, Sloane and I packed up the camp. I kept half of my attention on the grass swaying in the night breeze as I worked, just in case something slipped past the wolves.

Sloane spoke up again as we worked. "I still think that he's getting weaker. Those zombie spiders didn't stand a chance."

"Only because we weren't asleep. If they'd caught us off guard, we all would've been dead before we knew what happened," I said as I shoved things at random into packs.

"Look who's cranky this morning!"

"It's not morning, and that's the problem," I grumbled.

"Well, I still think that this relatively lame attack is a sign that we are wearing him down." Sloane sounded irritatingly chipper for someone who hadn't gotten a full night's sleep in about a week.

"Maybe. Or maybe those things," I pointed at the charred remains in the fire, "were the only corpses he could find today to reanimate. Or maybe he's lulling us into a false sense of security."

Sloane snorted. "He's been on the run for almost a week now, with no provisions and very little rest. No matter how powerful the lich is, he has to be feeling the effects. You need energy to do magic, and he is flinging around some pretty big spells by turning dead Fae creatures into zombies two or three times a day. His energy and his magic have to run out sometime."

"I could say the same for us and our energy," I pointed out dryly. "How long can we keep up this pace without making a mistake? As you said, Kroxius isn't letting up the pressure. We never know when the next attack is coming."

Sloane fastened the last of the straps on the last bag. "Fae has done weird things to you, Cam. Not sure that I like all of them."

"Well, Fae is a weird place," I retorted.

"You don't have to tell me that. I spent a lot of time here when I was younger. There's a reason I got out as soon as I could," Sloane said with a little shudder, the smile fading slowly from her face.

"You haven't ever talked about your time in Fae before. Not really," I said.

"That's because it sucked. Big time. And after the kind of discrimination that my people faced?" She shuddered. "Would you want to re-live the most traumatic events of your life repeatedly?"

I reached out and grabbed her hand, squeezing it reassuringly. "No. And you don't have to. Not with me at least. Just know that I'm here if you need me, however you need me."

Sloane squeezed back and nodded tightly. "It's just hard, you know? Being back. I never thought I'd be back here and now that I am?" She bit her lip and cast her eyes around furtively. "It's bringing back a lot of old memories. Not many of them are good."

"Yeah, based on the past few days, I'm getting an inkling of why you wanted to leave. The truth behind the fairy tales isn't all princesses and glitter, is it?"

"Not even close," Sloane said seriously. Memories chased the good humor from her eyes and her face clouded over with anxiety that she'd never fully divulged before. She blinked and shook her head before offering me a bright smile. "But you should hear the stories the fae tell about humans. Those manling tales are crazy! I bet you'd laugh til your sides hurt if you heard some of them."

"Sounds like you're volunteering to be our entertainment tomorrow night," I said, trying to lighten her mood.

"Well, I don't know about that. It would be much better if we could find a bard or something. One of the traveling musicians would do a better job than I ever could!"

"Great. I'll just tell Kroxius that he needs to make a pit stop in a fae town so we can grab a pint at the pub and listen to the local gossip," I said sarcastically.

"Wow! Attitude much? Want me to remake your bed for you so you can wake up again and get out on the right side this time?" Sloane's smirk belied her words as she hefted a bag onto her back. Her teasing made me feel better.

"Yeah, that'd be great, thanks. While you're at it, can you also make some breakfast and a nice cup of tea?" I said.

"Sorry, the kitchen is closed," Sloane grunted as she shifted the bag to a more comfortable position.

I ignored the bags for now. They could wait until the werewolves got back from their scouting. Instead, I focused on searching the darkness for any signs of ambush. I pulled a shadow blade into existence. It was harder when I was fully awake, which I found strange. Whenever I tried to use my magic instinctively to form a shadow blade in Fae, it worked easily. Like slicing a butter knife through thin air. However, when I concentrated on *making* the magic happen, it felt more like forcing a butter knife through hard-packed snow. It worked. Eventually. It just took a hell of a lot more effort.

The hilt of my new shadow sword thudded comfortingly into the palm of my hand. I smiled. It had formed a little faster than last time. Before I congratulated myself on my slight magical accomplishment, a thin, striped leg tipped with five glistening claws flashed out of the long grass on the edge of the campsite.

I yelped in surprise and jumped back. The claws swept through the space where my knees had been just a moment before. If I hadn't reacted so swiftly, I'd be about twelve inches shorter now.

"Cam!" The desperation in Sloane's voice was clear. I took a quick look. She scrabbled at the straps of the bag, trying to get it off her back so it wouldn't encumber her fighting. The straps didn't move. She shot me a wild look of fear as she redoubled her efforts.

"Get behind me, but stay near the fire. Use it as a shield if anything comes at you," I hissed.

Sloane nodded. She hurried to follow my directions, still struggling with the bag.

I braced myself in front of her with my sword uplifted. Another bandy leg whipped through the grass at me. This one was much larger than the spindly things attached to the smoldering spider-tigers in the fire. I threw myself over the leg in a diving forward roll. I lost control of the blade in the frantic move to escape. The sword melted back into shadows as soon as my focus wavered. Which is when the body attached to the clawed legs lumbered into view.

A rasping yowl curdled my blood as the beast rose out of the long grasses. It was a dark smear against the night, making it difficult to see details. However, I could tell that it was big. Much bigger than I imagined. Compared to the little spiderlings who'd attacked us first, this thing was huge. They were kittens compared to a saber-tooth-tiger. Mixed with a spider. Damn metaphors! Too hard to make properly when I was jumping over legs with clawed tips.

It swiped at me again, coming closer to the fire, and I finally got a good look at the creature. The sloping dome of the narrow body wasn't very high, but it was wide. Eight thin legs attached to clawed paws sprouted from the creature's thorax. Bristling orange and black fur covered the entire beast, and it smelled like it had never had a bath in its life. But that wasn't the worst part. The giant spider monster's face was covered in eyes of all shapes and sizes. It locked every single one directly on me.

And I no longer had a weapon.

Also By

<u>**Smoke and Shadows Series**</u>

Shadows and Relics - Book 1

Pixie Pranks (exclusive novella)

Felons and Fangs – Book 2

Bones and Blades – Book 3
Tempest and Treason – Book 4 (coming in 2023)

About the Author

L.L. Gray was born in Wisconsin and split her time being a musical theatre nerd, a book worm, and a burgeoning coffee addict. She began writing her debut novel after obsessing over fantasy books for most of her life. When she's not writing, she can be found playing soccer (or football for you non-American folks), singing loudly to any and all showtunes, or traveling the world in hopes of trying out new coffee shops. L.L. Gray currently lives in Abu Dhabi with her husband and two daughters.

**Psst, it's me. L.L. Gray. Nice to meet you! Connecting with fellow lovers of the written word and crazy adventure stories is important to me. If that sounds like your cup of tea (or coffee, or other beverage) please hop over to my website (www.llgray.com) and join my newsletter where you can grab a FREE, exclusive goodies or hang out with us on my Facebook readers group.

However, if email is more your speed, then please feel free to drop me a line at info@llgray.com should the mood strike.

I hope you stay in touch!

L.L. Gray

Acknowledgments

First, I need to thank my fabulous team. They have become like a second family to me. I couldn't do it without die-hard supporters like them.

I'd also like to thank you, the reader. I hope you enjoyed reading Cam's wild adventures as much as I've enjoyed writing them. If you'd like to stay in touch or be kept up to date with upcoming releases, please head over to my website. If you'd like to hang out with some like-minded readers on Facebook , come and join our wonderful community.

And last, but definitely not least, I'd like to thank my wonderful husband. Without your support, none of this would have been possible.

9 781958 873052